Golden Dawn

Mark Garrett

Golden Dawn

Matador
9 De Montfort Mews
Leicester LE1 7FW, UK
Tel: (+44) 116 255 9311 / 9312
Email: books@troubador.co.uk
Web: www.troubador.co.uk/matador

ISBN 978-1906510-404

Mixed Sources
Product group from well-managed
forests and other controlled sources
www.fsc.org Cert no. TT-COC-2082
© 1996 Forest Stewardship Council
FSC

Typeset in 11pt Stempel Garamond by Troubador Publishing Ltd, Leicester, UK
Printed in the UK by The Cromwell Press Ltd, Trowbridge, Wilts, UK

Matador is an imprint of Troubador Publishing Ltd

For Alison. Keep smiling.

The Glass Mountain

She could not be sure, not that the passage of time meant anything to her, but it had been a considerable period since she had last been to Glass Mountain. As usual he had arbitrarily made her begin the arduous climb from the very bottom. The summit was unlike the sharp, jagged, ice-like sides with a perfectly flat top exactly one hundred metres square. The surface resembled a highly polished mirror that was dazzling to look at. At the centre sat a small, exquisitely proportioned, white crystal pagoda and she climbed the steps to enter without invitation.

"You have come then?" he greeted. His face was lined with a great age, but not heavily, while his short white hair was impeccably brushed. He was dressed in a loose fitting white smock that draped from his shoulders, almost to the floor.

"Obviously you don't mind that I have to climb all the way up?" Chimelle replied, as she ran her fingers through her short jet-black hair to smooth it.

"I was not sure you would come."

"Is there ever a choice?" she countered, her vivid purple eyes almost flashing in anger.

"If you really require one," he replied, spreading his hands as if showing a range of unseen wares at a market.

"You've so little faith in your daughter."

"Oh never. Cannot an old man see his beautiful daughter to lighten his spirit?"

"I'm supposed to be meditating and get precious little time for it. You're playing with Paul Sayers and want to know what I think."

His eyes widened in surprise. "How do you know it is he?"

"You've taken a liking to him. His attraction to the Guardian, Rebecca, has warmed your cynical old soul." She glanced outside the serenely-lit pagoda to an unseen horizon. "You see what Charlotte's allowed as an opportunity to put right previous wrong happenings."

"I am aware of the mistakes made in the past."

"No one soul is a god," she said, in a softer tone.

"That was said at the time the Talid rebels were sentenced to infinite banishment."

"That was a long time ago Father. It is considered only a myth now."

"Let it be considered so. There exists an ideal opportunity, one which might not come again for an age of time, to make things right again. Paul's relationship with Rebecca will provide the new start needed."

She raised a perfectly-trimmed eyebrow. "Just because it has happened once does not mean it cannot be prevented. Anything is possible, Father."

He smiled. "I would like it to happen."

"Yes, I know what you'd like, but there'll be an infinite number of dangers along the path. With evil stalking the way too, even you cannot totally predict the outcome."

"I know that better than you my dear. However, I know that this will be right given any change of event."

She turned, her purple dress sparkling in the reflected light of the pagoda.

"If you've already made up your mind on the matter it's pointless asking me here."

"There is one other thing, something very important, that I have summoned you here for, Chimelle. I need your help."

"To do what?" she replied, softening her tone and stance.

"Your mother," he said, almost in a whisper. "She has need of aid in the mortal realm she inhabits." As he spoke he held out his hand and she firmly took it. "I will show you what will happen and leave it to you my dear to devise a solution."

Without word she closed her eyes and opened her mind so

that he could show her the possible path. A moment passed before she opened them and looked directly into his. The love he felt for the woman he had loved many ages before was still strong.

"Don't worry, Father," she soothed. "I'll see to it alterations are made. She'll be safe."

"Good. I know you will be discreet."

She tenderly squeezed his hand before turning to leave. Streamers of pure golden light were pouring into the interior of the structure from the distant sunrise. It illuminated the mountain in dazzling brilliance.

"Another golden dawn Father," she sighed, feasting her eyes on the pure beauty of the scene. "Don't play too many games with Paul Sayers and the Guardian, Rebecca."

"I will not, but he is strong and will become stronger."

"You've gifted him?" she asked, surprised by the weight of his statement.

"Yes, in a way that cannot be seen. But it is a talent he already possesses."

"Is that with brains instead of brawn, Father?"

"Whenever he needs clear rational thought, and decisive thinking, the unused area of his reasoning will boost his mind. It will be invaluable."

Chimelle looked at him, quizzically. "Did you say it was a gift he already possessed?"

"Yes."

"How?"

"He was a child of the Talid."

"The Guardians believe the Talid to be a myth. Does Charlotte know of his potential?"

"She does not believe in the myths, but is aware of his hidden strengths. Caroline is a believer and has passed on such beliefs to her. Only time will tell if it is to have an effect on how they treat him."

"Let's hope she treats him well," she said, before slowly walking the short distance back to the point she had climbed over. She gazed downwards at the almost sheer drop as it fell away below her feet. "I suppose I have to climb down," she muttered, momentarily studying the almost impossible descent. In a flash the vivid purple dress she was wearing glistened in the golden light and was replaced by a figure hugging cat-suit in a bilious multi-coloured pattern. She slipped easily and confidently over the precipice without waiting for further word from him.

With a feeling of contentment he gazed out at the golden radiance bathing the summit. It was breathtaking and he had never grown tired of it in all the eons of time he had dwelt there. While others spent time searching for the ideal place to meditate, or renew their spiritual energies, he knew he had found the perfect setting. As he stared she appeared in a momentary sparkle of bright yellow light. The little girl wore a knee length dazzling red dress, but with no shoes upon her feet, and carried a small brown teddy bear in her left hand. She had golden blonde hair in loose curls around her face, which brushed the tops of her shoulders. Her depthless blue eyes twinkled in fond recognition.

"My dear Ruth," he beamed, as she entered the pagoda. "Have you completed the task?"

She smiled. "Paul was in the corridor waiting for his body to recover. I believe I left him in a rather confused state, but I am sure he will be fine."

"Then we both have a period of waiting ahead of us. Let me teach you some more."

Together, old man and young child sat down directly opposite each other. Once settled they closed their eyes and began a conversation needing no words, only thought. The expanding of her education and knowledge continued.

Chapter 1

Sunday 6th December 1992

The blue Rover 820 saloon turned down the short driveway before passing through a set of tall metal gates which fronted a private estate. A prominent sign, affixed to one of the brick pillars, read; 'Pelham Hall. No public access. Strictly private.' Mixed amongst the lofty poplars lining the drive were smaller trees, various tall bushes, and shrubs. The purpose of the well-planned planting was to mask the grounds from prying eyes. After a distance of just over half a mile the avenue of greenery fanned out on both sides and encircled the rear of the main house. The back of its three stories looked down upon a spacious parking area, in the middle of which sat a circular pond. The Rover drew into a vacant spot next to several other cars, including a mixture of off-road vehicles and a luxurious black BMW saloon. The driver locked the car and made his way along the hedge bordered path to the front of the house.

Sited north of Harrogate, Pelham Hall had forty rooms ranged over three floors and extensive cellars. Originally set in over five hundred acres of private grounds, it had been built in Victorian times for a wealthy Leeds mill owner and looked out over an impressive vista. The neatly kept gardens fell away to lawns, and eventually trees, before rising up into the low distant hills. Elements of the landscape were hidden by further groupings of tall trees, but behind them, further towards the horizon, sat the majestic Yorkshire Dales.

Anthony Scott-Wade stopped briefly at the foot of the steps leading up to the main entrance doors. He gazed at the view as the first hint of low cloud from the Pennines brought splashes of rain on a typically cold winter's afternoon. Out of formal uniform, the

Chief Constable of the North Yorkshire police force felt more at ease in a casual suit and tie. For such a high ranking officer he was short, a little over five feet six, and several pounds overweight. Only in his late forties, his hair had greyed prematurely; giving the air of an older man, and this impression was added to by a neatly-trimmed beard. As he took in the splendours of the estate he noticed, on the lower lawn, a Bell Jet Ranger helicopter.

'Yes,' he thought to himself, as he surveyed the house and its associated trappings. 'Storn certainly does alright for himself.' This seemed to be the case whether events went in his favour or not. But, then again, his underlings always saw to it he was kept happy. Again he looked out towards the Dales, rapidly being cloaked by the misty fall of approaching rain. It was just after three-thirty. He was not late, he knew better than to even think of being that, but was the last to arrive. Knowing the gloom of evening would soon settle he was glad at least to be staying the night.

The doors at the top of the steps were open and he entered the well lit reception area. An orderly row of lamps on the walls of the cavernous entrance hall illuminated the way and cast light upon the various landscape paintings and portraits adorning them. At the end of the carpeted hallway stood a highly polished staircase leading up to a gallery landing and the first floor. Just inside, standing next to a displayed suit of armour, a dark suited man closed the door behind Scott-Wade. The muscular built man was one of Storn's personal guards, Payne. There were only two trusted men, both ex-military, trained killers, whom Storn let chauffeur him and stay in his presence. Payne said nothing as Scott-Wade entered the house, only replying in kind to the curt nod of the head he had received from him. Hardly pausing he handed the guard the keys to his Rover.

"There's a case in the boot. See to it that it reaches my room."

Payne nodded. "It'll be done."

Scott-Wade adjusted his tie and ran his fingers back through his hair. He occupied a privileged position in the organisation and knew the value of appearing to be in control of every aspect of his affairs. Neatness was a rule which he judged everyone he met by, it meant they were in control. Untidy people were not to be trusted.

The dining room occupied most of the east side of the ground floor and the centrepiece of it, a long, exquisitely-polished table, had been set for thirteen diners. A thick pile carpet made the floor feel luxurious underfoot while an ornate Louis XIV crystal chandelier cast delicate light all around. There were eleven people inside, gathered in small groups, and all turned to look when Scott-Wade entered. A smartly-dressed young woman sprang to his side offering him a drink from a silver tray. He readily accepted and made his way over to the closest group of four. The nearest was a woman, five feet ten tall, in a tight black dress which ended at her knees, with black nylons and matching high-heeled strapped sandals. She was slender in build, in her late thirties, and had long raven coloured hair brushed loosely down her back. The dress showed a well-proportioned figure and Scott-Wade had more than a passing fancy for her. Myra Stanford rolled a sherry glass between her palms, displaying the scarlet painted nails adorning her fingertips. Along with her now deceased husband, Richard, she had been deeply involved with Storn's failed venture at Kirkham, but had survived his wrath. Instead she had strengthened her relatively high ranking in the organisation. Despite her husband's failure a few weeks earlier, a price he had paid for with his own life at Storn's hands, she had become Storn's closest advisor. Intelligent, but equally as cold and calculating, Myra was exceptional at what she did.

Beside her, involved in some seemingly deep conversation, was Philip Carter. Scott-Wade knew the man was a detective constable and considered to be a shining light in the organisation. Carter stood six feet tall, but was not heavily built; the light blue suit he wore fitted him well, making it plain to see he took time over his appearance to make the right impression. His face was thin and clean shaven, passing for a man in his twenties rather than his true age of thirty-two. His dark brown hair was tightly trimmed in a military fashion, due to Storn's influence. Most of the younger men within the organisation worshipped Storn and it showed in their copying of his choice of hairstyle. Carter was animatedly explaining something to both Myra and the other man in the group. The second man stood slightly back from them and Scott-Wade knew him only by his first name, Harry. If he had a surname nobody knew it and that was the way it had always been. He was short, with large hands, a wide girth, and wore an ill-fitting grey suit. Despite his appearance Harry was perhaps the most important man in the room, because he was the accountant. As such he was solely responsible for laundering the entire monetary input of the organisation. This included keeping records of all the illegal as well as legal dealings they undertook. Also he was the only one amongst them who had a complete overview of every strata of Storn's empire. Scott-Wade knew some of it and was privileged to be in the top echelon. It brought with it certain perks as well as the opportunity to work with Storn on his far reaching projects. Below their level sat several layers of organised crime including fraud, drugs, prostitution, and arms dealing. Those below knew nothing of those above, for good reason, and had to earn the right to move up. The layer beneath though was important as it carried its weight of professional people who made Storn's schemes function. Their evil was controlled and fed by him, purely to keep them loyal and subservient.

The last person in the small group Scott-Wade thought looked oddly out of place. But then again he believed she always had. The girl was Persephone, Myra's daughter, and she had just turned sixteen. It had been her seeming closeness of spirit to the man who had wreaked havoc at Kirkham that had seen her placed under Storn's personal care. Scott-Wade felt that she existed among them in the form of an unpredictable danger. She was a follower who did not belong and someone he vowed to keep a watchful eye on. If there was ever to be a traitor in the camp he knew exactly where to go to first.

Persephone stared blankly at the floor whilst nursing a tall glass of orange juice, appearing to take little notice of the conversation next to her. Like her mother she wore black, a tight-fitting mini-dress that accentuated her youthful curves and trim figure. A pair of stiletto-heeled shoes took her height to almost six feet, but she kept her legs bare. Her ash-blonde hair had been severely cut back in a style almost as short as the men's and it showed off her childlike, attractive face. She wore little makeup and did not need to as her jade-green eyes were the first thing most men spotted.

"Hello Tony," Myra greeted, cutting Carter off in mid-conversation as Scott-Wade joined them. "Looking forward to a late lunch?"

"My dear Myra," he replied, pecking her on the cheek. "You look well. Call this a late lunch? Surely it's early dinner?"

"Take this meal as you find it. Storn'll eat when it pleases him."

Beside her Carter held out his hand, which Scott-Wade shook firmly.

"Philip, it's good to see you again."

"And you too, Sir."

He waved dismissively. "No 'Sir', Tony will suffice. It's good to see you've earned a place here with us."

"I only hope my input will please our Master and serve us well."

Scott-Wade then turned to Harry and shook his hand, briefly. As always it was limp and felt clammy.

"My dear Chief Constable," Harry began, in an effeminate tone. "How pleasing it was to see your much publicised promotion coming through at last."

"It was pleasing for me too."

"So it should be, my dear fellow, it didn't come cheap."

He smiled, knowing exactly what was meant. "I'm sure you'll get value for money."

"I do hope so," Harry quickly countered.

Further conversation was interrupted by a member of the staff ringing a small bell.

"If you'd kindly take your seats, we're about to serve,"

With an unspoken understanding of their various positions of seniority, they took places at the lavishly set dining table. The honour of being on the right of Storn went to Scott-Wade, with Myra opposite. Beside him sat Harry, while Persephone had been elevated from never being present before to a position next to her mother. The other eight, including Carter, were ranged either side towards the bottom. The burble of chatter soon began to rise again as Scott-Wade cast an eye down the table. At the very end sat a middle aged, dark skinned woman. She was not tall, but had a build which showed she took care of her fitness. Always immaculately dressed, he had seen her before at such gatherings, but, like the others, he had never been introduced. No one seemed to know her first name, not even Harry. When spoken to she said little, or nothing, preferring instead to listen to their conversations. When she did speak it was in a low voice which had led to the others labelling her 'mumbles.' She was Storn's trouble-shooter, but off-limits. Whenever he had posed questions to him about her they had been dismissed without an answer. His sideways study of her, and the chatter at the table, was ended when the main door opened. As one the dozen arose from their seats as a mark of respect, and in many of them also a measure of fear, for the daunting individual who strode casually into the room.

Chapter 2

Storn was an imposing figure, over six feet tall. Dressed as always in all black, the entrance was a piece of theatre in itself, with shiny leather trousers, calf high laced boots, and a roll-neck sweater. The cape over his shoulders he dumped in the arms of the nearest girl serving at table. As if in the presence of royalty, she bowed and backed away. Still in silence the assembled followers waited for him to make his way to the high backed chair at the head of the table. The man acting as butler pulled it out so the closely shaven, white haired, Storn could take his place. Once comfortable he studied each of his disciples in turn, giving them equal measure of his soulless black eyes. Satisfied his authority had been instilled in them, once again, he casually used a hand to show them they could be seated. A clap of the hands followed and the staff knew it was time to serve the starter course.

The sumptuous meal began with a soup of Stilton and wild mushroom. All portions were generous and had been prepared to the highest standard by Pelham's resident chef. The diners readily ate their fill apart from Persephone, who picked uneasily at her food. As was becoming a more frequent occurrence she felt an inward discomfort when in Storn's presence. For some unexplained reason he was having an effect on her that she could clearly feel. A dessert of raspberry torte, with lemon sorbet, followed the main course of venison steak wrapped in pastry. After the table had been cleared they all sat drinking coffee, warmed by an open fire in the huge grate on the back wall. A member of the staff attended to it and replenished it with several dry logs. A brief lull in the conversation allowed Storn to dismiss the waiting staff. Once they had departed, silence again returned to the room as they waited for him to speak. With deliberate ease he settled back

11

into his chair and pressed his fingertips together in a mock manner of prayer.

"For those of you who were not directly involved in the setting up," he began. "The facility at Padrigg is now in use."

Scott-Wade had been aware of the facility for some time, as they all had, but had presumed Storn would not want to use it so quickly after losing the one at Kirkham.

"May I ask if it is occupied?" he asked, tentatively.

"The first is there now," Storn replied. "It is my intention to remain here at Pelham for some time to come. Therefore you are aware I need to regenerate my being, regularly, so as to sustain my presence here. As the facility is now ready I intend to use it, immediately. I can see no reason for unnecessary delay. Of course you will all be present at the required time to share in the rituals."

A light ripple of approval went around the table at his invitation.

"I agree, there should be no delays," Scott-Wade replied. "What sort of catching tactics is the team using?"

"Latham has control over the team," Storn replied, indicating to a middle-aged man, with receding fair hair, who had just lit a cigarette, at the end of the table, and invited him to speak.

"We've begun by using a random pattern all over the country, but not within a hundred miles of Padrigg. Dumping too will take the form of a chance nature. Also, because the type of catch doesn't matter, we're faced with the good fortune of not having to look for certain individuals. We can pick from a wide assortment, be it men, women, children, young or old."

Scott-Wade nodded. "You're taking every safeguard I assume."

Latham was a man experienced in such matters and had been snatching people for Storn for many years. Some of those they had taken, used, and then dumped had still not been found by anxious families.

"Of course, the usual safety checks are in place," he began. "The operation will run safe at my end, I guarantee it. We're even using the coded bags and covers to mask our movements from the Guardians."

"That is of paramount importance," Storn interrupted. "I am

12

satisfied with arrangements and will allow Latham to continue until I instruct otherwise. Clear?"

They all agreed, knowing that if they thought differently it was hopeless to say so. Whatever he demanded he received, totally, and usually without fail. The price of failure was a swift death at his hands.

"Now, onto another matter," he continued, as if conducting a regular business meeting, and took a mouthful of brandy from his glass. "Carter has intelligence information on the troublesome Guardian lackey who disrupted the operation at Kirkham a few weeks ago."

"He didn't die from his injuries?" a woman opposite Latham asked, in a surprised voice.

"The Guardians played a hand in the result. I have yet to discover why, but he made a full and rapid recovery."

Carter pushed his chair back and recovered a briefcase from under the table. From inside he removed some sheets of paper and began passing them around.

"No doubt you're all familiar with the video footage taken at Skelwith farm," he began. Several of them murmured and nodded.

"Thanks to Scott-Wade, who spotted the tax disc in the windscreen of the old car he drove, we've easily traced the man. Luckily it fell into my area, Cambridgeshire." When everyone had been passed a file he held one up. "Inside are two recent photographs I've had taken, along with a set of personal details I'll quickly outline."

Myra studied the colour photographs of Paul Sayers. One was a head and shoulders shot, while the second was full length. Both had been taken secretly, at a distance, with a zoom lens. Silently, she again familiarised herself with him whilst cursing endless misery and misfortune upon him. He had been the one whom she saw as solely responsible for her husband's death. The evil streak of hatred in her wanted to extract a terrible revenge for it. Beside her, Persephone too had thoughts about the face of the man she had seen in countless faded dreams. They were distant images of a life shared and lived a long time past. It had been, she always felt, a better one than the one she now had. Each time the faded memories surfaced she tried to grab them, but she always failed to hold on long enough to make any sense of them. For a fleeting moment, as she stared into the familiar face, the pungent aroma of salty air flooded her senses. In her ears she could almost hear the distinctive sound of surf rolling onto some unseen shoreline.

Unaware of what was going through the minds of the others, Carter continued.

"His full name is Paul David Sayers; born nineteen-sixty-four, so he's twenty-eight years old. Single and lives alone in a detached house in the village of Sawston, near Clayborough. He works at a local vegetable packing plant where he handles sales and is quite adept at running what information tells us is a very successful business."

"If he's so good we should have him on the team," Harry interjected.

"That's a disgusting remark, even coming from you," Myra spat at him.

"Have you anyone on the inside?" Scott-Wade quickly asked, to deflect the argument about to start next to him.

"On the whole the workforce is made up of very casual, low-paid labour. It's typical of the area. I've placed Sabir inside. He's a good operative who'll blend in and stay as long as necessary."

"Good," Storn added, sounding pleased with what he heard.

"I've also searched deep into his family history. It would appear he has no close relatives at all."

"That's unusual," Myra commented. "Isn't there anyone we can use as a lever?"

Carter shook his head. "No, no one. There are no brothers, sisters, aunts or uncles. The grandparents on his father's side are alive, but they've never spoken to him. Abduct them and Sayers would probably thank you for doing it. Even after this many years, people in small Fen communities still remember and talk. It appears his parents marriage wasn't a popular one, especially with his father's side of the family." He shrugged. "His father died just before he was born and his mother of cancer twelve years ago."

"Jesus, I don't believe it," Scott-Wade whispered.

"You have something to add?" Storn asked, looking questioningly at him.

"How did the father die?" Scott-Wade asked, turning to Carter.

"David Sayers died in a car accident, January nineteen-sixty-four. Apparently he plunged off the road into a water filled dyke and drowned. However, the police report I found of the incident was sketchy and incomplete."

"So it should be. I made it so."

"You mean you knew him?" Myra blurted.

"Briefly," he replied. "We had an underground business operation going on in the Norwich area, back in sixty-three, sixty-four. It was very lucrative as I recall. I was a novice copper back then in the old county of Huntingdonshire. It's where Sayers lives now. Sayers senior was a reporter for a daily newspaper. Somehow he got wind of the scheme we were working and investigated. He became a dangerous nuisance and was paid off to keep his trap shut. He readily took the bribe, but came back for more, threatening again to expose everything." He paused and took a drink from his brandy glass. "They set him up on a quiet Fen road and I ran him into a dyke. The rate of fatal accidents on those roads was quite high and it wasn't considered out of the ordinary. It took no effort to cover my own tracks and fake a senior officer's signature on the report." He looked again at the photographs. "I thought it was ancient history. Now it seems the son's here to trouble us too. It's certainly a small world."

"It's a pity that the bitch who gave birth to him wasn't in the car," Myra spat, turning to face Storn. "If you know where he is why not deal with him?"

"Because," he quickly replied. "He is going to prove very useful to me alive."

"In what way?" she retorted, placing the papers and photographs down on the table, where a spillage of wine tuned the edge crimson.

"Since Carter has been watching Sayers, one very special individual keeps visiting him."

"The woman, Rebecca," Persephone interrupted.

"You know?" Storn asked, turning his attention to her for the first time.

15

Unabashed, she shrugged. "I do, somehow. What they share must be very special. Otherwise they wouldn't take such an enormous risk for each other would they?"

"Precisely!" he forcefully added. "The visitation of Guardians has never been predictable, until now. This one comes regularly to see the same individual. This error of judgment, because of the bond they share, will be the downfall of them both. I plan to entrap Sayers in what will seem like a perfectly legitimate way, so nothing will be suspected until it is too late. When we have him she will feel the need to come to his aid and then we shall take her." He punctuated the last words with a clenching of his right fist, before turning to Myra. "After which, my loyal friend, you may do to him whatever you wish."

Her face broke into an evil grin, as her mind began to actively dream up endless tortures for Paul to endure.

"When do you plan to start this?" Scott-Wade asked.

"Straightaway," Carter replied, at Storn's indication. "We're instigating a twenty-four hour watch on his home. Whenever he does something we'll know about it. We can activate the plan within hours, it's our choice. We control it without his knowledge."

"Excellent," Myra commented, as next to her Persephone shifted uneasily in her seat. "The sooner the better I say. Can you tell us more of this plan?"

"We will talk at length on this later," Storn replied, in a dismissive tone. "You will all take the opportunity to relax here for the remainder of the day and take advantage of the facilities. Tomorrow we will go to Padrigg."

Knowing that the discussion had ended they rose to their feet in respect as he strode from the dining room.

Scott-Wade turned to Carter. "I hear you're a decent snooker player Philip. Let's go to the games room and see if it's true."

The two men left, leaving both Myra and Persephone deep in their own thoughts.

Chapter 3

Monday 7th December 1992

The convoy of four had followed the BMW all the way from Pelham Hall to the isolated valley of Padrigg in the Lake District. It was quiet, the winter seeing only a fraction of the tourist trade that the busy summer months did. The hamlet consisted of only a dozen cottages and offered little to the tourist trade due to the lack of a through road. It served only to interest the countless walkers, whose boots trod the numerous paths to the higher fells beyond. It had been chosen for its remoteness and a core of Storn's followers had gradually moved into the parish where property had been purchased to accommodate them. They lived and worked as if everything was normal. At the very end of the valley, as the ground began to rise up into the surrounding fells, was Holthwaite farm. It was over half a mile from the nearest cottage in the village and was also in their hands. In the last Range Rover, Persephone surveyed the surroundings as they came to a halt in the farmyard. The grey clouds hung low over the tops of the fells, shrouding the dark craggy flanks in glistening mist. The visible terrain was a mottled mixture of greens, grays, and rusty browns, interwoven with the silver streaks of water-filled streams running off the tops. Dotted infrequently, sometimes in small groups, were the white blobs which on closer inspection proved to be the hardiest inhabitants of the Lakes. The Herdwick sheep were on the high fells throughout the district.

Holthwaite was a typical farmhouse with three small bedrooms, a modest kitchen, and two downstairs rooms that outwardly leant it a quite austere look. To a passer-by, or even knowledgeable local, the farm gave the impression of being just that, a working Lakeland property. However, it held a dark secret. Unbeknown to the select group who had assembled the facility at Kirkham, Storn had put into construction another, away from the Pennines, in the Lakes. As soon as Kirkham had been lost, emphasis had been immediately switched to Holthwaite. The rapid change took many of the followers by surprise. However, it had the effect of quickly lifting deflated spirits and redirecting their efforts in only a few short weeks.

The cars began disgorging passengers, the elite group from Pelham Hall. Persephone stepped from the warmth into the cold damp air. An involuntary shudder ran through her as clinging mizzle, carried on the wind, washed across her face. Without casting another look at the landscape, for which she had no love, she pulled the collar of her leather jacket up tight. The others were huddling together and she went to join them. The wind was deathly cold and she rammed her hands deep into her pockets, cursing the lack of gloves and a scarf. As they milled around, a man and woman quickly appeared from the house. They made an immediate beeline towards the BMW that had halted by the barn at the far end of the yard. The barn looked in pristine condition when compared with the house. The walls had been rebuilt with the removal of the windows. A new roof had been added, along with strong wooden doors at the front. Across from it sat another barn, much older and run down. The faded and splintered doors were open, revealing a rifle-wielding, cigarette-smoking guard inside. They had learned from the mistakes made at Kirkham. He scanned the visitors with casual interest and chose not to go out into the cold to be with them.

The couple from the house managed to reach the BMW just as the driver opened the rear door. The tall menacing figure stepped easily from the car and casually threw his cape over his shoulders. Randall, the man in charge at Holthwaite, greeted him with a slight bow.

"Everything is prepared I trust?" Storn asked, firmly.

"As instructed," Randall replied, as they crossed to the new barn.

A smaller door was set inside one of the two larger ones and the woman of the farm, Rhen, was busy speaking on an intercom. Again, it was a sign of the lessons they had learned. Without delay the door opened and a guard stepped out. He was wearing combat type fatigues and respectfully lowered the muzzle of his assault rifle when he saw who was approaching. Storn was first through the door, quickly followed by Scott-Wade and Myra. Persephone managed to be the last one in just behind Harry. When she was inside an all too familiar sight greeted her. While the rest looked on in spellbound pleasure, issuing low words of praise to each other, she could only feel revulsion in the knowledge of the building's use. Above their heads, suspended inside the open roof area, a circular gantry of halogen spotlights sharply lit the interior. The barn was half as big again as the one at Kirkham, although it had not primarily been constructed as a holding point. She took several steps further in as the door was closed and locked behind them. Already she had entered a twenty foot diameter circle of gold embossed codes, swirls, figures, and symbols that had been exactingly marked out upon the smooth, black, marble floor. Inside the centre of the large ring sat a smaller one that was surrounded by a multi-pointed star. The tips of the golden star touched the inner edge of the larger ring and it reflected the halogen light in dazzling brilliance. The centre of the smaller ring was clear, deliberately so, and the array of codes upon the floor were there to form an invisible shield, to hold just one individual. It was clear Storn wanted again to possess the Guardian woman called Rebecca. Upon the walls black velvet drapes, smothered in the selfsame gold coloured codes, hung from the ceiling to the floor. The only real difference Persephone could see between the new place and the one at Kirkham, was the addition of what seemed to be an altar. Just beyond the outer circle, towards the back wall, a raised area had been constructed. On the stage was another such section, seven feet in length and made from a huge block of black marble. At the base of the altar, forming a complete ring around it, sat a double row of unlit candles placed in stubby brass holders. Her study of the chilling scene was interrupted by a hand at her elbow guiding her to the corner. It was the woman, Rhen, and she spoke quietly in Persephone's ear.

"Your robes are over there with the others. It's the last peg on the right."

She nodded. "Okay."

Rhen gave a brief smile; she was already dressed in her robes and turned to make her way over to the altar. Persephone watched her as she crossed to the pedestal area and produced a cigarette lighter. Systematically, she quickly began the task of lighting the individual candles in the ring. With an inward sigh of resignation, Persephone went to get changed. Already most of her fellow travellers were in their robes and a low buzz of excited chatter filled the air. Without their evil enthusiasm for the ritual killing to come, she discarded her leather jacket and slipped the brown robe over her head. She knew it was nothing more than perverse ceremony for them to wear the things, a dreary brown monks-style habit. The rest, even her mother, to her dismay, revelled in the familiarity of it all. As she knotted the rope cord around her waist the circle of spot lamps in the roof were dimmed. What was to follow she had witnessed for the first time when she was just fourteen years old. It was an honour, or so her mother and father had instilled into her at the time, but there was no privilege in seeing the others take delight in the ritual killing of a helpless human being. The dreadful truth though was that there was no escape from it, now that she was older and under Storn's supervision. In fact things had worsened since he had taken so much interest in her and the fragile mental links she had with Paul Sayers. From that moment at Skelwith farm she had never been allowed anywhere on her own. One of Storn's personal guards continually shadowed her and she realised always would. The worst thing though was the guilt, the feeling that she was contaminated by it and would never be clean. But, even though the evil repulsed her, she was still with it by association.

The murmur of conversation died away, only to be followed by a low hum that they took up, one by one, as they made their way to the edge of the circle of candles. Systematically they began to spread themselves around the raised altar's base, keeping their heads bowed. The last light above winked out and the slow repetitive beat of a single drum began issuing from a set of concealed speakers in the roof. It sounded hollow, eerie, a low bass note echoing through Persephone's head. One by one the circle of followers fell to their knees around the altar. As they did, each took up a single word chant in turn.

"Chandra! Chandra! Chandra!" they repeated, loudly, as the call increased in time to the beating of the drum.

Persephone dropped to her knees and at the same time pulled the cowl of the habit over her head. She too took up the ceremonial chant, while inside she silently screamed out for them to stop the insanity they were indulging in.

"Please God, save me from this," she whispered

A quiet-running motor drew a series of long black curtains around them. The drapes, embellished in a maze of swirls, lines, and codes, completely enveloped the altar area. A similar patterned cover enclosed the space above them. The chant altered.

"Chandra comlea! Chandra comlea!"

For over five minutes they continued while the curtains shimmered around them in the light of the flickering candles. Then, in an instant, the chanting and the drum ceased. The silence was palpable, for almost a minute, before the curtains were pulled aside at the back of the altar. Storn appeared, as commanding as ever, basking in the devoted admiration of those around him; while feeding them his bidding in a way they would never understand. Their freewill was gone; it was purely an extension of his. The floor-length cloak he wore flowed out around him, masking the tall muscular body beneath. Emblazoned across the back of it was an intricately-embroidered golden sword, coiled around which was a colourful green serpent. He held out his hands, turning them palm upwards.

"Arise, my trusted disciples."

As one the circle rose, returning the gesture, arms outstretched.

"We come to you with nothing!" they called, in unison. "Give to us and we will humbly serve!"

"I will give to those who follow." From beneath the cloak he withdrew a long sword, gilded with gold. He turned and laid it upon the altar stone raising his arms skywards. "Witness the power of the serpent!"

"We are your devoted followers!" they immediately replied. "Let us respectfully stand before you and witness the power you command!"

He clapped his hands loudly above his head and briefly brushed them across the blade. In silence they watched as a bright glow encased it. Within a few seconds the light dispersed to leave a writhing green serpent wrapped around it. In awe they gazed at the apparition, unaware that Storn was simply playing an illusionary mind game with them.

"Bring to me the soul chosen to sustain me!" he commanded.

Behind him a gap appeared in the curtain. Two followers, dressed in their drab garb, semi-dragged the victim towards the altar. Tessa Fisher had been abducted two weeks before, on her way home from a night out. The operation, by Latham and his team, had been swift and unseen. Now, dressed in only a sheer-white slip, she was half-carried, half-dragged to the altar for Storn to execute. The drugs that had been administered throughout her incarceration had the desired effect. She could not speak, had no rational thought, and had no idea of what was happening. As they hoisted her up onto the cold marble slab she could see little through heavy eyes, while her body felt like jelly.

The followers moved closer, in eager anticipation, as Storn raised the sword above his head.

"The soul within is mine! And mine to take and use for the supplication of those who follow me!"

"We are those that follow. Take the soul that is not worthy of anything other than to nourish your absolute ascendancy!" they replied, in one voice.

The dullness that passed for thought in Tessa Fisher's head would not clear. It was a scant blessing, an escape from the awful reality around her. She could make out candles. Monks? Was it a monastery? She could not grasp it. As she looked up at the ceiling the blackness was only broken by the golden swirl of codes and figures glinting in the light. Then a face appeared over her, someone with a sword in their hand. Her eyes cleared a fraction and she could see who it was. Why was a middle-aged woman brandishing a sword in a monastery? What did it mean? What was she saying? What were those around her saying?

The circle of followers again dropped to their knees. Persephone too, as she looked on in wide-eyed horror, drawn to the dreadful sight. Helplessly trapped, she could only listen to Storn babble away in ritual verse while those around her responded, forcefully, on cue. Then they went silent. Storn carefully placed the tip of the sword just under the girl's ribcage and pushed it into the flesh. She did not utter a sound as the serpent uncoiled itself from the blade and slithered into the hole made by it. Once it had disappeared inside her he thrust the sword further into her chest and straight in her heart. The white slip rapidly turned crimson as the blood escaped from the fatal wound. As she died Tessa Fisher's head flopped to one side, leaving her to stare vacantly at those around her. Persephone felt her stomach heave over and fought to stop the rising vomit from entering her mouth. Moments later something unexpected happened, the like of which she had never witnessed before. From the dead girl's body a glowing sphere of light, the size of a small fist rose into the air. Persephone watched, fascinated by the spectre, acutely aware that the others could not see it. The sphere's upward motion was halted and it was drawn towards the open arms of Storn. She rapidly began to understand what it was that gave him his life and power. There were always ritual killings when he was there, his feeding as they called it. He fed on the souls of those he killed. Then, inexplicably, she saw a smaller sphere break away from the main one, just before it was drawn inside his body. The detached globe did not deviate and shot at high velocity straight towards her. Persephone was so taken aback by the sight of it she had no chance to avoid it. At the same moment that Storn devoured the soul of Tessa Fisher, a small part of it entered Persephone's spirit.

Storn removed the sword and passed it to one of those attending. The ritual was over. He stood over the inert body and crossed his arms over his chest, bathing in the surge of energy it had given him. Around the altar the followers looked on, pleased that all had gone well. Persephone felt different too, as a warm feeling flared inside her.

Chapter 4

Monday 21st December 1992

Paul Sayers lived in the small rural village of Sawston, in the Fens of Cambridgeshire. Most of those who lived in the village worked on the surrounding farmland. Paul was no different. Just twenty-eight years old, and single, he worked less than a mile from where he lived. At five feet ten he did not stand out in a crowd, although his build well matched his height and a love of fell-walking and rock climbing kept him reasonably fit. Although no one would ever see him as being athletic, he possessed a measure of strength and stamina and had steel-blue eyes that held a trace of tenacity. He never entertained the idea he was good looking and could live with the fact that women did not run to be in his company. One older female friend had once told him that he was 'pleasant to look at', and it was a description he could live with. It was a Monday and no different from any other weekday morning. It was a little after six and, as he stirred, he adjusted his eyes to the dim light. Almost at once he became aware that someone was sitting on the end of the bed. Without looking he reached out and flicked on the bedside lamp. The gloom was instantly replaced by a soft white glow. With her depthless blue eyes, Rebecca studied the man she loved and smiled, warmly, at the sleep-worn face looking at her. Rebecca carried no lines on a well-defined and evenly proportioned face. Her skin was soft, clear, and devoid of any blemishes. Paul would readily admit her face held no discernable age and she could pass for anywhere between sixteen and thirty, depending on what she wore. Nearly as tall as he, she had shoulder length fawn-blonde hair in loose curls around her face.

"Good morning my darling," she greeted, her voice musically

light on the ear while her whole being radiated endless affection for him.

"It is now," he countered, casually propping himself up on one elbow.

Although he had not seen her for three weeks she looked as if she had just woken with him. She looked so beautiful, so assured, and he savoured the moment. Seductively she crossed one shapely leg over the other, revealing the flesh of her thigh. She wore a sheer black negligee, with lace edging, that left nothing to the imagination and revealed the sensual curves beneath. With a wicked smile she could easily sense what he was thinking and well aware that he could see everything of her naked body through the wisp of material. She took pleasure in the fact he was enjoying every second of it and could feel the sexual tension that seemingly existed in the space between them.

"Such thoughts, you naughty boy," she warned, in a not very convincing tone.

"Well, sexy lady, you shouldn't come to my bed dressed, although I should say hardly dressed, like you are." He reached out and began to draw her towards the pulled down duvet.

"No," she warned, trying to resist. "You should not Paul."

"Then why come here in a negligee displaying a gorgeous pair of breasts and pert nipples if you had no intention of getting close to me?"

"Such rude talk," she replied. "It is my body you are talking about."

He opened the duvet and she was quickly under it, lying on top of him with only the wisp of clothing between them.

"What are you doing here at this time of day?" he asked, slightly puzzled by the early morning visit. "I've got to go to work you know."

"I had to come now and let you know I will not be able to make it this weekend."

He was genuinely disappointed and tried hard not to show it.

"I am sorry my darling. I know it means a lot to you, it does to me too, but there are some things I must do." She ran her fingers lovingly down his cheek.

Resigned to it, he sighed, kissing her on the forehead.

"I know you wouldn't break our time together lightly. But what am I to do for company this Christmas? I thought for once I'd have someone special to share it with."

"You will."

"Like who?"

"Rosemary," she replied, as if he should already know. "She is going to phone you later."

He knew better than to question her. If she said Rosemary would call, she would. Yet he appeared indifferent to the suggestion that he should go to the Pennines, and the town of Begdale, for Christmas.

"Go on," Rebecca urged. "You should go. I have a special present she will need."

"Oh alright then," he finally conceded. "I'll go. It'll be a good excuse to dig out the boots and rucksack."

She smiled as he looked into her depthless, sparkling blue eyes. "A present for Rosemary you said?"

She nodded.

"Where's mine then."

"It is just me."

"Everything I ever wanted," he said, slipping his hands up the lace hem of her negligee. She shuddered at the intimate touch as he reached her naked bottom and lightly caressed the smooth, firm, flesh. "Stay awhile and before I go to work I'll take the wrapping paper off."

"You will be late."

"Who cares? It'll run without me for an hour or two."

"No," she warned, and tried to wriggle free. "You know we must not."

"Don't be a spoilsport," he retorted, pulling the flimsy negligee up to completely uncover her bare bottom. "Anyway, it's usually you who gets carried away with it all."

"I know," she said, stifling a giggle.

"Is your bag safe?"

"I wondered if you would spot that I do not have it," she replied, showing him her right wrist. She had on a silver bracelet, less than a centimetre wide, that was a perfect fit. It was studded with small blue and white crystals that twinkled brightly.

"After my episode at Storn's hands, Charlotte decided we all needed something less vulnerable. Bracelets have been used before, but now we all have them."

He took hold of her wrist and admired the sparkling piece of jewellery.

"How does it work?"

"Too complicated to explain, but all I have to do is touch a particular spot on it and I am safely away."

"If you'd had it a few weeks ago Stanford wouldn't have got you."

"You are right," she replied, lowering her wrist. "It feels so much more secure and has restored my confidence."

"Well, feel secure with me," he added, pulling the duvet right over the top of them.

Rebecca giggled as they cuddled up together in the warmth.

"You just be careful not to get carried away. You know the promise you made to Charlotte."

"Yeah, but it didn't say anything about not being able to fool around under the covers."

Chapter 5

It was exactly nine-thirty, two and a half hours later than usual, when Paul arrived at the vegetable packing plant. A chill wind lazily cut across the puddle strewn car park as he headed towards the office block. Gary Malins, his old friend, appeared without warning from the nearest packing shed and made a beeline straight to him.

"Head down mate," Gary warned, as he reached Paul's shoulder. He wore faded jeans, an old bomber jacket, and boots. A little over six feet tall, he was powerfully built. Moving heavy sacks of vegetables all day was better than attending a gym. Although born in the Fens his parents were originally from Trinidad.

"And a very good morning to you too Gary," Paul cheerily threw back, clearly ignoring the advice.

Gary placed a chunky hand on Paul's shoulder and pulled him up.

"You're late, on a Monday morning. It's four days to Christmas, at our busiest time of year. Longsdale's steaming, excessively, and you're happy. If I didn't know your love life better I'd say it was a woman keeping you in bed this morning."

Untroubled by the firm grip, Paul turned to face Gary and raised his eyebrows.

"You sly bastard," Gary said, almost in disbelief at the inference, allowing Paul to continue on his way to the office. "Anyone I know?"

"No. And tell that motley crew you have working in those sheds; if all production quotas are met this week I'll personally guarantee the bonus will be doubled."

"Seriously?" he called after him. "You'll never swing it. He's in a foul mood because he's got to fly to Australia to visit family. You being late will only worsen it."

"I guarantee it. Take bets on the outcome if you like. I'm about to prove you can get blood from a stone."

Gary stood in the middle of the wet car park and laughed. Only a few weeks earlier Paul had gone missing for three weeks. There had been trouble, but the whole workforce had been behind him.

"You daft bugger!" he called out. "We went on strike to get you your job back. Don't blow it now."

"I won't. It's time I paid everybody back for what they did," Paul replied. "Anyway, we both know Longsdale couldn't organise a piss up in a brewery. He needs us to handle this place."

"You can say that again," Gary answered, in a low voice, as Paul disappeared inside the office block. "And it's good to see there's a woman in your life too. Especially if it puts a smile on your face."

"Good morning, Jenny," Paul brightly greeted the baby faced teenage receptionist.

"Good morning Mr. Sayers."

"Paul, Jenny, you can call me Paul," he added, as he went through the glass door into the corridor. Briefly, he stopped at the first office on the right and poked his head through the door. It was occupied by his personal secretary, Sally Marcroft. She was dependable, professional, and kept the rubbish from his desk. It was as if she had a sixth sense when it came to calls and callers. She would instantly know those he needed to talk to and those he did not.

When she saw him she took off her glasses and put down the folder she was engrossed in.

"You're late Paul," she informed him, seriously.

"So everyone keeps telling me," he replied, smiling happily. "So it really must be true."

"I called, but your phone was engaged. We're you alright?"

"I was busy."

Sally was pretty, with a clear complexion and soft blue eyes. She got up and crossed to where he stood. At five feet eight she was nearly as tall as Paul and, if she wore high heels, she looked him straight in the eye. The hair was brushed back from her face and cut short, yet she dyed it blonde.

"Longsdale's in a foul mood," she whispered, and poked her head around the door to look down the corridor. "Even for a Monday it's a bad one. I'm sure he'll blow a blood vessel one day." She looked at him, concerned, which amused him. He always got on well with her, their ages were the same, even though she came from the 'posher' end of town as Gary called it. Her local accent was much clearer than his Fen one. He had attended the local comprehensive, with Gary, but she had gone to the Catholic school.

"It's not funny," she added, seeing the amused expression on his face. "Tread carefully."

He continued to smile, failing to be dimmed by the dire warnings. For a change he felt alive and relaxed by the morning interlude with Rebecca.

"I'll have the delivery order totals, a decent cuppa, a sandwich from the canteen, and this morning's phone messages please. And in that order Sally."

She followed as he made his way to his own office. The lights and heating were already on, she had made sure of it, and he threw his jacket over the chair.

"I'll make you a fresh cup of tea rather than get one from the machine. It'll taste better."

He winked at her as he sat down. "Good girl, you do look after me."

"Sayers!" a deep voice bellowed from the far end of the corridor, causing Sally to jump.

"I did warn you," she whispered.

"I now have the delightful task of informing our much-loved employer he's paying double bonuses this year. Now, be a good girl Sally and get that tea and sandwich before the roof blows off."

"Suicide," she muttered, and quickly disappeared.

"Sayers!" Longsdale bellowed again.

"I'm busy!" Paul shouted back, refusing to go to the raucous beckoning. "What do you want, yelling down the corridor? You'll wake up half the production line if you're not careful."

Moments later the sound of heavy footsteps came clumping

down the corridor. Already Paul had breathed in and was counting to ten. As he finished, Longsdale stepped into the office, filling the doorway with his portly bulk. His face appeared bright red, stretching up to fill his balding, white haired head. After a short pause Paul glanced up from the sheet he was studying, but remained seated behind his desk.

"Good morning Neville. Working up a good head of steam for a second heart attack I see."

"You're late," he shouted, pointing accusingly at him.

"Bollocks."

"What?" Longsdale spluttered, unprepared for the reply.

"Bollocks," Paul happily repeated. "This place runs twenty-four hours a day, six days a week, and twelve on Sunday. The simple fact is I regularly put in sixty odd hours a week. Of which I only get paid for fifty. Therefore, when I turn up or leave is of little or no concern. It's you who works a short shift."

"It's Monday," Longsdale stated, incredulous at the response.

Paul picked up the desk calendar and studied it, animatedly.

"So it is. I'm so glad you're here to tell us these things."

"Don't try sarcasm with me, Sayers, I won't stand for it. You being late has meant turning down an order for Harvey's."

"You've turned down an order?" Paul asked, picking up the telephone and tapping in a number from memory.

"Hello," he greeted, as the call was answered. "Brian Shaw, please. Yes, Elaine, it's Paul Sayers."

"You won't work it," Longsdale added. "It's impossible."

"Morning Brian, it's Paul here," he began. "I believe there's been some confusion over an order you wanted to place." As he spoke, Sally squeezed past Longsdale and placed a mug of tea on the desk.

"I know what was said, but there were some crossed lines at our end. No, I'm not trying to sweet talk my way out Brian. I'll put it right because it's my fault. Tell me what you require and I'll guarantee it." Paul took some notes, repeating "okay" several times. "I'll see you have it at your distribution depot by seven this evening. Many thanks, Brian, there'll be something special sent as an apology, have a good Christmas."

31

Paul replaced the handset and immediately picked up the internal line to Gary's factory floor office. With a shake of the head he again looked up at Longsdale.

"Our biggest and best paying customer and you turned them down. What possessed you? Make sure you send him a decent bottle of whiskey today by courier."

"We can't cope with an order that size," he replied.

"You don't know how to sensibly deal with the people around you, Neville, that's why you can't cope," Paul bluntly told him. "If you treated them with a little more respect and some good manners you'd get on better."

Longsdale was stunned by the obvious character assassination, while Sally looked on, uncomfortably.

"Gary," Paul said, lazily into the phone. "I'm afraid there's been an urgent review. I need twenty tonnes off line one, four off two, four off three, and two off line five. Use a standard weight mix in Harvey's own label and put the lot on a wagon to be at their depot by seven this evening." There followed a pause while he held the phone well away from his ear. Gary's verbal tirade could be plainly heard pouring out from the other end. If the office window had been open they would have possibly heard him without the use of the phone.

Paul smiled at Sally. "When you get me that sandwich send a couple over to him. Put it on my tab."

"I will." She smiled and left, deliberately avoiding eye contact with Longsdale.

"See, Neville, treat people right and they suddenly cope for you. Are you paying the bonus this week?"

Grudgingly, he nodded as Paul again spoke to Gary. "And tell everyone the double Christmas bonus is being paid this week. Yes, Neville's in the office with me right now, he's just Okayed it."

Word spread instantly, before he had replaced the handset, and they clearly heard a cheer go up from the packing shed nearest to them.

"A happy workforce, Neville," Paul added. "How do you do it?"

Longsdale's eyes had grown, like saucers, and he tried to speak, but no words came out.

"Go and sit down Neville," Paul urged, while trying to disguise his obvious pleasure at his predicament. "You'll need the rest or you'll spoil your Australia trip."

Sally re-entered the office just as he left it and Paul quietly laughed as she placed a packet of sandwiches on his desk.

"There you go Sally, blood from a stone."

"You've a call," she said, leaning across to pick up the right phone and hand it to him.

"Who's it this time? Not another unhappy customer?"

"No," she replied. "Personal. Rosemary?"

He quickly took it from her. "Good morning. How are you keeping Rosemary?"

"Hello Paul," she happily answered, glad to hear him in good cheer. "I'm just fine, you?"

"Couldn't be better," he replied, and visualised her sitting at the bottom of the stairs in the hallway of Fell cottage. He had stayed with her in the Pennine town of Begdale, a few weeks earlier, and they had become very good friends.

"What can I do for you?" he asked, well aware of what it was she wanted, thanks to the prior warning from Rebecca.

"What are you doing for the holiday?" she asked. .

"Feet up, I suppose."

"Will you come and stay with me for a few days Paul? I'd love your company."

"That's just what I need. Should I bring anything special?"

"Just yourself," she said, with a laugh in her voice. "Oh, and something smart to wear. I've got tickets for a dinner dance in Leeds on Christmas Eve."

"Okay Rosie, sounds great. I won't be late, see you soon."

As he hung up he could see Sally looking at him, a disappointed look on her face.

"I wanted to ask you to come to mine on Christmas Day, Paul. I know you often spend the holiday alone," she said, brushing at her hair as if wiping away an imaginary tear.

He attempted to sound sincere. "You never said, Sally."

"I was going to, today, when we had a quiet moment."

"You usually spend Christmas with your parents. I don't think they'd appreciate me being there," he said, truthfully. "Rosemary's going to spend Christmas alone if I don't go. I can't call back now and say no, can I?"

"No, I understand," she mumbled, defeated. "I just wish I'd have asked earlier."

"Next year" he encouraged, warmly.

"You bet," Sally quickly answered, feeling more enthusiastic. "Why can't we ever get ourselves started Paul? What's the reason?"

He knew the answer, but she never wanted to hear it.

"It wouldn't last Sally. I could never get myself committed to a relationship. If it's not work it's old cars or walking. You know me. You're a pretty girl Sally. You're wasting your time waiting for me. I mean it. Leave me to meander through life as I am."

Briefly, he held her eye, seeing she was an attractive woman, yet knowing that there was nothing there for him. He could only love her as one friend could love another. Love of an intimate kind would never take place between them. He only wished she could see it the same way. Her parents would never accept him and he did not want the same thing to happen to him as had to his mother before him.

"It's not a waste of time, waiting for the right man to realise what's in front of his eyes," she said. "Ask any girl."

He shook his head. "You're still not listening."

"What about Rosemary?"

"She's a very good friend. No more than that."

"Good," she almost whispered. "Was she with you a few weeks ago when you were away without word? You've never fully explained what happened."

He shrugged. She was right; he had not because he did not want to. Only Gary and his wife, Gaynor, had been told of what had happened at Kirkham.

"No, she wasn't. There's little to explain. I just needed to get completely away from everything. It was like a depression. I couldn't tell you because I didn't understand it."

"And your left hand?" she added.

He held it up. The little finger and part of the hand with it was missing. It had been crudely hacked off with a spade by one of

Storn's men in the yard at Skelwith farm. There was no way he would ever tell her the truth.

"I told you. I went to the Lakes to get away from it all and slipped in some sharp crags."

"Okay Paul, I believe you, if that's what you're saying." She left without further word.

He watched her leave. Everyone else believed the story he had concocted except her. In fact every time he repeated it, it sounded better and better. Perhaps it was the Alice in Wonderland effect coming into play. Say something that is a lie three times and it becomes the truth. He shook his head and opened the packet of sandwiches. Moments later he was lost in paperwork and making the first phone calls of the day. The routine, as usual, sucked his attention.

Forty miles away the police were still undertaking a detailed examination of where Tessa Fisher's remains had been discovered. Their task, and the grisly one being undertaken by the pathologist, had set them on the road to discovering her killer. Many avenues of inquiry would be opened, but it would take months to finally solve. Paul had seen the television news over the weekend and had caught the initial reports of the murder. Like so many other things he had taken little notice of it, a daily occurrence, something that had happened to someone else. He was blindly unaware that her death, like those to follow, the police investigation, and his life, were heading towards a deadly meeting point.

Chapter 6

Thursday 24th December 1992

The house at the bottom end of Chapel Lane, Fell Cottage, was familiar to Paul. The house was detached, with five bedrooms, and Rosemary used it as a bed and breakfast establishment. Like the rest of the houses in the lane she kept her frontage immaculate. He drew onto the driveway in his Vauxhall Cavalier and parked next to the powder blue Mercedes convertible that was outside the garage. There had been a second fall of snow that morning and the drive had been meticulously swept. A similar brushed swathe ran to the front door. It was decorated with a holly wreath and the front windows were crisscrossed with multi-coloured fairy lights. He smiled at the cheeriness of it all. He had not bothered with such things for years. It never seemed worth it just for himself.

A sharp winter chill sent an involuntary shudder down his back. The warmth of the car had fooled him into a false sense of what it was like so close to the Pennines. The grey skies appeared full of snow and dirty-coloured clouds cloaked the hills. The tops were completely masked from view, but he hoped the weather would clear whilst he was there. His winter walking gear lay in the boot of the car and he had every intention of using it. The front door opened and Rosemary trotted out. She was in a long denim dress and thick woollen cardigan. At forty-two years of age Rosemary was a widow, her husband being a much older man when they had married. She always complained about being overweight, but was not, and possessed a curvaceous figure. Her long dark hair was lightly streaked with grey. The days of colouring it had passed.

"You've made it," she greeted, her grey eyes flashing joy.

He embraced her in a warm hug and spun her off her feet. She kissed him on the cheek.

"It's good to see you Paul."

"Thank you for having me."

"It's my pleasure. There's no point in being alone when we can share the time together."

"Too true," he replied, looking round at the failing light. "Sorry for being a bit late. It won't mess up going to the dance?"

"Not at all, we've plenty of time. What held you up?"

He answered, while at the same time extracting two large travel bags from the car. "Nothing, really, it was a good run up, but I had to attend a funeral this morning."

"Oh dear," she sighed. "Someone close?"

He half shrugged as he walked to the front door and placed the bags inside.

"She was a neighbour, Mrs. Eastwick. She's lived next door since before I was born. My mother and she were good friends. She baby sat me for many years."

"Was she getting on then?"

"She was in her early seventies, but still sprightly for her age." As he spoke he lifted out another holdall. "She wouldn't let me do a thing for her though."

She took it from him. "How did she die?"

He hefted a large plastic crate from the boot before shutting it.

"She was run over crossing the road in the village. The bastard failed to stop."

"Oh dear. Was there family?"

"I never saw anyone, regularly, but some daughter of a cousin turned up out of the blue for the funeral. Funny woman, hardly spoke a word to any of us there, but said she intended to move into the house with her husband as soon as possible."

"You'll have new neighbours then."

"Yeah, but I'm not expecting much in the way of neighbourliness."

"Any more bags?" she asked, as he followed her.

"No, just this load of veg."

She closed the door and deposited the bag with the others. "You shouldn't have."

"You forget what I do for a living," he said, grinning, as he went through to the kitchen.

"Not working today then?"

He placed the crate on the table and laughed. "We're supposed to be, but Longsdale's wife finally persuaded him to take her to Australia to see her sister."

"So the cat's away, etc," she said, with a smile.

He nodded. "Sally confirmed with Heathrow yesterday morning that they'd taken off, so I closed the place down and we went home at noon."

"Will he find out?"

"Who cares," he replied, sitting down. "Bonuses have been paid and everything's been delivered. Gary and I have fiddled the worksheets to make it look as if we have."

Rosemary filled the kettle. "Would you like a cup of tea?"

"Please, I couldn't be bothered with the motorway services."

"So you've had your bonus then?"

"Not until April."

"Why's that?"

"When Gary and I started to put the factory back on its feet, ten years ago, I had it written into the contracts that we'd receive no bonuses. Instead we get one percent of the financial year's profit at the end of the tax year."

She turned, a surprised look on her face. "But Longsdale's is a big business. You pack for several chains don't you?"

He pulled a pre-pack of carrots from the plastic crate and showed them to her.

"I've just secured the new Ferndale contract this week. We'll increase our business by a quarter next year. Then the next new thing will be organically grown stuff, if it'll ever take off."

"You'll be busier than ever then?"

"It keeps growing. From two run down packing sheds and a caravan for an office we've moved to nine sheds, washing plant, weighbridge, loading bays and haulage fleet. Apart from plastic bags and packaging we do everything ourselves, on one site." He smiled, but not really at her. "It sounds strange, but I love the place and hate it as well. It's like a child who's grown up, but you can't let it go. For those first few years we put in countless hours, for peanuts money. The buyer walked out after six months, the next after two, and the one before me after a week with Neville Longsdale."

She laughed. "So how do you tackle him? You couldn't have been more than a teenager."

"True, it's all I was. But I'd learnt from school how to ignore the ignoramuses around me. Insulting me is like water off a duck's back. I'd no father, so had heard them all before I was twelve."

"And Gary?"

"He had it worse. Parents from Trinidad and the only coloured face amongst dozens of kids. We've had the last laugh though. We took dead end jobs in a place that was a whisker from closing down, but between us we turned it around."

"Dare I ask how much profit you made last year?" Rosemary tentatively asked, as she handed him a steaming cup of tea.

"You could've read it in The Financial Times, but it was around four-point-seven million," he replied, casually.

"Then you got forty-seven-thousand pounds each," she exclaimed.

"Something like that. About two and a half years worth of wages in one payment. That's why I believe Neville's forgotten about it. It's paid direct from the company accounts and not by him personally. We've had similar amounts for the past three years now, but, with the Ferndale account, it'll rise.

"Doesn't he notice your lifestyle," she added, taken aback by his frank disclosure.

"We both keep quiet and invest the bulk. Gary wants to retire early and live a lazy life."

"And you Paul," she added. "What do you want from life?"

"A quiet one," he replied, truthfully. "Anyhow, don't talk to me about lifestyle when there's a Merc sports car sitting on the drive."

She feigned hurt. "I do have some nice things. If you're a good boy, I'll let you drive it later," she tempted. "We'll be eating tonight, at the do, but would you like a snack now?"

"Any chance of a bacon sandwich?"

"I've already prepared some. Are you sure you can dance?"

Before she reached the fridge he was on his feet and taking her in his arms. With half a dozen light steps he took her around the kitchen and spun her on the spot.

"Alright, I believe you," she said, as he bowed and kissed her hand. "You can dance."

"Lots of work related stuff revolves around dinners, socials, and posh events. It pays to be able to whisk some client's wife around a dance floor."

"I don't doubt it."

"I served at Clayborough's finest," he added. "The Alison Harris School of Dance."

She went to the fridge. "Don't tell me. Gold medal standard, right?"

It was his turn to appear hurt. "Gold Bar I'll have you know."

As she got his sandwich he went into the hallway and retrieved one of the larger bags. She watched as he took out a parcel from inside.

"This is for you Rosie," he said, handing it to her.

"Thank you, but shouldn't presents wait until tomorrow?"

"It's a gift from Charlotte for nursing me back from death's door. You'd better have it now, for obvious reasons when you see it."

Rosemary eagerly pulled the wrapping apart and caught her breath as a shimmering red evening dress spilled out into her hands. The material glinted in the kitchen spotlights and threw off sparkling flashes of colour.

"Oh Paul, it's gorgeous," she gushed, as she held it up to the light. "I'll just have to wear it tonight."

"It's a copy of the one Charlotte and Rebecca wore when we shared that meal together."

"I told her at the time I adored her dress. Strapless, backless, and split to the top of each thigh. How sensual, and in my colour too. How did she know my size?"

"I've been told to tell you to never let anyone else have it. It'll never fade, crease, or stain, while you have it. And, no matter how your figure changes, it'll always be a perfect fit."

She looked quizzical as she held it close to herself. The hem was level with her ankles.

"How can it do that?"

He shrugged. "Don't ask too many questions, just accept it."

"I will. Thank her for me."

"I already have."

She carefully laid it over the back of a chair. "I've put you in the room you had last time, okay? Water's hot if you'd like a soak before going out."

"Sounds great," he replied, as she handed him a sandwich. "I bet I put on weight while I'm here."

Chapter 7

"Well then," Rosemary began, breaking the twenty minute silence that had prevailed since leaving the hotel complex. "Did you enjoy yourself?"

Paul glanced sideways at her seated beside him, dressed in the shimmering red evening dress and a full-length sheepskin coat. She had done her own hair, leaving it loose, with a minimum of make-up.

"It was a wonderful evening Rosie," he replied, honestly. "It's been a long time since I've had such a carefree evening in such lovely company."

She demurely blushed. "I've never had such a first-rate evening out before. Thank you for taking me. And you danced really well."

"I was a bit rusty to start with, if you're truthful."

"Nonsense," she chided. "Everyone was looking, whenever we danced."

"It wasn't me they were looking at," he laughed. "With those splits in that dress as high as they are and your cleavage, I was invisible."

She visibly blushed again. "Oh Paul, I really do feel good in this. It's like I'm not really wearing anything. You just can't feel it on your skin. I expected not to have to wear a bra with it, but when I slipped it on I just had to take my knickers off too." She giggled, closing her eyes. "It was as if the dress rejected them. I'm naked under this."

"Don't tell me things like that."

As the Mercedes rounded the next bend on the winding road back over the Pennines to Begdale, he saw the old lady in the middle of the road in front of them. Dressed in a sensible tweed skirt and jacket, she had only a knitted shawl to keep out the cold winter night. Surprised to see someone in such conditions, at two in the morning, Paul braked hard to avoid running her down. As he did he could feel the back end of the German sports car twitch on the slushy road.

"Shit," he muttered, as it slid almost sideways to a halt.

"What's the matter?" Rosemary asked, pointedly, as she opened her eyes.

"It looks like Miss Marple standing in the road. God knows what's she's doing here."

"What does she want?" Rosemary asked, almost to herself, peering out through the windscreen. The wipers flicked back and forth in an effort to clear the falling sleet. Paul opened the door as the woman shuffled her way through the slush to them.

"You'll get killed standing there!" he called out. "What's the matter?"

She pulled the woollen shawl tighter around her shoulders as the sleet ran down the sides of her wrinkled face. Her hair was grey, although dripping wet, and her voice held age, yet was perfectly clear in tone.

"There's a van around the corner. A young woman's been abducted by three men. I fear they mean to kill her."

"Have you rung the police?" Rosemary asked, leaning across Paul.

She shook her head. "No phones up here."

"Are you sure about this?" Paul quizzed her, uncertain of the situation but feeling with some inner sense that she was genuine.

"Yes I am," the old woman replied in a more urgent, almost pleading tone. "Please will you do something to help?"

Again he looked to Rosemary, who simply shrugged.

"Quickly, please," the old lady again pleaded.

"Alright, I'll take a look." Slowly, he eased the car into gear and set off carefully in the sleet. As they went round the bend he glanced in the rear-view mirror and saw the woman following them. In front they both saw a white van. Paul flicked the headlamps to main beam and drove into the lay-by. Halfway along its length sat a battered Transit van. It was unlit, but the tyre tracks it had made were visible in the slush. It had obviously not been there for very long.

"Well it's here," he said, quietly, to Rosemary.

"Be careful Paul," she warned. "It seems very odd to me."

"Yeah, I know what you mean. It's Christmas morning for heavens sake. Where's the good cheer and peace of the season gone?"

He stopped ten yards short of the van and flicked on the front fog lights. The powerful beams brightly illuminated the area between the two vehicles.

"What now?" she whispered.

Paul removed his tie and jacket and slipped on his fleece.

"Time to see if anyone's in," he replied, somewhat more determined in manner, as the adrenaline began to pump in his body. From the centre console he unclipped the fire extinguisher from its bracket.

"Just in case," he added, taking it as a weapon. "Keep the engine running, Rosie, and slip in behind the wheel."

"Why?"

"If it gets silly put your foot down and get out of here."

Her face immediately flushed with concern. "No way, Paul, I won't leave you behind."

"Don't argue with me Rosie. Just make certain you get away."

He gave her no time to object and stepped from the car. As he did he glanced back the way they had come. The old lady was just visible, making her way towards them through the steadily falling sleet. He zipped the fleece up to his neck to keep out the elements and crossed to the back of the Transit. The sensation was odd, but he knew for certain he could trust the woman. Everything was clear at that point, except what she was doing on a deserted high Pennine road in such appalling weather. Inside he could feel his heart rate quickening. The windows in the rear doors of the van had been painted over and he caught the sound of voices coming from inside. Consciously he relaxed, wiping the clinging wet from his face. There was no time for pleasantries and he banged the base of the extinguisher hard on the door. The voices inside fell silent as he took two steps back. Both doors burst open, with a metallic wrench, and banged loudly as they came into contact with the sides. The dim interior lamp was overpowered by the lights of the

Mercedes and the inside of the van was filled with brightness. The scene that greeted Paul was unmistakable and he felt revulsion. Inside were three men, in their twenties, surrounding a young woman. She had been forced down onto a filthy tarpaulin, spread out across the rusty floor of the van. In the light he glimpsed the cold, stark, fear induced look of terror on her face. It chilled him more than the air temperature ever could. Most of her clothing had been either removed or ripped to one side. Her eyes, wide with fear, stared out at him, either with dread that he had arrived to join in, or in some vain hope he was there to help. He could not tell which.

The first of the three attackers, a rough shaven man in jeans and denim jacket, sat smoking a cigarette on the right hand wheel arch. The second, on the left hand side, had his hair in a ponytail and wore glasses. He was knelt next to the girl, pinning her arms above her head. The third was crouched at the rear and had opened the doors to discover who had intruded on their crime. He was a spotty faced youth with coloured spiky hair and a cigarette between his lips. It was obvious he was in the act of lowering his trousers.

"What the fuck d'ya want?" the one on the wheel arch spat at Paul. "Piss off before we giv ya some trouble!"

Outwardly Paul remained calm, belying the tension he could feel rising in his body. He was truly sickened and would never leave anyone in such an appalling predicament. There was going to be trouble for sure, because, as usual, he was going to be the catalyst for it.

"You know what you're doing is incredibly wrong, by any stretch of the imagination," he said, coolly. "Why not stop before it really does go too far." In his own mind he knew his words were falling on deaf ears. They had little intention of stopping the rape or allowing him to walk away.

"I'm gonna cut you up first," the dark haired one spat.

Paul saw the glint of steel as a knife appeared in his hand. 'Party time,' he mentally whispered. The night air was bitterly cold as a swirl of wind whipped the sleet up around them. The pause was momentary; the assailant with the knife sprang out of the van. He landed in a crouching posture a few inches from where Paul stood.

Despite the situation he almost laughed at the misjudgment. It was clear they were only able to pick on defenceless women when in a gang. Without any thought of restraint he whipped the extinguisher into the side of the attacker's head. He stood no chance and, without a noise, fell sprawling in the slush at Paul's feet. The knife fell harmlessly to the floor and he kicked it away into the darkness. Without waiting, Paul covered the short distance to the van in two long strides. He again took a firm grip on his makeshift weapon. The spiky haired youth, who had been nearest, was standing up with his trousers around his ankles. He was vainly trying to pull them back up before Paul reached him. The delay was costly and he reached inside, grabbing him by the shirt front. Even Rosemary heard the youth yell, in complete surprise, as Paul wrenched him out. With his lowered trousers he had no balance and tumbled out headfirst. With one powerful swing Paul swiped him across the back of the skull and he ended up in an unconscious heap.

Paul was not even breathing hard as he turned his attention to the last one. The man with the ponytail stared at him in outright disbelief while the girl struggled against his restraining grip.

"Out!" Paul ordered, his face a threatening stare as the sleet ran freely down it.

The man failed to respond and only continued to hold onto the girl.

"Who the hell are you anyway? You ain't the police. What's it to you?"

"Go on, make it hard, you piece of filth," Paul barked.

Without replying he let go of the girl and turned his full attention to Paul. The girl, free of restraint, scuttled away, desperately pulling the remnants of her tattered clothing around her.

"Out!" Paul repeated, as he stepped back. This time the man stepped forwards and jumped out onto the ground in front of him. As he landed he took one huge swinging lunge at Paul, trying to catch him off-guard. However, Paul had taken a measure of him and ducked easily out of the path of the fist. As he went down he lashed the extinguisher into the man's right kneecap. The effect was instant. He immediately forgot the assault and screamed loudly in pain as a fiery sensation shot up his leg. Without waiting, Paul grabbed him by the collar of his leather jacket and slammed him against the side of the van. The jolt winded him enough, but Paul was following it up with a knee to the groin that doubled him over with an audible gasp.

"No more," he managed to say, but Paul slammed his fist straight into his stomach. It had the effect of dropping the hapless attacker to the ground. Paul was in no mood to show any sort of mercy and wrenched the winded man back up onto his feet by his ponytail. He pulled his head back and forced it into the side of the van.

"No more, please," he gasped, again.

"Can't take the medicine you so happily dish out to others?" Paul said, slamming him into the van. "Takes three of you for one girl?"

The broken assailant weakly nodded and Paul roughly pulled the leather jacket off his back. He then turned him round and pushed him back against the van.

"Now everything else off," he coldly instructed.

Still shaking, and short of breath, his eyes widened. "What? No way am..."

Paul rammed a fist deep into his stomach for a second time.

"Wrong response. In case you've not been paying attention, I don't play by the rules."

The man was bent over and Paul smashed a knee into his face, knocking him backwards. Blood poured from his nose as he sank to the ground. Then, coughing and shaking, he slowly began to undress.

Seated in the still running Mercedes, Rosemary watched in disbelief as the last of the three young men began to undress. Paul's quick and clinical despatch of the first two had been a surprising revelation. The subsequent treatment he had handed out to the third had been almost too much to watch. His ability to look after himself against greater odds, in difficult situations, was quite evident.

Paul stood impassive as the man stood completely naked and shivering violently, in the freezing air. Strangely, he could not feel one scrap of pity for the distressed assailant. He pointed down the road.

"You'd better start walking."

The man looked agonised, adding to his paling features and the blood running down his face. "You can't do this," he bleated. "I'll freeze to death."

"Learn a lesson. Don't pick on defenceless women. Now walk"

He shook his head, but Paul smiled, without humour.

"I don't much care what you do, sunshine, but walking you might stand a chance, unconscious you won't. Understand?"

He did and quickly began to run down the road. Paul waited until he had disappeared from sight before picking up the leather jacket and discarded jeans from the ground. Then, without looking directly at the semi-naked girl, he tossed the clothing to her.

"If you pop those on we'll take you home or to the police, your choice."

Shaking, with a mixture of shock and the cold, the girl tentatively picked up the leather jacket and put it on, closing it tightly around herself. Then, as she slipped on the trousers, Rosemary appeared, carrying a tartan car rug.

"My name's Rosemary," she said, lightly, to the cowering girl and held out the unfolded blanket. "You're in good hands. This'll keep you warm."

Seeing Rosemary sparked something in the girl and she quickly went to her. She gingerly jumped out of the Transit and shied away from where the two men were lying face down on the ground. Almost at once she started sobbing as she fell into Rosemary's welcoming embrace and was led away to the warmth of the waiting Mercedes.

Paul removed the ignition keys from the van and flung them far into the darkness. After opening the bonnet he ripped out the distributor cap and ignition leads. On returning to the car he found Rosemary, on the back seat, with her arm around the blanket clad young woman. Thankfully, she looked less drained and had almost stopped sobbing. But on her face he could see some red marks and knew she would have bruises for several days to come. He slipped in behind the wheel, thankful to be back in the warm and dry, and glanced at them both.

"Are you ready to go?"

Rosemary nodded and pointed to the two men being gradually covered by falling snow.

"Are you going to leave them there?" she asked.

"They won't get far if they wake up. I've disabled the van and thrown their shoes away. If they think they're big and hard, picking on women, let's see how tough they really are."

"They would've killed me," the girl whispered. "They said as much because I'd seen their faces."

"Then let's go," he added.

Rosemary looked out of the rear window, peering into the darkness, and then questioningly back at him. "What about the old lady who flagged us down?"

"Don't know, Rosie. I saw her just before the trouble started, but not since."

Paul turned out of the lay-by and headed back the way they had come. The road had almost turned white as the snow fell steadily in the illuminating fans of the headlights. After a mile and a half they had seen nothing and he gradually picked up the pace. Lower down the snow again turned to sleet and it became marginally better to drive on.

"No," he finally concluded, breaking the silence. "She's not along here."

"Odd," Rosemary added. "I wonder who she was."

Back at the lay-by something stirred in the trees. The old lady pushed her way through the tangle of branches and stepped onto the snow covered road. With a self-satisfied smile she made her way over to the two prone figures. She was pleased that her task had been completed in a faultless manner. As expected Paul had not failed in protecting the girl. Unseen, and in the blinking of an eye, the old lady shimmered and took on the guise of the true person she was. Chimelle took one last look at the men and laughed in good humour. Then, in an iridescent flash of purple light, she was gone.

Chapter 8

"What's your name?" Rosemary asked, as they negotiated the road to Skipton. The car was warm, but Rosemary still held a reassuring arm around the girl's shoulders. "There's no need to worry. We'll take you to the nearest police station."

"Heather," she eventually stuttered, as if it had been a struggle to recall.

"I'm Rosemary, as you might remember, and this is my good friend, Paul."

She nodded, looking nervously at her hands clasped together in her lap. "I want to thank you for what you did."

"Glad to help, Heather. It was some old lady on the road who told us you were in trouble. We'd have driven past if it wasn't for her. She's the one you should really thank."

"I work as a waitress in Halifax. I never saw any old lady," Heather replied.

"Well it doesn't matter now," Rosemary added.

Despite the dismissal of her, Paul was intrigued by the old lady. How could she have known what was happening on that high Pennine road when the abduction had clearly taken place miles away? He guessed they would never really know the answer and it was pure chance they happened to be passing at the right time.

"We'll drop you off in Skipton, Heather," he said, speaking to the girl for the first time. "If that's alright with you? The police station should be manned at this hour. If not we'll go through to Leeds to be certain."

"That's fine."

"They'll at least get the two we left behind."

"One of them grabbed me from behind as I was getting into my car after work. They drove me around for what seemed like hours, making threats and knocking me around." She paused, staring into space. "All they really wanted was sex, no more than that, and to be violent. I'd never seen them before. Why pick on me? What gives them the right to ruin my life? Why be so evil?"

Paul considered the question, but could think of no real satisfactory answer. "Some people are evil because they choose to be. Others are easily led. I don't think there's an easy explanation to it. It's in all of us somewhere."

The remainder of the journey was undertaken in silence. The roads in the town were clear, having been gritted, and it took them just minutes to find the police station. Even though it was past three in the morning, lights shone brightly from within the building. Before Heather got out of the car Paul handed her a scrap of paper.

"There's the number and whereabouts of the van. Tell them one of the men ran naked from the scene, heading west." He handed her two wallets. "That's out of the pocket of his jacket. There's a driving licence in it. Only one of the other two had one. I disabled the van, so if they're not suffering from hypothermia they'll be on foot."

She managed a weak smile. "Aren't you two coming in?"

"No," he replied, glancing at Rosemary. "If you don't mind I'd rather not get tangled up with the police in this part of the world."

Rosemary nodded.

"Anyway," he added. "You don't need us. You've got enough to put those three away. You will do so won't you?"

"I will," Heather replied, positively. "And thank you again."

"No trouble," he added, as she and Rosemary climbed out. They walked to the door of the police station together and he watched as they exchanged a few brief words. As Heather entered the building, Rosemary quickly returned and jumped into the seat beside Paul. She closed the door as he drew off.

"We'll have to go the long way home," he said. "We can't go back the way we came."

"It doesn't matter."

"Will she be alright?"

"I think so, Paul," she replied. "She must be feeling better because she asked me where I bought the dress from."

51

He shook his head. "That dress sure has an effect. You'll be in it for another hour though. It'll take that to get home."

"I said it doesn't matter," she repeated, and leaned across to squeeze his hand. "What you did for her was extraordinary. You saved her life."

"I did what anyone else would've done in the same circumstances."

Rosemary kissed him on the cheek.

"What was that for?"

"For being you."

Chapter 9

Christmas Day 1992

The orange glow of the open fire bathed the room in flickering light, complimenting the rainbow of fairy lights woven through the branches of the Christmas tree. Paul sat on the floor with his back against an armchair and his feet aimed squarely at the fireplace. The coal fire gave off a relaxing heat that was quickly sending him off to sleep again. Despite the early hour they had returned to Fell Cottage, Rosemary had eagerly woken him just after eight. She had been up for over an hour, lighting the fire and presenting him with a cup of tea in bed. When he had slipped on his dressing gown and gone downstairs he found the stereo playing carols. It all added to the atmosphere, but he would have happily stayed in bed for an extra hour or two. Rosemary sat on the other side of the fireplace in a long baggy tee-shirt. She was busily adding to the pile of discarded wrapping paper lying between them. Her hair had not been brushed, but she seemed not to care. For her the magic of Christmas, which had been lost for so many years, had suddenly returned with all of its childhood wonder. There were presents to open and she was excited. Paul had brought her chocolates, perfume, jewellery, and even a china doll. All had been neatly wrapped with ribbons and bows, courtesy of Gary's wife, Gaynor. The oddly shaped parcel in her hands was the last one to unwrap.

"What can it be?" she asked, as she picked at the brightly coloured paper.

"Something I'd said I'd bring the next time I was here."

She looked at him as realisation dawned.

"Of course, the teddy bear that saved you from passing through the corridor when you had your near-death experience."

He nodded at her description of how he had nearly died at the hands of Storn's followers only weeks before. It had been something much more than a near-death experience though and he was slowly beginning to have some recall of the time in that corridor.

"I said I'd bring him."

With extra care she pulled the paper off to reveal a twelve inch tall brown bear. One leg and an arm had been sewn back on with cotton after a childhood mishap. In places the fur had worn through to the backing below, but it was still soft to hold and had a pleasing face she instantly adored.

"Paul it's wonderful, but I couldn't possibly take your childhood memories from you."

"He doesn't belong to anyone really and only lives with me."

"Don't say that for my sake."

"I'm not," he truthfully replied. "He deserves a change of scenery and you can give him that. You'll treat him much better than I do. I only keep him in a drawer back home."

She held it to her chest. "He'll have pride of place on my dressing table."

"Then just think of some of the wonderful sights he'll see."

She held up a finger to stop his next comment and carefully placed the bear in the corner of the sofa.

"Now," she said, standing up. "Time for breakfast and the turkey to go in the oven."

"Sounds good, but can you make it light?"

She smiled. "Eating too much?"

"I don't want to be overweight these days if I can help it." He glanced out of the lounge window. "It looks clearer this morning. Mind if I go walking for an hour or two?"

"Not at all," she replied, as she went through to the kitchen. "I'll make dinner for one-thirty."

As she busied herself he sat warming himself by the fire and began slipping into a doze again. In an effort to wake himself up he focussed on the cards lining the shelf. There was one that piqued his interest. He picked himself off the floor and went to it. The front of the card was a depiction of the crib scene, while along the top, in gold letters, it read; Happy Christmas Grandma. He opened the card and went over what was written inside. Apart from the printed verse, there was neatly written; *Thinking of you and wishing you a peaceful time. Love P xx*. He carefully replaced the card and went through to the kitchen.

"It'll be a minute," she said, as he entered.

"No rush," he replied. "I see you've had a card from a grandchild."

She did not stop. "Oh that. I've had one now for the past couple of years even though I've never met her."

"I didn't think you'd had children, let alone grandchildren."

"I haven't. Remember? I told you my late husband, Jack, had a daughter by his first marriage, Sandra. She's about my age, but never approved of me or the marriage." The toaster popped up and she removed the slices and began buttering them. "Sandra and her husband move about a lot. I never know where they are, not that they'd ever tell me. All I know is they have a daughter who must be a teenager by now." She handed him a plate with toast on. "I don't even know her name. She just signs 'P'. I guess she knows where I live because she sends a card. Strange isn't it? We've no blood ties, but I suppose I'm some sort of step grandmother, or something. She must feel the need to be in touch."

"Perhaps she'll visit when she's older."

"Perhaps," Rosemary said, returning to her preparations. "What of your grandparents?"

"None on Mother's side that I ever knew, just like I never knew my father, but both on his side are alive."

"Do you see them?"

He shook his head. "A bit like you really. They never approved of Mum and certainly not of their son marrying her. They've made it quite clear they don't want me in their lives, so we never speak."

"That's sad."

"Is it?" he asked, honestly. "It's their choice. I was too young at the time to understand and still don't. The only time I can ever recall grandma Sayers speaking to me was to call Mother a slut."

Rosemary grimaced. "Oh, how awful."

"That's the way of it, merry Christmas."

She smiled. "You too."

As Paul began eating his toast he crossed to the kitchen window and stared out over the garden to the fells, less than a mile distant. The cloud had lifted just enough to reveal a few of the snow covered peaks. Strangely though, his usual desire to climb deserted him and was replaced by a feeling of dread. The tops were no longer friendly and welcoming. Instead they were jagged icy pinnacles waiting to snare him. The sensation mercifully passed, but it left its mark. He knew he would have to climb at least one fell that day for peace of mind.

Chapter 10
Saturday 22nd May 1993

It was eight-thirty and, for Paul, a typical Saturday morning at Longsdale's vegetable packing plant. As usual he had arrived in the office at six-thirty, an hour before Sally Marcroft started. She always went in on a Saturday and did three hours, even though she did not need to. Also following the norm, Neville Longsdale had not arrived. If he did it was never to do any work. Paul assumed it was just to see if they were working or that they had not burned down the factory. A second mug of tea, along with a bacon roll, went some way to putting Paul in the right frame of mind for the rest of the day. As he lounged in the swivel chair, with his feet up on the desk, a familiar face appeared around the edge of the door.

"Working?"

He shook his head. "Not if I can help it."

Gary Malins broke into a broad smile as he stepped into the office. "Lazy sod."

"Watch your filthy boots on my carpet," he countered. "The lady that does isn't in until Monday."

"How's your sex life?"

"None of your business. If you've come in here to start pissing me off about the way I live my life you can go back to the factory floor where you came from." As he spoke he indicated to the buildings opposite with a thumb over the shoulder.

"Nothing of the sort," Gary cheerily replied. "We're having a barbeque tomorrow afternoon at our place. The usual crowd. Gaynor thought you might like to drag your sorry arse over and join in."

"I'd lay money she didn't use those words, but why? What's the occasion?"

"There isn't one," he offered, with a shrug of his broad shoulders. "It's just an excuse to eat and get plastered."

Paul laughed. "I'd better bring a bottle of lemonade then. Someone'll have to remain sober to deal with the cops when it gets out of hand."

"Are you saying...?" Gary began, in defence, before his words were cut off by the rasping sound of a powerful car outside. He quickly moved to the window to look, as did Paul.

"Phew," Gary expelled in a long whistle of genuine admiration. "That's one of those Bugatti EB110's. Are they importing them?"

Paul too watched as the highly-polished blue sports car drew into an empty bay on the far side of the car park. The Italian supercar sat low on fat tyres and looked impressive. As it stopped the engine growled and he smiled as he saw the two women getting out.

"That's certainly some car," Gary continued, as the driver, a tall redhead, and her passenger stepped from the car. "And wow, that's some good looking woman!"

"Contain yourself Malins," Paul interrupted. "That's my girl you're talking about."

"Which one?" he countered, staring hard out of the window.

"The blonde."

"Well that's okay mate, it's the redhead I fancy," he replied, as he looked longingly at Charlotte, elegantly crossing the car park towards them. She wore a pinstripe skirt, with a high split, along with a neat matching jacket and white blouse. A cascade of loose radiant red hair flowed untied down her back and across her shoulders.

"Oh mother," Gary continued. "I'm in love."

Paul could hardly keep from laughing, aware of the effect Charlotte was having on him.

"You're drooling all over my carpet."

"Who cares?"

"You're married."

"Get a lawyer. I'm divorced and gone to heaven."

Outside, Charlotte and Rebecca moved out of sight around to

the front of the building. As if a spell had been broken, Gary breathed out and turned to look at Paul.

"You said, 'my girl', the blonde?"

He nodded. "Rebecca."

"Guardian angel? Tanker crash and rescue from the devil Rebecca?"

Paul raised his left hand, showing the missing little finger. "Oh yes, that Rebecca."

"And the redhead?"

"Charlotte," he replied. "Angel too."

"Crap Sayers, you're unreal," Gary blurted. "But wow, they're good looking women. Your sex life can't be lacking, you lying sod."

Their conversation was interrupted by Sally, tapping on the open door.

"Paul I've two women here to see you. They don't have an appointment and won't say what it is they want to see you for."

"It's okay I know them. Please send them in and bring us a decent pot of tea."

She looked at him, oddly, without moving from the doorway. "Who are they?"

"Just send them in."

Sally paused, a frosted look crossing her face, before returning to the reception area.

"Uh oh," Gary exclaimed. "You've gone and upset matron now."

Paul snorted. "Don't be rotten. Haven't you got work to be going back to?"

He looked sharply at him. "Don't start that crap on me now Sayers. Introduce me, introduce me!"

He pointed to the door. "Then you go."

Moments later Sally reappeared with Charlotte and Rebecca. He hadn't seen Rebecca for three weeks and, in that moment, he felt as if they'd spent a lifetime apart. She looked businesslike in a dark trouser-suit and her hair neatly gathered up in a bun. He greeted them in good mannered fashion as if they were there on business.

"Come in ladies, do take a seat."

They smiled, carrying on the pretence while Gary stood with a silly grin on his face. He was rooted to the spot, staring wide-eyed at Charlotte.

"I'd like you to meet Mr. Malins," Paul began. "He's our production line manager."

"My pleasure." Charlotte softly replied, taking his hand. Almost instantly his eyes glazed over and his legs turned to jelly. He stammered for something to say as she turned on her most alluring smile. Paul found it difficult not to dissolve into laughter as he grabbed Gary and propelled him towards the door.

"You'll have to excuse Mr. Malins, ladies. He's had a challenging week."

Without word, Gary staggered out of the office and disappeared from sight.

"Go after him Sally and make sure he gets back in one piece."

She looked unsure. "Don't you want me to stay?"

"Go!" he insisted, pointing to the door. Without reply she again gave him a frosty stare, before going. He closed the door behind her and turned to find Rebecca standing behind him. It took no effort to lift her up off her feet in a warm embrace.

"I've missed you."

She kissed him on the lips. "I have you, my darling."

"And in such gorgeous company," he added, turning to Charlotte, Rebecca's senior. At over six feet tall she towered over him and the split skirt revealed a shapely thigh. The jacket too was cut to accentuate the exquisite curves of her body. She had a clear complexion, fiery red hair, and depthless green eyes that sparkled.

"You are looking well, lover," she said, with affection, and kissed him on the cheek.

"You too, as always. What did you do to poor old Gary?"

She broke into a broad smile. "His thoughts were an open book. That is why I gave him the pleasure of an entire night to remember in one brief pulse."

Paul shook his head and chuckled. "No wonder his legs went."

"He will get over it."

"And the Bugatti outside?" he asked, as they all sat down.

"What else would I choose?" Charlotte replied. "You would not wish us to travel in anything less than style?"

"Of course I wouldn't. But where did it come from?"

She simply clicked her fingers with a devilish smile.

"Well, I could talk cars all day if necessary. But seeing you two together means this isn't a social visit."

Charlotte shook her head. "You are right Paul. It has a lot to do with you and Rebecca though. Also I believe you can help us with something that is happening in your world."

"Sounds a bit deep," he said, turning to Rebecca. "Do you know about this?"

"A little, but not everything."

There was a tap at the door and Sally entered carrying a tray of tea and biscuits.

"Would you like me to sit in and take notes?"

"No thanks, Sally," he replied. "That'll be all for now. I don't want to be disturbed please. Is that clear?"

"Very clear," she replied, emphasising the words. She gave him a hard stare, and looked down her nose at the two women before leaving.

"She is upset," Charlotte said, as the door slammed shut behind them.

"No doubt," he said, returning his attention to them.

"Storn is conducting a campaign of evil here," she said, getting straight to the point.

"I guessed as much."

"How are you aware of it?"

He shrugged. "There's a programme on the television where they recreate crimes in the hope of finding those responsible. About a month ago they restaged an appalling murder. The body had been dismembered."

"I see. What pointed you to Storn?"

"I didn't know they were into chopping up their victims, but the means of disposal gave it away. They showed some plastic sacks the body parts were found in. They were covered in those crazy designs that were on the floor at Kirkham." He glanced to Rebecca. "I saw them and realised that it was his followers' handiwork."

"Did you not say anything?" Rebecca asked.

"You can hear me ringing them up saying; 'it's some kind of devil who can't be killed doing it. Oh, how do I know? Because I'm in love with my guardian angel, who saved me from certain death and in return I rescued her from the clutches of this evil being. He's tall, dresses in black, and looks like he's stepped out of a horror movie.' It's that clichéd."

"Sorry."

"My hands are tied Rebecca."

Charlotte interrupted. "We know how things are for you, yet would like to find out why he is indulging in this latest outpouring of evil."

"How many has he been responsible for?"

"Four," she replied. "Starting with a girl called Tessa Fisher. They take a victim and hold them for two weeks before he ritually kills them for the pleasure of his followers. They wait for a further two weeks and repeat the process."

"So, it's one a month? Why so regularly and ritually?"

"The ritual part serves no purpose for Storn. It is only to satisfy the evil pleasure of his closest followers. He only requires the soul."

"What?" he interrupted, incredulously.

"For a reason unknown to us, Storn is attempting to exist in your world for an undetermined length of time. To do this he must have the energy of a living soul fed to him on a regular basis."

"But the victims aren't the same?"

"The energy of the spirit is always the same, Paul. The age, size, sex, or race is unimportant," Rebecca explained.

"That makes sense, but I still can't go to the police with this."

Charlotte smiled briefly. "I know you cannot Paul. However, we would like you to find the place where these ritual killings are taking place and retrieve the latest victim."

"Is that all? Don't you know where?"

"They have been most thorough in their cover of the location. The shield they are using must be similar to the one used to hold Rebecca. Unless we look at it directly we cannot pinpoint it. There is no leakage to give away its position and we cannot spare the time to undertake such a wide-ranging search."

"So you need me to narrow it down and then go in."

"Yes."

"Why haven't you been able to follow the victims?"

"It is not easy," Charlotte replied. "Storn has taught them well. Because it is so random we cannot pre-empt the abductions. Somehow they manage to shield the victim at the moment they take them. So, unless we are watching at the particular moment, there is no chance of following their movements."

"And with millions of people, you can't watch everyone all the time," he added, with some sympathy for their task.

"Exactly, and we have many more duties to perform than just watching here"

"So it's down to the man on the ground."

"Will you help?"

"You know I will. Who's the latest victim?"

"Jason Galloway," Charlotte replied, seeing that he recognised the name.

"He's the boy who went missing from Norwich a few days ago. Are you saying he's been abducted by Storn's lot?"

"He was yet another random snatch. Taken and shielded before we even knew of it."

"I know he's a child, but why do you want me to start looking now? Why's he more special than those who've gone before?"

"All souls are precious Paul," Rebecca said, truthfully. "Tessa Fisher was a great loss to us as well. She was destined to become a Guardian. She had it within her."

"Sorry."

Charlotte quickly continued. "There are two reasons for looking for the child. Firstly he is destined to become a man of medicine. He will be instrumental in developing a cure for a disease that has not yet affected this place."

"And the second?"

"He is related, by birth, to both you and Rebecca. In effect, Paul, your great, great, great grandson."

He looked at her, astonished, before turning to Rebecca. She too seemed equally taken aback by the statement. "I did hear right? Didn't I?"

Charlotte nodded. "Yes."

"Care to explain?"

"The soul moves from one mortal life to another, not always in the same realm, but it travels. The previous existence, and the one to follow, is never remembered or known. You, Paul, were born on the fifth of July 1880 and lived as James Cooke. You had a twin sister called Annie. Rebecca was born on the thirteenth of October 1881 and was known as Rebecca Ekins. Both of you were brought up in the village of Saltmarsh."

"North Norfolk," Paul added, looking at Rebecca and realising it was news to her too.

"Correct. You were married in August of 1898 after being childhood sweethearts."

"So we have been together before," Rebecca said, smiling at him.

Charlotte nodded. "Therein lies the explanation for your love for each other. The bond created by love can transcend life and death. In May of the year 1900, Rebecca Cooke, you in effect, Rebecca, gave birth to a daughter, Ruth Cooke."

"The same Ruth as in the photograph?" Paul quickly asked.

"Correct. The very same one as in the picture I gave you."

Briefly, he recalled the scene after his flight from the barn at Kirkham with the unconscious Rebecca. Charlotte had sent him to Rosemary's with the photograph of a girl called Ruth. She had never explained anything about her or the fact that it was his handwriting on the reverse of it, with Rosemary's address in pencil.

She continued speaking, unaware of his momentary distraction. "However, in truth, it was you who gave the photograph to me."

"You never made that clear."

"It will become so later."

"Why not now?" Rebecca asked. "Will it really do so much harm for us to know?"

"Possibly. I will not take the chance it will not."

Paul shrugged. "Oh leave it; please continue with what you can tell us."

"Sadly, for James, Rebecca died in childbirth leaving him to bring Ruth up alone. Along with Rebecca's older brother, Albert, they shared a fishing boat. They were out at the time and returned too late for James to see Rebecca before she passed on."

"How sad," Rebecca added, commenting on her own previous demise.

"It was at this time Rebecca had been selected to become a Guardian. I was her Guardian then and saw the potential within her. I was right; she has become a fine one."

She visibly blushed at the compliment. "What became of James?"

"With the help of family, especially his twin sister, Annie, who had married Albert just a week before Rebecca's death, he quite ably raised Ruth. Later James enlisted in the Army, along with Albert, and fought in what you call here, The Great War."

"Your voice took a downward note," Paul said, scribbling notes on a desk jotter.

She nodded. "After initial good service, James was shot for desertion in June of 1916. It was just before The Battle of the Somme. Do you know of this?"

"I've heard of it of course. It was something of a massacre, but it eventually ended in defeat for the Germans. Why did he desert?"

"I cannot tell you."

"That means you know why."

"It means I cannot tell you."

"The photograph of Ruth that I wrote on the back of" he mused, as Rebecca gazed at him with a new understanding of her love for him. "If James and I are the same person, surely his handwriting would be identical. Did he write the address? But how would he know it?"

Charlotte only smiled and he realised he would get no further with her on the details of that meeting which had already occurred in the past. Or was it to occur in his future?

She continued. "Ruth Cooke married Charles Deane, at the age of eighteen, just at the end of that war. They too had an only daughter they named Ruby. One of her daughters, Florence, had two girls. They still live in Norfolk and both are married. Susan to the vicar of Saltmarsh, David Pryce, while Anne and her husband, Samuel, live in Norwich. They have a daughter of eight named Michelle and a son of ten..."

"Jason Galloway," Paul finished for her.

"Not only that, your daughter, Ruth, is still alive and lives in the same house you and Rebecca had in Saltmarsh."

"Really?" Rebecca started. "She must be well into old age by now."

"Ninety-three," Paul added.

Charlotte nodded. "She is extremely well, both in body and mind. Her subsequent family marrying and having children young has given her a depth of generations few here see."

"What of Charles, her husband?"

She turned to Rebecca. "He saw both of his great granddaughters marry before passing on peacefully in 1984, aged eighty-six."

"Not a bad innings," Paul concluded.

"That," Charlotte said. "Is a very brief history of the family you began in a previous life. The picture becomes complete when you were born in 1964 Paul. Unaware of the previous connection, because certain past life events are blocked when Guardians are selected, Rebecca was chosen to watch over the spirit of the son born to Pauline Sayers. Only after the birth, and her immediate feelings of love for you, did I discover the spirit link which joins you. Both of you had been devotedly in love before and that could not be broken by the passing of time or separation of souls."

"Did you not try to part us?" he asked, quietly.

"By nature of the selection, once the bond has been created it cannot be reversed or altered. As I told you once before, Paul, you can only ever have one Guardian. But it would not have altered the fact Rebecca was in love with you, Guardian or not."

"It was an instant feeling of love, almost consuming," Rebecca added.

"I could not change things," Charlotte said. "The chances of it happening are so infinitely great it is hard to believe it really happened. However, there may be other forces at work here that we are unaware of."

"It all seems too much like coincidence to me," he said, truthfully.

"But who else could interfere with such matters?" Rebecca asked, wanting to know of the other forces she referred to.

Charlotte spread her hands. "Not everything that happens in mortal realms, or that guides it, can be fully explained. Some events just have to be taken as they transpire. It is the way of it." She looked to Paul. "We come full circle back to you. You have the accident where you should have died, but Rebecca's love saves you. Then we have you confronting Storn and his followers to get her back. You are aware of us and what we do. Now, like then, you are in a unique position."

Slowly, he rose from his seat and turned to look out of the window.

"Now I have to go up against him and his people again."

Charlotte was about to reply when the office door opened and Sally stepped inside.

"Paul I've..."

"Can't you knock?" he snapped, without turning. "I told you no interruptions."

"But..."

"None!"

The door closed with a bang and she left.

"Was that necessary?" Rebecca asked, surprised by his sharpness.

"Probably not, but I need a few minutes to think this through and digest a whole new piece of my life. This place'll survive that long I'm sure."

After a brief pause Charlotte spoke again. "Do you have any ideas as to where we might be able to find the boy?"

"You're the mind readers," he replied. "Look at Storn's people."

"They are not ours to watch," Rebecca replied, quietly.

His response was blunt. "That didn't stop you with Stanford."

She looked down, a sense of shame instantly filling her with embarrassment. "I am sorry for that. I thought I could do some good there."

He shook his head, regretting the rash words. "Sorry precious, I didn't mean to be nasty, it's a lot to grasp in such a short time."

"I know."

"Talking of which, how much do we have?"

"Monday week, your time," Charlotte answered.

"I won't rush into anything straightaway, not when there's time to plan. I learnt my lesson at Kirkham."

"I fully understand," she replied. "Rebecca is here to help whenever you need her, on the clear understanding she is not placed in any sort of danger."

"That goes without saying," he replied, sincerely, and winked at her. "We'll be extra careful, believe me."

"So where do we begin?" Rebecca said, expectantly.

"I'm going with instinct, because something tells me to go to Saltmarsh." He looked at them both. "Address for Ruth?"

Without saying it, Charlotte scribbled on the corner of his jotter pad. "I would prefer it if Rebecca did not meet with Ruth."

"Why?" she quickly asked.

"It is not the time my girl, believe me."

"Then meet me at seven this evening," Paul added, winking. "Wherever I might be."

"Only if it is convenient. Anything you would like me to do?"

"Find Myra and Persephone. Storn, or where he's operating from, won't be far away."

Charlotte stood up, effectively ending the discussion. "I hope we can reach a satisfactory conclusion."

"I'll do my best Charlotte. I've still got a book of addresses from the Fox. If they're Stanford's cohorts we'll get some leads."

She kissed him on the cheek as he opened the door for them. "Good luck lover."

"Do angels believe in luck?" he asked, but she only smiled. He warmly embraced Rebecca. "Safe trip, precious, I'll see you later."

Affectionately, she patted his bottom. "You too, my darling."

In a professional manner he escorted them back to the main reception area.

"Thank you for your time," he cheerily bid them, as they left.

When he had shut the door he turned to find Sally waiting, arms folded tightly across her chest.

"And just who were they?" she began.

"Does it matter to you?"

"Of course it does," she angrily retorted. "I've a right to know who comes into this office."

"Sorry, Sally, but you're not my keeper. It's none of your business who I see privately in my office. You only work here."

"How dare you speak to me like that," she spat, in a tone full of hurt.

"I dare," he snapped. "So get back to whatever it was you were doing."

Her face flushed red and she stalked back to her office. The door slammed, echoing her obvious anger to all in the building. With a tinge of regret he shook his head and followed. The receptionist, Jenny, had kept quiet during the whole scene and casually glanced up at the clock; it was ten past nine. From outside she heard a rasp as the Bugatti started and rapidly exited the car park. As Paul returned to his office he stopped briefly outside Sally's. He could see her through the glass panel, sitting with her back to the door, and reached for the handle to go in and apologise. However, she either heard him or sensed he was there. Without turning she simply raised her hand and gave him a middle finger salute. Smiling, he continued to his office and tore the top page off the jotter. He had already decided to leave. There seemed little sense in trying to finish mundane tasks, especially when there was a child to be found. An instantly recognisable voice called loudly from the other end of the corridor.

"Sayers!"

Paul ignored it, aware that Longsdale had arrived.

"Sayers!" he boomed again.

Quite deliberately, Paul closed the office door and began walking away. Behind him Longsdale appeared from his own office.

"Come back here!" he bellowed. "Don't pretend to ignore me when it's quite obvious you can hear me."

Slowly, Paul turned. "Half the county can hear you."

69

"Funny," Longsdale, countered. "Who were those two women I just saw leaving? Marcroft says she doesn't know who they were."

"Well you're both in the same boat then," he said, calmly, and headed to reception.

"Who were they? And where do you think you're going?"

"None of your business on both accounts," Paul replied, without stopping or turning.

"Just you wait up, Sayers. Where do you think you're going at this time of day? There's work to be done."

"You wouldn't know the meaning of the word, Neville."

"How dare you."

"Not another," Paul muttered, as he looked his employer squarely in the face. "Have you forgotten who baled out this sorry excuse for a business? Gary and me turned this place round, rid you of a crippling overdraft, and made you a millionaire. What more do you want? To treat us all like casual labour? I've spent the morning on next week's schedules, Monday's orders, and the dubious task of trying to placate half the workforce. And why? Because you've interfered again and cocked-up the holiday roster." He pushed the main door open. "So, for the first time since before Christmas, I'm off home early instead of the usual twelve, one, or God knows when."

With his last word he exited the building and headed off to the car park. When he reached his car he saw that Longsdale had followed him. Adjacent to them, on a low wall, were several groups of workers. They were closely observing the byplay between the two men as they indulged in a morning break.

"Sayers, you're on very sticky ground!" Longsdale shouted.

"What've I done to deserve this?" Paul muttered, under his breath. "The ground's sticky from all the crap you keep shovelling in my direction!" he replied, loudly.

"I can make life hard for you around here."

As the workers looked on with glee at the exchange, they heard Paul laugh.

"The only thing you make around here Neville is a bloody mess. Chaos and confusion surrounds everything you do."

"I can take that little perk away for starters," Longsdale warned, pointing at the nearly new company car.

Paul casually tossed the keys to him. "Keep it. It obviously means more to you than me."

As he walked across to the road the workers began an impromptu round of applause which he acknowledged with a slight bow. In wordless anger Longsdale watched his departing employee while the keys to the Vauxhall lay at his feet. One of those who had witnessed the exchange and, more importantly, the arrival of Charlotte and Rebecca earlier, Sabir, rose from his seat on the wall. He stubbed out his cigarette and made his way over to the rear entrance of the office block. Something important had happened and he knew there could still be clues inside.

Paul was about half a mile down the road, heading back to his home in Sawston on foot, deep in thought, when the sound of a motorcycle slowing down drew his attention. With a growling roar, the green and white Kawasaki braked to halt right next to him. The dark tinted visor snapped open and Gary spoke loudly above the sound of the idling engine.

"Gonna walk all the way?" he asked, indifferently.

"That's the intention," Paul replied, unconcerned. "Obviously news travels fast."

"Word of what you've done has spread through the factory like wildfire. What a morning! Angels, Sally giving me the silent treatment, and Longsdale steaming mad."

Paul shook his head. "I'll no longer suffer him in any form. I don't need it. We've made him rich. Why does he think we'll keep taking it?"

"That's the way it's always been mate," Gary replied, slipping the spare helmet he was carrying off his forearm and passing it to him. "You can't change an old dog's ways."

"Teach an old dog new tricks you mean," Paul said, fastening the chin strap of the helmet tight.

"Whatever."

Paul straddled the pillion seat and grabbed the rear carry rack firmly with both hands. "Keep it legal!" he shouted, as the engine level increased with Gary's liberal use of the throttle. "I'm fed up having my balls catch up ten minutes after I arrive."

Above the noise he heard Gary's laughter as they roared off in the direction of Sawston.

Chapter 11

The spacious ground floor kitchen at Pelham Hall was quiet. The gas fired range had been left lit and it added some warmth to the damp feeling of the room. Outside it was overcast and little natural light filtered in through the high windows. Seated at a table that took centre position on the flagstone floor was Persephone. She was showing only moderate interest in the cheese sandwich in front of her, whilst Myra was busily making more. As she went about the task she was oblivious to her daughter and, likewise, her thoughts. Persephone sighed, inwardly, bored with yet another day stuck inside. She was trapped within the dull confines of Pelham when she wanted to be out on her own. There were so many other things she wanted to do than just be waiting on Storn's bidding. She glanced at her mother and knew that she did not want to end up like her. She too was trapped, but by choice, by the evil that had come to control all their lives so completely. Her mother was totally held in Storn's aura and in turn it held her too. She again looked down at the sandwich. She was not hungry, not for food anyway. The hunger she felt was for freedom, the space to become herself. At Pelham she was only being groomed to be Storn's tool, a useful object to achieve an aim. The fact that her sixteenth birthday had passed just a few weeks earlier with only scant acknowledgement from her mother had hurt. There was no party, presents, friends, not that she had any, or even a solitary card to mark the passing of the date. Her school days had been sporadic, mostly private tutoring with the other children of Storn's followers. These too were quickly stopped once her empathetic link to Paul Sayers had been discovered. She was considered too valuable and closely watched. Within days of the incident at Skelwith farm, where her evil father had been killed, both she and her mother had been installed at

Pelham Hall. For her mother it was the ultimate promotion within the organisation, while for her it was imprisonment.

The sound of light footsteps briefly brought her out of her thoughts. Payne, one of Storn's personal guards, entered. She detested the way the men wandered about the house trying to keep quiet, or, as she saw it, sneaking about. She often found her personal belongings had been gone through and they frequently attempted to spy on her whenever she went to take a bath. As usual he was dressed immaculately, in a dark suit, with the bulge of a pistol beneath the jacket. Without word he crossed to where Myra was preparing sandwiches and took two. As he made to leave, he briefly stopped to look down at Persephone, catching her eye. A leering grin lifted one corner of his mouth before he continued on his way out. She turned away, closing her eyes, and saw in her mind exactly what was going through his, the picture he had of the two of them together, sexually entwined. With an involuntary shudder she shook her head, more frightened by the thoughts Payne had than her recently conceived ability to see into minds. The 'unwanted gift,' as she called it, seemed directly attributable to her first encounter with Paul Sayers. Then there was the small part of Tessa Fisher's soul that had somehow entered her own spirit. She could feel it within herself if she relaxed her thoughts and it seemed to boost her newly found talents. She had told none of the others what was going on inside her mind, it would be dangerous. The sound of footsteps again broke her thoughts, although this time they were heavier. Myra turned as the imposing figure of Storn strode purposefully in. Dressed in black denim trousers and a loosely buttoned shirt, he sat down opposite Persephone. Without being asked she immediately poured him a cup of coffee from the pot.

"Sayers has been visited by the Guardian woman this morning," he began, accepting the steaming cup from her.

"The blonde one we had?" Myra asked, moving closer.

"And the one called Charlotte too."

"The senior one?" Persephone asked, surprised by the news.

"I have been expecting them to make a move and believe they are asking Sayers to do their work for them."

"Are you sure?" Myra added.

"News from Carter confirms it. His contact informed him that Sayers left quickly after his meeting with them. At present there is a discreet tail on him."

"How does this connect to us?"

A cold smile crossed his face. "The Longsdale contact got into the office Sayers uses right after he left. Although the top page of the note pad was missing there were some names still clearly impressed on the page beneath, one of which was Jason Galloway."

"The boy now at Padrigg," Myra blurted. "They know."

"Yes. Obviously he has some value to the Guardians," he continued. "They are risking using Sayers to try to find the child, but will only serve to place him in our hands."

"Could he possibly discover Padrigg?" Myra asked, sitting down at the table.

"There is no chance of it. The Guardians have no time to search for it and Sayers will have no idea of where to start looking."

"You sound confident," Persephone said, quietly, much to her mother's surprise.

"Of course," he replied, unperturbed. "Sayers will be in our hands within days."

"You're going to put Carter's plan into action?" Myra asked. "How do you know he'll be away long enough to implement it?"

His cold expression never changed. "It appears his intended destination is Norwich, to see the boy's parents. Possibly in an effort to glean more information."

"Will you have him followed all the way there?"

"No," he replied, more thoughtful. "Carter does not want to rattle Sayers in case he spots the tail. There was no time to set up a complicated set of following vehicles so the original one will peel off shortly. Carter is setting up another one to pick him up on the road into Norwich."

"So you figure he'll be away long enough for the evidence to be planted?"

Lazily, he leaned back. "Yes."

Myra stood up. "I can't help but believe this plan is too complicated and unnecessary. Nobody would miss him if he simply disappeared. Grabbing him now is surely the best plan?"

"I am aware of your personal need for vengeance, but it will be done this way. Not only will it destroy Sayers, it will completely take any possible investigation away from us."

"The evidence will never hold up," she added.

"It does not need to for very long. Carter calculates that they will charge Sayers within hours of his arrest. That is when we will take him. The police effort will switch to a manhunt and we can alter the evidence as we see fit. Remember, Carter is on site to make sure it runs smoothly."

"Not everything runs smoothly where Paul Sayers is concerned," Persephone warned.

"This will," Storn replied, confidently, and returned his attention to Myra. "Tell Carter to implement the full plan with immediate effect."

"Very good. I'll set up the control room and alert all those who need to know."

After she had left, Storn rose from his seat while still looking directly at Persephone. For once she held his eyes, surprising herself that for the first time she was not petrified. Strangely, she felt his presence was more subdued, as if she had just found the space to accommodate it within her. Without a doubt the very thing she had feared, until then, she sensed coming from him. The evil he possessed was like a buzz of energy that she could almost smell.

"And you my child," he said, quietly. "What is your opinion?"

She continued to hold his gaze. "There are difficult times ahead."

"Oh there are," he replied, with certainty. "For Sayers and the interfering Guardians." Without further word he spun on his heels and strode, self-assuredly, from the kitchen. As he left, Persephone picked up the sandwich and began eating. She knew in the days to come she would need the energy.

Chapter 12

The black, nineteen-fifties Wolseley Six-Eighty saloon slowed as it entered the village of Saltmarsh. The afternoon sun glinted off the highly polished bodywork and chrome. Even in its day it was a reasonably rare car; the curved lines of the body were equally matched by a long front end and tall chromium radiator grille. Underneath the bonnet sat a powerful six-cylinder motor that gave the big saloon a fair turn of speed and made distance traveling comfortable. Paul had restored the car himself after discovering it lying unused and unloved in a farmer's outbuilding. He had spotted the square tower of the church just before entering Saltmarsh. A small green in the centre had a typical Norfolk style carved wooden sign and he slowed to a crawl. There was only one village store and he turned by it into the appropriately named Church Lane. There was a crowd of people milling around outside the church and the verges were filled with an assortment of vehicles. To avoid conflicting with the guest's cars he parked the Wolseley in a gap near the vicarage gate.

The vicar of St Peter's, the Reverend David Pryce, was occupied in polite conversation with one of the wedding guests when he noticed a stranger enter the churchyard. It was a busy parish and he was also responsible for three other smaller churches in his ministry. However, he prided himself on personally knowing the majority of residents who lived in the village. The man was unfamiliar, but perhaps he was studying his family history, it was becoming more common. However, an inexplicable chill ran down his spine as he watched the stranger move through the jumble of headstones. With well-practiced ease, David continued the conversation while still watching Paul. He saw him halt amongst the memorials in the oldest section of the churchyard. In part it

77

was because of the chill feeling he had experienced, but he was more than a little interested in the newcomer because he knew all the people who tended graves in that particular spot.

Paul totally ignored the happy sounds emanating from the wedding party and was unaware he was being observed. Lost in thought he walked slowly up and down the ranks of old gravestones. Finally, he paused near a few and stopped at the very one he had been looking for. Someone remembered, someone still cared, possibly Ruth, but it was his first time there and he regretted not knowing about it until then. He had holidayed many times in the area without the knowledge that the mortal remains of the woman he loved, or was going to love, were lying close by. The words on the polished stone marker were in silver script. A deep, distant sadness flared inside him, that of another man, another life that was his own, yet was not. *'Rebecca Cooke. Darling wife of James. Died in childbirth. May 10th 1900 aged 19 years.'* Then, underneath, in a smaller script was written; *'Also in memory of James Cooke. Lost somewhere in France. A victim of The Great War.'*

Paul mused over the vague notation of his own former demise. It felt odd that he had held and kissed Rebecca that morning whilst her previous remains now lay under his feet. Lost in thought, he unwrapped the flowers he had brought and began arranging them in the vase.

David Pryce made his excuses to the wedding guests and crossed over to where Paul was kneeling. As he drew closer it became clear which grave he was at, surprising him because he knew the Cooke plot first hand.

"Good afternoon," he greeted.

"Hello," Paul replied, glancing around, before returning his attention to the flowers.

David halted a couple of steps behind him, partially casting a shadow. He could see he was putting red roses on the grave and was intrigued to know the connection.

"Do you know the Cooke family?" he asked.

"Just a little," Paul answered, unaware that the question was anything more than just passing interest.

"Oh really," David added. "I've not seen you here before."

"I only learned of Rebecca's final resting place this morning." David was puzzled by the casual answer and tried to gently push him further. "She died in childbirth. Do you know of the child?"

"Ruth, I know of Ruth."

"What of Rebecca's husband, James? Do you know what became of him?"

"I was shot for desertion before The Battle of the Somme," he answered, without thinking, not realising what he had said.

The words did not quite sink into David's thinking. He was fascinated that the stranger knew of James' fate. It was something few knew of.

Paul stood up. "I was hoping to find where Ruth lives locally. It was really her I was hoping to see."

David suddenly went on the defensive. "If you're some journalist or tabloid digger, here to pester Ruth and her family about Jason, you'll get no joy. The locals and her friends will see to that, I can promise you."

"I'm not a reporter," Paul replied, turning to face him for the first time. As their eyes met David felt rooted to the spot. The same chill he had felt minutes before ran colder down his back. It felt as if a door to the past had been opened inside him when it was meant to be kept shut. It was cold, despite the sun, and he realised he was staring, but he could not help it. Then the statement about James' death finally caught up with him, slamming into his stationary thought processes. Immediately his mind began turning over a series of important questions he needed to ask. Several things he had been aware of for many years were falling into place. Something quite extraordinary was happening and he was there to experience it. The face had taken David aback, but now he had time to study Paul further. Despite the age of the photographs and the colouring defects too, the image he had of James Cooke matched the man in front of him almost to the fine detail. The shape of the face, the eyes, nose, and mouth, were so very much alike. Even the smile had the same upturn at the corner of the mouth and was full of genuine warmth. However, what was different was the look in the steel-blue eyes he now studied. James had been just a fisherman. The man in front of him was much more than an ordinary working man. Behind the eyes lay a determination and strength of purpose he had seen in few men.

"I'm not a reporter, honest," Paul repeated, anxious to end the silence between them. "I really do have family connections and would dearly like to speak to Ruth."

"Yes. I believe you." David eventually said. He did not look like a typical vicar. He was tall and stoutly built, with a full head of tight curly hair. "Why did you say, 'I was shot for desertion' when I asked you how James died?"

"Did I? It must've been a slip of the tongue," he casually replied, while gesturing with his left hand. David caught sight of the missing little finger and quickly took hold of his hand.

"Dear Lord," he whispered, before looking Paul straight in the face. "That was no slip of the tongue just now. You really did mean to say 'I', didn't you?"

"No, it just slipped out."

"And how did this happen?" he continued, holding up Paul's hand.

"It was hacked off by some nutter..."

"...with a shovel, in a farmyard." David finished the sentence, leaving him puzzled.

"How did you know?" Paul asked, duly surprised by his knowledge of something so personal.

At once David felt at ease with the stranger who had walked into his life that day. He thrust out his right hand. "David Pryce."

Paul readily took the offered hand and shook it, firmly. "It's a pleasure to meet you David. Paul Sayers."

"Now tell me, Paul. Just what's your connection with Ruth Deane?"

"You wouldn't believe me if I told you."

"I think I know your story," he said, assuredly. "Do you believe it?"

"I do, David," he replied, with equal conviction. "In fact I'm one hundred percent sure of it. If I wasn't I wouldn't be here."

"I see your point," David said, and placed a hand on Paul's

back to guide him away from Rebecca's grave. "First thing though, let's go and talk to the person you came to see, Ruth. Then we can sit down together and exchange stories. I'm sure we've got some fascinating things to learn from each other."

He nodded in reply. "I guess that much will be true."

Together the two men left the churchyard to the wedding party, still in carefree chatter, and strode down the street towards the vicarage.

Chapter 13

A spacious anteroom at the rear of Pelham Hall had been converted into a control room to oversee Storn's operations. A set of French doors looked out over the secluded rear garden and access to it was challenging. There was plenty of natural daylight and a high degree of privacy. A table took up centre position and on it sat computer monitors with all the necessary hardware, and, more importantly, a link into the police network. The vital link was well paid for and gave them enviable access to a vast wealth of data and communications. Next to the door a small table had been pushed up against the wall. Persephone was sat on it, with her legs crossed. She had fixed her hair up and changed into black denim trousers and a light grey sweater.

For once Storn appeared noticeably subdued when he strode into the room. Seated at the table, Myra glanced up from the screen in front of her.

"Anything?" he asked.

She shook her head. "It's obvious he never took the Norwich road. They've doubled back to check but no joy. There's a watch on the Galloway house, but he hasn't turned up there either."

"A different route?"

"Whatever the route, he'd have been there at least an hour ago."

"Where did he go then?"

"Anywhere," she replied. "We're pretty thin on the ground. It's impossible to go searching without a plan. The people we can trust are in Clayborough with Carter."

"I see," Storn said, quietly. "And what of his plan?"

"Like clockwork so far. All the evidence necessary to implicate Sayers was placed inside the house a little over thirty minutes ago. He wants me to make the call to the Marcroft woman."

He nodded. "Very well."

"I think it's unnecessary," she added.

He smiled, a cold evil edge coming with his reply. "We must keep Carter happy."

Myra picked up the nearest phone and dialled in the number written on a pad next to it. It rang four times before being answered.

"Hello. Is that Ms Sally Marcroft?" she waited. "Yes Sally, Gina Howe here. I'm personal secretary for Mr. Albright of the Savefare supermarket chain. We're here with Paul Sayers discussing an urgent business matter regarding our changing to Longsdale's as our main supplier." She paused again. "Yes Sally, that's right, we're with Paul at his home. He's busy and asked me to call you. Could you possibly pop round? He'd like you to sit in on this."

Both Storn and Persephone watched as she went through the falsehood to lure Sally into the trap that had been laid by Carter.

"Good, Sally," she continued, in a cheerful voice "We'll see you in a few minutes." Without waiting she dialled again. "Carter, Myra, she's on her way." She put down the phone and looked up at Storn. "Everyone's in place watching the roads back into Clayborough. As soon as he reappears we'll make sure the police are notified. If we're lucky they'll arrive at the same time and he'll be arrested."

"But where is he?"

She shook her head. "He could be anywhere."

"The sea."

They turned to face Persephone. She appeared to be asleep.

"Say again," he said.

"The sea," she repeated, without opening her eyes. "He's gone home to the sea."

Myra looked puzzled, yet Storn only appeared neutral, as if he had not heard. He folded his arms across his chest and slowly walked over to the window. It was just after two. Persephone got up and crossed to one of the maps. When she was quite sure she had her mother's attention she pointed to it, tapping her finger on the centre of the North Norfolk coast.

"Home," she simply stated.

Myra looked doubtful, but Persephone did not care. She knew

where Paul was and could feel him there. He was taking a journey into the past, a past they shared, she could feel that too. She only wished she could join him while he took that voyage of discovery.

"I'll fetch some coffee."

"Good idea," Myra replied, as she watched her leave the room. Something was happening that she could not understand. She glanced at the imposing figure of Storn, standing with his back to her. Just what influence was he exerting over her daughter?

Chapter 14

The afternoon was bright, filling the small kitchen of the end cottage with warmth. As she glanced out of the window a distant piece of the past caught up with Ruth. She had read the letter countless times. The promise it held seemed so definite, so full of guarantee. Yet, over the years, she had gone from believing it to dismissing it as simply a last cheery message from a loving father. Every summer brought the same promise, every summer ended with the same desperate disappointment. Yet this time he was there, it had to be him, walking up the garden path with David, as he had promised in 1916. Hastily, she turned off the tap and left the kettle sitting in the sink.

They were almost at the back door when Ruth opened it. Paul slowed up as a sense of recognition stirred somewhere deep inside. Despite her years Ruth was still reasonably fit and came out to eagerly meet them. Without word of greeting she embraced Paul firmly around the waist. She was only a couple of inches shorter than he was, with snow white hair, and, after a brief moment, gazed into his face.

"I just knew you'd come one day."

He smiled, seeing Rebecca in the lined face and blue eyes. "It's lovely to meet you Ruth. But you'll have to forgive me for not really knowing you."

She took a step back, taking his hands in hers, and looked him up and down.

"You're here," she said, positively. "The why's and how's don't matter just now." She glanced at David. "Where did you find him?"

"At Rebecca's grave."

She looked back at Paul. "No surprise there I guess. And you are?"

He smiled. "Paul Sayers."

"Well, Paul Sayers, you've a knack for timing. The kettle was about to go on. Come in and sit down."

Ten minutes later all three of them were seated in the front room of the cottage. Paul was studying several framed photographs on the wall above the fireplace. His cup of tea and slice of homemade sponge cake were sitting beside the armchair he had briefly occupied. Behind him Ruth and David sat on the settee, studying him, fascinated by the man who now stood before them. In only the space of a few months Paul had become used to taking any number of surprises, or shocks in certain cases, almost in his stride. What had been his sense of reality before he met Rebecca had been completely dismissed and a new one had replaced it. Therefore, seeing an old sepia toned photograph of himself in a suit, along with Rebecca in a flowing white lace wedding dress, seemed perfectly plausible.

"You would've liked to have known her," Ruth said, aware of whom he was looking at in the pictures.

"I do," he replied, without turning. His interest was drawn to the other girl in the photo with them.

Ruth and David looked at each other and she mouthed to him, 'How?'

Paul looked over his shoulder, unaware of the silent exchange between them.

"It was more or less she who told me where to find you."

Ruth looked wide-eyed. "She's dead you know. Even I didn't know her."

"Just because you're not here doesn't make you dead. She died giving birth to you."

David moved to the edge of the settee. "Just what are you saying Paul?"

He held up a hand. "The chance of us getting really confused is becoming greater by the minute. I'll explain first and then it's your turn."

They both nodded as he returned his attention to the wedding photograph on the wall.

"Before that though," he began, pointing to it. "This girl, the bridesmaid, can you tell me who she is?"

"That's Auntie Annie. She was James's twin sister," Ruth quickly replied. "She kept it in the family and married Rebecca's older brother, Albert Ekins. He was best man at their wedding."

A piece of his own jigsaw fell into place and Paul felt a warm sense of relief.

"They shared a fishing boat," David added. "Didn't you know about Annie?"

"I knew a bit about her, but not the connection I had with her. She doesn't use that name now. She's a teenager called Persephone."

David was about to speak again when Paul stopped him. "My turn first."

They both smiled. "Agreed."

"About a year and a half ago I met and instantly fell in love with a beautiful girl. I lost her for a few days, but she returned when I was doing something incredibly stupid. She saved me from certain death." He tapped the photograph. "Rebecca. The reason she did it was because she's my guardian angel. At the time I didn't know she was one. Also we were unaware that we'd been together in another life."

David said nothing while Ruth appeared eager to hear more.

"An evil force lured her amongst us and seized her. I wasn't aware of this because she'd been forbidden to see me. She'd broken her Guardian laws by saving my life. However, another Guardian visited me and I went to help Rebecca."

"You succeeded?" Ruth blurted.

He nodded, holding up his left hand with its missing little finger. "It wasn't without its dangers though."

"Thank heavens you did," David added. "But how does that bring you to us?"

"Since I rescued Rebecca we've been allowed to see each other, but it comes with a price."

"You mean they're fighting evil amongst the living?" David asked, astounded.

Paul shook his head. "Not in the biblical sense. You have to understand that they're not allowed to. They seem to be governed by laws and constraints of their own. Their basic task is to guide on souls after death."

David let out a low whistle.

"Shouldn't you doubt me?"

"You're talking to a man of God about the fight between good and evil and the guidance of souls." He spread his hands wide. "Why should I doubt?"

Paul went to the vacant armchair and sat down.

"I'm glad you see it like that so easily. I agonised over it for months."

"And so did I before I decided to join the church," David added. "Please continue."

"For what good it may do, I'm trying to help the Guardians."

"A trouble-shooter?" Ruth offered.

"Sort of," he replied. "She gave me this just after I rescued Rebecca." From his wallet he took the photograph of Ruth as a young woman and gave it to her.

"I sent this to my father. Where did she get it from?"

"It would appear that when James Cooke was shot for desertion in 1916 he demanded to see the senior Guardian before being guided on to his next destination. He wrote the name and address you see on the back and told her to give it to me when I needed it."

"Did you?" she asked.

"Oh yes, it fitted in perfectly, Rosemary was waiting for me. Apparently Cooke said more, but she won't tell me what. Although how he knew about what was going to happen seventy-odd years into the future is a mystery. What's also strange is the handwriting. It's mine."

David glanced sharply in Ruth's direction and saw that she knew what he was thinking. He turned back to Paul.

"Ruth's father's story is one that's fascinated me since I became part of the family. In some respects we've never had any answers until possibly now."

Ruth had retrieved a large brown envelope from a sideboard and proceeded to open it while he continued.

"James was quite old to join up, in his thirties, but he wanted to do his bit. He was part of the new army, not conscripts, men who'd volunteered. He joined the Norfolk Regiment and became part of III Corps, 12th Division. They were stationed in the

Somme area before the great battle began. James was a good soldier by all accounts, even getting a mention in despatches a month before his execution. Just days before the initial bombardment started in June 1916 he deserted for no good reason."

"Was none given?" Paul asked.

"James was found in a nearby town, drinking at a cafe. The arresting officer reported that he insulted the King, amongst other things. Later, he said he was tired of the fighting and only wanted to find Rebecca before it was too late to save the child."

"Strange," Paul whispered.

"Exactly," Ruth interjected. "There was no rational reason for Dad to desert. He wasn't unhappy, his letters prove it. Life in the trenches was hard, but he had the strength to deal with it. Albert had been with him for some time, but had been sent home when he was shot in the chest. He lived and couldn't understand it either."

"Why did he want to find Rebecca? And save whose child?" Paul asked, absently.

"Mother had died some sixteen years earlier giving birth to me. She wasn't there to find. Also there were no other children and I was old enough to take care of myself."

"Battlefield stress?" Paul mused.

"Unlikely," David countered. "As Ruth's already said, he was too strong of character for that sort of thing. The other strange thing was he sat down and wrote a letter to Ruth in front of the padre the night before his execution."

"Why was that strange? Wasn't it normally allowed?"

Ruth unfolded a discoloured piece of writing paper she had taken from the envelope.

"Father was a lovely man, but suffered from a lack of education. He could neither read nor write a word, save sign his name. Soldiers in his platoon always wrote the letters to me for him."

David took the paper from her and studied it next to the photograph. After a few moments he handed them both to Paul.

"Well, the mystery has always been how did James suddenly acquire the ability to write a last letter to Ruth?" As Paul took the two items from David he continued. "It would appear, Paul, it was you who wrote that last letter."

"That's impossible," Paul whispered, as he too studied the letter. However, David had been correct in his appraisal, it was indeed his handwriting. Quietly, and with them looking on, he read the letter from father to daughter.

'Dearest Ruth. Little of this will make any sense. The situation I find myself in is the fact that I have to find Rebecca and save the child. Surely That And Strength IS CHancing A Miracle BEtween Rights. I will return to you one summer's day afternoon and everything will become clear. Your loving father, James.'

He looked to them both. "Any theories?"

"The man who wrote that letter and died at the firing squad the following morning wasn't James," David replied, with all certainty. "There's almost a rambling manner to the whole thing. What does it mean? Also, why put capitals in such wrong places?"

"It's obvious it was you Paul," Ruth answered, without doubt.

"How can you be so sure?"

She pointed to the letter. "It's your handwriting. Father couldn't have possibly written it. The photograph I sent he would've had on him at the time. Therefore only you would know the address of Rosemary, Father wouldn't. Likewise, 'I will return to you one summer's afternoon' points to you."

"How?"

"Because you're the only one who really knows you're coming here."

"If that's truly the case, I'm trying to get a message across to you in this rambling bit of the letter."

David leaned forwards. "I've never thought about it like that. You could be right."

"Perhaps you're missing the obvious," Ruth added. "You could be trying to get a message to yourself." She handed him a notebook and pencil. He took them and began writing out the letters that were boldly picked out in capitals. He put a line between them and showed it to David.

"STASIS/CHAMBER."

He shook his head. "No idea, Paul. Have you?"

"No. It proves little. There's a lot more to be explained before we can say it was me back then."

"Not really," David began. "You see, Paul, another piece of this intriguing puzzle is your hand."

He raised it again. "Of course, in the churchyard, how did you know how I'd lost it?"

A serious look crossed David's face.

"There was, and still is, a lot of misguided thought on the act of desertion in the face of the enemy. A good many needless executions were carried out during The Great War. James Cooke was one of them and records of it are, at best, sketchy. After some considerable effort I managed to trace the platoon sergeant who was present at the execution."

"He was still alive then?"

"Yes, up until the late seventies," David continued. "He'd survived the war but was reluctant to talk to anyone about it, according to his family, until I asked."

"Why you?"

"The story he told me goes like this..."

Chapter 15

The 23rd of June 1916

Sergeant Patrick Buchanan entered the small courtyard next to the farmhouse. The occupants of the once quite grand estate had long since departed. The Royal Norfolk Regiment was using it as a temporary headquarters. He had brought eight men from the platoon, in a truck, from their frontline position. After marching the men into the yard he stood them at ease before entering the house via the open front door. A sentry in the entrance hall showed him to one of the rooms, knocking lightly on the door before leaving him to enter alone. Inside sat a desk on the bare floor. Behind it was a young lieutenant, resplendent in a crisp clean uniform, attending to some paperwork. Buchanan came to attention in front of him, saluting smartly, and quickly appraised the young, clean-faced officer. 'Bloody typical,' he said to himself. 'Always immaculate because he's never been near a trench, let alone the frontline. He gets a warm billet, with good food and clean sheets on the bed at night, but calls in the squaddies off the front when there's dirty work to be done. Bastard.'

The lieutenant finished signing a document before looking up and returning the salute. "Good morning Sergeant. I assume you have the squad with you?"

"Yessir," was the sharp response. "Present and correct in the courtyard." 'Silly bugger,' he thought. 'Up at four in the morning. Walk a mile and a half, then two over rough terrain in a truck to be there at six-thirty and he asks if I've brought the men.'

"Okay, Sergeant. Wait with the men outside and we'll get this over with ASAP."

"Sir," Buchanan acknowledged. "If the Lieutenant would kindly allow. I wish to speak with Private Cooke before he's brought out."

The officer appeared puzzled. "An unusual request, Sergeant. Why?"

He looked him straight in the eye. "Because he's one of my men."

The lieutenant considered it for a moment before nodding. "Very well, Sergeant. You may have a couple of minutes with him, but I want no delays. Understood?"

"Perfectly, Sir." Buchanan saluted and wheeled around to march from the room.

The guard opened the door to one of the small cellar rooms that had been set aside for use as a cell. Makeshift bars had been fixed to the only window in the top of the wall and sturdy locks fitted to the door. It was dimly lit and it took Buchanan's eyes a few seconds to adjust. What he saw were bare brick walls, streaming with damp, the exposed heavy beams of the ceiling supporting the floor above, and a simple fold up bed under the tiny window. On it laid James Cooke. Beside him, on the floor, were an empty plate and a half consumed mug of tea. On seeing him enter, Cooke swung his legs out and sat up.

"Good morning Sergeant Buchanan. I've been expecting you."

He stepped inside, surprised by the cheery greeting. It was hard to believe; there he was, only twenty-two years old, with every soldier in the platoon younger than him except Cooke. He was a good ten years older and they all looked up to him for support and advice. To a man they called him 'Pop' out of a loving respect. What had brought him to this?

Cooke could see the quizzical look on his face and held up his hands. "Don't ask."

"A lot of the lads get tired, Pop, but why desertion? We're raring to go."

He stood up and crossed to where Buchanan was standing near the door.

"It's not easy to explain Pat. But I have to find Rebecca and save the child. Staying here would mean being too late to do anything useful. There's much more at stake here than a life. There are loose ends to tie up too and I'm afraid I have to do this to James Cooke to succeed."

Something bothered Buchanan, but the reason eluded him. "Wouldn't it be better to at least die fighting?"

"Can't guarantee that Pat. This way works and keeps history straight." He took him by the shoulders. "Don't worry Pat. You'll get through all the carnage and bloodshed to come and live to be an old man."

"You guarantee that, Pop?" The look on Cooke's face chilled him.

"Oh I certainly do Pat. One day, when you're a lot older, a vicar named David Pryce will call in on you. He'll ask you about this time here with me and I hope you'll tell him everything."

He grabbed him by the hands. "I will, I promise..." his voice tailed off as he examined Cooke's left hand in his own. He had seen him only a day or two earlier, yet his little finger was missing and the scarring was perfectly healed. "How on earth did this happen?"

"Some nutter with a shovel in a farmyard," Cooke began explaining, before he was cut off by the lieutenant in the doorway.

"Okay, Sergeant. You may escort the prisoner outside."

In silence they marched to an area at the back of the house. The men of the firing squad were already assembled and Buchanan crossed to them. As he did he glanced up at the drone of aircraft, passing overhead. An early morning patrol of RFC fighters were over a thousand feet up in the partially cloudy skies, climbing out over the frontline. He looked back to where Cooke was being readied. For some reason he seemed indifferent to the events going on around him, as if he was detached from reality. He too was looking up at the passing biplanes. A short conversation was taking place between Cooke and the officer, but Buchanan could not make out the words. If anything he was refusing a cigarette and the blindfold. The lieutenant then retreated back to the rank of men.

"Carry on, Sergeant."

The eight rifles came upright, on command, and took aim.

"Shoot!"

The order was instantly followed by a volley of shots that all found their target. Without a sound, Cooke fell backwards against the wall and slid to the ground. Then, as the echo of shots died away, the lieutenant stepped forward, along with Buchanan, to examine the body. It was evident, from the tattered holes in his chest and the growing stain of blood on his tunic, that the firing squad had been efficient. However, the officer unclipped his service revolver from its holster and fired twice into the head of Cooke. Blood and gore splattered over the wall and he seemed satisfied. He said nothing more to Buchanan and re-holstered the pistol. For a few moments Buchanan stood staring down at his executed comrade, thinking of the waste of life. Something again drew him to Cooke's left hand. He almost gasped out loud, but caught himself. The little finger, which had been missing only minutes before, had miraculously reappeared.

Chapter 16

Paul placed the empty teacup back on its saucer. "And that's what he told you?"

David nodded. "I taped my conversation with Patrick Buchanan back in nineteen-seventy-six, when he was eighty-two years old. I've listened to it often, it's fascinating. You've heard it the same way he told me."

"Did he tell you where they buried Cooke?"

"He asked the lieutenant for permission to remove the body but was refused. They were sent straight back to the frontline and no-one ever divulged the information to him. It paid him not to press the matter further. I've done some checking with the MOD, but they're reluctant to give anything out. I've also checked with the Imperial War Museum records. They confirm the execution, yet give no place of internment."

"What of the Norfolk Regiment's headquarters?"

Again David shook his head. "It seems it was just a temporary headquarters. The exact location, or the name of the farm, appears lost." He looked across at Ruth. "We'd love to bring him back so that he could lie next to Rebecca."

Paul managed a half smile. "Yeah, I guess he'd like that."

"So it now seems, somehow, you were there instead of James," David concluded.

Paul rubbed at his forehead. "Maybe it'll explain itself one day. Maybe."

"But isn't that why you're here?" Ruth asked.

"Not really," he replied. "I only learned of James and your existence this morning. I was only told of the connection because of Jason Galloway and his abduction."

Ruth and David looked at each other, a sudden realisation that they'd momentarily forgotten the boy's plight. So much had they been caught up with Paul's arrival thoughts of Jason had temporarily taken a back seat.

"You say abduction Paul," David said, quietly. "The police are only treating it as a missing person's case at the present."

"Sorry to tell you this, but it's an abduction," he said, gravely.

"Apart from the twisted family connection, Paul, what else do you know about Jason?"

He shrugged. "Little. Only that he's alive."

"You can be certain?" Ruth asked.

"Yes, because I know who's holding him and why."

David lightly slapped his forehead with the palm of his hand. "Of course. It has to be this evil force who took your Rebecca."

Paul nodded. "For some reason, everything I've done or seem to do is linked to this evil thing or the Guardians. That means now, in the future, or even the past, it all appears to be part of one big puzzle. It must be my lot in life to piece it together bit by bit. Even what happened to Cooke in the war is linked to me, as if it's my fault he died."

"It isn't," Ruth added.

"What can you do?" David asked. "The police are looking for him."

"The problem is the police can't be trusted."

"Can you find him?"

"I believe I can," was the positive reply. "I have a head start on knowing where to begin the search."

Chapter 17

The sun had been reduced to a harmless red disc, slowly fading from sight behind a low bank of cloud close to the horizon. A light breeze drifted lazily over the waves, stirring the air, but not diminishing the warmth left in the day. A small group sat chatting outside the 'Fisherman' public house, under the shadow of the windmill at Cley-next-the-sea, reveling in the evening light. One of the men put his glass down and pointed at the black Wolseley that was slowing down to round the corner. Paul had driven along the coast road after leaving the vicarage at Saltmarsh. After a long conversation with Ruth and David, he had made his excuses and left for his meeting with Rebecca. A mile past the village he turned down a track to the shingle beach. At the end of it was a secluded car park that he knew well. Rebecca was already waiting for him and, on seeing the car, waved. A flash of headlights returned the greeting. Paul felt the usual rush of joy he always experienced whenever he saw her. She was sitting on a short stretch of fencing, running beside the track, dressed in white slacks, blouse, and a fawn coloured jumper. Paul jumped out and breathed in the salty air. The sound of waves lapping onto the shore could be heard on the other side of the high shingle bank. He met Rebecca, effortlessly lifting her off the ground and spinning her in his arms before putting her back down. Their lips met as her feet touched the ground.

"Hello darling," she greeted.

"Good evening, precious. You look gorgeous."

"Did you have an interesting afternoon at Saltmarsh?"

"Did you look in?"

"No. I did not have the time," she replied, honestly. "Did you learn anything?"

"A great deal, but nothing that's going to be a help with

finding the boy. It also threw up many more questions than answers. Let's talk about it later though." He let go of her hand and opened the boot. As she stood there he passed her two tartan blankets and also took out a wicker picnic hamper. Hand in hand they climbed the high gravel bank that spanned several miles of the coastline in each direction as a sea-defence. Once on the top they descended the other side to the shingle beach and walked along the shoreline. A ceaseless wash of waves rolled rhythmically in and out at their feet as they crunched along on the wet gravel. Only a frothy line remained as a marker of each passing. After few hundred yards Paul spotted a niche in the stepped edge of the banking that was only thirty or so feet from the sea. They steered towards it and found it dry enough to spread the blankets on. Once they had settled into their spot he began delving into the hamper and bringing out an assortment of food.

"Help yourself."

She looked half-heartedly over the spread.

"I don't need to Paul. It is just that we do not eat and do not when here. I am never here long enough to use the mortal energy of the body to feel the need to replenish it." She gently squeezed his arm. "I am just not used to it my darling."

"Then you don't have to. I'm not forcing you."

She slid her arm around his waist as he ate and sensed that he felt he had not done enough to please her. However, that was wrong. He always did more than enough to thrill her and she had never once felt let down. It was only as she sat there that she realised how much it was an important part of being together, of being a couple, even in their short periods of time together. Reaching out she took a sandwich and examined it.

"If I am going to spend time with you, my darling, I had better get used to eating. I will need to fuel my body with the energy it needs."

He patted her knee. "And what a gorgeous body it is."

"Forgive me."

"For what?" he asked, looking at her and seeing the concerned look in her depthless blue eyes.

"For being so thoughtless at the effort you have gone to."

"There's nothing to forgive," he said, truthfully. "We've so much to learn about each other it's going to take time. Especially when we live such totally different lives."

She squeezed him tighter. "I know what you mean Paul. Watching you for all those years was never easy to endure. Being with you is special, yet just as hard."

"You're not kidding."

"Now tell me what you learned this afternoon."

He finished his sandwich before launching into an explanation of how he had been to the grave in Saltmarsh churchyard and the subsequent conversation with David Pryce. She listened without interruption, especially when he recounted the reunion with Ruth and her recollections.

"Did you really know nothing of our past life here?" he finally asked.

"Not until this morning. Obviously during my induction my past was somehow blocked. Charlotte had her reasons for keeping it from me, all valid I am sure, but I did not know. At least now we have an explanation for the way we feel about each other."

He nodded. "But, whatever was blocked, love transcends everything, even death. There are so many more questions yet to answer though."

"Like the photograph of Ruth?" she asked.

"And the writing on the back," he replied, seriously, as he stared out to sea. "David's convinced that I lived as James Cooke in the last few hours of his life. He reckons it could be the only explanation for the missing finger. Also because of the fact that James couldn't read or write, but wrote a letter to Ruth in my handwriting."

"It said you would return one summer. Yes?"

"Amongst other things. It would seem my predecessor knew of this day before I did. Or I could've written it because I now know of this day too. It means that at some point still to come I have to go back." He gazed at the glowing red clouds of sunset and rubbed his forehead. "Oh I don't know Rebecca. I've had to come to terms with so much lately. I guess it's better to leave everything to unfold in time."

She stroked the back of his hand. "That is the best idea my darling. It will be explained in time I am certain. Try not to let it trouble you."

He drew up his knees and rested his chin on them, letting out a long breath. "I think I found out why I feel so close to Persephone."

"Myra Stanford's daughter? I know you said you felt something when you were close to her. What do you think it is?"

"When I'm near her I feel a great sense of attachment, love even. It's as if we can sense what each other's thinking and feeling. Ruth had a picture of what was our wedding in 1898. James' twin sister, Annie, was bridesmaid. It was quite clear Rebecca. Persephone's the spitting image of Annie."

"Really," she said, intrigued by his discovery. "Do you believe that the bond, often shared by twins, can be carried into the next life? Even if born apart?"

"If love can transcend death maybe other feelings can too." He looked at her. "If you Guardians can't answer these questions how do you expect me to? Especially with Charlotte keeping secret some of what she knows."

"I wish I could help you more with figuring things out."

"I love you," he whispered, as their lips met in a long lingering kiss.

"And I have always loved you."

The orange glow of sunset finally dipped below the horizon, leaving the light to lazily tone from blue to indigo and then to inky black. The air on the beach remained warm as pinpricks of starlight appeared will-o-the-wisp fashion amongst the high altitude streaks of cloud. Paul wrapped Rebecca in one of the blankets and she snuggled up in his arms. The warmth of love and affection she felt lazily drifted through her thoughts like the waves across the shingle. In the early hours of Sunday morning Paul gathered several pieces of wood and an old fish crate, found on the beach, and built a small fire. Together, disturbed only by the lapping of the waves close to their feet, they shared the night. Paul opened a bottle of wine and even Rebecca enjoyed the picnic. For Paul the peace of that night would be long remembered. Elsewhere events had overtaken them.

Chapter 18

It was late evening at Pelham Hall. The phone rang once before Myra swiftly snatched it up.

"Yes?" she greeted, curtly. A moment or two passed, in the ensuing silence of the room, before she said; "Okay," and replaced the handset. She looked across at Storn. He had stood unmoving and unspeaking, looking out of the French windows, for hours. To an outside observer he could have been a statue. Beyond, the evening light was fading to darkness.

"There's been no sign of Sayers since this morning and the car hasn't been spotted either," she said, genuinely exasperated. "The bastard's disappeared."

Persephone had returned to her position sitting on the table. Her eyes were closed and in her mind she was reaching out with her senses to experience another person's feelings. It was a new and delicate talent that needed patience simply to begin to even understand. Somewhere she could sense, and nearly see, the waves gently foaming as they broke against a gravel shoreline. There was also the smell of salty air. Beside her, as if she was sitting there too, she could feel someone next to her. They were sharing an intimate moment the like of which she had never experienced before. The love was like a wash of dazzling colour passing through her heart.

"He won't be back for hours yet," she muttered.

Myra glanced at her. "How can you be so sure?"

By the window Storn did not move or say anything. Myra continued to study her daughter. Despite her young years she appeared to be maturing, rapidly, in front of her eyes. There would soon come a time when she had no control over her at all.

"Why won't he be back for hours?" she asked.

Persephone opened her eyes and smiled.

"He won't rush away from the arms of his lover. Would you?"

She raised an eyebrow, taken a little aback by the surprise answer. "Pure guesswork, Daughter, surely?"

"No, Mother," came her positive reply. "Pure feeling." With that she got up and went to the door.

"Where are you going?"

"I'd like to go to bed. It's been a long day." She paused, looking directly at Storn. "It usually takes a few minutes to find where they've put the miniature camera to spy on me."

Again Storn did not move or say a word and Myra was surprised by her forthright stance with him. Persephone said no more and left the room to the two of them.

Chapter 19

Sunday 23rd May 1993

The big silver airliner was just settling into its approach for landing at the airport. Inside, sitting in a window seat of unusually large proportions for even First Class, Gary Malins was fervently anticipating the landing. It was to be the holiday of a lifetime on a tropical island. Still gripped in his hand was the football pools cheque for four million pounds. By some quirk of fortune he had become the biggest winner in its history. This he found quite unbelievable, because he had never filled in a coupon in his life. Still he did not want to ask too many questions, as he thought it better not to look a gift horse in the mouth. Without warning, the passenger next to him began shaking him by the shoulder and shouting at him.

"Get off me," he cried, turning to look at the offending culprit. Quite frighteningly, he found himself staring into the face of his old junior school headmistress, Clarissa Parker. He gave a half strangled cry of recognition.

"What are you doing on my holiday?"

"Wake up Gary!" the familiar voice urged, as the shaking increased. Slowly, the grey fog of sleep lifted and he came to, lying in bed next to Gaynor. Her long dark hair hung loose over her shoulders and her pretty brown eyes looked sleepily at him. "Are you awake?"

"No."

Gaynor was the only child of a Jamaican father and Welsh mother. She had inherited her stunning good looks from her mother and her dark complexion from her father. She was tall and slender with proportioned curves that gave her a model-like appearance.

Gary had pounced on her the moment she had arrived at the factory. At the time she was a packaging-materials salesperson. A whirlwind romance ended with a wedding six months later. Afterwards, she had gone back to being a hairdresser and was self-employed.

"Gary!" she again urged. "There's someone banging at the front door," she said, more urgently. "You go."

"Why don't you?" he replied, closing his eyes, anxious to be back on the tropical island.

"I can't go because I'm naked, you idiot. Don't you remember pulling off my nightie last night?"

"Why does what I did last night have to do with now?" he said, sleepily, as downstairs the loud knocking could be heard again.

"Go Gary!"

Reluctantly, he struggled up. "What on earth's the time?"

"Seven-thirty," she replied. "It could be urgent."

"Urgent? On a Sunday morning at this hour?" he blurted. "It's the only day I get a lie in."

"It could be someone arriving for the barbeque," she added.

He looked at her, puzzled. "That's this afternoon. Why this bloody early? If we ignore them they'll go away."

She tossed him a dressing gown. "Put that on."

There was further knocking as he descended the stairs.

"Alright!" he called out. "Give us a break. It's Sunday you know."

As he opened the door he was greeted by a couple in their fifties. A vague recognition stirred in his thoughts, but the effects of sleep meant he could not quite grasp it.

"If it's religion you're selling, I've already got one, voodoo," he said, firmly.

The tall woman, with slightly greying, dark curled hair stepped closer.

"We don't choose to intrude Mr. Malins, but our daughter's been out all night and hasn't been in touch. It's not like her to stay out without at least..."

"Wait, wait, wait," Gary interrupted, holding up his hands in surrender. "I ain't awake I know, but what's your daughter got to do with me?"

She took a step backwards. "We're Sally's parents."

He still looked at them groggily.

"Sally Marcroft," the man said. "What Brenda's trying to say is; Sally's spent the night with your friend Paul Sayers. We've been round to his house but can't rouse them. Both their cars are in the driveway."

"Well I put Paul's there yesterday lunchtime. He'd gone out by then."

"Sally was called yesterday afternoon. Apparently he had some important business contact there and needed her to go round to help him."

Gary shook his head. "Sorry, but that doesn't make sense. Paul doesn't do business at home, it's not his style."

"Well the curtains are drawn so someone must be in," Brenda added.

"Perhaps they're having a lie in. They're both adults, so why worry?"

"I don't find that funny," she retorted. "She's been out all night and Sally isn't that sort of a girl."

He shrugged. "If she's with Paul she won't come to any harm, believe me, give it a couple of hours."

She continued, as if she had not heard him. "Look, Mr. Malins, I've been worried sick all night. We've phoned, dozens of times, and keep getting fobbed off with a machine. And we've been round there knocking. Even his neighbour said he'd seen them both there yesterday evening."

"Then why call on me?"

"Because you're his friend," Brian Marcroft began, trying to calm the conversation. "Would you please come with us and try?"

Gary shook the sleep from his head. Gaynor was standing on the landing in her dressing gown. He was not sure how much of the conversation she had heard.

"I'm just going to pop round to Paul's," he said, with a wink. "Apparently Sally's been with him all night and they can't be woken."

"Oh."

He turned back to Sally's parents. "I'll see you down there, okay?"

Brian nodded. "Thank you."

Back upstairs Gary hastily pulled on a pair of jeans and sweatshirt. Gaynor sat on the end of the bed watching him.

"Can't they give the girl a break?" she asked.

He shook his head. "She's an only child and Catholic to boot. They won't let her out of their sight." He pulled on his motorcycle boots as he spoke. "Anyway, it doesn't add up. Paul wasn't there yesterday when I took the car back. Also he'd seen that Rebecca bird hours before and he's potty about her as you know."

"The angel?" she said, sceptically.

"The same, but I'll tell you something, she was beautiful. If Paul's truly in love with her, as we know he is, why sacrifice that for sex with Sally?"

"Why did she go round there?"

"That doesn't make any sense either. He's supposed to have called her because he had an important meeting going on. It's bullshit. Paul doesn't do business at home, ever."

"Then what's this all about?"

"I haven't a clue," he replied, kissing her on the lips. "Just keep the bed warm."

Within minutes the Kawasaki motorcycle was heading in the direction of Sawston. With experienced ease, coupled with a healthy turn of speed, Gary pulled up outside Paul's house scant seconds after the Marcroft's had arrived in their car. He kicked the side-stand down, turned off the engine, and climbed off the bike. For a couple of seconds he studied the red brick house. He had been there many times before and had known it as a place of welcome since childhood. All the curtains were drawn and, parked on the drive where he had left it, was Paul's Cavalier. Stood behind it was Sally's Ford Escort. Gary reached the front door at about the same time as the Marcroft's. Without pausing, he loudly rapped on the frosted glass door and pressed the bell. After waiting a few seconds he repeated the exercise.

"You see," Brenda said, in a victorious tone. "They're not answering."

Gary shrugged. "Perhaps it proves they're not here at all."

"He called her yesterday afternoon. Where can they be without a car?"

"As I said before, I returned his car yesterday and he wasn't here then."

A wall bordered Paul's property and it ran close to the side of the house. Gary used it as a bridge to climb up onto the flat garage roof while they stood and watched. The window on the landing had been left ajar. The security catch was not on and he pulled it open, before pitching his large frame inside. He knew the house, intimately, and went straight to the front bedroom.

"Paul! Are you in?"

His hand paused over the handle, before he pushed the door open. It proved what he already knew, there was no one in. The bed though had obviously been used. The duvet was almost on the floor, while the bottom sheet was all creased up. The pillows too were scattered about and one lay at his feet. However, his eyes quickly locked onto the top of the bed. Attached to the brass bed-head were two pairs of silver handcuffs. A blue dress, white panties, and a bra sat on a chair next to the dressing table.

"Shit," he whispered. "What've you been up to?"

A speedy search of the other rooms proved fruitless. He went downstairs and used the kitchen entrance to the garage. It was empty. Paul had taken the Wolseley. But where had he gone? Was Sally with him? Unable to answer his own questions, he went to the front door and found the other two still waiting.

"There's no one home."

"But their cars are here," Brenda repeated.

"That's funny," Gary said, as he bent down to retrieve the set of keys lying on the doormat. "I put these through yesterday. It looks as if he's not been home at all."

"Then where've they gone?" she asked.

"It looks like he left yesterday, in the Wolseley, and didn't come back. There's no other explanation."

"But he rang Sally from here. That's why she came," Brenda insisted.

"Did he ring himself?"

"No. It was the personal secretary of the business contact he was meeting."

Gary shook his head. "None of this makes any sense. He didn't make the call himself and I don't believe he's been here since yesterday morning."

"Let me look," she said, pushing her way in. Gary followed and Brian brought up the rear. The lounge was in darkness and Gary drew back the curtains. The room instantly filled with sunlight.

"They're not here," he repeated, as they all stood in the centre of the empty lounge.

"Well I'm worried," she said, looking directly at him.

"You'll have to wait and see," he replied, with a shrug. "I've done my bit."

"Then I'll wait here," she said, firmly, and sat down on the sofa. "I've something to say to Paul Sayers concerning good manners and behaviour."

Gary crossed to where she sat. "Hey, I only came to look at your insistence. You can't expect to wait here without invitation. That wouldn't be good manners either."

She looked daggers at him. "I'd expect you to stand up for him. Sally's been carrying a torch for him for years. Yet he's never had the decency to take their relationship further. He's a waste of time, but still keeps her hanging on a string."

"Wait a minute," Gary retorted. "Paul's never had her on a string at any time. In fact he's repeatedly said he doesn't want a relationship with her. He knows it wouldn't work, but she won't believe it."

"So you say."

"And when did you ever think anything of him anyway?" Gary added. "You've hardly made him welcome, even as one of her friends. She's said as much herself."

Brenda pushed her nose in the air and turned to look away from him.

"I think it's time you left and waited at home," he said, quietly, as he brought himself back to a level of calm.

As the exchange had taken place Brian Marcroft had wandered about the room and found himself back at the sofa where his wife sat. He took Gary's attention and pointed to the gap between it and the wall.

"Look, he keeps bags of rubbish in the lounge."

"What?" Gary began, as he too looked. "That's odd."

Brenda twisted in her seat as Gary stepped round to where the four black sacks were standing on a sheet of clear plastic. He leant over the nearest one and pulled at the tied neck of it. The bag though was heavier than he had expected it to be. With a wrench he pulled harder, only to have the side rip open before their shocked eyes. The blood drenched mess of hacked up flesh and bone that spilled onto the floor was not recognisable as being something human. However, the clear plastic bag that contained the severed head of Sally Marcroft was, instantly so. The sheer horror and revulsion that jerked through Gary's body at that moment would sadly live with him, and haunt his dreams, forever. He turned, with a lurch, and scrambled to empty the contents of his stomach into the empty fireplace. At the same time, cutting through his head like a jagged blade, came the long inhuman scream of Brenda Marcroft.

Chapter 20

It was one o'clock in the afternoon and Paul was enjoying the steady cruise back from the coast. They had enjoyed the morning in Sheringham together and, although the drive home was relaxing, he was eager to get on with the task of finding Jason Galloway.

"You're stopping for a while when we get back?" he asked, glancing across at Rebecca as she comfortably occupied the passenger seat.

"Of course, Paul. I have some time to spare and Charlotte's blessing too."

"Grab it while you can."

She leaned across and rested her hand on his thigh, while at the same time passing a burst of affection that he could easily feel.

"I spend too much time away as it is. After last night I have realised how much we deserve to have a little time together."

"And in a good cause too. We'll need to talk over some sort of plan for locating the boy."

"Do you have something in mind?"

"Not at the moment," he replied, with a shrug. "I'll think clearer when I've had something to eat."

"You and your food."

The Wolseley negotiated the biggest roundabout on the Kings Lynn by-pass just as the sun broke through the loose puffy cloud cover. A Rover police car drew out of the A10 feeder road and took up position behind it. Paul saw it, but took little notice.

Inside the patrol car the uniformed officer in the passenger seat thumbed the microphone to speak to his controller. "Charlie Alpha to control."

"Go ahead Charlie Alpha," came the almost instant response.

"That black Wolseley we had word of this morning. We've just pulled in behind it"

"What's your position?"

"We're just joining the A47 at Kings Lynn, heading towards Wisbech."

"Roger, Charlie Alpha," the controller replied. "We're alerting all available units in the area. Stay behind him until we've set a roadblock on the road ahead of you. This man's considered dangerous and could be armed. Do you acknowledge?"

"Understood control," the officer replied. "We'll just keep tabs on him. Be advised he's carrying a passenger."

"Can you pass a description Charlie Alpha?"

"It's a white female, with fair hair."

"Roger, keep with them Charlie Alpha."

The officer replaced the handset and turned to his colleague. "Is the adrenaline starting to flow Steve?"

The driver nodded without taking his eyes off the Wolseley. "Let's make sure this goes as smooth as possible."

Paul was talking with Rebecca and, for those few minutes, oblivious to the police car behind.

"If Storn's followers have taken Jason, for him to feed on his soul, then surely he'll be kept in the same place as the others were."

"Yes. It will be a holding facility equally as remote as the one I was held in. There is a ceremony involved so the place is important to them. The ritualistic element is purely contrived, to please the followers, and has no real importance in the taking of the soul. Storn only requires that the soul is contained upon the death of the subject."

Paul shuddered. "It hardly bears thinking about. At least I've got that black book from Stanford. There're bound to be some leads in it. Perhaps we can see if there are any groups of followers in the same area. There were plenty of them around Kirkham. It could be the same elsewhere. Did you locate Sephie and Myra?"

"I thought you said you had no ideas. They are at a place called Pelham Hall."

"I did a little thinking last night. Where's Pelham Hall?" As he spoke he glanced in the mirror and noticed the police car, still behind. He briefly looked at the white faced speedometer. They were travelling at a steady fifty mph.

"Something wrong Paul?" Rebecca asked, noting his sudden shift in interest.

"I don't think so," he replied. "I don't think I've done anything wrong."

"What makes you think you might have?"

He indicated over his shoulder. "He seems to have an unhealthy interest in keeping behind us."

She turned and looked out of the oval rear window. As she studied the patrol car and its two uniformed officers, a Range Rover, with its blue lights flashing, pulled in behind too. Paul saw it in his mirrors and instantly knew something was amiss. She turned back to him, concern on her face and in her voice.

"There is something wrong."

"Obviously so, precious," he replied, dividing his attention between her, the road, and the police. "Why do I get the impression something very serious has happened in the last few hours and we've been saddled with it."

"Storn," she said, with conviction.

As he looked in the mirror he saw a third police car draw into the trailing posse.

"Shit," he whispered. "It's bad Rebecca. You'd better be on your way back."

Anxiously, she looked across at the man she loved. "I want to stay with you."

"That's not advisable. You know we can't prove who you are."

Slowly, she nodded. "If you put it like that, I will go."

He reached over and squeezed her hand, affectionately. "I don't want you to go. But, if something's happened involving Storn, I want you as far away as possible." He pulled her hand up and kissed it. "It'll be easier for me knowing you're observing from a position of safety."

"I understand darling."

"It would appear I'm going to be arrested, so keep a close

watch. If I'm still being held, three days before Jason's due to be killed, try and get me out without endangering yourself."

"I will. I love you."

"I love you too. Now scrunch down in the foot-well before you go. They must've seen you. Disappearing from sight could prove hard to explain."

There was plenty of room in the front of the Wolseley and she slipped below the level of the windows. "You are going to have to explain my disappearance anyway."

He shrugged. "I'll deny all knowledge. They can't prove a thing without you."

Rebecca clasped her hand around her bracelet and smiled, lovingly. "Take good care, my darling, I'll be watching."

With a cheery smile he winked back, but in that split second she was gone.

"Safe trip," he whispered. Now he had only his own predicament to worry about. Ahead the single carriageway was opening out to two lanes each way. It was a stretch he knew well, as did the police. In the distance was a roadblock. He took his foot off the accelerator pedal and began slowing down. The one certain fact was that he had not done anything wrong. But the police obviously thought otherwise. There seemed no sense in giving them reason to think he was anything other than innocent. The three cars behind fanned out to block any idea of turning around and pushed him into the others.

"Whatever it is they think you've done Sayers, it must be pretty bad," he whispered, under his breath, as he rolled to halt just twenty feet short of them. Behind him the cars stopped and the policemen inside instantly leapt out and went for cover behind their vehicles.

'Whatever can they be thinking?' Paul asked himself. Then he saw the two officers in the blockade ahead of him wearing flack vests and carrying pistols. Quite worryingly the guns were pointed in his direction.

"Let's not be hasty gentleman."

An unseen loudhailer rang out. "Driver of the car! Turn off the engine and step from the vehicle along with your passenger!"

Paul switched off and slowly pushed the door open. Once he was outside the officer called again.

"Walk away from the car and put your arms in the air where I can see them. Tell your passenger to do the same!"

He moved to the side, several feet, without shutting the door and shook his head.

"I haven't got a passenger!"

"This is no time for games!" the officer warned. "Tell her to step from the car!"

Paul shouted again. "There's no one else in the car!"

There followed a pause, before another order was called. "Step four paces forward and lay face down on the ground with your arms clearly out to the sides. Now!"

Without comment or delay he did exactly as directed. As he lay on the warm tarmac he heard footsteps approaching from all sides. At least two of them were at the Wolseley.

"Where the hell did she go to?" he heard one astonished officer say to another. The reply went unheard and Paul smiled at the clever piece of deception. In the following moment his hands were snatched back and a set of handcuffs went on. A low chatter of conversation was taking place, beside the Wolseley, but he could not hear what was being said.

"Anybody care to tell me what I've supposed to have done?"

A shadow fell over Paul and two pairs of hands roughly dragged him to his feet. A ring of policemen had formed around him and the men with the guns were the closest. A sergeant spoke first as another officer searched Paul's clothing.

"Where's your female passenger?" he demanded and indicated to the Wolseley.

"Why do you keep asking about a passenger? I'm on my own."

"He's clean," the officer carrying out the search said, and stood back. The sergeant stepped up to him so they were just inches part.

"You were chatting to her when she ducked out of sight."

Paul smiled and shook his head. "If you can find a woman in my car I'd like to meet her. She can help pay for the petrol."

The officer's face did not alter and his professionalism impressed Paul. But with Rebecca he held all the cards. He knew they had seen her, yet without her they could do nothing.

"Don't get smart, laddie," he warned. "Where'd she go?"

He remained calm. "You've been following me. So if she's not here she must've got out. Right? She hasn't, which means she was never there in the first place. If you want to search for someone who doesn't exist be my guest." He paused to draw breath and allowed the point to sink in. "Now are you going to tell me what it is I've supposedly done to warrant the heavy-handed approach?"

The officer who had searched him handed Paul's wallet to the sergeant. He took it and removed the driving licence.

"You are Paul Sayers of twelve Low Road Sawston?" he asked, looking him up and down.

"Yes."

"Well, Mr. smart-arse with the disappearing passenger, you're being placed under arrest for the rape and murder of Ms Sally Marcroft."

Paul's eyes widened in outright disbelief as the shocking revelation hit him. It was beyond his wildest imagination. Sally had been murdered and he was somehow being framed for it. The officer continued with the necessary cautioning and the reading of his rights, although he did not hear him. His thoughts were racing away with all the possible implications and consequences.

"When did this happen?" he interrupted.

The officer said nothing and only finished the necessary caution.

"You'd better get yourself a lawyer sunshine," he eventually said. "Because you're going to need one."

Paul realised that saying something would probably do him more harm than good, in the circumstances, and decided to shut up. The sergeant signalled to two of his men and had them lead Paul to the nearest car. The roadblock was being moved and a car sat ready with its doors open. Without ceremony he was pushed into the rear seat and sandwiched between two men. The sergeant slipped into the vacant front seat beside the driver. Within moments they were speeding away from the scene with another car as escort. Paul glanced over his shoulder at the rapidly disappearing Wolseley. It was bathed in afternoon sunshine and was being coned off where it sat.

Chapter 21

The dome shaped room that was the return chamber glowed iridescent red for several long moments before a blue flash lit the interior with a brief, high intensity pulse. Again the walls dulled to red, before settling back to a soft white glow. In the centre of the floor, on the energy grid, Rebecca stood for a moment with her eyes closed. As always she waited for her senses to steady from the swirl of tangled shapes and vivid colours. She opened her eyes, relieved that the return had been successfully completed. Whilst many of her Guardian sisters enjoyed the sensations of transfer, she did not and was unhappy with their mode of travel. Dismissing her feelings, she quickly exited the chamber and discarded the cardigan she was wearing. She was in a hurry and dashed along the illuminated corridors and down three levels to the area set aside for viewing. Her senses told her that the first one was the one with Charlotte in. Almost falling over, she burst into the chamber, anxious for news. Charlotte was inside and turned to see her arrival, surprised at how quickly she had gotten there after leaving Paul.

"Slow down Rebecca," she said, holding her hands up in a halting gesture. "Rushing around will not solve anything."

If she could have been breathless she would have been, as she spoke in a hurried tone.

"Paul is in serious danger. I had to leave him."

"It was wise of him to send you back."

"Do you know what has happened?"

With a wave of her beautifully manicured hand Charlotte motioned to the events being displayed upon the viewing chamber wall. Also in the room was another of their Guardian sisters, Annabelle. Although Rebecca knew everyone, she did not know her closely. She was almost identical in stature to Charlotte, wearing the same one-piece white gown, but displayed her red hair in a series of multi-platted strands. Rebecca moved to stand with them and gazed at the picture being played out on the port. It was as if they were there too, standing at the side of the road observing, unseen.

"Whatever is it they think he has done?" she asked, in a tone filling with dread.

Annabelle turned to face her; a look of sadness was etched on the features of her pretty face. "Without warning, yesterday evening of their time, one of my charges was taken from me in an evil act."

"Who?" Rebecca asked, only momentarily taking her eyes from the events on the wall.

"Sally Marcroft."

"Paul's friend from where he works?" Rebecca said, astonished. "How?"

"In an act of deception, she was taken, raped, and then dismembered. It was fortunate I was able to bring her away before any serious harm came to her soul." Annabelle replied.

"Storn."

"Not personally," Charlotte added. "However, from what we have already learned, he is behind it. It was one of his followers who did the deed."

"Why has Paul been brought into it?"

"I fear some sort of diversion is being created by them, or that Paul is being subjected to a revenge attack. The body of Sally was placed in Paul's home and found there while the two of you were away. They have also placed inside the house material to link Paul to the abduction of Jason Galloway and the others Storn's followers took. I suspect they may also be hoping that you will go to his aid and have some plan to take you."

Rebecca shook her head. "Paul would not allow it. But if you knew of this last night, when we were together, why did you not warn us?"

Charlotte tried to smile. "My dear girl, Paul is in enough trouble as it is. No doubt he will lie about being with you. His position would be worse if he had known of Sally's death. It was better for him not to know. He can deny it and appear plausible."

"But what can we do now Charlotte?"

"Absolutely nothing at present," she replied, truthfully, and returned her attention to the view port. "For now we have to be patient and see what develops. Only then can we decide what we can do to help Paul."

"Then let us hope something develops soon," Rebecca said, as they watched Paul being driven away.

Chapter 22

The grey door of the secure interview room swung inwards and Paul glanced up to witness the arrival of the two detectives. He had been waiting several hours for the questioning to begin. The trip to Clayborough police station had been conducted in silence. On arrival he had gone through the process of being searched again, his fingerprints and samples for DNA being taken, and a lengthy form filling exercise. They had taken his wristwatch, along with the other things he had been carrying, so he could only guess at the time. He sat back in the simple plastic chair and watched as the two of them sat down. The woman had short dark hair and looked to be in her early forties. She was not unattractive, but determined blue eyes and a sense of toughness showed through. If she had a sense of humour or a likeable side, he guessed he would not be seeing it. There was a darkening under the eyes and the telltale signs of aging. The stress of dealing with the underbelly of society had its drawbacks. She removed her smart grey jacket and hung it over the back of the seat. She then began shuffling through a file of papers on the desk.

"You've refused to have legal representation present at this time," she said, looking up.

Paul nodded and she studied his expressionless face.

"You may still call for one to be present during this interview," she continued, in an accent he couldn't place, without taking her gaze from him. "This interview will continue if you do not and will be taped. Is that clear?"

Again he nodded.

The other detective was setting up a tape recorder. He was surprisingly short, just five feet six, with close-cropped fair hair. He was younger than her, only in his mid-twenties, and appeared both lean and fit. He set the machine running and spoke clearly into it.

"It's seven-thirty p.m. Sunday the twenty-third of May 1993. The subject being interviewed is Paul Sayers. Conducting the interview is DCI Helen Bradshaw, with Detective Constable Steven Wiles."

Helen saw no change in the expression of the man she was facing. He was unshaven, but not the sort who warranted a second glance in normal society. If anything he was simply an ordinary bloke. The steel-blue eyes though struck her as being extra attentive, possessing a certain amount of character. Her first thought was that he was not the sort of man capable of the charges being levelled at him. He did not fit the profile they were rapidly building of him through the statements they had been taking throughout the day. However, experience also told her faces rarely fitted the mental picture people had of men capable of committing such gross acts. She knew they would have to work to break down the barriers he would erect in his defence to get to the truth.

"These are extremely serious charges being brought against you, Sayers," she began, in an authoritative tone. "Is there any reason why you don't want representation? One can be provided."

"I haven't done anything, so it could possibly imply defence of the guilty."

She paused, having not heard that particular reply before. "Are you saying you're not guilty of the murder of Sally Marcroft?"

Paul crossed his arms over his chest. The game of words had begun and they were the experts while he was just an amateur.

"I know for a fact I didn't kill Sally."

"No legal representative then?" she again asked, ignoring his statement of denial.

"I wouldn't know who to trust."

Helen turned the page of a blank jotter and took out a pen. Wiles did the same. It was going to be long, demanding, and mentally draining, but Paul knew he would have to go through it.

"Tell us about your movements on Saturday the twenty-second of May. Yesterday," Helen began.

It was precisely then that Paul realised just what a predicament he was in and how those who had chosen to frame him had picked exactly the right moment. They must have been watching him all along. How could he explain that he had been visited by two guardian angels, one of whom he was in love with and shared a relationship of sorts, and another one who had described to him how he had lived and died during The First World War? There was also the fact he was searching to find where a devil had taken their abducted, great, great, great grandson, before his soul was taken. He knew it was true, but, like those who had set him up knew, if he tried to use it as an alibi the police would consider it deranged ranting. He really was in a spot and would have to tread carefully.

"I arrived at work about six-thirty."

"Was Sally Marcroft there at this time as well?" Wiles interjected.

He shook his head. "Sally only does seven-thirty to ten-thirty on a Saturday."

"Did," Helen corrected.

"Alright, did."

"So you saw her then?" Wiles continued.

"When you work in the same office it's hard not to," Paul replied, sarcastically.

"Did you discuss anything in particular? Or argue?" Helen quickly asked.

"Not that I remember," he said, casting his mind back, and realised they had. "Only work stuff."

She removed a sheet from her folder.

"The receptionist, Jenny Smith, gave us a statement in which she says you and Sally Marcroft exchanged 'cross words', as she put it, at ten past nine. This was following a visit by two unidentified females to your office." She paused, to look directly at him. "Is this true? Did you argue with Sally?"

"A disagreement."

"Over what?"

"The visitors," he replied, straightaway, and mentally cursed himself for not thinking before opening his mouth.

"You then had an argument with your employer, Mr. Neville Longsdale," she continued, as if he had not spoken. "There were several witnesses. Are you naturally argumentative Sayers? Does your temper often get the better of you?"

122

"Arguing with Longsdale is the only way to communicate with him. You can ask anyone at the factory."

"Why did you argue with Sally over the two female visitors?" Wiles quizzed.

"She wanted to know more about them and I refused to tell her."

"Why?"

"It was private," he replied, realising the questions were coming quickly from them both.

"There are no records of these two women. No appointment was made and they didn't sign in. So you'll have to tell us who they were and what their business was. We'll need to speak with them," Helen said, preparing to make notes.

"They were friends, stopping by for a chat," he replied, knowing he was painting himself into the first corner with little resistance.

"Names?"

He looked straight back at her. "I don't remember."

"Really," Helen said. "A stunningly beautiful, long-legged redhead as your friend Gary Malins describes her, and an equally attractive blonde, driving a Bugatti, and you can't remember their names. Just what kind of friends are these?"

"Casual?"

"Casual?" she repeated. "They were in your office. Names!"

"I don't remember," he repeated, calmly.

"Were they high class hookers?" Wiles added.

Paul's face remained expressionless, but inside he winced. "I don't remember."

She shook her head and laid down the pen. Paul sat back and mentally pictured himself, with a shovel in his hands, eagerly beginning the task of deepening the hole he had slipped into. They were winning the opening rounds handsomely.

"How did you loose the finger?" Wiles asked, pointing to Paul's left hand.

"Hacked off with a spade," he replied, deadpan.

Wiles said no more as Helen again started with more questions.

"Let's see what else you can or can't remember. Why did you leave work early?"

"Overtime isn't compulsory at Longsdale's. It's just a necessity that gets on top of you at times. I'd had enough for one day and went home early."

"Why?"

"There was something on my mind?"

"What?"

"Private thoughts."

"How long did it take you to drive home? Did you go directly there?"

He shook his head. "I went straight home, but didn't drive."

She glanced at Wiles and then back to him. "What then?"

"I walked part of the way. Then Gary gave me a lift on his motorbike."

"Then how did your company car end up on your driveway?" Wiles interjected.

"Ask at the factory, or perhaps Gary knows. The argument with Neville ended up with him threatening to take away the 'perk'. So I tossed him the keys and told him to keep it. I haven't been home since just after ten yesterday so don't know how it got there."

He looked at them both as a silent pause followed. "Check if you like, I last saw it on Saturday morning."

Wiles made some notes on his pad. "Then what did you do at home?"

"I packed a few things in a picnic basket and drove the Wolseley to the Norfolk coast."

"Did you take it because you'd lost the other car?"

"No," he replied, truthfully. "I would've taken it anyway. I rebuilt the top end of the motor and did some bodywork on it during the winter. It needed a good run and I took the opportunity."

"Why a picnic?"

"I planned to be away all day."

"Where exactly did you go?" Helen asked, as she took the questioning from Wiles seamlessly.

Paul sat dumb.

"Where were you on Saturday after you left work? Did you see those two nameless women again?"

124

By choice he did not want to bring Ruth, David Pryce, and their families into what was happening to him. To give Storn a lever was something he dreaded. They were better left out of it, even if they could prove his innocence. It would make it worse for him, but that was something he could deal with. He would face Storn and his followers if necessary, but David and Ruth would never see them coming. Inwardly, he shrugged at the decision. It was the only way.

"I can't tell you because it's private," he finally replied.

"A name and a place," Helen simply added.

"I don't remember," he heartily threw back at her, determined to be as difficult as possible with them. If the set up was good they would have to work hard to make it stick. Perhaps the two he was facing had nothing to do with it; there was no way of knowing. Storn had people everywhere, especially in the police force, and no one could be trusted.

Helen again took time to study the man in front of her. He was not stupid, yet his answers seemed ridiculous. If anything he was not even going to make much of a defence.

"This isn't helping, Sayers," she said.

"That's your opinion."

"Very well," she continued. "Where were you between eight p.m. and ten p.m. last night?"

"On a beach."

"Whereabouts?"

He replied truthfully, seeing no reason to lie. "On the shingle bank near to Cley."

"Alone?"

"Yes. All alone," he lied.

"Why go to a beach to be alone?" Wiles asked, as he rejoined the interview.

"To find some peace and quiet. We don't all lead fast lives and spend our time down the pub. Sometimes it's nice to sit in solitude and consider what else there is."

"Very poetic," Helen interrupted. "What time did you leave?"

"I didn't."

The two detectives glanced at each other, but she spoke. "Do you expect us to believe you spent the night alone on a beach?"

"Believe what you like," he replied, casually. "If you ever get the chance, lay on a beach or mountain top, at night, and gaze up at the stars. Believe me; it'll give you a whole new outlook."

"Then what time did you leave from this night of self-imposed solitude?"

"Not until this morning."

She smiled, but it did not contain any trace of humour. "I don't believe a word of this. We have witness statements that state you were at home yesterday afternoon and that you called Sally Marcroft to go to your home. She was seen entering your house during this time."

Paul shook his head, wondering just who the so-called witnesses were.

Helen continued. "At some time between seven and nine in the evening, you brutally murdered her in an unrestrained, violent attack, and left her body in your living room. There's evidence to show you raped and assaulted her during the time before her death. Is this not so?"

He shook his head as a cold empty feeling of sadness went through his blood at the thought of Sally's savage death.

"Denial's pointless, Sayers," she continued, in full flow, while lowering the tone of her voice. "Witnesses place you and Sally at the house together. The murder weapon was found in your dishwasher with blood still on it. The plastic sheet you used to protect the floor from blood was left bundled up in the garage." She paused. "Do I need to go further?"

"Feel free." Inside Paul fought hard to keep calm, but wanted to hear all they had against him. Harder still though, it seemed impossible such an atrocious act could be committed in his own home and that Charlotte had made no attempt to warn them.

"I will continue then," Helen said. "Perhaps the most disturbing aspect of this case, Sayers, is that you videotaped the events of yesterday evening."

Surprising her, with what appeared a cold attempt at humour, he laughed.

"Now I know you're talking a load of bollocks. You mean to say you've got a video of me raping Sally?"

126

"Oh yes," she replied. "Your video camera, complete with cassette, was found hidden in your loft, along with other material of a disturbing nature."

"Like what?"

"Extreme, hard pornographic videos, books, magazines and photographs. Most of it from foreign sources. There's a considerable amount of child pornographic material too." She looked at him, coldly. "But you must already know this. You must know we've searched your house, thoroughly, and found this vile filth."

"Is that right?"

"Yes!" she forcefully retorted. "Or are you denying that we found this filth in your possession?"

"I'm not denying the fact you found it," he replied. "The fact is I didn't put it there. I don't own a video camera. So why don't you show me this film I've supposed to have made of myself raping Sally."

"You're just an animal," she added, disgusted.

"If you've seen it, tell me just what it is I get up to and where."

She shook her head. "This is going to be a pointless exercise if you continue with the all too obvious denials, Sayers."

"So you want me to admit to a crime I didn't commit?"

"But this is one you did commit," she said, firmly.

"Then show me the video and I'll admit to it," he said, leaning forward, with a fire in his eyes that took Wiles by surprise.

"I have no intention of showing it to you," Helen snapped back.

"Then it can't be that damning," he said, and leaned back.

"Tell us again about your movements on Saturday morning," Wiles began, again, after a moment of frosty silence.

Paul shook his head. The questions had come full circle and it would be a long session.

Chapter 23

Helen Bradshaw sat behind her desk, picking haphazardly through the piles of paperwork scattered in front of her. It was already eleven p.m. and had been a taxing day since early, when they had been called to the house in Sawston. She drained the dregs of cold coffee from the cup and again looked at the photographs from the murder scene. It would be better if she went home and got some much deserved sleep. Experience told her progress would be made with Sayers, the following morning, when she was fresh. Yet that notion troubled her. He appeared so confident and determined; even though it was clear he was hiding something from them. Then there was his house. It too had something not quite right about it that she could not put her finger on. The video that he made such a point about wanting to see was not right either. Sighing, she went to switch off the desk lamp when there was a tap at the door.

"Come," she said, to the shadowy figure behind the frosted glass. It was a detective she had worked with before.

"Sorry to intrude at this late hour Boss," the tall, dark haired detective began. "But might I have a private word?"

She made a point of rubbing her eyes, and glancing at her wristwatch, in a show of tiredness. "Make it quick Mitcham. I'm about to go home for a few hours sleep."

"I know I'm not on this investigation, but is it true you're holding Paul Sayers in connection with the Marcroft murder?"

"Yeah, it's no big secret."

"Rumour has it that the Norfolk uniforms lost his passenger while following the car."

"Someone got their wires crossed. They thought they saw a

blonde in the car with him, but, when they stopped it, there was no sign of her. Sayers denies ever carrying a passenger."

Mitcham's eyes widened. "Well he would."

"Is this leading anywhere, Detective?" she asked, point-blank.

"Was he driving an old Wolseley at the time?"

"Yes," she replied, exasperated. "Just what are you driving at, Detective?"

Without invitation, he sat down opposite her. "Do you remember, about a year and a half ago, the tanker crash on the orbital road? Three people died, two of them in a sports car. There was a huge fire that caused a lot of damage and closed the road for days."

"Vaguely. Didn't someone have a miracle escape from..." her voice tailed off as a piece of the jigsaw fell into place.

He nodded. "None other than Mr. Paul Sayers driving an old Wolseley. Apparently he drove straight through the inferno without harm to himself or the car."

Helen stood up and crossed to the window that overlooked the car park below. In the station floodlights she could see two uniformed officers, talking by a patrol car.

"I knew I'd seen that name somewhere before, even though he hadn't got prior," she said, as she surveyed the scene outside.

"No charges were ever brought against him, due to lack of real evidence. But I believe reckless driving was responsible for the deaths of the two lads," Mitcham added.

"Are we talking about a personal vendetta here, Detective?"

"Far from it, Boss. If there's no evidence that's the end of it as far as I'm concerned, despite what my gut feeling may be. There's so much else to do it's pointless pursuing something that's dead in the water."

She shrugged. "So what's this all about?"

"Witnesses who saw Sayers' car, just before the accident, claim they saw a blonde in the passenger seat beside him."

Helen moved back to the desk. "He saw a blonde on Saturday morning as well as the mistaken sighting in his car. Did you interview her at the time?"

"That's the whole point. She wasn't seen by anybody after the accident. Uniforms arrived minutes later and there was no sign of a passenger."

She looked down at him. "You must've interviewed Sayers at the time. What did he say about her?"

Mitcham smiled. "At first he denied all knowledge of her."

"But...?" she coaxed.

Strangely, he looked hesitant. "You won't laugh?"

"No," she replied, despite her tiredness she was intrigued by his seriousness.

"Until I heard what happened today, I thought his eventual confession was fanciful."

"Which was?"

"Sayers said the blonde was called Rebecca. She could appear and disappear at will and had saved him from dying in the inferno because they were in love."

"Why would he say something like that?" she mused. "And how could this Rebecca save his life in such a miraculous way?"

"I've seen plenty of guilty people lie before. Instinct usually tells you when they are. I looked at the evidence, the crash scene, and the only explanation is the bizarre one he gave. Also his entire tone and manner showed he believed it too."

"Then who did he say she was?"

"She's his guardian angel."

Helen shook her head. "No, Detective, it's too fanciful."

"It's not my case, Boss," Mitcham said, leaving the folder he'd been holding on her desk and standing up. "If you can find this Rebecca you'll unlock Sayers."

She stopped him before he reached the door. "Do you have a reason for bringing this to my attention?"

He paused, looking wistful for a moment. "I've met some weird characters in my time, but this was one case that didn't fit into any category. Sayers is just someone I've never forgotten. Did you know he was so well thought of at Longsdale's they went on strike to get him his job back?"

"No, I didn't know that."

"Everything I did is in that folder; reports, statements, and photos. I'll leave you to draw your own conclusions because I never came up with a satisfactory answer. The guy actually drove through a wall of solid steel, engulfed in flames, at high speed, and lived. There wasn't a scratch on either him or the car. He should be dead. I know it and more to the point he does too."

"Leave this with me," she said, quietly. After he had left she sat down on the corner of the desk. She took another look at the time and then opened the file he had left.

Chapter 24

Monday 24th May 1993

The holding cells were below ground level and not afforded the luxury of windows. The only light was artificial, coming from a florescent tube hidden in the ceiling and protected by a metal grid. Paul lay on just a bare mattress that possessed a lingering smell of both urine and vomit. It had been a grueling night in the confines of the cell. They had made no attempt to turn off the light or even provide him with a drink. It was as if they were deliberately wearing him down and he felt sure it was not wholly the norm to treat suspects in such a way. However, he had kept his spirits up and managed to grab a few hours of much needed sleep. His one advantage was in knowing that Rebecca was watching. He would have to suffer the ordeal, but knew she would not let him down. His mind went back, only a few hours, to the time on the beach and the feel of Rebecca's warm body next to his. It was a far cry from the incarceration he now endured. The lock clicked and the door swung inwards, allowing further artificial light to stream in from outside. A constable entered carrying a plate of fried breakfast and a steaming mug of tea. A second officer followed and Paul noted he was much more powerfully built. He sat up as an uneasy feeling ran through his stomach. The first one said nothing and just handed him the tray with the food on before leaving. In silence, Paul studied the tall officer who had entered his enclosed world and decided that acting dumb was the only way of dealing with him. It was only when he dropped his gaze from the hard looking face that he saw something that made him give an involuntary shudder. The officer wore no tunic top, only a short sleeved shirt with epaulettes and his number. There were tattoos all over his arms, with the most prominent one being a golden sword with a green serpent coiled around it. It was identical to one he had seen on both Persephone and Richard Stanford. It took an effort of will for him to take his gaze off it and look back into the face of the officer. He knew he was seeing one of Storn's men.

"What d'ya think you're looking at you worthless son of a bitch?" he barked.

Paul remained silent, a sense of achievement, tinged with a healthy amount of anxiety, filled him. He had been right from the outset. Storn had been behind the moves to put him in the perilous position he now endured. The standoff continued as he stared the big man down with a totally neutral look. Without warning he lashed out and kicked the tray from Paul's hands. It flew from his grasp, depositing the food and drink all over the cell. Paul sat dumb, refusing to say or do anything. Instead he continued his neutral study of him, much to his annoyance.

"We'll be back for you Sayers. There's no escape from here." The big man spat, before leaving the cell. The door slammed heavily behind him with a loud metallic clang.

Afterwards, Paul sat for several long seconds, shaking from the encounter. There was some relief at escaping a beating, but he guessed there was more trouble to come. Unless he could get out the next move would be theirs.

Chapter 25

It was two-thirty in the afternoon and Helen Bradshaw met up with Wiles outside the interview room.

"Any progress Steven?"

"Sort of, but it's just adding confusion to the picture. I've spoken again with Gary Malins. He confirms he took the company car round to the house at about midday. The keys were still on the doormat when he went in on Sunday morning. It was his opinion Sayers had not been home."

Helen shook her head. "Well you can make anything of that. What else?"

"I spoke with an old chap who lives at the end of the village. He was doing his garden all Saturday morning and saw Sayers leave in the Wolseley around ten o'clock."

"What about the forensic team?"

"They're working it through as fast as they can, but DNA will be at least two weeks," he replied, passing her a file. "Here's the latest."

She glanced at it, briefly, before indicating to the door. "Let's see what he's got to say today."

Paul looked up as the two detectives walked in. He had been waiting for over an hour and was surprised not to have been questioned that morning. He fingered around the collar of his tee-shirt. It felt grubby after being worn for three days and he smelt of body odour. There was stubble on his chin and he felt unclean. At no time had he been allowed access to washing facilities or the opportunity to get clean clothes. He guessed it was all part of the gradual wearing down process. He also assumed he was being denied some basic rights, but said nothing. It was either a deliberate policy or Storn's insiders to blame. Either way he would not allow them to manoeuvre pressure against him. Without word Helen sat down while Wiles crossed to the tape recorder and set it up.

"You're still entitled to have legal representation," she said, looking into the unshaven face.

He shrugged, his attitude seemingly indifferent. "I don't trust anyone."

She continued to study him. Just why he had such apparent confidence and calmness was a puzzle. Most people facing such charges would have been screaming for a lawyer at that point. Wiles sat down next to her as she began the session with a question to immediately catch him off-guard.

"Tell me about Rebecca."

"Who?" he casually replied.

'Good,' she thought to herself as she saw the fleeting movement traced across his eyes. 'But not good enough.'

"The blonde woman who's sometimes seen with you yet can never be found at crucial times. That Rebecca."

He idly scratched at the stubble on his chin. "I really haven't a clue who you're talking about."

"Is this the same woman who visited you at work on Saturday? The one you couldn't remember the name of?" Wiles added.

"I don't know who you're talking about," he repeated, while inside he was dying to know how they had come by her name.

"Is this the same blonde who visits you at home, but isn't seen leaving or entering by any door?" Helen asked.

"Not a clue." His mind was working overtime, trying to piece the bits together. Were there any clues? How had he been so expertly watched without him even being aware or suspecting? How had they traced him? And why had he not been dealt with? They could have done so easily without the charade.

From underneath her papers Helen withdrew a blue folder.

"Now then, Sayers, are you going to tell us who she is and where she is right now?"

"I haven't a clue who you're talking about."

"That's funny," she began. "After an accident, eighteen months ago, in which I may add three people died, you were seen with a blonde then. Mysteriously, you couldn't produce her then. You even denied all knowledge of her. Isn't that so?"

Inwardly he cursed his own lapse. He had totally forgotten about the accident with the tanker and the fact he had been interviewed. Someone had remembered his involvement, putting two and two together to make Rebecca. As a defence he feigned indifference and opted to keep quiet. However, with assured confidence, Helen continued to play her winning hand.

"I've spoken with DC Mitcham, the investigating officer at the time. He interviewed you didn't he?"

Without thinking Paul nodded, as the vague memory of the man crossed his thoughts.

"Just what did you eventually tell him?"

"I don't remember," he ran out, parrot-fashion.

"Now, Sayers," she urged, pulling a plastic bag from another folder. "You can remember, can't you? Weren't you driving that old Wolseley of yours then?"

Denial seemed pointless. "That's no secret."

Quite deliberately she held the clear plastic bag between them, allowing him to see it. "Know what this is?"

He shook his head. "Not a clue, but further incriminating evidence I should imagine."

"Exactly," she replied, firmly. "To be precise, several strands of blonde hair recovered from your car, the blanket you claim to use for picnics, and also from the back bedroom of your house."

"So, it's a crime to have blonde hair upon your person is it?" he said, sarcastically.

"Would you care to tell us the same story you told DC Mitcham at the time of that so-called accident?"

"You've read his report. If he made notes of what I said there's no need to."

"I'd like to hear it first hand," she said, and smiled.

"If you believe I'm going to plead some sort of insanity charge, and own up to a crime I didn't commit, think again. What I told him then is as true as it is today."

"Then tell us what you said," she repeated, in a firmer tone.

"Piss off."

She looked indifferent to the casual remark.

"Don't you want your guardian angel to give you an alibi? Won't she appear now to get you out of here? Just who do you think she is?"

Paul looked at her. "I don't think she's anything. I know what she is. You've looked at the evidence. You're the experts. So you tell me how it's possible to drive through a solid wall of steel at seventy miles an hour. When you've worked it out, tell me."

They both looked at him without reply.

"Until you do I'm sticking to what I know."

"Did she tell you she was a guardian angel?" Wiles added, after a pause.

"She didn't have to."

"Was it she who came to your office on Saturday morning?"

"Yes."

"Was she in the car at the time of the accident?"

"Yes."

"What about the other woman with her on Saturday. Is she an angel too?"

"Yes."

Helen shook her head. "Then why don't they come here and prove it? Maybe show us a trick or two."

"They're not a circus act," Paul replied, shaking his head.

"No, but you are," she retorted. "Isn't it time you started telling us the truth about what happened and how this woman's involved. Is she the one who phoned Sally on Saturday afternoon?"

For a moment he was puzzled, and then it struck him. "So you're saying it wasn't me who phoned Sally?" His question was met by silence and he smiled. "So a woman called her. It wasn't me. I knew all along."

"She was told you were conducting a business meeting at your house and that you needed her there," Wiles added.

"Crap," Paul said. "I never conduct business at home. I wasn't there, I never called her, and it's not me in the video you won't show me. When you can prove I actually raped and murdered Sally, I'll own up to it."

"Where's Jason Galloway?" Helen suddenly asked, harshly.

It took him a surprised moment to reply. "What the hell's he got to do with this?"

"Stop playing games, Sayers," she angrily cut back. "We know you're more than a little involved in his abduction. Now where is he?"

He was taken aback by the fresh allegations and the surprise showed on his face. Wiles was studying him closely and noticed it too.

"How am I supposed to be involved?" he demanded to know.

"Along with the other vile filth found in your home we discovered the sweatshirt the boy was wearing at the time he went missing."

"Bastards," Paul swore, under his breath. The frame-up was a masterful piece of work. At every turn there was something new to confuse things and put him in deeper.

"Who?" Wiles asked, catching the remark.

"Nothing," he replied, shaking his head. It seemed hard to believe the lengths they had gone to just to nail him. They either feared him or again hoped to trap Rebecca. "Don't tell me," he added. "You've also found evidence linking me to the other abductions and ritual killings that have taken place since before Christmas."

"Precisely," Helen interjected. "But then you already knew that."

Paul found time to laugh. "Christ, this frame-up's good."

"Who'd want to do this to you?" Wiles asked.

"It's the same evil bastard who's been doing it from the start. They want me out of the way or, worse still, Rebecca."

"Why her?"

"Because she's a Guardian, that's why. And they must also believe I can find the boy before the two week period is up."

"Why would they know you're looking for him?" Wiles asked, as Helen sat back and watched the exchange between them.

"Charlotte asked me to help them look for him," Paul said, without thinking.

"Charlotte?"

"The other Guardian who came with Rebecca," he explained.

Helen sat, shaking her head, amazed at how readily he pursued the fantasy he had created. Paul was already saying more to Wiles.

"She told me the boy wasn't missing, but had in fact been snatched."

"Why can't they tell you where he is?"

"Because they're as blind as you are if the soul's been masked."

"How's it done?"

"They set out a series of codes, like those on the bags you've found. It creates a barrier that the Guardians can't see through. A shield if you like."

"Then how can you succeed where they've failed?"

"Because I know who I'm dealing with."

"So you believe Jason Galloway's being held in a shield, as you put it, now?"

Paul nodded. "I've no doubts about it. The cycle has much to do with the evil controlling it, it's rigorous, has to be. Jason's alive for the two week period after his abduction."

"So why did you go to a beach in Norfolk?"

"I needed thinking time. I met up with Rebecca and we spent the evening together. The following morning you caught up with us outside Lynn."

Helen could contain herself no longer. "You do tell a good fantasy, Sayers, I'll give you that. I've heard some choice pieces of bullshit in my time, but you're a gold medal winner." With a cold stare she looked straight into his eyes, but failed to ruffle his calm demeanor. "You're the killer. There was no night on a beach with an angel who can't come forward. She's an accomplice. It's clear there's more than one person involved. Is she with the boy now? Was she there when you brutally raped and murdered Sally Marcroft?"

Slowly, he shook his head.

"If the boy's alive you'd do better to tell us where he's being kept. At least it'd put one good point in your miserable favour."

Paul was strangely impassive as she trooped out the condemnation and Wiles noted it.

"If, as you say, I lured Sally to my home and killed her, why leave the body and calmly go away for the night with her car on

139

the driveway? Surely it would've been better to prop her up behind the wheel and torch the car somewhere quiet. At least then I'd dispose of all the evidence."

"Perhaps you went to scout a suitable location to dispose of the body."

He leaned across the table towards her. "I'm really so cold and calculating then? After weeks of successfully abducting and killing others, up and down the country, while at the same time evading the attention of the police, I decide to kill a friend in my own home. I video the deed, leave it and her body lying in the house, along with enough evidence to put me away for centuries, and coolly keep a low profile in a forty year old motor car. And then I wait for someone to come looking for Sally at my place." He paused, but she said nothing. "You call my story fantasy, fair enough, I wouldn't expect it any other way, but yours is equally so to me."

"You'd do much better telling us the truth," she again said, ignoring his view of their case against him.

"I want to see the video."

"Why won't you trust a lawyer?" Wiles asked.

"I want to see the video," he demanded."

"Why won't you have a lawyer to arrange these things for you?" Wiles repeated.

"If I point out where the flaws are someone will make sure they're pasted up."

"Then why not allow it to fall apart?" Helen added.

"That's the intention. They just want me out of the game long enough to do whatever it is they've got planned. But if things start to fall apart I'm dead. Even in here."

"Rubbish," she spat.

"Far from it," Paul immediately replied. "I've already been threatened since I've been in here."

She looked far from convinced. "By whom?"

He smiled. "No way. I know at least one to look out for. Anyway, I like to know which direction trouble's coming from."

Helen began gathering her papers as Wiles rolled up his shirt sleeves. Paul quickly noted he had no tattoos on his arms and surmised he was probably not one of Storn's followers.

140

"Do you think you could die for someone after only knowing them for a brief few moments? After only one kiss? Do you believe love could be so strong?"

"No," she replied, truthfully. The only man she had ever loved had let her down badly. She felt there was no need for love in her life.

Paul held up his mutilated hand. "That was sliced off last September, by someone whose name I didn't even know. I had bullets in my legs, a fractured skull and several broken ribs. And all because I dared to rescue Rebecca from the same evil bastards who've got Jason Galloway. They're also responsible for the other killings and for putting me here now. Rebecca saved my life that day on the ring road and I fell in love. I repaid it by saving hers and will never do anything to endanger her."

Wiles stared at him, acutely aware that he was not ranting or raving. There was a firmness of conviction in his manner that unsettled him.

"So you prove I killed Sally. I'm not about to confess to a crime I didn't commit. Nor am I going to plead insanity."

"How do you think it sounds then?" Helen added.

"I'll sit here and take any shit coming from you as long as she remains out of reach of those who want her. But, be advised, I'll try anything to find the boy. Despite the oddities of life and death, he's family, blood, and while he's still alive there's a chance."

Helen stood up. "Very touching, but you're totally unconvincing. Your stories won't wash here. The evidence points to you and you alone. When we're through you'll be inside for the rest of your life." She opened the door. "The interview's over for now. Escort the prisoner back downstairs."

Wiles began collecting his papers as Paul got up.

"At the time Sally was killed I was a hundred miles away. And I still want to see the video."

Without reply, Wiles watched him being led away by the constable.

Chapter 26

As Wiles made his way back up the stairs he found Helen waiting for him.

"Opinion on this nutter?" she said, openly.

"I don't think he killed her."

She looked surprised. "What makes you say that? He can't be all there."

"Com'on, Boss. The video will be thrown out in court. It's laughable. The only way we can say for definite is when the forensics comes through."

"What about the items from the other murders?"

"That's another line of inquiry. We're here to get Sally Marcroft's killer aren't we?"

She nodded. "But you must have other reasons to say you don't think it's him."

"It's what he said about disposing of the body. He said if he was going to do it he'd leave her propped up in her car and torch it. No one's told him she was cut up. He believes she's in one-piece."

"That's flimsy, Steven."

"So is our evidence at the present. He didn't call her personally. Even her parents confirm that. Also, Malins returned the car and it wasn't moved."

She smiled. "I think Malins is the key. I'll get him in here and see if he can talk some sense into him."

"I doubt it'll work. This guy isn't going to fold and put his hand up, Boss. We've got to prove he did it."

She shrugged. "We'll do it the hard way if necessary. What about the vanishing lady?"

"I talked with the two uniforms from Norfolk earlier. They swear blind she was in the car. They're trained to observe these things."

"Explain then."

It was his turn to shrug. "I can't."

A face appeared over the rail at the top of the stairs. It was the front desk sergeant, Harris. "Sorry to intrude Ma'am. There's someone to see you about the Marcroft case."

"What's the connection?" Helen asked, looking up.

"A woman who claims to know Sayers."

"How does she know we're holding him?" she asked, puzzled.

"Apparently it was on the news earlier. Someone's leaked his name to the media. There's even been a picture on the TV," Harris replied.

Helen shook her head. "Damn, that'll make it hard. Who the hell let it out?"

Wiles only looked neutral. "There's little we can do about it now. Do you want me to speak to her?"

"Yeah, Steven, if you would, see what she's got to say. I'll send word to Longsdale's and get Malins back here." She again looked up the stairs. "Harris. I've just sent Sayers downstairs. Get him back into a room in half an hour. We'll be talking again."

"Okay Ma'am."

Chapter 27

Steven Wiles entered the interview room and found Rosemary waiting. She had seen Paul's face on the television that morning and heard the charges being levelled at him. In a rush, of almost panic, she had jumped into her car and raced down to Clayborough. She had no idea what she was going to do or say, but felt the need to show some support.

He smiled. "I see they've given you a cup of tea."

"Yes, thank you," she replied, feeling a little nervous. "Are you dealing with these quite dreadful charges against Paul?"

"I'm one of the investigation team. And you are?"

"Rosemary Newall. I run a B&B in Begdale."

"I'm not familiar with it."

"Dales, Lakes border town."

"Sorry, I'm more a sunshine and beach man. How can I help?"

"Are these charges against Paul true?"

"They are. Do you know him well?"

"He's stayed with me. He's a nice feller and certainly not the sort of man to do the things they're saying."

He nodded. "The problem is, even close friends of murderers and rapists don't always know. Unless you're here to provide him with a credible alibi for Saturday evening, you're wasting our time. I'm afraid charges aren't dropped because someone says they're a nice feller."

She shook her head. "No, I'm not able to provide an alibi for Paul."

"Then what do you hope to achieve here?"

Again she shook her head. "I don't know. I just rushed here when I saw it on the news. I know he didn't do it, wouldn't do it, and wanted you to know."

"Well, we have your details. If there's anything you can help us with we'll be in touch."

"Can I see him?"

"No. I'm afraid that's not possible at the present time."

Chapter 28

Paul had no sooner returned to the cell when he was again returned to the interview room. The door opened and the two detectives entered. Behind them he saw Gary and nodded in reply to his raised hand greeting, but the gesture was lacklustre.

"Please take a seat Mr. Malins," Helen said, indicating to a vacant chair. Wiles sat down next to him while she remained standing where she could see the two men sitting face to face.

Gary half smiled. "You okay?"

"I've had better days."

He saw the weariness in Paul's face, the unshaven drawn look that showed how hard it had been on his friend.

"How are they treating you?"

"It's interesting. But not an experience I'd recommend."

Again Paul saw the brief smile cross his friend's face, showing the tension he obviously felt. There followed a nervous silence which he eventually broke.

"Are you the trusted mate who's supposed to talk sense and get me to confess to the crime?"

Gary glanced down at his hands, locking and unlocking the fingers together. Paul could see it was not easy for him, but thought, 'what the hell'. It was no picnic for him either.

Gary slowly nodded. "Something like that."

Paul looked towards Helen and saw her studying him. "Evidence not so good then? Need the confession do we?"

She looked indifferent to his remark. "If Mr. Malins can talk some sense into you it could save us all a great deal of time."

"Instead of looking for who really did it?"

"So you're saying there's an accomplice or two?"

He smiled. "Sharp."

Gary spoke, deliberately cutting off their exchange. "Why won't you have a lawyer Paul? I can sort something out. I'm here to help." He saw Paul look directly at him with a cold stare. It sent a shiver down his spine. It was still his friend sitting opposite, yet he had changed. But, then again, he knew he had changed before that day, when he had first met Rebecca.

"As an old trusted friend," Paul began, seriously. "I'll give you some solid advice. Things are going to get really nasty before they ever get better."

"In what way?"

"Doesn't matter, they just will. I want you to keep away from me and have nothing to do with me. Understand?"

"Why?"

"Self-survival, Gary. You've got to protect yourself and Gaynor."

"From who?" Helen interrupted.

"From everyone," he replied, without looking at her.

Gary nodded, he understood. "I see. Do you want me to get you someone?"

"No."

Helen turned her attention to Gary. "Mr. Malins, please, remember what we discussed."

He glanced at her and nodded. He turned back to Paul, only to find him smiling, but not humorously. "This is like selling my soul. Do you understand what I'm saying?"

"You're doing the selling mate, not me. Personally I wouldn't sell mine so cheaply."

"Did you kill Sally?" he blurted out the question as if it was a foul taste in his mouth.

"If you have to ask the question it shows you've no idea who I am at all. That's twenty years of friendship down the pan, mate."

Gary shook his head. "No, it's not like that."

Paul cut him off. "You've got nothing to say that I want to hear. You've done as you were asked." He turned to Helen. "There's no confession today."

"That's not what this is about," she replied, calmly. "I asked

147

Mr. Malins here to try to talk some sense into you. Won't you even listen to a friend?"

He crossed his arms and looked Gary straight in the eye. "He's no friend of mine anymore."

"Because of this?" Gary asked.

"Selling yourself to the coppers simply to do a mate in? You must want my job so badly you can't get it any other way. You ain't worth bothering with," Paul added, with a sneer.

"I thought we were friends."

"Not anymore, Judas. Piss off."

Gary leant across the table. "No, sunshine, you're wrong. You're the one stuck in here, so screw you!" He turned his back and looked at Helen. "I'm done here."

She nodded and ushered him out of the room. Without conversation they walked to the far end of the corridor.

"Have you done with me?" Gary asked, stopping at a drinks vending machine. "It's just I've got a lot to do at work. I'm trying to do two jobs at present. Know what I mean?"

For a few moments she studied the heavily built man and in particular his bright intelligent face. One thing was certain, he wasn't a fool.

"That was a pretty good act you two played in there. You've done it before I assume."

His reply was a puzzled look. It did little to convince her he was telling the truth.

"I don't know what you mean."

"Yes you do. That last little scene was for our benefit. I deal with truth and lies every day of the week. I've seen dozens of different scams, from people a lot better at it than you two are."

"Is he pulling a scam over the death of Sally then?"

She smiled. "Isn't it obvious? Sayers is trying to concoct a story so bizarre he'll be considered insane. He's not the first to try and by no means will be the last."

To her surprise he laughed. "Daft he might be, but insane? Never."

"Then you believe his outlandish fantasy?"

His face became serious. "I told you exactly what he told us eighteen months or so ago and what happened last September. It all happened to him back then, Detective. It's not something that's just been cooked up in the past few hours."

"It could all be part of some long running delusion that's culminated in the murder of Sally Marcroft. You did say he'd been under a lot of stress."

Gary snorted. "You just go on believing what ain't true. I met Rebecca and her friend, Charlotte, on Saturday. Beautiful wasn't the word for it. If they're not angels, I'd like to know where exactly they come from."

"Then you believe him?"

He nodded. "If, at midnight, on the darkest night in winter, Paul told me the sun was shining outside, I wouldn't need to check."

"You're that certain," she said, resigned to his convictions. "What gives you such confidence?"

"We've had too many years of genuine friendship for me to think otherwise. We've been through some tight spots together, mostly at school. Back in the seventies I stood out like a sore thumb around here, racism was the norm for school kids then. But when he looks at me he sees me, there's no black and white between us."

"Most wives are ignorant of the fact their loving husbands are rapists," she added.

"We're not married."

"True. So you go on strike to get him his job back, even though he disappeared for nearly three weeks."

"I told you what he told me."

"But serious injuries like you described don't heal in a matter of days Mr. Malins."

He shrugged. "Well, if he's correct in his belief about Rebecca, she's got good contacts."

"Including a doctor called Margaret Salter?"

"That was the name as I remember it."

"Well we'll see about that. Personally, Mr. Malins, I know enough about the criminal mind to be able to tell you he did kill her."

"Look, whatever you believe, I can't alter it. But, likewise, you can't change what I believe about my friend. Paul's one of life's good guys and always will be. He believes in honesty, truth, and is as soft as shit with people, especially women. If he says it's a stitch up, believe me, it will be."

"Alright, I realise you can't talk any sense into him. Thank you for your time."

He simply nodded. "There was no pleasure in it."

"We might need to talk again."

"You know exactly where to find me."

He stood and watched her go and waited until she was nearly at the door before calling after her. "Have you thought about how you're going to feel when he's proved innocent?"

She stopped, momentarily in her stride, before pushing through the double fire doors without replying. He saw them swing shut and crossed to the vending machine. There he stood against it and tapped his forehead on the glass panel.

"Shit, what a mess," he cursed, to the empty space around him.

When Helen returned to the interview room Wiles was waiting for her, alone.

"I've sent him back."

She nodded. "Yeah, there're a few things we need to check out. Malins failed to come up trumps for us."

He smiled. "I told you Sayers wouldn't roll over."

"You're still convinced he didn't do it?"

"Let's wait for the forensics. Any further word?"

"I'm rushing them through as quickly as I dare push Maggie."

"It pays not to upset her."

It was her turn to smile. "No way, we need her expertise. What did the Newall woman produce?"

He shook his head. "It was a waste of time. He spent some time there on holiday and she reckons he's a nice guy. She could be seeking publicity."

"My nights with the killer, I can see it now. Keep her on the file though, you never know."

"Are you going to show him the video?"

She shrugged. "Possibly, just to watch his reaction. Let him stew overnight."

Chapter 29

Tuesday 25th May 1993

Paul was unsure of the time, but assumed that it was early morning. He was deep in thought, having slept little. Bradshaw had been far from convinced by anything he had said, but he felt sure he had planted some doubt in Wiles' mind. There was still the knot of anxiety in his stomach though. It was taking time to sort out, precious time he could not afford to waste. Storn was calling the shots and he was playing the game according to his rules. It was his people who had seen to it that he had been arrested and incriminating evidence planted in his home. The thing that infuriated him most was Sally's brutal death. He would make them pay for it. The heavy cell door swung open and he turned to see who it was. The knot in his stomach tightened at the sight that greeted him. As was usual, where Storn's followers were concerned, trouble was about to start, and he was the catalyst for it. The big constable who had threatened him the day before was back and had been joined by two others. All were stripped of their tunic tops, they were Storn's men, of that there was no doubt as they had the same tattoo, and their evil determination betrayed their allegiance. He tried hard to relax, breathing calmly in the forlorn hope he would take the beating better that way. Resistance seemed pointless against the overwhelming odds and he turned over. The clump of heavy feet, on the bare concrete floor, drew up to the side of the bed. In the ensuing silence he could hear them breathing.

"Tell us if the Guardian woman knows where you are!" the big man barked in a gruff, unbending voice.

Paul remained silent. Storn's interest in him was all too apparent, the reasons clear. He still had designs on Rebecca and wanted her through him.

"Tell us now or you'll regret it," he added. "Storn demands to know how you summon her and when you're going to send for her again."

The tone sounded somehow desperate. There was harshness in it for certain, but it also contained a trace of nervousness. Had the three of them been seen coming down to him? Were they fearful of being disturbed? Paul could only hope so.

"Sit up, you stupid bastard!" the officer shouted. At the same time he used his hands to drag Paul's legs off the bed.

He twisted round and sat on the edge of the mattress. Quite deliberately he looked up into the face of Storn's bullyboy and saw something that made his blood run cold. It was filled with hate, an intense hatred that wanted him dead. In his own mind he knew there was a beating to come, but they weren't there to kill him. While he was alive Storn still had an eye on Rebecca. They had lost Stanford and he was, now, the only known link. He would be kept alive just long enough to get her.

"Where's breakfast?" Paul asked, and sharply brought his right foot up between the man's legs. Without restraint he rammed it savagely into the groin and he doubled over in front of him. Storn's man expelled air, in a loud groan, taken by complete surprise, and it allowed Paul the space to grab him by the ears. He twisted them, hard, and pulled his head down. He shrieked in pain, before crashing backwards, as Paul butted his forehead into his face. Blood began pouring from his broken nose as he fell heavily onto the bare concrete floor.

"Tell Storn to go fuck himself, along with you!" Paul cursed, as he got to his feet.

"Kill the bastard!" the man on the floor screeched to the other two.

They, however, were already reacting and the one on the left lashed the side of Paul's head with a long baton. The blow was enough to send him crashing to the floor. His head was ringing and his sight blurred, allowing them to continue the assault. The second officer launched a kick, straight into his ribcage, filling him with an agonising pain that rocketed across his ribs. The following one went under Paul's chin, sending him into unconsciousness. Thankfully, he was oblivious to the ferocious barrage that rained down, in a frenzy of violence, from the two officers.

"Stop this nonsensical behaviour now!" Helen screamed at the top of her voice, as she appeared in the doorway. With her were Wiles, the duty sergeant, and another constable.

"Renton!" she barked, at the man on the floor. "Get up on your feet!"

The other two, who were dishing out the beating, stopped and turned to face her. Their expressions showed how conscious they were of the consequences of being caught. Renton was too, for their careers and the wrath they would suffer from Storn. As he struggled to his feet he knew they had badly botched their handling of Sayers. He was well out of it on the floor and in return they had learned nothing.

The duty sergeant pointed to the two men standing over the prone figure of Paul.

"Matthews! Barker!" he ordered, sternly. "Out! Be at my desk in one minute!"

The two men, both sweating, defiantly brushed past them, leaving some measure of space in the cramped cell. As they passed her, Helen took the baton. The sergeant left with them, shaking his head and muttering. "Reckless stupidity."

Wiles moved over to where Paul lay. He carefully lifted his head and saw blood seeping from the corner of his mouth.

"He's well out of it," he said, turning to Helen. "We'd better get a doctor here, quickly."

She turned to the constable who was eagerly studying the scene from outside.

"Go call the doctor. And also request an ambulance just to be on the safe side."

He nodded and disappeared. Renton had finally got up and was wiping at his face with the back of his hand. The blood dripped in scarlet drops down the front of his clean white shirt. However, his stance showed defiance, almost as if he felt he had nothing to fear from the situation he had created. In fact he stood several inches taller than Helen and tried to intimidate her by his sheer physical presence. She would not let him put her off her stride and stared him hard in the face before he conceded and looked down.

"Just what in God's name did you think you were doing?" she calmly asked, in a low, commanding tone, never letting her gaze wander from his bloodied face.

Renton sniffed, loudly, as if he had stepped in something nasty.

"The son of a bitch knows where that boy's being held," he spat, in a quite convincing tone of disgust.

"And you believed this sort of gross stupidity would help?"

"An evil bastard like him only knows one language, violence. It's the only way to get anywhere with his sort." He drew breath. "It was decided this would be the quickest way to find the boy."

"Who decided?" Wiles asked.

The burly officer chose to say nothing and instead stared aimlessly at the ceiling.

"Get out of here," Helen ordered, breaking the momentary silence. "I'll speak with you later Renton. So don't go home until I've sent for you."

His face twitched, once, which she noted with satisfaction, before he brushed past her. He kept his thoughts to himself. Already the lies were forming in his mind, as well as those he would use to placate Storn. They would be the hardest excuses of all to find. Helen watched as he strode away.

"Irresponsible, bloody fools," she cursed. "They'll wreck everything with this sort of behaviour."

Wiles shook his head. "It makes no sense. They know the evidence is in our favour. Why do this?"

"What are you getting at Steve?"

He glanced down at Paul. "He did say they were out to get him. Even in here."

"Coincidence," she offered.

He again shook his head. "This case gives me the creeps Boss, I don't mind admitting it. Ritualistic killings, abduction, rape, pornography, you name it we're dealing with it. But can it be just one man with no previous form?"

154

"He's just another weirdo."

"But this guy doesn't fit any of the profiles I've ever seen," he added, and again looked down at him. "None of it adds up. There are too many unanswered questions"

"Com'on Steve," she coaxed. "You've seen the evidence and heard his fairytale alibi. He's not all there. He'll break. They always do."

"I'm not convinced," he replied. "I'll wager that this guy's innocent."

Chapter 30

The white coated technician motioned Helen into the X-ray room. She nodded and followed the young woman in. Inside, standing next to an illuminated display machine, was the senior consultant. He extended a hand as he took off his glasses.

"Do excuse me for calling you in, Ms Bradshaw."

She shook the offered hand. "Helen."

"Graham Farlowe, Orthopedic Surgeon," he said, and indicated to the young woman closing the door. "And this is Pat Baxter, our Chief Technician."

"I assume this has to do with Sayers," she said, getting straight to the point.

"Yes. I think we need to talk about him."

"I was informed he's physically okay."

"Oh yes. A few minor cuts and bruises, a headache no doubt, but you may take him away when ready."

"Good. Now how can I help?"

Farlowe selected an X-ray and clipped it into a machine. "We did a full set of pictures, just to check, and found something the like of which we haven't seen before."

Helen looked at it, although not knowing exactly what it was she was supposed to see.

"Your Mr. Sayers is very evasive about some of the injuries he's received in the past."

"It doesn't surprise me."

"He's told us he was treated privately for some minor fractures last October."

She nodded. "A Doctor Margaret Salter. Do you know her?"

For a moment he looked thoughtful. "There was a doctor by

that name at Northampton General a few years ago. I did a stint there. It might've been her."

"So why would he be cagey about being treated by her?" Helen asked.

"Does he walk with a limp?"

"Not that I'm aware of."

"Well he ought to," Farlowe added, tapping the X-ray. "This area around the knee; the bone's been shattered, possibly by a bullet, into many fragments."

"It's been replaced then?"

"No. Someone's quite literally welded all the separate pieces back together." He pointed out the detail. "It's superb. You can see every reconstructed break and even the holes have been somehow filled. I've examined him and he has a perfect kneecap"

"It's unusual then?" Helen asked, studying the picture. "Can it be done privately?"

"Not that we're aware of," he replied, and changed the X-ray for another. "Here too his skull has received the same technique on a large area of damage at the back." He again tapped the picture. "This severe blow, to the back of the head, should've killed him or at least imparted serious brain damage. It's as if someone removed this section of his skull, repaired it, and then put it back."

She looked at him, astonished. "Is that possible?"

"It's beyond anything we've seen before. If indeed these injuries were sustained last October, under normal surgical conditions I'd expect him to be still convalescing. It's a miracle he survived the trauma."

In a moment of quiet, Helen recalled her conversation with Gary Malins earlier. He had told her of Paul's time off, the previous October, and how he had been sacked. However, a strike by the workforce had seen him reinstated, just a week or two later.

"He was back at work in November," she told the surgeon, matter of factually.

"That's just not possible," he exclaimed, and the technician nodded in agreement.

Helen turned to the door. "We'll go and have a word."

He agreed and led the way to a private room, just off the

casualty department. Helen said nothing as they walked, her thoughts were elsewhere. If she was truthful medical matters were not really her forte. It was usually just a necessity linked to a lot of the cases she dealt with. Even then it was the norm for them to be interested in the victim, not the accused. Within a minute they were in the isolated room. Farlowe drew the curtain to one side and she saw Paul sitting on a bed, handcuffed to the metal frame. He was also flanked by two uniformed officers.

The surgeon smiled. "You're to be released from us. There are no serious injuries."

"Glad to hear it. Fit enough to be sent back for them to have another go at me."

"The matter will be dealt with," Helen replied, businesslike.

"Hmmm."

"The injuries you sustained last October," she began. "You say they were treated privately. Where and by whom?"

He shrugged. "Somewhere up North. I can't remember exactly where."

"Who then?"

He saw no point in lying, they could never trace her. "A Doctor Salter."

Helen saw Farlowe nodding and realised they would get no further.

"Okay," she gestured to the two uniformed men. "Return him to the station."

A few minutes later Helen sat behind the wheel of her car outside the main entrance to the casualty department. She watched as Paul was ushered into a waiting police van, accompanied by the officers. With two escorting patrol cars the small convoy quickly departed. Once they had gone she picked up her telephone and called the station.

"Bradshaw," she began. "I want a search on a Doctor Margaret Salter. Try Northampton General to start with."

She replaced the handset and sat wondering why she was even pursuing that angle when there was so much else to do.

Chapter 31

It was eleven-fifteen in the morning. Steven Wiles hated an untidy desk, preferring instead methodical working practices and neatness. However, the sheer weight of material involved in the case meant that some of his usual methods had been dispensed with. The frosted office door clicked open, unannounced, and he glanced up from a desk littered with files, statements, and numerous pieces of paper. Everything was relevant to the case, but needed his ordered touch. Across from his, Helen's desk looked no better and in the corner sat several boxes of personal papers gathered from the house in Sawston. Wiles immediately recognised his colleague, Philip Carter, as he stepped into the office.

"What can I do for you Phil?" he asked, in his usual friendly manner.

Carter smiled. "I was just wondering if you're up for a frame or two of snooker in the social club later."

The shake of the head said it all. "Sorry, everything's on ice at the moment."

"Is it that heavy?"

"Yes."

"I guessed it would be," Carter continued. "I've been told I'm being assigned to the case, as of tomorrow, to help with the load."

"Welcome to it, and you really are."

He looked at him, quizzically. "You're still going ahead with the court session tomorrow afternoon aren't you?"

Wiles shrugged. "We might."

"Most of us thought it'd be earlier, what with all the evidence you've got on this nutter."

"Don't take it as read, Phil. Those stupid bastards first thing didn't help matters."

"Feelings are high mate."

Wiles looked directly at him. "Don't condone behaviour like that. It makes us no better."

"Only a perv would video himself," Carter added, trying to gauge his colleague's reaction to the evidence.

"It'll never stand up in court. Anyway, Sayers reckons he can easily pull it apart."

"No way," Carter replied, while inside he felt uneasy. It was never designed to take severe scrutiny. It was assumed Sayers would be quickly transferred to court, where the vital part of his plan would be enacted. They were already a day behind his estimations with a further one to go. Then there were the three clowns who had taken it upon themselves to risk everything for personal glory. All had been transferred there in the previous few weeks to aid him. Now he no longer had credible back-up in the station and was on his own. "Mark my words Steve, he's a nutter. In a day or two it'll be curtains for Sayers. The psychotic bastard deserves hanging."

"Yeah, something like that," Wiles replied, as a sudden thought struck him.

"You don't sound convinced," Carter said, picking up on the down tone in the reply.

"I'm not."

"Why ever not?" he asked, aware of the implications of it unraveling before they had Sayers.

"Everyone considers him crazy, although I'm not so sure. It could all be part of some deliberate frame-up. Although the reasons why certainly aren't clear."

Carter cursed his powers of perception and realised, if he started digging, that was the end of his scheme. "I think…"

Wiles cut him off. "You've cracked it Phil."

"Cracked what?"

"You said a moment ago it was curtains for Sayers."

"So what?" he replied, suddenly confused.

"Something about that video's been bugging me since we first saw it."

160

"The guy's a pervert mate, has to be."

"No, wait a minute," he continued. "The curtains are pulled in the bedroom, if it really is Sayers' bedroom, and they're a yellow and blue striped pattern. When we went in the house on Sunday they're a dark green colour."

"So?" Carter quizzed, sounding unconvinced while inside his mind raced in thought. The video had been put together several weeks earlier after the house had been thoroughly checked out. By some quirk of chance Sayers had obviously changed some furnishings since then. The whole plan was hanging by a thread and he would have to act to salvage it. He needed Wiles out of the picture and himself next to Bradshaw. Then he could manipulate the evidence to suit their needs. After the apparent escape by Sayers, on the way to court, he could continue to add more discrediting evidence and bog down the case for months.

Wiles continued chatting, unaware of Carter's thoughts. "The rape, if that's what it really is, didn't take place at the house. It was filmed elsewhere."

"I wouldn't speak to anyone else about this just yet. Check out the house, Steve, and get the facts right before you go telling Bradshaw. We can meet up later this evening and thrash out what you've got."

"Okay, Phil. I'll check the house out after I've spoken with Sayers' grandparents."

"You're seeing them?"

"Bradshaw wants background, if there is any." He grabbed a notepad and his jacket from the back of the chair as Carter held the door open. "I'll see you for that frame of snooker after all."

He nodded. "I'll see you at seven-thirty Steve."

"Cheers."

Carter waited until he had disappeared before pulling a mobile phone from his pocket. After just two rings it was answered.

"Yes?"

"Carter."

"Problem?" she curtly asked.

"You're the emergency back-up, right?"

161

"I create solutions," she replied.

"Detective Wiles is about to go and interview Sayers' grandparents. Later he's going to the house, where he'll find evidence that the video's worthless. He'll pull it all apart by tonight at the present rate."

"A foul up?"

"Possibly," he reluctantly replied, knowing that the buck stopped with him. It was his grand plan. "Most of it was only superficial. He should've gone to court by now. The delay's unexpected."

"That's not my problem," she replied, unsympathetically. "Anything else?"

"Apparently Sayers spent Saturday evening on a beach in Norfolk. He was possibly with the Guardian woman."

"Romantic."

"Can you deal with Wiles?"

"Yes. Storn will have to be informed."

"I guessed that," he said, quietly. "Will you tell him?"

"I'll need the go ahead from him for this action."

"Will you ask Storn...?" Carter began, but the line was buzzing at the other end. As he broke the call at his end he realised his hands were shaking.

Chapter 32

A large painting of an unnamed woodland scene filled the wall space above the fireplace. Seated in a leather armchair, Wiles glanced from the picture and around the neatly furnished lounge of the bungalow. It was just past midday in the West Fen suburb of Clayborough, two miles from the city centre. He carefully placed the empty teacup back on its saucer.

"As I was saying, Mr. and Mrs. Sayers, I was hoping you might be able to give us some background on your grandson."

Across from him, Alice Sayers sat with a hard expression on her lined face. She had almost white hair and clear blue eyes like her grandson. In her hands she had a copy of the morning newspaper, with its front page picture of Paul and the headline story of his supposed crimes.

"And as I've told you, Mr. Wiles, we have no contact with Paul Sayers. We want nothing to do with him or the evil things he gets up to."

Beside her, John Sayers said nothing and Wiles noted he had said little since his arrival. He could see in the face and build of the older man where Paul got his own features from. The family resemblance was quite striking.

"Can you tell me the last time you saw him?"

"We haven't spoken," Alice replied.

"Since when?" Wiles asked, making notes.

"Ever," she spat, shaking her head to emphasise the statement. "That little bastard's slut of a mother stole my son from me and killed him. I won't ever forgive her."

"But didn't your son die in a road accident before Paul was born? Do you think she was responsible?"

"He fell asleep at the wheel of his car after working God

knows how many hours to keep her in her tarty lifestyle."

"And Pauline Sayers?"

"The bitch died when he was sixteen. Do you know that bastard managed to manoeuvre the solicitors so that he could inherit the house?" She looked bitter. "That was our retirement nest egg down the drain. He denied us that."

Wiles deliberately closed his pad and slipped it back into his pocket. He had only spent a few minutes with them, but had heard enough to know he would not get any useful information regarding the investigation.

"Well, thank you for your time," he said, politely. "I'll be in touch if I need to know anything further."

"After what we've read, the little pervert wants stringing up," Alice added, pointing to the newspaper.

"That's paper talk, Mrs. Sayers. I wouldn't believe everything you read."

"I do. He's not right in the head."

Without further word Wiles got up to leave, closely followed by John Sayers.

"I'll see you out," he said, as they went to the front door. Wiles let himself out, only to be followed down the path by the older man. When they reached the gate, John spoke.

"Did the boy do it?"

"Do you really care?" Wiles asked, turning to face him.

He looked back at the bungalow and then to Wiles. "I don't know how it ever got to be like this. Alice didn't approve of David's choice of wife and perhaps never would've done any woman. You see, she lost three babies before David and then couldn't have anymore. Quite simply she became too possessive and tried to control him, even when he was an adult. But Pauline was different; she was the type who wouldn't be controlled. Alice's attitude was pure bitterness towards her and it only got worse after David's death. This of course extended to the boy. It became infectious, somehow, and I treated them the same. You can't blame Pauline or the boy for fate, but we did and Alice still does." Again he looked towards the bungalow. "Time's only made it worse for her to accept, with everything now becoming blurred, and the hatred has somehow got stronger. The house was Pauline's anyway, left to her by her mother, we had no right to it, ever, but still we tried to deny the boy a home when he needed it most. It's unforgivable how we've treated him."

Wiles realised how difficult it was for him to relate the details of their past and admit their mistakes. "I see, Mr. Sayers."

"These past few years I've come to totally regret what we've done. We've lost the valuable years we could've spent with our only grandson, the sole blood link with our son. And it was for no good reason."

"It's never too late," Wiles added.

John shook his head. "It is for us, Detective. My wife will die a bitter woman and myself full of regret. So that's why I have to ask you again. Has he done these terrible things we've read about?"

"I believe he's innocent."

"Thank you for your candour."

Without further word Wiles crossed the road back to his car. He was thankful to be away from the hostile attitude of Alice Sayers. Once settled in behind the wheel he looked back at the bungalow to see the front door closing. No wonder Paul Sayers had said he could trust no one, he mused. When his only family thought little of him what chance did he have? With a sigh he retrieved his phone from the passenger seat and tapped in a familiar number. As he did so the low battery warning flashed at him.

"Control room," was the crackled reply.

"DC Wiles here. Can you relay a message to DCI Bradshaw?"

"Go ahead."

"Tell her I've just spent twenty minutes in the company of Sayers' grandparents and there's no joy here."

"Any particular reason?"

"Granny would gladly place the noose around his neck if asked," he explained, without humour.

"Anything else?"

"Tell her I'm off to visit the crime scene again. My phone's about to go down, so if I'm required page me."

"Understood."

Wiles tossed the phone back onto the seat and glanced at the time. He felt hungry and decided to visit his favourite fish and chip shop before driving to Sawston. As the car started he took one last glance across the road before drawing off. He was lost in thought as he drove down the tree-lined avenue. Behind him a green Isuzu Trooper pulled off the opposite kerb and followed. She had arrived minutes before, following the information received from Carter. The one thing Storn demanded more than anything else was competence. Carter wasn't to know she was this close to the operation, with a contingency for most problems. At a discreet distance the big 4x4 tailed the Vauxhall as it picked its way through the lunchtime traffic.

Chapter 33

A rapping at the frosted glass awoke Helen from her thoughts. She looked up and saw the silhouette. "Come in."

The door opened and the duty sergeant leaned in. "Sorry to disturb, Ma'am, but we've a young lady to see you."

"What does she want?"

"Something about the Sayers thing," he replied.

"Can't Wiles speak to her?"

"Sorry, Ma'am, but he's out."

She scratched at her forehead. "Oh yes, he's gone to the grandparents."

"She say's she's come a long way."

"Oh alright, Sergeant," she sighed, resigned to another interruption. "Where is she?"

"I've put her in number two. Would you like a WPC present?"

"No, that's not necessary," she said, shaking her head. "I'll see what she wants first. She could be another timewaster like the last one."

"Okay Ma'am. I'll say you'll be along in a minute." He turned and left her to sort through some more of the papers on the desk. After a few minutes she rose from her seat and gathered a notepad.

Down on the ground floor, outside the interview room, she paused to straighten her long black skirt and brush her fingers through her hair. Deciding she looked organised, she pushed the door open. Inside, a young woman sat at the desk with a cup of tea in front of her and a handbag and a plastic carrier bag beside her. Helen smiled as she sat opposite and quickly studied the piece of paper handed to her by the constable outside.

"Now, Ms Barnes," she began. "What do you want to see me about?"

Heather Barnes felt nervous, and sounded it too as she answered. "You're in charge of this case involving the man called Paul Sayers aren't you?"

"I'm overseeing the entire investigation and as such I'm very busy. Any distractions can prove costly in many respects," she said firmly. "Do you understand?"

Heather smiled, weakly. "I understand what you're saying, but felt that I should try to repay a good deed."

"To whom?"

"Bear with me please," she said, pulling a slim scrapbook from her bag and handing it to Helen. She took it and opened it on the desk in front of her. In silence she scanned through the news cuttings, gleaned from several local Yorkshire newspapers as well as a couple of national ones. After a few minutes she looked back up at Heather.

"So, Ms Barnes, it seems you were abducted by three men who attempted to rape you, but instead you were rescued by a 'Knight in shining armour', as several of these reporters chose to put it."

She nodded in reply.

"But," Helen continued. "I fail to see what these three miserable sods have to do with my case. These cuttings say they've been put away."

"It's not them I've come about," she replied, more confidently. "They would've killed me after raping me. Of that I've no doubt."

"Then what do you want me for?"

"My knight in shining armour. The man who dealt with the three rapists."

Helen felt a little bewildered by the conversation. "Well, if you couldn't find him last December, how do you expect me to do it? I'm extremely busy with other matters right now."

Heather pulled a newspaper from her bag and handed it over. The headlines were the same on every one that morning. Someone had leaked the story and they even had a picture of Paul that filled the cover.

"You've got my knight in shining armour," Heather said.

Helen glanced at the open scrapbook, then to the picture of Paul, and finally back to Heather. "You're joking."

She shook her head. "I won't ever forget that face inspector, especially after he dealt so easily with three men intent on raping me. At the time he said his name was Paul."

Helen once again picked up the scrapbook and quickly reread the cuttings. After ten minutes silence she closed it.

"You're sure it's the same man?"

"Absolutely."

"Why come forward?"

"I really don't know how much of what I've read in the papers is true, but Paul Sayers saved my life. He had every chance to rape me after he'd dealt with them, but didn't. I was kept warm and taken to the nearest police station."

Helen studied the young woman carefully, sensing that what she was saying was the truth. However, it upset the picture she had formed in her mind of Paul Sayers. Why would he do such evil, yet also something equally as good? It unsettled her in a strange way. Less than an hour before, after returning from the hospital, she had allowed him to see the video evidence. Surprisingly, he had sat in silence throughout. She was expecting a vigorous defence, but instead he had said nothing except a 'thank you' for allowing him to see it. If anything, the puzzle was getting more complicated rather than easier.

"If my coming here helps him, then I'll have repaid the debt I owe," Heather added.

"Why didn't he stop and give a statement?"

"They didn't want to get involved with the police."

"They?" she asked, instantly aware of the change of description. "Are you saying he wasn't alone that night?"

"There was a woman with him. She sat with me and provided a blanket."

Helen was eager to hear more, expecting Rebecca to be the one with Paul.

"Can you describe her to me?"

"She was older than him, darkish hair, trim build, but a full figure. She had a gorgeous dress on, something you'd simply die for to have."

Helen felt let down. There was no Rebecca. "Strange you should remember a dress."

She shrugged. "It's funny what you do remember. The dress was exceptional, even with the state I was in. She said her name was Rosemary if that's any help."

She raised an eyebrow. "Definitely Rosemary?"

"Yes. Do you know her?"

"Vaguely," she answered, as she got up from her chair and went to a wall-mounted internal phone. "This attempted rape was Christmas Eve, right? Up in the Pennines?"

Heather nodded. "It was the early hours of Christmas morning to be precise."

"Hello," Helen said, into the phone. "Get Wiles back here quickly." There was a pause. "I know he's out. Call or page him, I don't care which, just do it." She replaced the handset and looked across to Heather. "Would you mind keeping this between us for a little while? I'd like it kept out of the newspapers if possible."

"Yes, if it'll help prove him innocent."

"It's doubtful it'll do that. You see, Ms Barnes, the evidence against him is strong and this doesn't give him an alibi."

"I know, but I needed to let you know he's a good guy."

She half smiled, they had heard that before. "This does give us an insight into his character though. Would you be prepared to give us a statement later if necessary?"

"Yes, of course."

Next to her the phone rang and she grabbed it. "Bradshaw." After a pause she replied. "I see. Make sure you tell Wiles and inform him I'll meet up with him there." She glanced at Heather. "It seems not everyone who saw Sayers' picture this morning thinks he's a good guy."

"What do you mean?"

"It won't do any harm to tell you as you'll hear about it later," she replied. "It appears someone has set fire to his home in a revenge attack."

In the following silence the two women looked at each other with differing thoughts running through their minds.

Chapter 34

It was nearly one o'clock when Wiles stepped out of the Golden Cod Fish Bar. It was on the edge of the city centre and his fruitless interview with the Sayers' had given him the opportunity to stop for his lunch before continuing on to Sawston. There he could put his curtain theory to the test and prove the worthlessness of the video himself. The pager in his pocket trilled at the point he was fumbling with the key in the door of the car.

"Bugger!" he cursed, as it momentarily startled him into dropping the keys into the gutter. He pulled it out and turned it off, putting the chips down on the bonnet. The Cavalier carried no radio and his phone was dead. A public telephone box sat just along on the opposite side of the road. He pulled some loose change out of his pocket and crossed over to it, idly wondering what could have developed in such a short space of time.

"Clayborough Police. How can I help?"

"DC Wiles here. I've been paged."

"Oh yeah, Bradshaw wants to meet you at the Sayers house."

"I'm going anyway to look at the crime scene," he replied, slightly mystified.

"Not anymore," came the reply. "You'd better get over there double quick. Someone's torched the place."

"For God's sake, didn't they have a uniform on it?"

"He was out front in the car. It looks as if someone went in through the back."

"The dozy sod. How bad is it?"

"It's been totally gutted."

"Bugger it," Wiles said, more to himself than the officer on the other end. "Tell her I'll be there shortly."

"Will do."

The money ran out just as Wiles replaced the handset. He stepped out of the call box, suddenly plunged into thought. It made no sense to destroy the house unless it was to cover something up, possibly the curtains. But who would do it? The only other person who knew was Philip Carter.

Parked a hundred yards behind the Cavalier sat the 4x4. It stood high off the ground on chunky tyres with a set of grotesque tubular bars protruding threateningly from the front. She sat, impassive, surveying the scene on the street in front of her. The detective was exiting the telephone box and would have to cross the road to get back to his car. It was not the first time she had killed someone in such a manner. The old woman, Eastwick, had been the last one, back in December. Then, like now, the opportunity had arisen through patience and the ability to select the right moment. With deliberate ease she selected drive on the automatic gearbox and drew away from the kerb. She was cold hearted, with a calculating mind, and worked everything out to the last detail. It was the reason Storn favoured her to do his cleaning up. She never let emotion get in the way and there were never any errors. A hit and run type of 'hit' was simple for her to execute, especially when the victim did not even know they were being targeted. When she saw him step into the road she accelerated, hard, covering the distance between them in a matter of a few brief, thoughtless seconds.

Instinctively, but much too late, Wiles looked up, startled from his reverie by the noise of the engine roaring towards him. The Isuzu was on top of him, its unforgiving steel bars scant inches from where he stood. There was no time to even scream out, only a blank moment as he froze in time and space. In a blur of red pain, that passed the instant it hit, he went crashing down under the heavy driving force of the Trooper. It did not stop and continued to accelerate down the street. He was quickly up onto his feet and running after the fast fleeing car. It was hopeless and he gave up after the first few futile yards of pursuit. He waved a fist at the unseen driver.

"You stupid bastard! You could've killed..." His voice tailed off. Slowly, he turned round and looked back to where he had run from. With horrifying clarity he stood witness to the scene unfolding in the bright sunshine before him. A badly contorted body and his own face staring lifelessly heavenwards as the tarmac turned crimson around it. From the shops close by, people were running out to where his mortal body lay.

"Oh no," he moaned. "You did kill me."

With the feeling of lead in his feet he returned to the scene of his own death.

"Hit and bloody run," he said, out loud, though no one saw or heard him say it. "Not in a blaze of glory, doing duty," he continued. "Just a bloody stupid accident."

He stopped short of where the people were gathering and instead glanced back to where the Trooper had fled. In that brief moment his thoughts became crystal clear and he saw everything.

"Philip Carter. I was taken out for trying to prove Sayers innocent."

"Quite right Steven," a soft female voice agreed.

He spun round, to be faced by the most beautiful young woman he had ever seen. Her dark blue eyes took his attention as they seemed to sparkle to limitless depths and complemented her flawless dark complexion. She wore a white cat-suit that displayed her slim figure to perfection and she radiated an aura of calm he readily accepted.

"Sayers was telling the truth."

"Yes," she replied. "I am Colette, a friend of Rebecca's. Paul Sayers is combating a great evil amongst the living of this place. You tried to help and have been despatched to us for that reason." She held out a perfectly manicured hand. "Do not be fearful, Steven. Please come with me."

Without any fear he took it and together they stepped into the light.

Chapter 35

The plush office of Superintendent John Cunningham sat on the top floor of Clayborough police station. A tall, wiry man, he still had a full head of brownish hair. At fifty years of age he had devoted his working life to the force and secretly enjoyed most of it. There was always a satisfaction in serving the wider community, even if expectations and practices were rapidly changing. He also sported a full beard, giving the outward illusion that he was an old-fashioned sea captain rather than a policeman. Because of this he was affectionately called 'The Skipper' by the officers who served under him. Not for the first time in his career he was subdued as he sat behind his desk. Across from him was Helen. He had been the bearer of bad news before, on numerous occasions, yet it still came no easier, least of all with close colleagues.

"I don't believe it," she said, shaking her head. "Run over in the middle of town."

He nodded, the sombre look never once leaving his face. "A tragic, unnecessary accident from what we can gather."

"Do you have the driver of the vehicle?"

"Not yet," he replied, picking up a single sheet of paper from the desk. "The vehicle description and number fits that of an Isuzu Trooper stolen in Manchester three days ago." He passed her the brief report. "A stolen vehicle involved in a hit and run. It'll have been torched by now. We both know the form."

She sank visibly in the chair. "Why did this have to happen now? It just complicates matters at a difficult time."

"I know," he said, quietly. "But, as bad as it sounds Helen, I need you to put personal feelings to one side and concentrate on the Marcroft case."

"I will Skipper," she said. "I was at the Sayers house when I was recalled."

He looked at her. "Bad?"

"It's been totally gutted inside."

"It's probably the best thing for it in the long run, if a little premature."

"But I've lost the crime scene," she added, with noticeable disappointment. "Whoever did it went in the back while our man was out front. It appears to have been a crude petrol bomb."

"The leaked story and photograph to the press fuelled that, I should guess," Cunningham said, rubbing his beard. "Still, when he gets put away he won't have any need for it."

A knock at the door stopped any further conversation.

"Come!" Cunningham called. The door opened and in stepped Carter, dressed smartly in a grey suit.

"Ah, Carter," Cunningham greeted. "Good to see you up here so quickly."

"Thank you, Sir," he courteously replied.

Cunningham turned to Helen. "As I'm sure you're aware, Carter was due to join the investigating team tomorrow."

She nodded.

"But, in the light of today's events, I think he should take over Wiles' position on the case and share your workload."

Again she nodded as she looked Carter up and down. He wasn't the first of his type she had seen, the newer officers making their way up through the ranks. Like the rest he looked ambitious, with a sharp haircut, stylish suit and polished shoes. Why were outward appearances more important to them than the quality of their work?

"We've not worked together before have we?"

"No, Ma'am," he replied, looking straight at her, conscious that he had been judged in those few brief moments. "I've only been here eight months, but your reputation is well known around the station." The flattery did not appear to work so he pressed on. "My caseload is light at present and I look forward to working with you. Even in such unfortunate circumstances."

"If you know my reputation you'll know it's based on hard

work and sound police practice. Officers with pin sharp suits and light workloads smack of slacking, Detective. If you're to work with me on this there won't be any nine to five. Understand?"

"Absolutely," he quickly replied.

"Did you know Steven Wiles?"

"We'd often share a frame or two of snooker in the social club."

"He's going to be a tough act to follow, Detective. You'd better move into my office and get yourself up to speed."

He nodded. "I'm on it. Would you like me to chase up on the forensic results?"

She shook her head. "They're not ready yet. I want you up on the basics of the case first, Detective. Don't start running until you've walked."

Silently, he cursed. The most important thing was for him to get hold of that evidence first and see what it said.

Helen got to her feet and Cunningham did too.

"I'll pop by later Helen," he said, as they turned to leave.

"Okay Skipper," she acknowledged, and followed Carter out.

Chapter 36

The long dining table at Pelham Hall was not set for a lavish meal to be enjoyed by a party of guests. Instead the five people who sat around the top end of it had only a cup of coffee each in front of them. At the head, as usual, Storn presided over his four followers. There were two on each side of him, attentive to his words, while he looked relaxed with his gloved hands clasped together. Next to him sat O'Neil, a thick set muscular Irishman with a full black beard and equally dark hair. He was sat lazily in a chair, his arms folded loosely across his broad chest.

"Your preparations are complete and are ready to go, I trust?" Storn asked, turning his gaze towards him.

He nodded, positively, coming upright in his seat, and his Dublin accent was noticeable in his reply. "We've been ready since Sunday morning, as instructed. The vehicles and weapons are secure at a farm just five miles outside Clayborough. The remainder of the team is leaving this evening with us and we'll be on standby from six in the morning."

Storn appeared pleased. "And what word of the escort to take Sayers to the hearing?"

"We've yet to hear confirmation from Carter. But, if it goes as expected, it'll be a van with a car and two motorbikes as escort. Once they're on the ring road we've a three minute window of opportunity in which to make the move."

"Will it be an armoured van?"

The Irishman shook his head. "We're expecting an LDV with just the normal window grilles."

"And the escorting vehicles?"

"Our vehicles will overtake and wedge in between the police

car and the van. The machine guns will easily take care of it and the two motorcycles following."

"But can you guarantee to stop the van with him inside?" Myra asked, from the opposite side of the table.

The dark skinned Jamaican sitting next to O'Neil, known only as Halo, spoke for the first time. "It'll stop."

O'Neil continued. "By then the van'll have halted and our car, containing Persephone, will draw up behind it." He casually indicated to her sitting next to her mother. "A small prepared charge will blow the rear doors and we'll kill every policeman inside the thing."

"And the others?" Storn asked.

"If necessary we'll kill everyone in the escort. It's their choice whether or not they resist."

"Good," Storn replied, seeming well satisfied with what he heard. "And how long will all this take?"

"From stopping the convoy to moving off with the target, fifty-two seconds," Halo added.

"It'll be just as you wanted, Master," O'Neil added. "It'll look like Sayers has been released by his accomplices, including the Guardian woman, of course being played by Persephone. It'll look right, especially if we can leave a copper or two alive to tell the story."

"It sounds perfect," Storn mused. "Sayers will be ours to lure the Guardian with. The police emphasis will shift to finding him, and they never will, how perfect."

"There's the investigation already underway," Myra interjected. "They've waited longer than expected to take him to court. If the frame-up's pushed too hard it'll not stand serious scrutiny."

He nodded. "There have already been some problems in that direction and they have been dealt with. Carter has been moved closer to the core of the case and will manipulate the evidence from now on. They will continue to believe what they already believe." A cold smile crossed his face. "And of course they will never speak to Sayers again."

Persephone sat unspeaking, but aware of what was being said. She was, on the whole, lost in thought as to how she would react the following day. The idea of being close to Paul again, perhaps experiencing further flashbacks to the time they had shared before, both excited her and filled her with unease.

"You may go now," Storn instructed those at the table and woke Persephone from her thoughts. "Assemble your team in position and be ready to move."

O'Neil nodded. "We'll be waiting for word from Carter."

Storn shook his head. "You will take your orders direct from Scott-Wade. He will be at Clayborough tomorrow to oversee the operation."

O'Neil exchanged a puzzled glance with Halo. Then, without further word, the two men, followed closely by Persephone, left the room. Myra watched her daughter leave with the rest of the snatch team.

"Is she capable of the task?" Storn asked.

"For one so young I believe she's more than capable. Too many are fooled by her quiet nature. She will perform her part, without fail, despite the risk."

"They are under no illusions, my trusted friend, they have express orders to keep her safe. It is not necessary for her to be part of the taking team, but I want her close to him from the earliest possible moment. She will prove invaluable."

"Then she won't let us down."

"I believe she will not," he added. "Now, Myra, you must arrange an immediate meeting with Scott-Wade at the usual contact point."

She nodded. "Straightaway, but why? Do you have doubts about Carter?"

"Some," he replied. "The delay in getting Sayers into court, and therefore our hands, has led to unforeseen problems."

"It was always too complicated and superficial," she interrupted.

"I have implemented several measures to get it back on track. With Carter close to the main investigation he can no longer oversee the taking of Sayers. That is why I am sending Scott-Wade."

"What reason will he have for being there?"

179

He pushed a folder across the table. "The reasons are in there. You will drive us to the meeting point." After she left he settled back into his chair and closed his eyes. "Soon," he whispered. "Very soon."

Chapter 37

With her spirit filled with a mixture of tiredness and emotion, from the loss of her colleague, Helen slowly looked up as the door to the office opened. It was nearly six o'clock and she was not surprised to see Cunningham step inside.

"Just checking you're okay Helen. Is everything alright?"

She nodded. "Yeah, I think so."

"How's Carter? Is he a help?"

"I've sent him home with a load of paperwork to catch up on. DS Maxwell is going through personal papers and checking names and addresses. Apart from the routine stuff it's slow progress." She ran her fingers back through her hair. "We're getting there, Skipper, but there're a lot of loose ends to tie down yet."

"You're doing good work Helen," he added. "Is something bothering you regarding the court hearing?"

"Not really. I'd have just liked another day."

"I don't believe it'll make a difference. You've enough to keep him here. Get through the hearing tomorrow and you can question him at your leisure. He'll eventually break or you'll get the forensics."

"I know, but that's not the main reason for concern. There's the Galloway boy to be found and three-quarters of the team are liaising with Norfolk over that. Then there's the evidence from the other murders. We're going to be questioning him for weeks yet. The boy probably hasn't got that long to wait."

"I'm aware of the complications Helen. I'm sure if you put it to him, in the right context, Sayers will tell us where he is, dead or alive," he said, quietly. "Encourage him that it might make things easier in the long run."

"We don't make deals, Skipper," she retorted.

"I know," he replied, with a knowing wink. "But he might think we will."

"It's possible."

"There are a couple of other things too, Helen. After the court hearing I'm allowing the other forces involved to send teams in to work with you. They can begin their questioning as soon as you're ready."

She nodded. "And the second thing?"

"Chief Constable Scott-Wade will be here in the morning to put some questions to Sayers."

"He's high ranking, Skipper? Can't they send a detective?"

"I've just received a request from his office. It's regarding a series of events that took place on his patch last autumn. It may not have any connection with the crimes we're investigating."

"I see."

"Scott-Wade is a senior man Helen. I'd like you to show him every courtesy, even at this busy time, your fullest co-operation. He's an old friend."

She nodded. "I will. We can make room for him in the morning. We've nothing planned in advance. In fact it might be useful to see how Sayers reacts to a different set of questions. How long have you known Scott-Wade?"

"We did some time here together in the early days. I stayed on, but he moved up North in search of better prospects. We'll end up talking about the old times over a pint."

"I hope you both enjoy yourselves," she offered, as he went to leave.

"Get some rest Helen," he urged. "I need you on top form. We're being watched on this one, big media interest, and I want Sayers nailed to the wall without any errors."

"What if he chooses to make a complaint about the assault in the cell?"

"We'll have to go along with it, because there's no other choice."

"What about the men responsible?"

He shook his head. "We're short handed as it is, Helen. As much as I'd like to do otherwise, I'm afraid I can't take them off duty. But it's another reason why I want this case cut and dried. If he wants to complain, he can do it from a prison cell serving life."

She nodded and he left. A glance at her watch told her there was still time before she needed to leave and she again began to flick through the paperwork. If anything, she was trying to make order of the chaos rampant on her desk. From the edge of it a small plastic bag fell to the floor. She picked it up and turned it over in her fingers. It contained several strands of hair.

"When will you turn up in all this, mysterious blonde lady?" she said, to the empty office. Moments later there was a knock at the door.

"Come in."

It was Maggie Watts, their leading forensic expert.

"Maggie? We don't usually see you about at this time of the day. What can I do for you?" Helen asked, as she beckoned her in.

Watts walked straight in and sat down, passing her a slim white folder. Maggie always reminded Helen of her biology teacher and was every bit the scientist. She was in her mid-thirties, unmarried, like her, and dressed sensibly in long skirts and plain jackets. As always she had her glasses perched on the end of her nose and peered over the top of them with intelligent grey eyes. She was considered attractive by many of her male colleagues, but Helen knew her spurning of their advances was because her interests in that area did not lie with men.

"Knowing how important it is, we've been working flat out. Therefore, I thought I'd better drop in with the initial findings myself."

"And?"

She cleared her throat. "It's been interesting to say the least."

"In what way?"

"We've sent away samples recovered from the body of Sally Marcroft for testing. The DNA results will take at least three weeks to come through. However, hair samples taken from her, consistent with the male who raped her and presumably murdered her too, are dark brown. They're different from samples taken from Paul Sayers. I've also blood typed a tiny sample of blood recovered from under one of her fingernails, again assumed from her attacker. It's not Paul Sayers'."

"Are you sure?"

"Hate to spoil your case, Helen, but my initial findings point to the fact that your prime suspect didn't rape Sally Marcroft."

"Anything else?"

"We made a thorough examination of the Sayers house before it was burned down. The rape didn't take place in any of the rooms there. Nor did the murder, she was killed elsewhere. It's highly likely that Marcroft wasn't in the house before she died."

"Damn. What about the video?"

Maggie laughed. "You didn't fall for that did you? The camera was part of a consignment stolen from a Milton Keynes warehouse over a year ago. There're no prints on it and the only tape found in the house was inside the camera. And the only footage shot was what you see. A partial print on the cassette matches no one on file."

"Meaning?"

"We've got to believe this guy's obtained a stolen video camera and used it only once. Sorry, I don't buy it. It won't stand up in court on its own. My conclusion is the camera's never been used and was placed in the house by someone wearing gloves. The guy, who made the tape, obviously on a different camera, wasn't so careful. You can't load a camera in gloves and get prints on the cassette."

"So the video's useless."

"You've been so wound up with what you've found you're not looking at the basics."

"Which are?"

"The post-mortem shows the killer was left handed, yet Sayers is right handed. The knife found in the dishwasher was used to kill Sally Marcroft, but matches none of the sets in the house. However, one partial print on the weapon is the same as that on the video cassette. I would say the killer attempted to clean the knife of prints, but wanted to leave it blood stained too. If Sayers had done it, wouldn't he have just switched on the machine rather than wipe it? Sayers' prints are all over the cutlery, but not the murder weapon. The handcuffs on the bed also had no prints on them. Also remember that the other victims, who'd been butchered, hadn't been sexually assaulted before death. And all had one fatal stab wound just under the heart. Sally Marcroft was strangled."

Helen shook her head. "Christ, Maggie, it gets worse."

She half smiled. "The porno tapes found in the house weren't used by Sayers either."

"How come?"

"There're no prints on any of them and none are originals. They're all copies in long play format. His video recorder is quite an old one and only has a short play facility. Helen, he hadn't touched them and couldn't watch them."

"How many people know of this?"

"My team," she replied.

Helen sighed. "Okay, I'd appreciate it if we could keep it that way."

"I will for now. But, in my professional opinion, you're keeping an innocent man locked up. If you don't sort this soon I'll go over your head. If you're trying to wear him down to make a confession it'll fall apart in court on the evidence."

"I understand."

Maggie nodded and left without further word, leaving Helen alone with her thoughts. She looked at the pile of papers and realised her case was falling apart. She smiled, Wiles had been right. However, she felt it was not over and done that quickly. There was still the evidence to link Sayers to the other killings and the abduction of the boy. Perhaps he was not working alone. An accomplice could have killed Sally and still be holding the boy. If, as the evidence showed, he did not kill her, why concoct a fantasy alibi? Who was the blonde Rebecca, if that really was her name, and why was he protecting her? She shook her head in attempt to clear it from the confusion of questions. If they could not get a charge against him regarding the other cases she would have to release him. But she did not want to, despite Maggie's threats. He was the key to unraveling the affair. With a sigh, she gathered her jacket from the back of the chair.

Chapter 38

At the same time, in the North Yorkshire countryside, a meeting was about to take place. The lay-by was quiet, secluded, and bordered by low trees. It had been used before when just a brief exchange was necessary. The dark blue Rover saloon indicated and left the road, stopping about halfway along its length. Scott-Wade scanned his surroundings before turning off the engine. It was, as usual, quiet and deserted. Only the sounds of traffic, passing beyond the trees, filtered through. He was satisfied and settled into a comfortable seating position. With one finger he pushed the cassette into the player and turned up the volume. As the first notes of Vivaldi's Spring movement began to drift through the speakers, he closed his eyes.

Ten minutes later the familiar black BMW, with darkened windows, pulled up behind the Rover. It had taken them less than twenty minutes to drive from Pelham Hall. Scott-Wade ejected the cassette and carefully replaced it in its case. Then, without delay, he walked the few short steps to the BMW and climbed in the rear. Languishing coolly in the back seat sat the imposing figure of Storn.

"You have kept abreast of the Sayers arrest?" Storn casually began.

"Of course," he replied. "Through official channels as well as our own."

"What is your view?"

"It seems to be going well. He's due in court tomorrow and the snatch goes into effect just before that. You should be talking to him by the evening."

"Not quite," Storn replied, in the selfsame casual manner.

"There have been some alterations in the planning. You will travel to Clayborough tonight and oversee the operation to deliver Sayers."

"Why me?" he asked, somewhat taken aback by the late change. "Surely this is Carter's show?"

"Not anymore," Storn added. "We have had to eliminate one of the detectives and burn down the house due to his lack of foresight."

"Anyone could see it was a far too complicated to ever work satisfactorily. Policemen aren't fools. If I go down there I could put my own position in jeopardy. Wouldn't it make better sense for me to keep out of the way?"

"No!" Storn barked. "It would not. You will go because I bid it. See to it personally, Scott-Wade, that Sayers is delivered to Pelham Hall without further complications."

"What possible reason do I have to be there?"

Storn looked to Myra, sitting behind the wheel. "Explain."

From the vacant passenger seat beside her she handed Scott-Wade a file.

"Inside are the details and photographs of the incident at Kirkham. It's all been altered and allows you the chance to question Sayers about his part in it. He doesn't know you, so it'll be up to him how he chooses to answer. We've put in a call as if from your office, requesting the chance to question Sayers. It's been accepted."

Scott-Wade nodded. "This hasn't been sorted in the last few hours. This was pre-planned."

"Of course," Storn added. "Every possibility has to be covered. Thanks to the evidence planted in his home, Sayers is due to be questioned by several other forces in regard to the deaths of those we have already taken. Another request was not considered out of the ordinary. As a senior officer you'll have full run of Clayborough station."

"This is a risky venture at best."

"You will go," Storn ordered.

"Carter is the only inside man left untarnished," Myra added. "The rest of our people are the snatch squad on the outside. Their side of things will go smoothly the moment Sayers gets into that van to go to court."

"It'd better," he said firmly. "Keep those other three dozy bastards at Clayborough out of my way and tell the snatch team to be extra alert."

She nodded and he got out. As he made his way back to his car Storn looked at Myra. "Our Mr. Scott-Wade appears peeved by the change in plan."

She had already started the car and was pulling past the parked Rover when she glanced in the mirror and replied. "The risk is giving him cause for concern. He's a valuable man. To lose his position would be a great loss."

"That is true. But it is sometimes necessary to risk such things to bring out the best in people. Do you not agree?"

Again she glanced in the mirror, but could not gauge his mood. "Yes."

He did not speak further, and in silence they sped back to Pelham Hall.

Chapter 39

The picturesque village of Cautely, several miles west of Clayborough, was unspoiled by development. There was only one public house, with a reputation for high-quality meals, and even for a Tuesday evening the Black Horse was busy. The bar was bustling while a chatter of conversation filtered through from the restaurant area. Helen had found the lounge reasonably quiet and had settled herself at a corner table. She had deliberately arrived early, for the prearranged meeting with Rhodes, and had partaken of a bar meal. A waitress had taken away the empty plate just before he had arrived and moments later he joined her at the table with a glass of orange juice.

"I'm not watching for drink driving," she said, with a smile.

He laughed lightly. "Sorry, wasn't thinking like that. In my position you never know when you might be suddenly called in. It pays to have a steady hand when you're wielding a scalpel."

"I wouldn't doubt it." For a second or two she studied the tall, distinguished looking consultant with the eyes of a woman and not a police officer. He was smartly dressed, clean shaven, with a full head of grey hair and a not unattractive face. If anything he was at least ten years older, but she dismissed the idea of any romantic entanglements with him. There was a gold ring on his left hand to show he had already been claimed. She watched as he took a sip from his glass and then looked at her.

"I'm glad you could spare me the time," she began.

"No trouble at all," he replied, placing his drink on the table. "It's all rather fascinating."

"Call me Helen. I'd like to keep it informal for now."

"Likewise," he countered. "Please call me David. I believe you've had some setbacks today."

She nodded. "The media are all over us at the moment and it's getting worse. The fact my colleague was killed in a road accident this morning hasn't helped matters."

"Then this is a bad time?"

"There's little to be gained by sitting and mourning."

"Then let's get to the point of this as quickly as possible."

Helen again nodded. "Okay. What can you tell me about Paul Sayers?"

"Not much I'm afraid. I only learned of him, like everyone else, through the media. It was only the fact that your people contacted my hospital regarding Margaret Salter that I put two and two together." For a moment he stopped and looked around where they sat. She could see he did not want to be overheard and it intrigued her further.

"However, Helen, what I'm about to disclose to you now is strictly off the record. I won't jeopardize the rest of my career over this. If this gets into the public domain I'll deny it, emphatically."

"Okay, it goes no further."

"Good," he said, leaning closer over the table. "Paul Sayers claims to have been treated for gunshot wounds and a head injury, amongst other things, last October. Correct?"

"Yes, but the surgeon who examined him this morning says he's been treated in a manner like no other he's seen before. He reckons he should be dead, brain damaged, limping, or simply still recovering. The fact is Sayers was back at work a scant few weeks after the injuries occurred."

Rhodes nodded. "I took the liberty of phoning Doctor Farlowe after our chat this afternoon. He explained his findings and on the surface it seems truly remarkable."

"Sayers reckons he was treated privately, by this Margaret Salter. Do you still have her on your staff?"

From his briefcase Rhodes removed a thick black ledger and opened it on the table. He took out his reading glasses and quickly flipped the pages over. He turned it so she could see and tapped the handwritten entry.

"There, on the first of October last year, Margaret Salter signed out an emergency pack, a first aid case and a sterile theatre pack. Also she took several units of whole blood and plasma. The name of the patient was given as Sayers and male. Injuries were

190

listed as gunshot wounds, rib fractures, severed finger, and head trauma. It's her signature on the sign-out."

She studied the page carefully. "So it's true, she did treat him last October. She must be some pretty clever surgeon then."

He shook his head, but not dismissively. "Wait a second, Helen, the ledger doesn't tell the whole story. At the time I did some quite thorough checking across the whole country. Paul Sayers wasn't treated at any National Health Service hospital or any of the privates. It beggars belief as to where this complicated operation, or series of operations, took place."

"Then what are you saying?"

"I clearly saw Margaret Salter in our supply room on the afternoon we're talking about. I can recall the moment vividly and I remember speaking to her. I also saw Margaret Salter die from cancer. I signed the death certificate and attended the funeral."

At once Helen looked deflated. "So I can't speak to her."

"No," he said, quietly. "You don't understand. Margaret died in the July of 1982. That's ten years before she signed this book and treated Paul Sayers."

Her eyes widened in pure disbelief.

"It's no joke Helen, I assure you. I saw her, the signature's genuine and the equipment was never returned. Paul Sayers was treated by a dead woman whose surgical skills had obviously increased tenfold."

"Are you sure?" she asked. There could be no logical explanation for what he was saying. Dead doctors did not treat living people, not in the real world.

Rhodes returned the ledger to his briefcase and snapped it shut. "I'm afraid I can't let you have this Helen, as I keep it safe at home."

"It doesn't make sense," she added.

"I still don't believe in ghosts. When I saw Margaret she was flesh and blood."

"Was she capable of attending to such injuries?"

He shook his head. "As I said, it would've taken a mega-leap in her abilities to do such things. It would be doubtful that Margaret had ever encountered a gunshot wound in her career. She was a good doctor, but first and foremost a pediatrician."

Helen took another drink, lost in thought.

Chapter 40

Wednesday 26th May 1993

Once again Paul was seated inside the familiar interview room and he was aware that it was Wednesday morning. After being allowed to see the video, he had been sent back to the cell and not seen again. The only other news was confirmation that he was due in court that afternoon. The door opened and he looked up, interested to see why they had come so quickly. Usually he was left waiting for an hour or more. This time it was less than ten minutes. Helen led the way, closely followed by Carter, Cunningham, and Scott-Wade. Both the senior men were dressed in their uniforms. Helen took the seat opposite Paul, but he noticed, for the first time, she was avoiding eye contact with him. Scott-Wade sat down next to her and began to take several items from a slim briefcase. Paul did not know either of the two high ranking officers and wondered why they were there. Carter went and stood behind him. Helen motioned for him to start the recorder and she spoke out loud to confirm the names of those present. Paul glanced at Cunningham, by the door, and then to Scott-Wade.

"Honoured company," Paul said, drearily, and noticed Scott-Wade scowl at him. A little light went on in his thoughts and he looked again at him. 'Bingo', he said to himself and smiled back. Richard Stanford's address book was a mine of information that he had only scratched the surface of. He had thumbed through it on many occasions and the name, Anthony Scott-Wade, had been written quite boldly. Even the telephone number was marked in red beside it. This alone had made it stand out from the rest. It proved that Storn had followers everywhere, in every strata of life. As well as the faceless ones who carried out his bidding there were also individuals like chief constables. He could not even begin to imagine how far his evil tentacles stretched, but Paul felt rather flattered, in a perverse kind of way. What game had he been sent to play with him?

"Chief Constable Scott-Wade is here to question you about events in his area during September and October of last year. Do you understand?" Helen began, breaking his reverie.

He nodded.

"The subject, Paul Sayers, has nodded his head," she said, for the benefit of the tape. "You still have the right to legal representation."

He scratched idly at the back of his neck. "And to a good kicking in the cells too I suppose?"

"The complaints procedure is open to you," Cunningham added.

"I'm glad to hear it," he retorted, and looked the senior man straight in the face. "I'll be complaining about the fact that every time someone brings food or drink into the cell they tip it onto the floor. And also about the lack of washing facilities and a change of clothes too."

"Shit like you always smells," Carter commented from behind him.

Cunningham looked sharply across. "Enough of that."

He shrugged, unperturbed by the rebuke from his superior and Paul did not bother to turn round to look at the detective. Instead he looked at Helen, who, for once, appeared decidedly uncomfortable.

"So the upholders of justice everywhere have already made their minds up? Whatever happened to innocent until proven guilty?" Paul added.

For a few moments there was silence, until Scott-Wade pulled the first sheet of paper from a folder. He did not want to be in the interview room with Sayers or in Clayborough either. If events turned out wrong for them he did not want to be there to answer difficult questions. His initial hope of not being able to carry out the fake line of questioning had been dashed when his old colleague, Cunningham, had made sure he saw Sayers straightaway. He could not back out of it once the request had been made, just as he could not back out on Storn's orders. He looked into the face of the man his master so greatly risked everything for and saw him looking back. The last time he had seen him was in the yard at Skelwith farm, when he had given him up for dead. Now he was sitting there with a look of determined calm on his face. What gave him such confidence to face them without fear?

"Were you in the village of Kirkham on Sunday the twenty-seventh of September 1992?" he asked, to end the silence.

"Yes."

For a second he was duly surprised by the answer and it showed in his facial reaction.

Paul saw it too and smiled. 'Good,' he said, to himself. 'I'll confuse you a bit more.'

"Did you enter the Fox public house on that same evening?"

"Yes."

"Do you recall seeing the landlord?" Scott-Wade continued, producing a photograph. "A man called Richard Stanford?"

"You don't need to show me a picture of that bastard," Paul quickly replied. "I remember him."

Helen was eagerly dividing her interest between the two men. She could almost feel an atmosphere between them. Paul appeared supremely calm, although he had never been overwrought in her presence either. His replies seemed to indicate he would not play games with Scott-Wade. If anything he appeared to have no regard for either him or his position of authority. She was also well aware of the fact that, despite the many unresolved questions; the man she was looking at almost certainly did not murder Sally Marcroft. It was the one point he had protested his innocence on from the start.

Scott-Wade laid a second photograph down and Paul immediately recognised the face. It was Quirke; the mountain of a man he had faced at the Fox and in the barn where Rebecca had been imprisoned.

"Did you become involved in a fight with this man?"

Paul deliberately picked up the picture, studied it, and placed it back on the table. "How many of the scumbags who died that morning have you got in there?"

Scott-Wade's eyes blazed in anger as he snatched up the photograph and roughly pushed it into Paul's face. "Did you fight this man?"

"He punched me around a bit, if that's what you call a fight," he answered, casually.

Another picture was swiftly produced and Paul recognised him as the man, North, another one of Storn's followers he had encountered at Kirkham.

"Yeah I saw him too, briefly, but your photo doesn't show him with the dead goat draped down his back. I thought he looked a right twat then and the picture just proves I was right."

Despite knowing that he should act better, Scott-Wade was feeling increasingly agitated by the interview. He wanted the chance to deal with Sayers personally. The restrictions of his position were suffocating his urge to strike out.

"These three men are dead," he continued. "Did you know that?"

Paul laughed and it caught all of them in the room off-guard.

"Why on earth's Storn sent you here, Scott-Wade? It must be one hell of an embarrassment for you to come and see me, dressed like the doorman from the Roxy." He paused, staring directly into his face, seeing it redden, and enjoying every moment. "Where do you get off on playing this silly game? Of course I know they're dead. You know they're dead, and we both know that each other knows' that we know."

As she sat beside Scott-Wade, Helen noticed him slowly clenching and unclenching his right hand into a fist. Opposite them Paul still seemed to be under no pressure at all. Whatever was taking place between them was something she could not fathom out and it only added to the mystery that surrounded her once prime suspect.

The next question from Scott-Wade was forcefully directed. "Did you shoot Richard Stanford?"

"No," Paul quietly replied. "But had I been given first chance, I would have and derived great pleasure from it."

"Who did then if not you?"

"You know."

Helen exchanged looks between them.

"How would I know?" he replied, with an open-handed gesture. "If I knew, the case would be solved."

"Because, if you weren't actually there at the time, you're sick enough to have watched the video made by that sad bitch with the camera," Paul retorted.

"Are you saying this killing was recorded on video?" Helen interjected, in surprise.

Paul grinned, humourlessly. "They're very fond of their tapes Helen. But you're already aware of that from the trashy one you've got as evidence. They can do much better than that if they try."

Carter too felt uncomfortable and realised things were not going well for them.

"He's lying," Scott-Wade snarled, never taking his eyes off Paul for a moment. "You shot Stanford because you believed he was having an affair with your girlfriend."

Paul snorted. "That's good. Did you just think that one up? Why's it taken you so long to come and question me then?" Silence followed and he realised he had scored points. "Com'on," he urged. "Let us in on the secret. How on earth has the death of Sally Marcroft connected me to your case? Why me? Why now?"

Scott-Wade seethed, having not expected to be painted into a corner by Paul. The man had been in custody, facing major charges, for several days, yet he looked untroubled by them.

"Richard Stanford had a brief affair with your girlfriend and you were insanely jealous. You confronted him at the Fox public house that night, in a violent temper, and regulars like Mr. Quirke and North stepped in to prevent your assault." He poured out the ready made theory in an attempt to block him and deflect the argument.

"Then why's it taken so long to come and question me?"

"In a rage, you killed the two of them later the following morning. Then you returned days afterwards to kill Stanford himself. Isn't that the real truth Sayers?" There followed a long pause while Paul stared back with total indifference. "Isn't that the truth Sayers?" he repeated, in a raised voice.

The grin that crossed Paul's mouth was icy cold. "Be careful how deep you dig that hole, shithead, because you're slipping into it yourself."

The patience that Scott-Wade had barely been controlling finally snapped and he lashed out. The blow half connected with Paul's cheek and sent him sprawling onto the floor. Suitably shocked by the turn of events, Helen shot to her feet as Cunningham quickly moved in. At once he placed his hands on Scott-Wade's shoulders and firmly pushed him back into the seat.

"What do you think this is Tony?" he blurted, shocked by his friend's violent reaction. "You don't behave in this manner during an interview."

In a show of mock calm he held up both hands. "Sorry Alan, but I'm on edge. I know this scumbag's a killer and there's still that boy to be found, remember?"

"I want him found too," Cunningham stated, truthfully. "But this isn't the way. You should know that better than anybody."

He nodded. "Sure Alan." He tried to sound convincing, but was cursing his own lack of self-control in a situation he knew he should have full control over. There was something inherently irritating about Sayers that he could not put his finger on, but he had gotten under his skin. Also he was dealing with the fact that somehow Sayers knew who he was and who had sent him. It was just another unexpected turn of events. The frustration would continue until he could find a positive conclusion to the session.

Beside him Helen had sat down again and was staring at Paul, sitting on the floor. Blood had again begun to seep from the wound he had received to his mouth the day before. However, he seemed unaware of it and did nothing to wipe it away. 'Just what's your game?' she thought, as she again saw the depth of purpose in his steel-blue eyes. If anything he appeared satisfied, as if he had achieved the desired reaction from Scott-Wade. She realised that what was happening between the two men had nothing to do with any police investigation, anywhere. It was a bitter confrontation that had begun elsewhere, at an earlier point in time.

Carter stood over Paul and reached down with an outstretched arm. Paul saw the lower part of his arm revealed from under his jacket and shirt. The tip of a golden sword and the head of the green serpent were just visible. He turned from it and roughly slapped the offered hand away.

"Hands off," he spat, getting to his feet, as Carter glared at him. "I know where you're coming from."

There was no reply, but Paul knew he had hit the mark. He turned and saw Helen motioning him to sit down. She was trying hard to return a degree of professionalism to the proceedings, while at the same time attempting to make sense of the situation herself.

"Your girlfriend, who had this affair with Richard Stanford, was it Sally Marcroft?" she asked.

"Sally was never my girlfriend. Haven't you learnt that much already? We were always just friends. She had nothing to do with what happened in Kirkham last year, absolutely nothing. There never was any affair. It's a load of crap."

"Then tell us who was the woman you were seen with and where I can interview her," Scott-Wade instantly asked.

Paul met the statement with another cold stare. "Do you honestly think I'd tell you anything about her? If you do you're stupider than you look."

Again Helen could see Scott-Wade clenching his fist beneath the table and laid a restraining hand upon his arm. However, Paul was not about to let up on him and she could sense it. Inexplicably her senses tingled as he spoke in a low voice that was filled with absolute surety.

"It took over a dozen of you to imprison one woman and beat her mercilessly. No doubt you went to that vile barn to gain some perverse pleasure from seeing her there, beaten and twisted. But I took her away from you and the rest of the filth that held her, despite your heavies with their guns. And it's still hurting isn't it?"

In the silence that followed, the eyes of Scott-Wade betrayed his innermost feelings towards Paul. His cheek twitched and Paul clearly saw his discomfort. He just pressed further, knowing that he would have to report back to Storn.

"You tried to kill me and failed, even though there were enough of you to do it. Stanford's failure was complete, because she went back to where she'll always be safe from you and any of Storn's lackeys."

Helen glanced up at Cunningham, but he was too engrossed. Paul was simply hammering home his words, uncaring of anybody that heard him.

"Both Quirke and North died in the blaze at the barn, taking any evidence of who did it with them. Anything else you'd have covered up to protect your own miserable arses. As for the Fox, you know Stanford torched the place to cover his own failings."

"Your deranged ranting won't get you anywhere," Scott-Wade began.

"No? Then let's have the evidence of how I killed them. Can you show me the bodies? Can you produce a post-mortem of Stanford and describe his wounds?"

"We're going to make sure you get punished for your evil crimes, Sayers," Scott-Wade continued.

"Produce the evidence then."

"You're totally insane."

"You can't, can you? Like the rest of it, Scott-Wade, it's a total shambles."

"Continue to spout your rubbish Sayers, as much as you like, because you'll never leave the justice system. It will punish you for your cowardly crimes."

Again Paul laughed. "You're priceless."

Scott-Wade saw the opportunity to end the session and quickly gathered up his papers. "I'm done here for now, Alan," he said, and headed towards the door. Cunningham followed, with Carter close on their heels. However, he stopped when he saw that Helen was still seated at the table. For a moment he seemed reluctant to leave her there.

"You can get back to what you were doing, Detective," she said.

He glanced at Paul. "I'll send in the uniform."

"No," she firmly replied. "You can tell him to wait outside the door."

"But..."

"Leave," she ordered.

Without further word he nodded, sharply, and walked out. Only then did she cross to the tape recorder and turn it off. "Just what sort of a game are you playing?"

"A highly dangerous one," Paul freely answered.

She leaned back against the wall. "Are you satisfied with the outcome of this morning's little drama?"

"Completely," he replied. "You saw how he lost his cool. It must say something if they've sent a senior man like him."

"Are you trying to tell me that Scott-Wade is part of this fantasy frame-up of yours?"

He nodded. "I'd watch your back if I were you, because so is your new bloke, Carter."

"Nonsense," she threw back, and straightened up.

"They removed Wiles because he had doubts. They needed to move someone close to you to keep an eye on what's happening. It's just in case you don't follow the obvious line."

"And Scott-Wade?"

He shrugged. "I can't answer that one. They must've something else going on to send him down here."

She again shook her head. "You can't expect me to believe this fantasy you've created. You'd be better off telling me the truth and letting me sort it out, whatever the alleged involvement of others."

He smiled, but all she saw was determination. "I've told you the truth, no matter how stupid it sounds. And I know it does, even as I say it. But where they're concerned they just want me to keep running with it. I bet they even know I've told you about Rebecca. The fact is they want me kept locked up and treated like a nutter while they know that it's true."

"I knew we'd get back to guardian angels again," Helen said, raising an eyebrow.

"I'm sure you'll enjoy meeting her," he cheerily replied, as she crossed over to the door. "The forensics proves I'm innocent, don't they?"

Only a brief pause showed he had scored a point.

"DNA takes weeks, so what makes you believe that?"

He laughed. "I didn't do it, that's why. Anyway, you must have some results by now. You'd be ramming them down my throat if you thought it was me."

"Really?" she asked, aware that she was standing in front of a man who had been through a lot whilst in custody, yet still appeared calm and rational. "There's a watertight case against you," she lied. "Any evidence we have is being saved for that case."

"And I'm supposed to be the one living in a fantasy. Do you honestly believe this'll go to a trial with no forensic evidence and that stupid video?"

She sat down. "We found vile, pornographic material in your home and evidence linking you to abduction and murder."

He leaned back. "It proves nothing and you know it."

"Why do you insist the video's rubbish?" she suddenly found herself asking.

"A few minutes of a man dressed in black, with a leather mask conveniently covering his head, knocking about a partially clad young woman with a black bin liner over her head too. Then there's footage of him having violent intercourse with her. Call that concrete? Is it supposed to be me and Sally Marcroft?"

"It's your house. The camera was found in your attic with the tape inside."

"So that makes it me? If I'm so sick and twisted surely I'd want to see myself in better action than that. And why didn't I video the killing too? Why would I want just a few minutes of cheap porno action and not see myself?"

She shrugged, conscious that what he was saying was clear to the entire investigation team. "You tell me. Sick people don't think rationally when they do these things."

He held up his left hand. "Mutilated, agreed?"

"So?"

"I'm right handed."

"So?" she repeated, knowing the killer was left handed.

"The people who made the film know I've a finger missing. It's why, apart from all the dark clothing and hoods, the guy acting in it is wearing gloves. He has to hide the fact he has all his fingers. If you look at him, holding the knife in his left hand, it's quite clear he's gripping it with all his fingers."

Quite unexpectedly she found herself nodding and realised he had been sharp-eyed in his observation of the video.

"Did you know that Sally had a very strict Catholic upbringing? That she was 'girls only' school educated?"

201

"Yes," Helen replied.

"Sally always wore a gold crucifix on a silver chain around her neck. The woman in the video doesn't have one. And she's wearing several rings on her fingers while Sally had none. Also, when she was nineteen, she got drunk with some old school friends, although her mum never knew, and had a rose tattooed on her left thigh, quite high up." Helen raised her eyebrows. "Sally told me the story, because we were good friends" he quickly explained. "Again, the woman in the video doesn't have one. Is that enough for you?"

"Is there more?"

"They obviously went into my place weeks ago and copied the layout for the video."

"What makes you say that?"

"I changed the curtains a fortnight ago."

"So the video's fake," she began. "But you still could've made it purely to throw us into believing you're being framed. It doesn't explain away your connection with the other murders. Whatever you may believe, Sayers, you're going to remain in custody for the foreseeable future."

"Whether or not you believe me, I don't much care, because I'm getting out of here before they decide I'm no use and do me in."

She shook her head. "No one's going to kill you in here."

"Really? When they've already killed one of yours?"

"Wiles died in a road accident."

He nodded. "Hit and run by a big 4x4."

"So what's your point?"

"My neighbours have so readily told you all about my movements, haven't they? I now realise they were planted there to spy on me."

Again she shook her head in desperation.

"My previous neighbour was a Mrs. Eastwick, who'd lived there since before the war. She was killed just before Christmas and the so-called relatives moved in days later."

"So now you're saying this old lady was murdered just so they could move in next door?" she said, astounded by his sheer gall.

"She was run down by a 4x4 while crossing the road outside the local shop in Sawston. The car and the driver were never traced. Now Wiles too, in the same manner. Is it pure coincidence? Or does fantasy begin to sound believable?"

"If so many people are out to get you, why are you telling me this? Couldn't I be one of them?" she countered, in an attempt to shake him from the delusion she thought he was living under.

"You're not."

"How do you know?"

He pointed to her arm and the semi-transparent material of her white blouse. "Your arms are bare."

"Say again?" she said, looking down to where he pointed.

"They're an evil bunch, Helen, and you'll do well to watch your own back. To show how they're all joined, and follow one evil master, they sport the same tattoo. A golden sword with a vivid green serpent wrapped around it. The three who did me over in the cells have one and Carter has one too. I should imagine Scott-Wade's got one under that fancy uniform as well."

She went to the door. "You'll remain here while I do some checking. Then you'll be prepared for the court appearance." She paused by the door. "If you can trust me, answer another question truthfully."

He nodded.

"The man Scott-Wade was talking about, Richard Stanford, did you kill him?"

"No, but I was there when he was. Quirke too."

"What about the third one?"

His reply was cold and truthful. "North? Yes. I caved his head in with a baseball bat and left no trace of evidence. Scott-Wade knows that much for certain and can't produce any against me. Not that he wants to."

The truth of his confession was all too evident to her. "Why?"

"My guardian angel, Rebecca," he began. "I know you don't believe it, but she was captured by the evil cult Scott-Wade is involved with. I had to kill North to get her out. It was the only solution at the time. I burned down the barn where they were keeping her. North and Quirke were inside; it's as simple as that.

Scott-Wade knew that long before he came here. He obviously didn't expect me to know he was one of them."

"How did you know?"

"Richard Stanford had a book of contacts, a small black diary type of thing." He looked at her, concerned. "You no doubt have it, having already been through my place. If you bring it along I'll show something to interest you."

She could not remember everything they had recovered, but felt sure she had not seen such a book. The only way was to check with DS Maxwell. She said nothing further and left him to his own thoughts.

Chapter 41

One side of the double glass doors swung inwards, as Rebecca strode into Clayborough police station. She wore a knee length white dress, with a blue jacket and matching flat soled shoes. Her hair was neatly gathered up and held in place with a band. She also carried a small holdall over her shoulder. The foyer was sparsely furnished, with just a few seats for those waiting to be seen and a single rubber plant in one corner. She crossed the smooth vinyl floor and went straight up to the front desk. Quite casually, she rested her bag on the part of the counter her side and discreetly removed a small white sphere. A sergeant in the office, sitting behind a desk, caught sight of her and went to his side of the glass partition. She greeted him with a smile and left the sphere visible in her hand.

"Can I help you?" he asked, taking no notice of it.

"Would you be a darling and let me through?" she asked, pleasantly.

"Of course Miss," he answered, with a smile, and quickly opened the security door.

"Thank you," she beamed, as she passed into the station proper.

"My pleasure, Miss," the sergeant replied.

The map she had etched in her mind unfolded neatly before her, as she made her way through the station corridors. The route led to several encounters with officers of various ranks and to each she offered a sweet smile whilst keeping her fingers around the sphere. Within a couple of minutes she stood outside a dark grey door marked number three. She stopped to straighten her jacket, before lightly tapping on it.

Inside Paul looked up as the constable turned and opened it. As she stepped inside he instantly recognised her and began to get to his feet.

"Who are..?" the constable started to ask, as Rebecca reached up and gently ran her fingertips down the side of his face. Without finishing the question, his eyes glazed over and he crumpled to the floor. She deftly closed the door before Paul reached her. He picked her effortlessly off her feet.

"Hello my love," she said, smiling. "Do I take it that you have missed me?"

"Just a bit." For several long moments he lost himself in her depthless blue eyes and their dancing pools of colour, before kissing her lovingly on the lips. She pulled away and ran a hand through his rough hair.

"You are a mess," she stated, with a shake of the head.

"A hotel it isn't."

"We have to get you out of here," she began, and laid her bag on the table.

"Can you do it?"

"I came in without much difficulty. The sphere is helping me take control of the surroundings. I need it because there are so many minds to mask from our true intentions. It has enough energy to spare to see us out safely and more besides."

"Good."

Rebecca looked towards the door. "Helen Bradshaw is on her way. Do you want to wait for her?"

"I think she can be trusted." As he spoke he dragged the unconscious constable into the corner.

"I have done some looking into her past and can persuade her you are telling the truth." Rebecca added. "You should also be aware that Rosemary came here."

He looked concerned. "Then we'll definitely wait."

A minute later Helen entered the room. Her eyes focussed on Paul, sitting on the edge of the table, and then to the officer slumped in the corner. Her reaction was immediate and she slapped the alarm band running at waist height around the room. Startled that nothing happened she hit it a second time, only to be answered by silence.

"It's a waste of time Helen," he gently told her. "Please come in and close the door."

She lightly pushed it shut, whilst keeping her attention on him all the time.

"This won't help you at all Sayers. You've really screwed up any chance you had."

He smiled and gestured behind her. "Fantasy time, Helen. I'd like you to meet my guardian angel."

She turned, slowly, and saw her standing with her back to the wall. As their eyes met Rebecca gave a wave of greeting.

"How on earth did you manage to get in here?" she asked, astonished.

"I walked in," she replied, in all honesty. "They were all very helpful."

"So you're the mysterious Rebecca. You're under arrest on the suspicion..."

Rebecca interrupted, cutting her off. "What Paul has told you is the truth, every word of it."

"This is nonsense," Helen began. "You're under arrest, blonde lady. I don't know what part you play in this sorry affair or if you're privy to his fantasy, but you're no angel."

Rebecca uncurled her fingers from around the sphere and met her tirade with a warm, welcoming, smile. "Relax Helen," she soothed. "We are going on a short journey into your past."

"What?" she started, but in the blink of an eye she found herself standing by a roadside, with Rebecca beside her. She was still dressed the same, but was no longer in the interview room. As she glanced around in disbelief, at the change of surroundings, she quickly realised she recognised the place. They were the streets of Leicester, the city she had grown up in. "How'd we get here?" she whispered.

"That is not important," Rebecca replied, indicating to the other side of the road. They could see a little girl, no more than eight years old, walking towards them. The girl was pretty, with a happy face and long chestnut coloured hair. "Do you recognise her?"

Helen stared in disbelief. "It's me."

"Do you remember what happened next?"

She reluctantly nodded. "Only too well, every little detail."

A green Vauxhall Velox saloon appeared at the junction further down the quiet backstreet. It turned and headed in their direction until it drew level with the young Helen. The driver's window was wound down by a middle aged man in spectacles. As he leaned out they could see he had a trilby hat pulled well down over his forehead to partially obscure his face.

"Where are you going?" he asked the young Helen.

"Home," she replied, continuing on her way.

Helen looked on in fear and disbelief, as she relived the haunting scene from her childhood. Tears began to prick at the corners of her eyes as the vivid memories came flooding back into her senses. They were feelings she thought had been long buried.

"I'll give you a lift if you hop in," the driver said, lightly.

Helen reached, desperately, as if to take hold of her younger self. However, her feet would not move. Rebecca gently laid a hand on the outstretched arm and lowered it.

"I am sorry Helen, we are only here to observe. You cannot change what has already happened."

"God, I know," she replied, in a choked whisper. "But I want to get my hands on that vile pervert. How many more little girls or boys did he harm?"

"Sadly, there were a few before he was despatched elsewhere."

Helen glanced at her. "He's dead?"

"Twelve years after this incident," she replied. As she did the door of the car opened and the man reached out.

"Come on. I've got some sweets in here. You can have some while I take you home."

The young Helen took two steps back, shaking her head. "Mummy said I mustn't."

"Run!" Helen screamed in desperation, and Rebecca squeezed her hand. The would-be abductor reached out and grabbed the child by the arm, dragging her towards the car.

"Get in," he barked.

From out of nowhere, Helen saw the woman, dressed in a snow-white jump-suit, appear virtually from thin air at a run. She covered the distance to the child and swiftly pulled her from his grasp. The car door slammed shut and he dashed quickly from the scene. The tall woman in white was quickly kneeling beside the young Helen and comforting her. She had curly raven hair that cascaded over her shoulders and striking, almost jet-black eyes.

"Where did she come from?" Helen asked Rebecca, in a whisper, almost afraid that the woman would hear her as they witnessed the drama from her past. "I remember her so clearly, those beautiful eyes. She saved me from that awful man and I never even had the chance to thank her."

Rebecca smiled. "Her name is Chantelle."

Helen nodded, knowing that she was telling the truth. It was as if she had always known the name and only needed reminding of it. There was something inside being touched, something basic in her existence that she would not normally connect with.

"This has to be a dream," she whispered. "How can I go back and see my past?"

"This was the defining moment in your life Helen. Without it you would not be the person you are today. Whether you believe it or not, it is entirely up to your own philosophy. I am here only to try and gain your confidence. Chantelle is your guardian and she was there to protect you."

"Why can't you save everyone?" she asked, with tears in her eyes. "Why did she save me? Why can't you be fair with everyone?"

"I cannot explain our laws to you. You were being watched at that moment and she came to your aid."

"I believe you," she said, wiping at her face. "But it's a lot to take in."

"There is more." As she spoke, the scene from Helen's childhood froze in time around them. For a brief instant it blurred, chaotically, before refocusing. The new scene was frozen too, even though they could move through it. Rebecca took her hand and guided her through the ring of people who appeared like statues.

"Where's this place? I don't recognise it," Helen asked.

"This is Skelwith farm," Rebecca began. "This is shortly after Paul rescued me from Storn and his followers."

Helen could only look in astonishment at the number of hate-filled faces and the guns they carried.

"Do not be frightened Helen. They cannot see us or harm us."

They paused in front of the menacing figure of Storn, who towered above them. Even in a state of complete stillness he was a frightening sight to witness. Helen found it impossible to stare into the cold black eyes. They seemed to cut through her like a blade.

"Storn," Rebecca simply replied to the unasked question.

"Where's he from?"

"Not from your realm."

"Is he an alien or something?"

Rebecca shook her head. "You do not need to look outwards to find other realms, Helen. Storn is a great evil that exists in many domains. He is using his powers in an attempt to overcome the Guardian realm that watches over them."

"Is he responsible for the ritual killings?" Helen asked, turning her head away.

"Storn finds it hard to exist here for any great period of time. He needs to feed on the soul of a living person at a regular interval to sustain a mortal form. That is why the deaths are at the exact same time-interval. Jason Galloway is next and very soon. The ritual side of it is not necessary to Storn. It is done only to please the followers who witness it. He controls them to release their evil potential and to serve him devotedly."

"It's not real," Helen mumbled. "This doesn't really go on in this country." She turned to look at Rebecca. "Why was Sally Marcroft out of sequence?"

"They desire me. By implicating Paul they disgrace him and have him held in one place," she replied, coaxing her to where the Wolseley sat. She indicated to the ground at the front of the car where Paul was lying. There was blood everywhere, his hand mutilated, and his head was streaming blood from the back. In the past Helen had seen many victims of violent assault, but none to match the ferocity he had been subjected to.

Rebecca could sense Helen's revulsion. "This is what they subjected Paul to, because he rescued me from them. He saved my soul. Can you understand?"

She nodded. "I believe I can now."

"It kills a part of me to imagine the pain he suffered." Rebecca wiped at her face. "I am sorry Helen, but you see, angels cry too."

"I don't really know what to say."

Rebecca pointed to the other side of the Wolseley, to a man in a flat cap carrying a rifle. Helen looked hard at the face before recognition finally dawned on her. "My God! Paul's telling the truth. It's Scott-Wade."

"He is one of Storn's highly placed followers. He is a very valuable man in his organisation."

"This is shocking," Helen gasped, in disbelief. "How could someone so high ranking be a party to something like this?"

"Storn has highly persuasive powers over those with weak minds or the propensity to lean towards evil. You see, Helen, every living person has it within them to be good or evil. Both tendencies are in the soul in equal measure. Storn's ability is to release the full measure of evil. It totally obscures the good. Once done, he controls them through the feeding of that evil. In effect, he owns their souls."

The scene again blurred. When it cleared Helen found herself back in the interview room. Paul was smiling.

"Well, Alice, do tell us about your visit to wonderland."

She rubbed at her eyes, as if tired. "I must admit it's taken me back a bit. I've just had my life turned on its head. I suppose it's like finding religion."

"Don't worry," he replied, motioning towards Rebecca. "This lovely lady turned mine upside down, but I don't regret a minute of it."

She smiled, shyly, in return.

"Who did kill Sally?" he asked Rebecca, directly.

She looked across at Helen. "Your man Carter did the actual killing."

"How do you know that?" she asked, stunned by the revelation.

"We see a lot of what happens here. It was one of the things seen as it happened."

"Couldn't you have stopped it?" she asked, in disbelief.

"No," was the simple reply. "The majority of events are mapped out long in advance and the paths they follow are clear. Other individual events, mostly those caused by evil, come more quickly and can rarely, if ever, be altered by us. There are things that even we are not allowed to interfere with."

"But you're obviously interfering now."

"Yes. However, I cannot explain to you why these particular circumstances warrant our inclusion."

Paul turned to Helen. "You'd best not ask questions about how they operate. I've tried it and just get knotted up in stuff I can't fathom out."

She nodded. "Have you proof he did it?"

Rebecca shook her head. "None you could use, but you will find it." She looked seriously at her. "You will have to act as if you know none of this. If they suspect anything other than what you believed before, it could prove fatal to you."

"I can see that."

Paul almost laughed. "The simple truth is, Helen, you can't tell anyone, not even your superior."

"Why do you say that?"

"Guardian angels? Seeing a recording of your past?" he began. "You reckoned everything I told you was a fantasy. You thought I was a nutcase."

She nodded.

"You'll be called similar if you tell anyone. As a defence it sucks, wouldn't you agree?"

"Agreed, but it means I'm stuck in limbo until I can get the evidence."

"No one said it'd be easy, but at least you know who killed Sally," he replied. "Plus I've got to find Jason."

"Why's he important to you?"

"It's a long story and I'll tell you when it's over."

Helen held out her hand. "Sorry, Paul, you're not going anywhere. You've got to give me the time to sort this out."

"Did I kill Sally?"

"No, I don't believe so. The initial forensics show you didn't."

"Then I'm out of here. I'm not going to sit in some cell until one of Storn's killers walks in and blows me away."

"But you can't walk out."

"Watch me."

"Look, sit it out for forty-eight hours. I promise you I can sort it in that time."

"I'm sorry Helen, but you're not in control of them. Would you still take me to court this afternoon?"

"I was planning to, before this happened."

"Even though you thought I might be innocent?"

"I was aiming to get you in court so we could formally get you held, indefinitely. I believed I could sort out all the oddities of this case, given time."

Paul shook his head. "What happened to fair play?"

She shrugged. "That's the way it goes. We're under intense media attention. You haven't known, but you've featured in every daily newspaper and on the television too. Your house was burned down in a revenge attack." Even as she spoke she realised she had said the wrong thing at the wrong time.

He looked at her, disgusted. "When were you going to tell me?"

She gazed at the floor. "I'm not sure."

He looked her directly in the eye when she raised her head. "I want one thing guaranteed."

"What?"

"Rosemary Newall is a dear friend. I don't want to see her used or hurt. I want your assurance that all mention of her will be removed from your files."

She nodded. "I guessed she meant something to you. I just hadn't gotten round to seeing her again."

"Then don't," he added, quite forcefully. "Do I have your word?"

"Yes," Helen replied, and looked across to Rebecca. "You'll get him out of here won't you?"

"We will simply walk out. But I had to get Paul out of here today anyway."

"Because of the boy?"

"No. Because they planned to take Paul on the way to court."

"How?" Helen quizzed. "There's police cover the whole way."

"Carter knows every move. They have men standing by on the

route with guns. The outcome was set. They would have succeeded in taking Paul and killing most of your men. Using someone who looks like me, they wanted it to appear that Paul had accomplices who would help him escape."

"Clever," Helen said. "Thanks for telling me."

"Me too," Paul added, winking at Rebecca. "I'll wager they were going to use Sephie to act your part."

She smiled, impressed at his foresight. "How did you ever guess?"

"It's a funny thing, but I thought I felt her close by this morning when I woke up."

"Who's Sephie?" Helen asked, suddenly at a loss during their personal conversation.

"No one for you to worry about," he replied. "She's our responsibility."

"What about me?" Helen asked.

"You won't feel a thing, I guarantee it," Rebecca said, as she stopped at her side. "It will not help if you simply sit here while we walk out. There will be too many questions to answer."

Helen turned to catch Paul's attention. "You do realise every copper in the country will be looking for you, as well as this Storn's men being on your back."

He shrugged, although the self-confidence and determination were evident in his manner and steel-blue eyes. The glint of challenge was there

"I love long odds, Helen. In fact I thrive on them."

"Yes, I bet you do."

Before any other words were exchanged, Rebecca deftly reached out and touched her on the back of the neck. Without uttering a sound, Helen crumpled to the floor. Paul caught her halfway and gently laid her on her side.

"Any after-effects?" he asked, checking her breathing.

"Both of them will have a bruise as if they have actually been hit. It is purely superficial, to pass examination, and the constable will truly believe he was struck from behind."

He looked satisfied. "Good let's get out of here."

Chapter 42

Paul stepped out of the interview room and into the corridor. He quickly surveyed its length, saw it was quiet, and beckoned Rebecca out. The sphere was turning a mottled grey and he looked down at it in her hand.

"Is everything okay?"

"We will make it Paul. It has plenty of energy left in it yet."

"Good. I need to go to Helen's office."

"Why?"

"Stanford's book," he replied, as they reached the end of the corridor and climbed the stairs. "I asked her to bring it, but she didn't. She said she couldn't remember seeing it."

Rebecca smiled. "I know you felt it was important. They have it, but do not know the value of it."

"Why not?"

"Charlotte managed to send down a covering field. When they look at the pages they see nothing to interest them."

"Well done," he said, as they reached the next floor and scanned the corridor ahead.

"How important do you think it is?"

"I'm sure Storn has his followers in groups all over the place. If it can place people or telephone numbers together we can start looking."

"Will it lead to Jason?"

"I hope," he said, pushing the fire door open. Making their way along the corridor it was clear they were between two separate rows of offices. It was fortunate the windows had frosted glass.

"The bottom one on the right," she informed him, reading his thoughts long before he asked the question.

Without warning, two officers exited an office and began to walk in their direction. Paul slowed up, the tension showing in his movements.

"Keep walking," Rebecca urged, expertly deflecting the thoughts of the two men. They continued on their way, totally oblivious of their presence.

"That unnerved me a bit," he admitted.

"I will tell you when to get worried," she replied, with a smile. "And it might be right now, because Carter is inside."

"Just the man I wanted to see."

Carter looked up as a rap at the door heralded an arrival. "Come!" he called, noticing the two people standing outside. "Come in!" he repeated, in a louder voice. The two blurred shapes stood motionless as if they had not heard. Another few seconds passed before he got up.

"Why don't you come in?" he said, snatching the door open. It came as a complete shock to the senses and momentarily froze him. "You...?" he stuttered.

Paul was prepared for him, burning with a desire to confront the man who had killed Sally. The mesmeric few seconds that the detective stood agape were all he needed to secure an advantage. Carter took a step back as Paul slammed his right fist hard into his face.

"That's for Sally, you murdering bastard!" he hissed, powerfully forcing his way into the office after the staggering Carter. Blood was running from his shattered nose as a second punch sent the stunned man down onto all fours. He gasped as he saw Paul bearing down on him again. A vicious kick under the chin drove him into unconsciousness.

Rebecca stood waiting in the doorway. "Hurry, we may not have long now."

"Where's the book?"

She pointed to a set of boxes on the floor, close to where Carter was lying. He quickly began rummaging through the first one. "After they've burned down my house, this and the Wolseley could be all I have left in the world."

At the bottom, beneath the clutter, he laid his hand on the

book. "Bingo. Let's get out of here before someone finds one of the bodies we're leaving littered around the place."

The corridor was empty apart from the sound of muffled voices coming from behind frosted windows.

"Which way?" he asked, glancing in both directions.

She pointed to the right. "We are on the ground floor. The entrance is that way."

He nodded and they made their way to the doors at the end. On reaching them, a woman police officer pushed her way through, backwards. She turned and they let her pass. Rebecca easily deflected her thoughts and she continued on her way with a tray in her hands.

"It's uncanny," Paul whispered, pushing through the doors.

"I read her thoughts. She is going down to the interview room. We had best hurry."

"Will she be aware when she gets there?"

"Totally," Rebecca replied. "I cannot hope to mask her senses at this distance."

He needed no further information to know that their time was limited and that speed was the only action left open to them. With gentle firmness, he grabbed her by the hand and they broke into a fast jog. The sound of their footfalls drummed around them as they burst straight through the security door. The duty sergeant rose to his feet to see what was happening. Rebecca deftly sat him back down with a quick alteration of his thoughts.

"Thank you!" she politely called, as they scurried past. The automatic door opened in front of them and they were running down the front steps and into the car park.

"We'll need a car," he urged, clearing the last step. "It's going to be tight and there might be some reporters outside the main gate."

She glanced down at the sphere and saw that its energy was diminishing. "I think we can manage."

Paul was still holding onto her hand as they hurried down the first row of parked cars in a desperate bid to find one with a driver. He breathed a sigh of relief and pointed to where a row of patrol cars sat.

"That one," he said, steering her over towards a damson-coloured Vauxhall Carlton.

Inside it were two uniformed officers, casually engaged in conversation.

"We'll need some money too if you can manage it," he added, as they approached the men from the side.

Inside the station, the woman officer had reached the interview room. Stepping inside, her eyes grew wide with comprehending shock. Both her uniformed colleague and Helen were laid out on the floor, unconscious. Within moments her professional instinct took over and she dropped the tray. As the china shattered across the floor, along with a shower of hot coffee, she clenched a fist and banged the alarm band. All around the station, heads jerked up and officers began to respond to the sound of the warning klaxon.

Chapter 43

The two officers in the Vauxhall Carlton smiled when Rebecca appeared at the window, unaware that their thoughts were being controlled.

"Would you both be darlings and give me your wallets and lend me your lovely little car?"

"Certainly Miss," the driver replied, getting out.

Paul needed no urging and slipped in behind the steering wheel. Rebecca climbed in while smiling sweetly at the wooden looking policemen. Paul was almost laughing as he fired the big saloon into life and reversed out of the bay. The two men stood casually aside while the sound of alarms going off inside the station could be heard.

"Close," Paul said, accelerating quickly away. Two camera crews and a dozen reporters were outside waiting for something to happen. With the influence of Rebecca and the sphere, they were blissfully unaware of the Carlton as it raced past them.

"How long before those two realise we've got their car?" Paul asked, pulling onto the main road.

"About a couple of minutes," she replied, replacing the almost exhausted sphere back in her shoulder bag. "Why did you want this car, Paul?"

He grinned, mischievously. "It's a three-litre Lotus Carlton with twin turbos. An unmarked pursuit car, and it's very, very, quick." As if to add weight to the statement he accelerated down the slip road to join the dual carriageway. With more than enough power to spare the Vauxhall moved swiftly into the outside lane, where it smoothly passed the one-hundred and twenty miles an hour mark on the speedometer and left all the other traffic in its wake.

"What now?" Rebecca asked, studying him.

"Dump this for something else."

She looked puzzled. "Why after going to the trouble of getting it?"

"We only needed a fast car to get away. This thing'll become hot property in about five minutes. Every copper in the area will be looking for it," he replied, glancing at her. "You look lovely today."

"Thank you. I love you too, darling, but you do need a wash and a shave."

He laughed "Don't I know it."

The Eastway Trading Estate came into view halfway around the ring road system. Paul knew the area and slipped into it via the link road. A little over four minutes had passed since they had left the police station. The forecourt they drove onto was that of Stamps Motors, the largest second-hand car dealership in Clayborough. The sign emblazoned across the main showroom window boasted of over five hundred used cars in stock. A huge assortment of models and colours were ranged in neat rows all over the premises. Paul halted in a vacant parking bay by the office.

"We'll get another here," he told Rebecca, as the engine died. "And leave this behind."

"Do you want me to use my influence?" she asked, as they both stepped from the car.

"Not this time, precious," he replied. "Save your talents on this one."

She handed him one of the wallets and he took out the cash, stuffing it in his back pocket. They had only walked a few paces when a salesman approached them. He intercepted them with an eager smile that looked too well practiced to be genuine.

"Can I help you?" he enquired, staring at Rebecca.

Paul looked down at himself and knew he looked a disheveled mess compared to her. "You'll have to forgive me," he explained. "I've just come off a long shift at work."

The salesman nodded, quickly returning his attention to Rebecca. "That's no problem. Are you and the young lady after anything in particular?"

Paul smiled. It was going to be easy to get a car with Rebecca to distract the salesman.

"Something for my friend, if you don't mind showing us something small she can do her running around in."

"Has madam a particular preference? I'm quite sure you have very good taste," he gushed.

She smiled, demurely pointing to the nearest row. "I like the little red one."

"Ah the Metro," he sighed. "That's an ideal choice. I'll fetch some keys." With a brief gesture he strode back into the showroom.

Paul looked sideways at her while they appeared to be looking around the forecourt.

"Why that one?"

She squeezed his hand. "There seem to be a few like it about, so it will not look out of place. Also it appears ready to drive straight out."

"Well thought out, precious. You're a little devil when you want to be."

"Do not talk to me about devils. Have you seen the way he has been looking at me? His mind is like an open sewer, undressing me with his eyes."

"Obviously, which means he hasn't really seen me."

"What next?"

"Get out of here," he whispered, as the salesman reappeared.

The man quickly launched into his sales patter, doing his level best to keep beside Rebecca and keep Paul out of the conversation. He opened the driver's door and tried to usher her in behind the wheel. However, she did the opposite and followed Paul around as he played the part of examining the car.

"Doesn't look bad for four years old," Paul said, as the salesman hurried to catch them up on the other side. He was just too late to see Rebecca jump into the vacant passenger seat and pull down the hem of her dress to cover her knees. Before he could again move closer, she shut the door and opened the window.

"I do like it, darling," she said, excitedly, to Paul. "Especially the colour."

The man leaned in the open window. "Does madam like all things red?"

While he was again distracted, Paul took the opportunity to hop in behind the wheel. The engine started readily and he revved it for a few seconds before allowing it to idle.

"What d'you reckon then? Not bad?" the salesman said, enthusiastically, through the open window.

"What do you think?" Paul asked Rebecca, with a wink.

She grasped his hand. "Oh darling, can I have it? You can make love to me all weekend if you say yes."

He heard the salesman groan and stifled a laugh. Instead he patted her knee.

"We'll see."

"I can do a cracking deal if there's no part-exchange."

Paul peeled the price sticker from the window and passed it to him. "Knock three hundred off this and we'll talk seriously."

His eyes lit up. "We may have a deal."

Rebecca smiled innocently up at him as he stared down the top two open buttons of her dress. "And you need not think about offering to knock another hundred off for the pleasure of photographing me in red stockings."

The salesman flushed in the face, totally embarrassed, but also shocked that his thoughts had been so comprehensively read. He was flustered and found it difficult to reply. But Paul spoke as if nothing had been said and managed to keep a straight face.

"You don't mind us going for a quick run do you?"

"Of course not," he quickly replied, glad of something to say. "I'll come with you."

Paul held up a hand. "If you don't mind I'd like to make my own decision."

Despite his embarrassment a hesitant look clouded his face. "It's not our usual policy to allow customers to take cars out on their own."

"Hang on," Paul said, taking the wallet from his pocket. He opened it and removed the driving licence and a credit card from inside. With a smile he handed them both through the open window, along with the keys to the Vauxhall. "I'm not about to leave you those and my Lotus Carlton and run off in a Metro, am I?"

He shrugged and then laughed. "No, I suppose not."

"Good," Paul grinned. "Give us twenty minutes. Once around the parkway and back through town. Okay?"

The salesman weighed up the potential of the sale along with the keys in his hand.

"Fair enough, but be careful."

"Sure."

Rebecca again smiled sweetly at him, causing him to redden once more. "You are a darling, thank you."

Once they were clear of the forecourt Paul burst out laughing and looked at her in amazement. "Where did all that come from? You can make love to me all weekend and don't think about photographing me in red stockings."

She managed to look completely innocent, even though he knew different.

"It took his mind off you, thinking about making love all weekend. And his ideas of lingerie are quite exotic."

"Mine could be too."

"Only too well do I know your tastes in what women should wear underneath."

Again he laughed. "Coming from someone who often wears nothing underneath, that's rich."

A smile crossed her lips. "Enough of that. How long do we have?"

"I'll give them thirty minutes before they get suspicious and discover what they've really got on the forecourt."

Chapter 44

Twenty minutes after leaving Stamps Motors, the Metro pulled up at a service station in the small Fenland town of Mereside St Mary's. Paul drew up against one of the pumps and casually put ten pounds worth of petrol in the car. Although it wanted fuel he also needed the shop.

"Stay here," he said to Rebecca, as he passed her open window and went inside to pay. A few minutes later he reappeared with two carrier bags and she opened the door to take them from him. Inside one were several cartons of fruit juice and milk. Also he had bought sandwiches, crisps, and sausage rolls. The second contained a pair of self-adhesive number plates and an assortment of letters and figures. Without hurrying, he turned onto the main road heading east. His intention was to get as far away from Clayborough as possible before dumping the car in Norfolk. They had travelled less than a mile when Rebecca held up one of the number plates.

"What are these for?"

"I thought you'd never ask. They're to change the registration. It should give us the extra time we need." He pointed to the assortment of figures in her lap. "Make them like the car in front. Just be sure you do them both the same."

She winked, laid them across her knees and got to work. After a couple of minutes she held up the completed plates for inspection.

"Perfect. Now, pass me a couple of those sandwiches. They starved me back there."

"Sorry, I should have thought," she said, reaching into the other bag. "Ham salad?"

"I don't mind."

She leaned over and gently pushed one into his open mouth. "There, that will shut you up for a little while."

Without reply, he simply raised his eyebrows and began to devour the welcome nourishment. A few minutes later they were heading into Norfolk and towards his intended destination, Norwich. At the first opportunity he pulled into a lay-by at the side of the road. A solitary Ford Mondeo sat in it with its driver asleep behind the wheel. Paul halted well short of it and motioned for Rebecca to stay put. Casually, he strode around the Metro until there was a lull in passing traffic and then quickly stuck the new number over the originals. Satisfied with the deception, he got back in and drove off. He hoped the change of plates would give them at least an hour or more lead. At the back of his mind though he knew Storn's followers would be mobilising to find him too. The one thing in his favour was the book that might or might not lead them to the boy. Also there was Rebecca, with her valuable skills. They had a chance, not much of one, but he felt confident. At the next junction he turned off and headed towards the town of Downham Market.

"Where do you plan going to?" Rebecca asked, when she felt that he was relaxed enough to engage in conversation.

"Norwich. I'm going to need you to stay with me for a while."

"I will stay for as long as you need me. Why Norwich?"

"We'll dump the car and get the train out to Sheringham. From there we'll walk to Saltmarsh and go to David Pryce. We should get there just after dark. I'm hoping for somewhere to sleep and time to work out how to find Jason."

She nodded. "That sounds good. You really have been thinking it through."

"As far as it goes," he replied. "I just pray that the book holds the key."

"I am sure it will," Rebecca added, and passed him another sandwich. In thoughtful silence they continued on their way.

Chapter 45

Alan Cunningham was inside his office and seated behind his desk, twiddling a pen between his fingers. Helen was sitting opposite, nursing a cup of coffee, trying to massage the niggling throb from the back of her neck. Over by the window, seemingly oblivious of the other two, Scott-Wade paced furiously up and down. Occasionally he would pause, look out of the window, and mutter oaths under his breath. All of them were lost in their own thoughts, but his face was full of anger and continued to redden every time he stopped pacing. Cunningham had known him for many years, but what he saw was a side of the man he had never known. It was a sight that did more than just trouble him. He turned to Helen.

"Are you sure you remember nothing?"

She shook her head. "I went back to see if there was any link between Sally Marcroft and the time Sayers spent in Kirkham. We had an hour before court and I thought I'd use it." She paused and took another sip from the mug. Inwardly she was satisfied with how the lie sounded, aware too that Scott-Wade would be taking note of everything she said. "I walked in and got hit from behind, everything went black."

Scott-Wade stopped, momentarily, and looked at her. She put on a suitably dazed expression and thought, 'buy it, creep.'

Cunningham sat back, a slightly bemused look on his face. "Our own foyer cameras show this woman walking in straight past security. Then, a few minutes later, they jog out together." He shook his head. "A building full of coppers, yet no one remembers seeing anything. Even the desk officer who opened the door recalls nothing. Did you see her Helen?"

"I saw no one," she lied.

Scott-Wade again began to pace up and down, renewing his assault on the carpet. "Why did he go up to your office?" he asked, without stopping. "Was it purely to attack Carter? Or was it to get something that was his?"

She shrugged. "No idea. Perhaps Carter was just in the way. There's nothing missing from any of the evidence we gathered." She again sipped at her coffee, surmising that Paul had gone for the black book he had asked her about. Also she was aware that Carter had been responsible for the death of Sally Marcroft. Perhaps Paul had vented his anger on him. Personally, she neither condoned nor condemned the action.

Cunningham turned to Scott-Wade. "Do you recognise this mysterious blonde, Tony?"

He chose not to look as he replied. It was easier to lie when not making eye contact. He knew exactly who she was, the highly regarded prize sought by Storn.

"If it's true Marcroft didn't go to Kirkham, as Sayers says, it's possible this one's the woman Stanford had the affair with. Whatever the tie with his or Marcroft's murder, she's obviously an accomplice."

Cunningham readily nodded. "Whoever she is, I'd like to meet her. She's got something about her that's for sure. How they managed to get the traffic lads to hand over their unmarked is a mystery." He shook his head, almost having to hide a smile that Helen alone saw. "They're hopping mad. The outside camera shows them handing over their wallets and Sayers driving away."

"What was their explanation?" Scott-Wade asked, even though he was aware of Rebecca's ability to influence thoughts and actions.

"They've no recollection of it. They've seen the footage and still can't believe it. Not even the press saw them."

The conversation was cut short by a sharp rap at the door and a uniformed officer stepped in, carrying a sheet of paper which he immediately laid on the desk in front of Cunningham. "The unmarked Carlton's been found, Sir."

"Where?"

Scott-Wade again stopped and turned his attention to him, as did Helen.

"At Stamps', Sir, the used car dealers."

"What's the story?"

"Apparently they went in on the pretence of buying a car and took a red Rover Metro out for a test drive. They failed to return. The staff became suspicious and found the Carlton to be ours."

"Didn't someone go with them?" Cunningham asked, studying the brief report.

"No," the officer added. "He left the keys as a show of good faith along with PC White's driving licence and credit card."

Cunningham stole a glance in Helen's direction. "Very clever wouldn't you say? No headlong race for distance."

She nodded, admiring Paul's bravado at so quickly swapping the Carlton for something so ordinary.

"Put it into the system," he added.

"It's already been done, Sir. We've also alerted all neighbouring forces."

"Good work."

As the officer left, Scott-Wade made his way to the desk and picked up the report. "May I?"

"Certainly, Tony."

He made to leave too. "I've a call to make."

Helen watched him go and breathed a sigh of relief. She knew who would be on the receiving end of the call. Storn's people would soon have the details and the long odds Paul spoke about would increase.

Cunningham stood up and crossed to the window. "Anything you want to tell me?"

"I don't think so," she quietly replied. She studied his back, framed in the light of the window. She knew he was driving at something and certainly nobody's fool.

Without taking his gaze from the scene below, he spoke again. "I got the distinct impression you don't like Tony. Am I right?"

"I wouldn't go that far."

"Rubbish," he said, and turned to face her. "What did you make of the interview earlier?"

"It was hard to read."

"Rubbish again, Helen. You're hiding something. That was like no other interview I'd ever seen before."

"It's true that Sayers was the calm one. If anyone was uncomfortable, it was Scott-Wade."

He nodded. "Now is there something?"

She sighed. "If it's not too unreasonable, would you mind showing me your arms?"

He looked puzzled.

"I know, but don't ask."

He went back to the desk and undid the buttons on his tunic. After laying it across the back of the chair he undid the cuffs and rolled up both shirtsleeves. With exaggerated motions, he openly displayed both arms. She saw there were no tattoos and was certain she was safe with the man she had known for years.

"Satisfied?"

"Yes," she replied. "I can't give you much proof about a lot of this yet Skipper. One thing is certain though, Sayers didn't murder Sally Marcroft. I'm also sure he's not responsible for the Galloway abduction or other murders."

His expression did not alter. "So what makes you say that?"

"There's an extensive frame-up and the cracks are becoming visible."

"Then why escape?"

"Because of the boy," she replied. "He truly believes he can find him and prove his own innocence."

"If Sayers is innocent, why not let us prove it?"

She shook her head. "If it's proven, the frame-up comes in the greater part from our people."

His eyes widened in disbelief. "Who exactly?"

She pointed towards the door. "Scott-Wade."

"Are you serious Helen?" he blurted, incredulously.

She nodded. "Wiles had doubts from the beginning, even expressed them round the station. He was targeted by the same people who are after Sayers."

"It was a tragic accident."

"Sayers' neighbour went the same way so they could watch him closely. You're forgetting the assault in the cells."

He returned to his chair and sat down. "It's hard to believe Tony's in on this."

"You saw how he reacted in the interview. It's hardly the way for a senior officer to behave. And since Sayers escaped he's been on edge and uptight. It's not his case or man, Skipper, but he's totally wrapped up in it."

"I need proof Helen, something concrete."

"I'll get it," she replied, confidently. "I'd like to test Carter's blood for a match and DNA without him being told."

"Why?"

"I'm certain it'll confirm he killed Sally Marcroft. If I arrest him we can fingerprint him and see if it matches the partial ones we've already got"

If Cunningham was stunned by the statement he did not show it. "I see. How do you propose to do it?"

She pulled an evidence bag from her pocket. It contained a blood spattered tissue.

"Sayers gave him a bloody nose before leaving. I retrieved this from the office."

"I hope to God you're right about this. If not there'll be serious repercussions for both of us."

She nodded.

"The search for Sayers will continue as normal."

"I know, and so does he."

"Did you know he was going to escape? Did you allow it?"

"I couldn't have stopped him even if I'd have wanted to."

For several long moments they both sat in silence, before she crossed to the door to leave.

"As far as I'm concerned, Helen, this conversation never took place. Understand?"

Without reply, she closed the door behind her.

Chapter 46

In the car park, below the window of Cunningham's upper floor office, Scott-Wade sat behind the wheel of his car. With the new information he had he was already busy on his mobile phone.

"Yes?" came the clear voice of Myra at the other end.

"Sayers has gone."

"Shit! How?"

"The Guardian woman," he simply added.

"It figures."

"I've arranged for all the available info to go to the police operations room in Harrogate. It'll seem routine and you can hack into it from Pelham. With our inside knowledge we should keep one step ahead of the game and get him first."

"Okay. I'll sort everything out from here. What about Sephie and the team?"

He took a swig from a bottle of mineral water. "I've sent them all back. I want no trace of anything at this end."

"I understand. What about Padrigg?"

He thought for a moment. "He's got no leads on it and I don't believe he'll try to find the boy. He'll be too busy dodging us and the rest of the force to get clever, but tell them to step up the watch nevertheless."

"Storn's not going to like this one bit," she warned.

A patrol car entered the yard as he stared out of the windscreen, thinking about what she had said. His reply was almost casual. "He'll have to live with it. This mess is down to Carter and his stupid plan. Whatever anyone thinks Sayers is going to do is usually wrong. He's running solo most of the time which makes him unpredictable."

"He's more so with that blonde bitch interfering too."

231

"True," he agreed. "It's a pity Storn's great prophecies never see her getting in the way."

"I'd better get started, Tony. I'll be in touch."

"Okay, Myra. I'll return whenever it's prudent for me to leave," he replied, and cut the line. In the solitude of the car his busy mind began to work on the new problems facing them.

Chapter 47

It was just past four-thirty, with the sun still managing to occasionally peek out from behind the puffy white clouds. Paul had been in Norwich for a little over ten minutes and had left the Metro in a vacant parking bay. The choice of one of the larger car parks had been quite deliberate. With its false plates he hoped to conceal the car for several hours or longer. After first buying a five hour ticket to see it legally through to the free evening period, he threw the keys into the nearest litter bin. His destination was the railway station, where, only moments earlier, he had dropped off Rebecca. On the way he stopped to buy a disposable razor and shampoo. At a clothing store he picked up a change of clothes too. Entering the station, he made his way directly to the toilets. Once inside he quickly washed himself, his hair, and shaved, before donning the clean clothes. The effect was immediate and he felt cleaner, respectable, and, more importantly, less conspicuous.

Paul had no prior knowledge of the timetable and found himself early for the train to Sheringham. To pass the time he sat at the end of the platform, nursing a plastic cup of tea and a packet of biscuits from the buffet. Rebecca had been inside too, with a perfect view of the entire platform. She could see him on a bench further down it, with his back to her. They had seen each other but had passed as strangers, as planned. The brief encounter showed he had taken time to freshen up and change. As for herself, she had removed her jacket, dumped it in a waste bin, and put on the white cardigan she carried in her shoulder bag.

At six o'clock on the dot, the train, which was a basic two-carriage affair emblazoned with a Network South-East logo, pulled up at the platform. A crackled voice called out over the announcement system, heralding its arrival and listing the subsequent stops. Inside the buffet, Rebecca took one last mouthful of tea before making her way onto the platform and joining the others boarding the train as the doors opened. At the other end, Paul waited until she had got on before stepping aboard himself. It took a further two minutes before the train finally pulled out of the station.

North of Norwich, at the vicarage in Saltmarsh, David Pryce switched on the six o'clock news as he sat down with his tea. Susan had left him a meal to be heated in the microwave, while she had gone to her sister's for the evening. They had also agreed that she would stay with her for a few days for support. The bulletin had hardly begun when Paul's face appeared on the screen. David became immediately alert. For several seconds he sat dumbly and watched the report. Rather belatedly, he flicked on the video and recorded the rest. His surprise redoubled when security camera footage of Paul's 'accomplice' was shown. An involuntary shudder went down his back as he stared at the fuzzy black and white picture that had been frozen to show her face. The item ended and they were quickly onto the next news story.

David put his meal to one side and fetched a photograph album from the sideboard. He swiftly flicked through to the page he wanted and rewound the video. Another shiver ran down his spine as he placed the open page next to the screen. His hand was shaking.

"It's you, Rebecca, it really is you," he whispered, to the empty room. After a few moments study he switched off the television and gathered up the newspapers they had amassed over the previous two days. Each one went into more lurid detail about Paul's assumed past and shocking crimes. He went outside and dumped them all in the dustbin.

"There," he said, slamming the lid shut. "Just as I suspected, judged and convicted by media jury."

Chapter 48

At ten past seven, the train from Norwich pulled into Sheringham station. Alighting from the last carriage, with a dozen other passengers, Paul stepped onto the platform and immediately made his way to the exit. As planned, Rebecca had remained at the opposite end of the train and had got off at the previous stop. The intention was that she would take a taxi to Weybourne and meet him later in the evening. From there they would walk the rest of the way to Saltmarsh. Paul knew the seaside town well and walked down the main street to the seafront. The only stop he made was to buy fish and chips. He sat on the promenade and, as he ate, watched the tide going out, leaving the shingle covered beach exposed. His preferred option was now to walk along the shore to Weybourne and avoid the majority of people.

Ten minutes later he was strolling along the beach. It felt good to be away from the confines of the police cell and stuffiness of the train. Freedom was indeed precious and the taste of imprisonment had been bitter. The salty air wafted around him while the frothy white waves lapped at his feet. He took them into his senses like a fine wine and beautiful music. North from the town a gravel bank rose up behind the beach. It was man made; the defences that made some attempt to keep the continuous onslaught of the sea from the land. It took him less than half an hour to walk to Weybourne. Its prominent windmill came into view as soon as he climbed the bank. As he got closer he could see Rebecca, sitting just below the top, facing out to sea. She had her arms over her knees, resting her head across them, and was not actually looking for him. In fact he quickly appreciated she was asleep. The experience was one she had not faced before, tiredness. It had caught up with her unexpectedly and, almost gratefully, she had

235

succumbed to it while waiting for him to arrive. It was after eight and the breeze coming off the water was turning chilly. He made a beeline towards her and slipped off his sweatshirt.

"Good evening, Miss," he said, softly, and laid it across her shoulders.

Her eyes flickered open on hearing his voice.

"What's a nice girl...?" he began, smiling. "You know the rest."

Aware that he could still use humour in such a trying situation, she got to her feet.

"I am waiting for a handsome knight to carry me away to his bedchamber."

Quite casually he glanced around where they stood, before slipping his arms around her waist. "Sorry, Miss, no white knights available. There's only me here."

In return she clasped her arms around him. "Well, if you are all there is, I suppose you will have to do," she replied, as if he were a poor second choice.

Their lips met. "Then I'm all yours."

"I know," she whispered.

He loosely tied the arms of the sweatshirt around her neck "It'll keep the chill out."

"What are we going to do now?"

"I don't fancy walking into Saltmarsh in daylight. We'll wait here."

She nodded and they sat down. Once together, she snuggled against his chest and felt the reassuring warmth of his arms round her. In turn, he hugged her close and lightly buried his face in her faintly perfumed hair. No words were spoken or deemed necessary as, together, they felt their shared love radiate its bond between them. For well over an hour they had only the ceaseless roll of the waves for company. Above them the sky turned through darkening shades of blue until darkness took over.

It was ten o'clock when Paul gently whispered into her ear that they should be going. The time spent, having the man she loved just hold her, was like a lifetime of pleasure for Rebecca. It had more than made up for the barren times when she could only watch him from afar, out of reach and always out of touch.

"I could stay like this forever," she whispered.

"Me too, but we must be moving."

She took both his hands and squeezed them. "We have not spoken words, my darling, but what your feelings have said to me has been truly wondrous. Thank you."

He kissed each hand in turn. "Com'on, reality beckons."

It did not take them long to walk through the quiet streets of Weybourne and out the other side towards Saltmarsh. Paul already knew the road from his previous visit and kept off it. Instead they walked in the fields, masked by the hedgerow. He knew he could take no chances with either the police or Storn's men. If the Metro had been found, either organisation could guess their intended destination and have men waiting on the off-chance they would turn up.

At eleven-thirty, under starlit skies, they finally reached the outskirts of the village. Everywhere appeared peaceful as they used the shadows to make their way towards the church. The churchyard seemed deathly still and a track from it led down to the vicarage. After running the last short distance, they stopped to catch their breath and Paul peered over the low hedge that skirted the side of the house. A light was on, illuminating the driveway, and he could hear the sound of voices from the front porch.

On the road sat a police car, with its orange flash vivid in the light cast by the streetlamp. He ducked out of sight next to Rebecca.

"Police," he whispered, in reply to the unasked question. "Someone's figured out we might come here. They might've found the Metro for all I know."

"What now?"

"Let's get round the back," he whispered, and led her by the hand until they were in the darkness at the rear of the house. The tall conifer hedging was dense and they had to search for a suitable point at which to crawl through. The whole of the garden was well shielded and they immediately went to the back door. He continued down the side of the house until he could again see the police car outside. The sound of voices still carried on the night air, but he could make out little of what was being said and went back. Rebecca was by the kitchen door with her hand on the handle. It was half open and he was surprised, but also grateful that it was not locked. He urged her inside and quickly followed. The room was in darkness except for a shaft of light coming through the partially-open door to the hallway. He made his way stealthily over and listened.

"I suggest you keep your windows and doors locked, he may just come in this direction. Call us if you suspect anything," he heard the deep Norfolk accent say.

"Very good, officer," came David Pryce's familiar tone in reply.

"Goodnight Sir."

"And to you."

Paul waited until the front door was closed before indicating to Rebecca to step back outside. She did so and acknowledged his finger-to-the-lips gesture for quiet. Still listening, he heard the chain go on and a key turn in the lock. When that was done he reached up to the shelf behind and took down a glass tumbler. He dropped it on the floor. The crash of shattering glass was followed by absolute silence, while he shuffled into the shadow cast by the door. A few moments later it opened, spilling more light in from the hallway.

"Is someone there?" David asked, in a faltering voice, as he reached out and flicked on the light.

Waiting only until he had stepped into the kitchen, Paul was on him in a flash, pinning him across the chest from behind and clamping a hand over his mouth. David stiffened in the restraining grip, but did nothing to resist. Paul sensed the lack of struggle and loosened the hold.

"It's Paul, David," he said, in a coarse whisper. "I'm not here to do you any harm."

David relaxed as soon as he realised who it was and nodded. Paul immediately let go and took the hand away from his mouth. David turned round and found himself looking into the face of the man he had met only days earlier. However, it was not as different as he had possibly expected. A desperate man on the run would surely look at least jumpy or even scared. Instead, apart from looking tired, Paul appeared assured and confident, with his steel-blue eyes filled with a sense of purpose.

"Do you think I killed Sally and am responsible for Jason being abducted?"

David shook his head. He had no doubts that Paul was genuine. From the first time they met he had sensed he was somehow set aside from others. His life had others destinies wrapped inside it. He was special.

"I don't believe a word of it."

Paul visibly relaxed. "Thanks, David; I need the help of a friend tonight."

"You'll always have friends here, Paul," he replied, patting him on the arm.

"Thanks," he said, and ushered Rebecca back inside.

As it had been with the picture on the television screen, David felt a tingle down his spine and the hairs rise on the back of his neck. The feeling was a sense of awe that she could easily feel within him and she nodded, to show that she understood. It was enough to allow him to regain his composure.

"It's a pleasure to meet you, Rebecca."

She gently squeezed the offered hand. "And you."

He glanced at Paul. "The police were just here warning me about you two."

"I guessed they might. It's why we came in the back." He smiled, weakly. "Sorry about the shock, but I couldn't be sure of your reaction on seeing me."

"No problem. I'm just glad to see you're okay. The hunt for you is nationwide. You've been on every news bulletin and will be in every paper again by the morning."

"Can we go into the living room? I hate to be in here with all the lights on."

"Of course," he replied, leading the way through. "Sue's gone over to Anne's, so you've picked the right moment to come."

Paul deposited himself on the sofa with Rebecca at his side. David sat opposite them in an armchair.

"Why come here? Not that you're not welcome."

"Friendly port in a storm and I need a breathing space before setting out to find Jason."

"Can you?"

"I think so," he replied, seriously, and leaned back. "We've only until Monday to do so or he'll be dead for sure. Either way it's going to be pretty tight."

"Depending on who gets to you first?"

Paul looked indifferent. "Storn's people are everywhere. No one's trustworthy. Even if the police get to us first his henchmen'll see to me while I'm being held."

"So you've nowhere to go?"

"Exactly. They'll also know Rebecca's with me."

She was acutely aware of what he meant.

"If they think there's the remotest chance of getting her they'll use me. But, whatever happens, they want me dead, I can feel it."

"So how can I help, Paul?" David asked, feeling a little powerless.

"For starters, you must always deny knowledge of knowing me. If they ever suspect we're connected they'll use you and your family against me."

David nodded. "So where do you start looking for Jason? We're all worried sick, me especially as I know what the boy's facing." he asked, standing up. "I'll put the kettle on."

"What a good idea," Rebecca said, enthusiastically.

Five minutes later he returned, carrying a tray of cups and a steaming pot of tea. Paul was laid flat out asleep on the sofa with Rebecca sitting on the floor beside him. She looked up at David and smiled, while tenderly caressing Paul's cheek with her fingers.

"He is really exhausted, David, and needs to sleep if we are to find Jason. I have settled him for now."

He laid the tray down on the coffee table as she produced the black book from her handbag. "This is the key to finding Jason."

He knelt down next to her. "What is it?"

"Storn's followers are in here. It is a list of telephone numbers. If we can group enough together in one area I can go back to my realm and look. If I find a masking shield then that will be the place."

"That easy?" he said, taking it from her.

"It is down to us David, Paul needs the rest for the time to come. It will not be easy rescuing him from them."

He glanced at her sideways. "Then let's start looking."

Chapter 49

Thursday 27th May 1993

Paul had learned much from his almost fatal encounter in Kirkham, when he had rescued Rebecca. Again they were alert to his possible arrival, but he had time on his side. The plan had a simple enough start though and he had, on the face of it, stolen David's Fiat Tipo. As agreed that morning, David would report the theft just after lunch so as to give Paul enough time to reach his destination, The Lake District. With Rebecca's help, David had isolated four pockets of Storn's followers spread throughout the country. After a brief return to the Guardian realm, she brought back the news they had hoped for. In the heart of the Lakes she had encountered a shield like the one that had contained her. The drive up from Norfolk had taken five hours without a stop and, knowing that the theft would not be reported until later in the day, it was fairly relaxing. Paul knew the area well and parked the car in Grasmere. The busy little tourist village made it an ideal place to pick up some gear and cross the fells to the intended target of Padrigg. A frontal approach into the isolated valley had been quickly dismissed and he planned instead to reach it on foot. Rebecca was in Grasmere too, having arrived by her own mode of travel just minutes ahead of him. As expected, their pictures were all over the media and traveling together had seemed unnecessary. Dressed in dark green corduroy trousers, walking boots and denim shirt, she had her hair tied up so she looked different to the pictures. She carried some things in a shoulder bag and wandered aimlessly among the shops, looking like any of the other tourists. Paul had spotted her as he headed for the nearest outdoor activity shop.

Once inside the store he quickly purchased a pair of lightweight boots, trousers, two fleece jackets and a rucksack. The young girl assistant took little notice of him as he paid for the items and several smaller things from around the shelves. Afterwards, he went to the mini-market for drinks and provisions. Twenty minutes after leaving Grasmere, Paul halted alongside a stone wall that was about a mile out of the village and over two hundred feet up. A brief study of the map showed him what he already knew; the route across the fells would eventually lead to the isolated valley of Padrigg. Without wasting time, he quickly discarded his jeans and training shoes for the new gear he had bought. The rest was placed in the rucksack and he felt ready for several hours walking. He was eating a packet of crisps when Rebecca appeared on the path below him and waved in greeting.

"Ready for a good walk then?" he asked, passing her a fleece.

"I think so."

"If we make good time we should be there before it gets dark."

She looked at him, seriously. "I will not be able to get close, Paul. The shield is very intense, probably the strongest ever."

They set off upward. "Don't worry, I wasn't about to suggest you go anywhere near the place. If I go in, I go in alone."

She fleetingly read his thoughts and saw the underlying determination to release the boy.

"Now we are this close, evil has obscured the path. Even Charlotte cannot read the possible outcome to all of this." She hesitated, before continuing. "I do not want to hold you up."

He laughed and grabbed her hand. "We're not out to break records to get there. As long as I can get a look at the place in daylight we've got time on our side. I'm not as much in the dark as I was when I went to Kirkham." Even as he spoke he automatically shortened his stride, to compensate for the increasing gradient. They had plenty of time and he knew it.

It was nine-thirty, and under cloudy skies, when they crossed the last summit of the rocky ridge overlooking Padrigg. The narrow valley was laid out below them and he breathed easier while quietly surveying the scene. By keeping the pace steady, so as not to tire Rebecca, Paul had succeeded in arriving somewhat fitter himself. In fact the walk had served to loosen him up better than expected. They sat down on a mound of soft grass amongst the grey rocks. The need for something to eat and drink was strong and he wanted to think about the next move. Quite deliberately they had not talked about the farm or what he might do on arrival. She could sense he would only act once he had firsthand knowledge of the area and the possible dangers. Moreover, she could also tell his mind had stepped up a gear and he was thinking clearer than she had ever known. How he had come by such a skill she had no idea, but there was no time to question him.

The village was small and surrounded by a few scattered farms. He found it hard to believe a place of such beauty could be a home to evil, yet the book had revealed that over half of the homes in the valley were lived in by Storn's people.

"Will they expect us on foot?" Rebecca eventually broke the silence, as he finished a sandwich.

He shrugged. "Which one is it? Can you feel it from up here?"

"Easily. I thought I might not at this distance, but the shield radiates strongly. From our realm it is a very precise area, but down here it is not so."

He followed her finger as she indicated down into the far end of the valley to their right.

"There," she said, pointing to a small cluster of buildings that were surrounded by fields and enclosed by walls.

"I see it," he said, nodding, and reaching out to lower her arm. "It's a long way off the main road, which means going in by car's impossible. It's also a fair way from the rest of the houses this end of the valley and half a mile to the nearest farm." He shook his head. "They've picked a good spot this time

"That is how they like it," she replied, gazing at the landscape below.

"Isolation keeps out prying eyes, but it's well within reach of a 4x4, clever. But it could work against them."

"How?" she asked

243

"With any luck they'll think I'm on the run and not walking in the backdoor," he said, lightly, to mask the already rising tension.

"You have a plan?"

"Working on it," he said, and got up. "It won't be long before darkness hides us from those below. Let's get up along the ridge and right above the place."

The cloud cover thickened as the last vestiges of sunlight disappeared behind the fells. Without further word they continued angling down across the fell side until they reached the dry-stone wall above their target. Once in place they squatted down out of sight.

"I can't believe there won't be extra security after last time," he whispered.

"I will have a brief look and see what I can pick up."

Together they peered over the top at the group of buildings making up Holthwaite farm. Furthest from them was the house, built from stone with a moss covered slate roof. Across a neatly laid tarmac yard sat a refurbished stone barn. Another barn, in obvious need of repair, was opposite it. Rebecca nodded in the general direction of the refurbished one.

"That has to be the place they are keeping him in. The field is so intense I fear I can get no closer than this."

He glanced at her and clearly saw the discomfort in her face. "That bad is it?"

She nodded and he squeezed her hand. "You stay here, it's safer. Now what else can you tell me about what or who's down there?"

She returned her attention to the target and the lights came on in the farmhouse. By instinct they both ducked under the cover of the wall.

"It's alright. I think it's only because it's getting dark," Paul whispered.

She breathed out and probed the area with her senses. "There are two men and a woman in the house. All three seem relaxed and not unduly apprehensive. In the small barn there is another man, younger, keeping watch over the yard. From his thoughts he is tired and bored, if that is a help."

"It is," Paul replied, and stole a glance over the wall in the ensuing gloom. "They're keeping better guard than last time and it'll make it difficult. I just wish I knew how many are in the main barn."

Rebecca shrugged and rubbed at the dull ache that was nagging at the base of her neck. "I cannot see anything Paul. Sorry."

"I know," he added. "I've been through this little scene before, crouching behind a wall trying to figure out the odds." As he surveyed the farm a powerful floodlight came on and swathed the yard in bright light. "I should imagine they'll have cameras and see me coming."

She realised he had come to the decision to make a move.

"If they find the Fiat in Grasmere, and I'm sure they will pretty soon, someone'll guess we're close by. The shutters will slam down so hard on this place it'll turn into a fortress we'll never penetrate."

They sat in a brief moment of silence while he mulled things over. She believed he had the makings of a plan, but nothing concrete to work on. All he knew was, like the time he had found her at Kirkham, whatever he did would have to be quick and decisive. The option was the same, straight in, hope for the best, and run away as fast as possible.

"Would you like some cover my darling?"

He looked at her, suspiciously, interested by her tone. "What sort of cover?"

She pointed skywards. "How does a good downpour and a flash or two of lightning sound?"

"Really?"

"It will not take much. The clouds are about ready for it anyway and it will only take a little enhancement from me."

"Great," he replied, slipping off the rucksack and fleece and handing them to her. "Find your way back up to the top of the ridge and wait for me there."

"How long shall I wait?"

"You'll know. Give me ten minutes before you start the diversion."

"I will," she said, and leaned across to kiss him. They both embraced. "Take good care my darling."

"You too. And get out quickly if it all goes wrong."

Once Rebecca had disappeared into the gloom, Paul scrambled over the top of the wall and began to make his way down to the farm. With her safely hidden in the darkness he had the luxury of devoting his complete attention to the task at hand.

Chapter 50

The first point Paul reached was the wall that bounded the rear of the buildings. The nearest barn had a Toyota pick-up truck parked behind it, next to a dilapidated tractor. From his position of cover he could see no one and, more importantly, no cameras. For the first time he glanced at his wristwatch and realised that Rebecca would soon begin the diversion. With that in mind he climbed over the wall, the last area of cover before the buildings, and sprinted to the pick-up truck. He paused to catch his breath and saw the scattering of items lying in the back of the truck that instantly piqued his attention. A bag of tools yielded a crowbar and, as he weighed it in his hand, the first splashes of rain began to fall.

"You're early," he whispered, and grabbed the two cans of petrol lying in the back. An inspired idea had struck him and he quickly opened the bonnet as rain drops began tapping on the metal roof of the truck. He found a gap in each side of the engine bay and wedged them in with the filler caps open. A socket spanner quickly released two of the glow plugs from the diesel engine and he hung one in each of the open cans, before closing the bonnet. If anyone attempted to start the vehicle he hoped his crude firebomb would disable it.

High up on the fell side, among the strewn rocks of the ridge, Rebecca sat in the dry as the rain purposely avoided her. In the enfolding darkness she concentrated on Holthwaite and the cosily illuminated farmhouse. Thankfully the clouds were heavy with rain and she used little of her own energy to make it fall. The only thing left was to generate the lightning and guide it to where it would do the most damage. The first objective was to deny them of power and create havoc in the house.

Inside the farmhouse, George Bell crossed over to the living room window. He grasped the exposed wooden beam above it and pressed his face against the glass. For only a few seconds he scanned the empty yard under the floodlight.

"Looks like another wet night," he commented to Rhen Stubbs.

She was in the corner, watching over a series of screens that showed what the security cameras were pointed at. A glass of red wine was next to her and she took a sip, winking at him. "At least we'll get a peaceful night. There won't be anyone stupid enough to be running about out there."

He looked at her with a sly grin as she ran a hand through dyed blonde hair. "Is that an offer?"

With another wink she lifted the side of her jumper to reveal a bare breast. "What do you think?"

"Wait till Randall does his turn at the desk," he added, picking up his own glass.

She nodded, keenly awaiting the end of her stint. Bell returned his attention to the window and pulled the curtains shut. At the same moment the lights dimmed and a brief snow of interference showed on the screens.

"Lightning," he said, helping himself to a glass of wine.

"It could turn into a colourful night," he added, and tipped the glass in a 'cheers' gesture at her.

She caught the meaning at once and began to laugh.

Chapter 51

Paul made his way to the rear of the barn with the sole intention of taking out the man inside. The only visible opening was a hole in the wall near to the corner, about three feet up. As he weighed up the distance a vivid flash struck high up in the fells about a mile from the farm.

"Nice one Rebecca," he whispered, and ran headlong to the corner. A demonic crash of thunder rode down from the hills like a juggernaut to accompany it. At the corner he sprawled onto the ground and into the shadows. The floodlight in the yard cast its glare in every direction and he caught sight of the camera as it panned past his position. For several seconds he pressed himself tight against the wall. All at once the rain began to hammer down with extraordinary ferocity. The sound augmented the fading echo of thunder. He prayed the camera had not seen him as the ground around him turned to muddy pools.

After a minute he poked his head around the corner and saw that the camera was pointed directly away from his position. Without delay he quickly discarded his soaking wet sweatshirt and pushed himself through the hole in the wall.

The road to the farm had a grass verge on each side. An accurately aimed, yellow-blue fork of lightning slammed into the wooden pylon carrying the overhead cables to the farm. The metal junction box fixed atop it exploded in a shower of sparks and debris. At the same time the powerful bolt of energy splintered the 'H' frame cleanly down the centre and it fell apart. As it did so it took the pole carrying the telephone lines too.

Inside the house, Randall ran into the darkened living room.

Rhen and Bell had been busy chatting, but were abruptly cut short when the lightning had struck in the lane outside.

"The power's off!" Randall hollered, as he flicked round the room with a torch. "Everything went with that strike."

"Better get outside," Rhen replied, retrieving a torch from the top drawer of the desk. In front of her the screens were black. "And fire up the generator. We don't want to be blind for long."

"I'm on it," he replied.

"I'll go too," Bell interjected, quickly following him out.

Rhen played the torch over the dead monitors before picking up the telephone with her free hand. She jiggled it, but it too was dead. Frustrated, she slammed it back down and swore. "Fucking weather! Phone's dead too!" she called after the two men.

The barn was in almost total darkness. Taylor slid from behind the wheel of the Land Rover and picked up the machine pistol from the passenger seat. He walked the short distance to where one of the large wooden doors had been left open. The rain drummed unceasingly on the roof as he looked outside into the darkened yard. After hours of boredom he was glad of the distraction and hoisted the gun over his shoulder. Across the yard he saw Randall emerge from the house, carrying a torch that feebly cut through the swathes of rain. For someone who had spent his entire life in the Lakes, Taylor was impressed by the sheer volume of water falling. The force was so intense it splashed back upwards in countless mini fountains. Randall saw Taylor and waved. Moments later he disappeared into the small outhouse built on the side of the house. Bell too emerged and sprinted to the open door after Randall. Seeing the two of them were busy, he pulled the mobile telephone from the pocket of his combat jacket. It was switched on, as always, and he simply pressed the first memory preset.

Chapter 52

Night had fallen on the other side of the Pennines, at Pelham Hall. Inside the control room, Scott-Wade sat on a stool, drinking coffee. He was aware of the feeling that he wanted to do something more positive, but what? Occasionally, as it had all day, the printer would spew out information. Along with Myra they would study it in an attempt to glean some useful leads, but up until then it had all proved useless. After so many years in the police force he was pretty good at assessing what the criminal mind was thinking and thought of Paul as being no different. The man was at a loss since his escape from custody. He had gone to Norwich, but not disposed of the car properly, and had been seen on the train to Sheringham. They also suspected him of sniffing around Saltmarsh, because the Reverend Pryce's car had been stolen. Perhaps he had gone there to plead his innocence, but could not afford to wait around. Whatever the reason, Sayers had to be lying low. With no family or friends to harbour him, it was just a matter of time before he surfaced. It was the waiting that angered Scott-Wade the most though. The hatred he felt after the botched interview at Clayborough still burned inside him. Myra sat nearby, seemingly ignoring the computer screens and fax machine sitting in front of her. Like him, she too had mentally planned her revenge on Paul and was filing her crimson-painted fingernails to sharp points. In the corner, seated in a sumptuous leather chair, was the commanding presence of Storn. Motionless, he sat with his eyes closed, contemplating his evil plans. He was diverting his thoughts while the wait for information continued. One of the phones on the desk sprang into life and Myra pounced on it before it had a chance to ring a second time.

"Yes," she sharply answered, and paused for several moments, listening. Then she covered the mouthpiece and looked up at Scott-Wade. "It's Holthwaite. Taylor say's there's a heavy storm raging over the farm and they've been hit by lightning. Apparently the power's down."

"They've got a generator?" he asked, standing up.

She nodded. "They're about to start it now."

"Good. Tell them to keep us informed and we'll get someone up there in the morning to put it right."

She relayed the message and replaced the handset. In the corner Storn remained silent, but began tapping his heel against the leg of the chair. Within the space of a minute the printer again chattered into life and Scott-Wade removed the single sheet.

"Useful?" Myra quizzed.

He glanced up. "It's from Norfolk. It seems the vicar's car has turned up."

"Where?" Storn barked.

"They've found it in a public car park in Grasmere."

"So, if Sayers did take it...?" Myra started, as the penny dropped with all of them.

Scott-Wade almost leaped to one of the maps behind her. The area was quite familiar and he immediately went to Padrigg, tracing a line with his fingertip.

"Oh, shit," he cursed. "Grasmere's only a few miles away from Holthwaite over the fells."

"What!" Storn bellowed, jumping to his feet.

Scott-Wade looked pained in reply. "The bastard could've been in Grasmere hours ago. How could he have found the facility so quickly?"

"We've underestimated him yet again," Myra angrily spat. "He could cause no end of damage there. We've got to kill the son of a bitch now!"

Storn slammed a fist down on top of one of the monitors and rounded on her. "The storm has been created by the Guardian woman. She is there with him. Inform Holthwaite I want them alive."

She snatched the nearest phone and dialled at speed.

252

"And tell them to kill the child immediately," he added, as if it was an afterthought. She nodded, waiting to be answered, but gave them a blank look. "The line to the house must be down too."

"Call Taylor back on his mobile! Tell him!" Scott-Wade frantically instructed, snatching up a telephone himself. "I'll alert everyone in Padrigg village and get them up there. After that, everyone we have in a hundred mile radius. We'll flood the area."

Storn nodded. "We'd better bring the helicopter up from Manchester in the morning. It'll give us better ground coverage."

"Good," Storn oozed, with evil confidence. "This time there will be no underestimating, no mistakes. Once I have the Guardian, Sayers can provide me with his soul. It will be fitting that such a pathetic irritation will feed me so that I can take his woman."

Chapter 53

At Holthwaite, Taylor stood watching the ferocious storm rage outside. The house held all of his attention as he waited for either Bell or Randall to appear from the outhouse. The wait was not long. Through the unremitting rainfall the sound of the generator starting up could be heard. A scant second later the lights inside the house and the main floodlight blazed into life. He breathed a sigh of relief and saw Randall sprint from the open doorway back to the shelter of the house. Taylor had no time to relax though. The atmosphere around him crackled with electrical energy. Outside, a fierce bolt of power slammed into the house as he stood rooted in helpless fascination. The side of it blew outwards and toppled into the roof of the outhouse below. Several huge sections of stone and mortar, followed by the tall chimney stack, crashed heavily through the tiles and onto the generator. It was accompanied by a rent of thunder, tearing the heavens open like a bomb, and the outhouse collapsed. The lights winked out in an instant, to return the rain-drenched yard to darkness.

Taylor took a long step backwards into the barn, shaking in shock, and with his eyes filled by the intense flash of lightning. It was something he had never seen before, or would ever do again, nature's unrestrained fury. Despite the shake up, his senses were alert enough to warn him that something was amiss and he spun round with the feeling someone was behind him. Unsure, he peered into the dark-filled shadows while he stood safe in the glow cast by the Land Rover's courtesy light. As his eyes adjusted he could make out the silhouette of a man standing at the rear of the car. A pool of water, growing at his boot clad feet, showed he was soaking wet. The face was not visible, but Taylor could see the crowbar in his right hand and guessed he was looking for trouble.

"Who the fuck are you?" he asked, coarsely, as his hand closed around the stock of the rifle hanging from his shoulder. "This is private property."

The mobile in Taylor's pocket trilled into life. For a reason he would never be able to explain, he looked down and used his free hand to reach for it.

Paul needed no other opportunity than the one handed to him by the distraction. Until the time he had rescued Rebecca from a similar situation, he would never have attacked another person without thought or good reason. But he knew how deep the evil ran in Storn's followers and had no such misgivings with them. He took two steps and slammed the crowbar hard into the hand gripping the rifle. Taylor screeched in agony as his fingers and knuckles splintered against the unyielding stock of the weapon. A perfectly executed crash of thunder masked the sound within the walls of the barn. The injured youth fell jarringly to the floor, dropping the rifle and telephone. It continued to ring and Paul stamped on it with his heel. Taylor looked up as it went silent, crying as the pain raged in his shattered hand.

"Call 'em back," Paul growled, and picked up the discarded machine pistol. He then looked down into the pale features of a youth who was little more than eighteen years of age. He was still freckled and had the makings of a beard, but the eyes stared at him in disbelief.

"Who are you? Why have you hurt me?" he whimpered.

Paul snorted, hardly able to believe him and knowing that he would have shot him without question, given the chance. Paul tipped Taylor's head back by putting the muzzle of the gun under his chin and pressing. The brown eyes widened further and his face drained of what little colour there was left.

"Didn't they tell you about some bastard named Sayers?"

Taylor nodded dumbly against the restriction under his chin.

"Well I'm here."

The face was recognisable and identical to the photograph they had all been issued with weeks before. Even in a shocked state he realised why Paul was there and of the significant fact that he had failed to guard against him.

"I know the boy's in the other barn," Paul continued. "And, as you've just found out, I'll stop at nothing to release him. Understand?" Although they had been told Holthwaite would never be discovered, the defences in place were considerable. Despite some of the senior members ridiculing Sayers, others still rated him a threat. Now Taylor believed it too, with his hand broken and no chance of turning the tables on his assailant.

"Now!" Paul snapped, digging the muzzle into his throat. "Make it easy or make it hard, I don't much mind which way you choose, how many are in there with him?"

"Don't hurt me," he bleated.

He jammed it upward another fraction. "How many?"

"Three," Taylor squeaked.

"Armed?"

Again he nodded, as the tears of pain, fear, and failure, ran freely down his cheeks.

"Is there a signal to get inside?"

"Yes, but I don't know what it is. Believe me," he pleaded, seeing the determination in Paul's face. "They'll never let you in," he added trying to gather his senses. "If you don't hurt me, and go, I won't say anything."

Paul half smiled. "As if."

Taylor could only wince, helplessly, as Paul whipped the butt of the gun into the side of his head. The pain exploded and he crumpled sideways in a heap. Unceremoniously, Paul dragged the inert youth from out of the path of the Land Rover and removed his combat jacket. It was dry and he slipped it on over his own sopping wet clothes. The pockets felt heavy and after a check he found a 9mm pistol in one and several spare magazines in the other. He shook his head and zipped them back up. There was no time to lose and he felt sure that whoever had been cut off on the telephone would be trying to make contact through other sources. Events had swiftly taken on a certain amount of momentum and he did not want to slow things down by considering plans of attack. He went to the main doors and kicked the closed one wide open. Outside the rain was still falling in a torrent and the yard was awash with water.

"Great special effects, my angel," he whispered, into the darkness. "But lay off a bit on the wet stuff."

The other barn was in darkness, the doors firmly shut, and there seemed no sign of life. Over at the house though, he could make out a figure clawing frantically at the pile of rubble burying the outhouse. Randall stopped for a moment and looked across, his face indistinct.

"Come here Taylor!" he yelled. "Bell's buried under this lot!"

Paul just heard what he said and realised that in the combat jacket he had been mistaken for the youth. They were not aware of him and he was going to take full advantage of the deception. He waved back.

"I'm on my way!"

Seeing the acknowledgement, Randall returned to the task of digging, oblivious to the danger. Paul turned on his heels and sprinted back to the Land Rover, while mentally thanking Rebecca for reducing the odds. Once in the driver's seat he started the sturdy 4x4. There were two large canvas bags on the seat beside him. Both were open and he quickly went through the contents. The first contained another machine pistol and several dozen magazines. He slipped several into a vacant pocket of his jacket and also pulled out two grenade type canisters crudely marked 'stun'. The second bag contained a pump action shotgun with several boxes of cartridges and a dozen grenades. Lying under the bags was a Russian-made assault rifle, with two magazines taped together ready to fire, and a polished wooden box.

"Bugger this," Paul said, with a low whistle. "The bastards are ready for war."

He leaned across and wound down the window before opening the wooden box. Inside was a dismantled automatic rifle, with hi-tech sights and a laser target illuminator. He clipped it shut and shoved it inside the canvas bag with the other machine pistol and magazines. For good measure he also put in it six of the grenades and zipped it up. It was forward planning and the only way he would ever be able to arm himself for an unknown future. With the engine ticking over he flicked on the headlamps and high-intensity driving lamps. The whole of the barn's interior was instantly illuminated as he engaged four-wheel drive and screeched outside.

Randall heard the squeal of tyres above the rain and, with a brick in each hand, turned to see what was happening.

"What the...?" he began, as the Land Rover, its lights blazing and dazzling him, careered across the yard. He held up a hand to shield his eyes as it slewed sideways to a halt only yards from where he stood. Puzzled, by what he took to be Taylor's strange behaviour, he studied it. In those few moments his puzzlement reached a perverse enlightenment when he saw the face of the man behind the wheel. He silently mouthed the name, 'Sayers', and dropped the bricks. Randall could have sworn that Paul smiled, when he said his name, but his eyes quickly focussed on the assault rifle poking through the open window. Turning, he leapt onto the pile of rain-soaked rubble as Paul emptied the magazine in one long slashing burst. With his heart pounding, Randall sprawled across the debris, unable to move, and felt the searing agony of pain blossom in his legs and waist. Above the noise of the storm he could hear the sound of another weapon being fired, this time from the house.

"Go on Rhen," he mutedly urged. "Kill the bastard."

The shots from the house caught Paul off-guard, for a second, and he ducked down below the level of the windscreen. The hail of bullets shattered the screen and peppered the bodywork. He quickly slammed into reverse and weaved backwards across the skidpan-like surface. The Land Rover came to a slithering stop back inside the barn. He poked his head over the dashboard and could see, in the headlights, the crouching figure in the doorway. She had stopped firing and was busy reloading. Paul took the opportunity too and quickly changed the magazine of his assault rifle. A moment later he felt the immense static in the air. Instinctively, he looked up at the storm-filled sky through the shattered screen. It seemed to be in slow motion, but the powerful bolt of electrical energy arced towards the house in anything other than a gentle manner. The sheer ferocity of nature was guided by Rebecca's hand and raked savagely into the already damaged roof. Paul watched, with cold fascination, as the woman tried vainly to get up and run. Above her the roof and part of the upper wall exploded in a shower of masonry, tiles, and woodwork. She had stood up, but he saw her disappear under the cascading torrent of debris.

Back at Pelham, Myra was still desperately trying to ring Taylor's mobile. Exasperated, she slammed the phone down as Scott-Wade finished speaking on the other line.

"His phone's dead," she told them both.

Scott-Wade smiled. "Don't worry, the bastard's cornered. All of our people in the village will be there in a few minutes."

She looked at him, but was unconvinced by his assured tone. Sayers was anything but predictable.

Chapter 54

Paul took a few seconds to gather himself before tackling the barn. He did not have the required signal to get in and was not about to go up and knock on the door. The choice was to ram the entrance with the Land Rover and take it from there. The right hand door had a smaller entry door built into it and he reckoned on it being the weakest point to aim for. Without delaying further, he gunned the Land Rover across the yard. Just before it hit he ducked below the windscreen. With the horn blaring like a strangled war cry, the bulky 4x4 smashed into the doors amidst the sound of splintering wood. With the doors demolished the car halted inside the barn, coming to rest on top of them. Paul took a deep breath and kicked open his door as the sounds of destruction gave way to that of rain thundering on the roof. Briefly, he peered over the dashboard and saw only one headlamp working from the battered front end. There was a flash to the left and bullets rattled into the side of the car.

"Nasty," he whispered, dipping backwards out of the seat. As he went he emptied the last rounds from the assault rifle just above head height into that side of the barn. Momentarily the gunfire stopped and he discarded the weapon for a machine pistol. Seconds later shorter bursts began issuing from the corner. He crouched beside the car and swiftly surveyed the surroundings in the poor light. Close to his right he could make out the edge of the shattered door and saw an arm, still clutching a rifle, sticking out from beneath it.

'One down, two to go.'

Another burst rattled into the other side and he silently cursed them. He knew it was accomplishing little, just sitting there, but he would not risk returning fire unless he became desperate.

Somewhere in the shadows was Jason and he could not risk hitting the boy just to have a go. Again he fired a burst over the top, to show he was not a sitting target, but was met by return fire of greater ferocity.

"Shit," he cursed, and leaned in low across the seats to salvage the two canisters marked 'stun'. They had pins in the top, like grenades, and he pulled both out at the same time, before tossing them into the corner. When they clattered against the wall he sprinted outside, using the car for cover. Even above the downpour he distinctly heard them go off. Without waiting he ran back inside. There were two figures, a man and woman, staggering into the light cast by the car. There was no time for niceties. He grasped them both by the hair and banged their heads together.

"Bingo," he cried, as they fell unconscious to the ground at his feet. The impossible had been achieved and he had dealt with all of Storn's guards. The victory celebrations, if that was what they were, were short-lived and he immediately began a frantic search of the barn.

"Jason!" he shouted. "Jason!"

At the rear of the barn he stumbled upon the altar where Storn partook of his ritual killings. He was sickened and felt the residual terror of those who had met their dreadful end there. On top of the polished black marble he saw the golden sword, lying waiting for the next victim, Jason. The feeling persisted until he tore himself from it and crossed to the other corner. In the darkness he stumbled upon a bundle on the floor and quickly knelt down next to the bound and hooded figure. It was Jason and he pulled the hood off his head. Thankfully he was still breathing, although it was clear he was either unconscious or drugged. With some reluctance he went back to the altar and retrieved the sword. The fearsome blade buzzed with static in his hand and he held it just long enough to cut the boy's bonds, before tossing it away. There was little time to waste and he carried Jason to the Land Rover. He laid him on the passenger seat and realised the rain was lessening outside.

"It's gonna be a rough ride kid," he warned, and reversed into the yard. A brief glance over his shoulder showed that there were lights in the road. The reinforcements alerted by Scott-Wade were fast approaching.

"Shit!" he swore, as shades of what had occurred after he had rescued Rebecca flashed through his mind. He reversed speedily towards the open gateway.

John and Clara Stubbs had been the first ones to be warned about the possible events taking place at Holthwaite. Within minutes they had raced up from the village in their Suzuki Jeep, determined to be the first there. Clara was still loading an automatic pistol when they reached the entrance.

"Power's down," he said, seeing the wires lying useless across the road. Then, without warning, the Land Rover burst into the light cast by their headlamps. It did nothing to slow down and hit them at an angle. The jarring collision forced the lighter vehicle sideways, into the wall and gatepost. They both sat stunned as it drew away and halted. Through the cracked, rain lashed windscreen, they saw Paul step out.

"Jesus!" Stubbs cried. "Get out Clara!"

"I can't," she wailed. "My door's jammed."

"Duck!"

Paul raked the front of the jeep with gunfire, tearing the tyres apart and shattering the headlights. The gate was blocked. He jumped back in and raced away down the yard.

Inside the disabled Suzuki, Stubbs sat numb with shock, as Clara buried her face in her hands and cried. He had recognised their assailant as Sayers, as warned, and he had come within a fraction of killing them both, but had chosen not to. Unsteadily, he climbed out. Steam issued from the sides of the bonnet where the radiator had been holed. Even with the lights out he knew the place well enough to walk into the yard proper. Clara had recovered her composure and followed with a powerful lantern. The stark white beam played upon the pile of rubble that had once been the side of the house. On another smaller pile lay the body of Randall, beyond their help and destined to die from his injuries. The front doors of the holding barn were down, with bodies everywhere and the boy gone. He shook his head in disbelief and saw Clara looking wide-eyed at him.

"We were lucky John."

He nodded. "Sayers is a killer. Just look at this mess. You'd think he was a bloody one-man army." He reached for the mobile phone in his jacket and pressed a familiar number. As it connected, the lights and sounds of approaching vehicles came from behind them. The telltale voice of Myra answered at the other end.

"It's not good," he began.

Chapter 55

The Land Rover flew through the farmyard, out between the barns, and into the fields beyond. It had not been in Paul's initial thinking to drive out, but the impending arrival of a posse of Storn's people left him no option. He had to put as much distance between himself and the farm before abandoning the car. However, it would eventually run out of momentum when the upslope of the fell became too much to cope with. In four-wheel drive mode the chunky tyres bit deep into the grass and found plenty of traction. What were left of the lights he switched off, not wanting to show those below which direction he was heading. There was some delight that it was quicker than walking, but none in forging a new path where one should not have been. The rain had been left behind and he sat dripping wet in the seat. His trousers stuck to him like a second skin and he played with the heater controls until the fan began blasting hot air.

"That's better," he said, out loud, as in the next moment the Land Rover ploughed through the upper boundary wall.

"Bugger it," he cried, bucking over and through the demolished wall, slightly losing speed. "I forgot that was there."

The incline increased further as he gained altitude and increasingly he had to zigzag to keep any sort of progress possible. Minutes later the car clattered and bounced into the jumble of outlying rocks that marked the crag line just below the ridge. That was the limit in the dark and he stopped. Silence invaded the car once the motor died. He clambered out and surveyed the scene. Down below, the lights of the village were easy to pick out although the farm was still in darkness. There were vehicles in the road outside and it would not take them long to clear the gate and he knew he would have to be moving on. He made his way to the rear of the car and stepped into one of the neat furrows the tyres had carved into the soft ground. Although he had left the lights off, to avoid detection, they could easily follow the tracks. A new sense of urgency gripped his actions, as a ball of fire erupted skywards from the direction of the farm. Moments later a dull 'boom' carried to the lofty position and he saw more flames. A smile of grim satisfaction briefly crossed his lips. The crude bomb he had left had been detonated. It was clear they were using the pick-up truck to save time; instead he had saved himself time and possibly more. The firebomb gave him another idea and he went to the passenger side. Jason was still out of it and he lifted him out and onto the grass. The canvas bag filled with weapons was laid beside him and he took two further grenades from the other. He then knocked the car out of gear and released the handbrake. Almost at once it began to roll backwards down the hillside and he ran beside it. At the last moment, he pulled the pins and tossed the grenades through the open window. He quickly dropped to his bottom to halt his descent and watched the Land Rover disappear rapidly into the darkness. Several hundred feet below, the two explosions occurred together. The car was moving fast and instantly turned into a fireball. Halfway down the slope it skidded sideways, flipping onto its side. The energy it contained still carried it downwards though, in a decreasing series of end-over-end tumbles, scattering burning wreckage in every direction. The largest section of chassis and engine finally crashed into the wall at the boundary, halting it.

At the farm, the followers were still struggling with those injured by the firebomb. They fled in all directions as the Land Rover exploded and headed towards them at speed.

"He's lost it!" someone shouted.

"Get some torches up there and check!" another called, when the wreckage finally came to a halt. Chaos reigned because not one of them chose to, or had the willpower to, take control. The initial success was indeed with Paul and Rebecca.

High in the darkness above Holthwaite, Paul had thrown Jason over his shoulder and was carrying the canvas bag in his free hand. On foot, he began the steady climb to the top of the ridge and

Rebecca. She had waited in the dry, sensing and watching the events unfurl below, knowing exactly when he was safe. Without him feeling it, she read his thoughts and got to her feet. With the rucksack on her back she began walking, sensing where it was they would eventually meet along the ridge. She was satisfied that things had gone well. However, she knew it was a long way from being over.

Chapter 56

The control room at Pelham Hall was quiet, apart from the occasional replies of 'yes' or 'no' from Scott-Wade as he answered various telephone calls. Myra was watching him, trying to glean the outcome of events by his mood. Persephone was sitting on the table by the door. She had heard that something was going on and had stopped to listen in. Sipping at a mug of milky coffee, she ventured no opinions until asked. The clock on the wall showed it was past midnight and Storn paced under it, menacingly. The news was gradually filtering through that it was not going their way. Behind the black, lifeless eyes his mind worked quickly on the unfolding series of events. Outwardly, to the others in the room, he seethed in anger and frustration, which disturbed them as it was supposed to do. However, in his own mind he was not overly concerned. There was frustration that Sayers had once again caused disruption, but it had to be accepted. He had help from the Guardians, which would give some advantage over his followers, but not in everything. The game of give and take would continue as he expected it too. The domination and victory he wanted to secure had been in the building for decades of mere mortals' time. It would come because he had the patience to succeed. In the meantime he would play the part for those gathered around to serve him. It kept them in a servile and obedient manner. They were weak of mind and feared his apparent, evil unpredictability. All of them had been deliberately selected because of their deeply rooted evil nature and he had cultivated them to the point of their sole reliance on his ability to feed it.

'Yes,' he said, to himself. 'Your time will come, Sayers.' But the others did not need to know that. They would see only a facade of anger and impatience to spur them on.

267

Scott-Wade replaced the receiver and looked across at him.

"Well?" Storn snapped.

"It's not good."

"What about the facility?" Myra asked.

"Useless for now," he replied, without looking directly at her. "The doors are down on the holding area. The house has been partially demolished on top of them. John Stubbs says his sister's dead, along with Randall, Bell, and Hughes in the barn. Sayers left some sort of car bomb that took out Parr and left three others badly burned." He then looked at her. "It's a total mess. With Randall gone there's no-one there to take control."

"Sayers?"

"Unsure. The boy's gone too. Moments after the car bomb went off, the Land Rover he'd escaped in crashed in flames. They're combing the wreckage, but haven't found anything yet."

Instinctively, Myra glanced at Persephone, who simply shook her head to the unasked question. "He got out."

"Are you sure?" Scott-Wade snapped, and spun round to face her.

She ran a hand through her blonde hair. "Positive."

"How can you be so sure?"

"She can be!" Storn bellowed. "It will be light in a matter of hours and he is on foot. Surround all the access points and roads in that area around the fells. Make it a six mile radius from Holthwaite and make sure there are no gaps."

"It's a lot of area to cover."

Storn fixed him in a cold stare that made him shiver. "I care not for the size of area. Now take control of this!"

Scott-Wade nodded and crossed to the large scale map of the Lakes. "He's carrying an unconscious boy. It'll slow him down. We can put a vehicle on each road and get teams of two roving across the fells from all the known paths."

"Can we use the helicopter?" Myra asked.

He pointed to one spot. "Get them airborne at first light and send them across to Castle Rake. Just here."

"Why there?"

"It's a difficult path down a cliff face in one area where we

268

can't get to quickly on foot. From there he could easily mingle with the regular streams of walkers who head up into the high ground beyond. If he's smart he'll go that way in an attempt to evade us."

"Not back across to Grasmere? It's quicker." Myra offered.

He shook his head. "He'll assume we've found the car. And, with crags each side descending back into Grasmere, we'll only need one vehicle there to keep watch."

"How about the reserve chopper in Cambridgeshire?" she added, picking up the nearest telephone.

He nodded. "It'll take the best part of the morning to get here."

"Just get on with it!" Storn barked, and immediately left the room.

In the ensuing silence Persephone slipped off the table and downed the last of her coffee. "I'm going to bed."

"Wait!" Scott-Wade ordered, as her hand closed around the door handle. "Just whose side are you really on, little Miss know-it-all?"

Slowly, without a trace of emotion on her features, she turned to face him. "Anger, tetchiness, and impatience won't catch Paul Sayers. His thinking has reached a new level. He's become stronger. If you continue to underestimate him, you'll fail again." She glanced across to Myra. "Goodnight Mother, I'll see you early in the morning."

She felt a new respect growing for her daughter and how she was turning into a smart, useful young woman. At first she felt aggrieved that Persephone was not like her, in possessing the skills of reading the Tarot. But somehow she had gained a different gift. One that was possibly more useful.

"We can't trust her," Scott-Wade said, when she had left.

Myra seemed bemused. "Don't be silly Tony, of course we can. She won't let us down. What you've failed to notice is that she's growing up."

"I haven't," he replied. "And neither have a lot of the others."

"I might've guessed."

"They're not happy to see her under Storn's protection, walking around untouched."

"It all boils down to sex, doesn't it? With Sayers running around unchecked, it's a pity they don't concentrate on him for a while and keep their trousers zipped up," she quickly replied.

He shrugged. "Just thought you'd want to know what's being said."

"I knew anyway," she said, and pointed to the telephones. "Com'on, let's get everyone organised and in place for the morning. If we can cover the fells he's as good as ours."

Chapter 57

Friday 28th May 1993

Paul woke just before the early light of dawn penetrated the sparse cloud cover above Rough Crag. Although he had never climbed Rough Crag before, he had explored the range to the east on a previous visit. In front of them lay the sprawling top of Dunter Fell, with its rocky summit and marshy grassland flanks. It was misleading to think it was uninteresting to either climb or visit. Beyond the summit lay the impressive cliff of Scythe Crag and a treacherous switchback path down its near-one-thousand-feet of face called Castle Rake. He had ascended the narrow, scree-covered slog just once, but it had been exhausting. It was, though, the quickest way down, onto a series of well-used paths where they could mix with other walkers. The plan would only work if Rebecca and the boy were up to it. He turned to look at them, huddled together in a bright orange survival bag next to him, and hoped they would soon wake. There was an urgency to be moving, but they could not travel far or fast with Jason still knocked out from the drugs. Rebecca had assured him that he was perfectly healthy, apart from a lack of food. The knowledge that Storn would put people into the area to search for them was at the forefront of Paul's thoughts. He needed the boy able to walk on his own and not have to carry him. If that became the case he knew they would have to dump the weapons. It was an option, but not one he wanted to take. The previous night they had walked over three miles across the fells in an effort to put distance between themselves and the farm. In the end they needed to rest and had found a sheltered hollow in which to make rudimentary camp. The two of them had shared the only means of cover, the survival bag, and he had simply laid down on the softest piece of ground he could find. Paul leaned across and lightly kissed Rebecca on the cheek. Her hair was tousled, but, despite the early hour and previous night's events, she looked beautiful. In an instant she came awake, her blue eyes flicking open like sparkling jewels to greet him.

"Good morning, my angel. You look gorgeous this morning."

"And you too ..." she began, but her eyes seemed to look straight through him. As he saw the expression on her face he heard the ominous 'click' from behind and cursed inwardly.

"Get your hands in the air now, Sayers. Stand up!" the gruff voice ordered.

Slowly, he rose to his feet and turned to face what he assumed would be an armed group. Instead, standing just a few feet away on the edge of the crag was a short, stocky man with his face smeared in dark camouflage cream. He was dressed in khaki trousers, jacket, and cap. A small rucksack was on his back and he had a rifle with telescopic sights levelled at Paul's chest.

"Don't move an inch," he calmly added. "I'll wound if I have to."

Paul said nothing, hoping that he was, as first appeared, alone.

"You've got a lot to answer for, Sayers," he continued, taking a couple of steps towards him. "They're queuing up to take a piece outta yer arse. Especially Myra Stanford."

"Another sad, twisted bitch," he replied, knowing she would never be far from the scene. The man simply snorted as Paul studied him in the early light. He was careful, calm, and obviously used to working on his own. Perhaps he was a hunter of some kind and used to stalking prey alone. This time though he was stalking a different game, not an animal, them.

"What got you out of bed so early?"

"A reward," he replied and stepped closer. "Just because you put a pair of boots, it doesn't make you an expert round here Sayers. I know the land like the back of my hand. You've been laughably easy to find."

"Then why aren't the rest of the rabid mob here then?" he asked, indifferently.

"No point in sharing."

'Big mistake,' Paul thought. 'You may be calm, but greed will be your undoing.'

The hunter stopped, just two paces from him, and looked him up and down. A set of perfect white teeth showed in a self-satisfied smile as he looked down at Rebecca and Jason, lying helpless in the confines of the survival bag.

"Just stay where you are, bitch," he growled. "Otherwise your boyfriend loses what gives you pleasure between the legs."

Paul could only watch as he pointed the rifle at his lower leg.

"You'll cause me no trouble when you have to hobble down the mountain, Sayers." An evil smirk crossed his lips. "Don't worry, I'll make it clean. You won't bleed to death." He again glanced at Rebecca. "Same goes for you, bitch. If you go anywhere, I'll blow his head off."

She only nodded while at the same time switched her concentration to a ball sized rock sitting on the ground close by. With a burst of raw energy, she propelled the jagged chunk of stone upward. The hunter was taken completely by surprise as it slammed into the rifle, tearing it from his hands.

"What the..?" he gasped, in alarm.

Paul was the least surprised by the turn of events and used the opportunity to leap at him. The hunter was too late to avoid being dived on. Rebecca quickly extracted herself from the confines of the bag as she saw the two men tumble out of sight over the edge of the crag. Hardly daring to look, she peered over the rock-strewn edge. Twenty feet below, where the grassy slope was dotted all over with projections of bare grey rock, she saw movement. Paul was struggling to his feet, rubbing at his bruised shoulder and elbow, and she breathed a sigh of relief.

"Are you all right?!" she called down.

He waved back. "I'm still in one piece!"

Beside him the hunter was laying on his back, staring into the sky, his neck broken by the jagged lump of stone he had collided with. There was only relief that he would not have to fight the man and started to go through his pockets.

It took Paul several minutes to climb back up through the rocks. He was delighted to see Jason sitting up and eating a packet of crisps. Rebecca was delving into the rucksack for more food and smiled as he approached.

"Our guest is feeling hungry," she explained.

"So I see," he replied. "Glad to see you've woken up Jason. We're not here to hurt you."

"I guessed that much," he replied, with a smile, and ran a hand back through his uncombed brown hair. It was clear he had not washed for several days, his clothes were dirty, but he appeared in reasonable health. He was tall for his eleven years, with a boyish face, freckles, and blue eyes that seemed to run in the family.

"Here are some more sandwiches. They're from our would-be captor down there," Paul said, passing him a foil wrapped packet.

"Great," he said, gleefully accepting the offered food.

From another pocket, Paul took out the mobile phone he had taken from the dead man. Rebecca glanced across at him, mentally checking him over to see if he was alright. He could almost sense it and smiled back with deep affection. She blew him a kiss while at the same time tried to tidy her tangled hair. Despite the early hour, he phoned the vicarage. It buzzed for a full minute before it was answered, by the sleep-filled voice of David Pryce.

"Do you realise the time?"

"I thought you'd be up writing the sermon for Sunday," Paul cheerfully replied.

"Paul?" was the suddenly wide-awake response. "Where on earth are you?"

"The Lakes. I've someone here who wants a word or two." He handed it immediately to Jason.

"Hello Uncle David."

"Thank the Lord. You're safe and well my boy?"

"Yes, Uncle David. Tell Mum I'll be home soon."

"I will, you're in good hands Jason, put Paul back on." He handed the telephone back and continued to eat the sandwich that was in his other hand.

"How's it going Paul?"

"We're getting there, but we're not out of the woods yet. There's a long way to go and the bad guys are already on our tails."

"Anything I can do?"

"Keep it in the family and keep praying."

"That goes without saying, Paul," he replied, in all seriousness. "When do you think you'll get here?"

"I can't be sure, but at least another day."

"Something's cropped up for Monday morning. It's something really important that we can't avoid."

"Like what?" Paul asked.

"We're opening the new village community centre and the American First Lady is coming to perform the ceremony."

"The President's wife? You don't do things by half."

"Someone did some research and found that her original family came from round here. The Parish council wrote to her. No-one expected her to come, it's a total surprise."

Paul shook his head. "Well, we won't ruin the party. I'll do my best to get Jason back to you by Sunday evening."

"Godspeed, Paul."

"Thanks." He flicked off the phone and looked at Rebecca. "Can you sense anybody else nearby?"

She shook her head. "I can feel at quite a distance, although it tends to get vague in identifying individuals." She pointed further along the ridge. "There are two men down there, some distance away, and they appear to be sleeping. After that there is no-one remotely near enough to see us."

"They'll be walkers, camping. Right you two, let's be going."

Chapter 58

The flat, rocky summit of Dunter Fell held no secrets on three of its un-forbidding sides and could be easily passed by without exploration. However, the east-facing side of its two and a half thousand feet altitude gave rise to the impressive cliff known as Scythe Crag. There was but one way either up or down, a narrow, scree-covered path that switched back and forth for over fifteen hundred feet. Carved out by long forgotten locals, Castle Rake suffered from severe erosion and as such was often bypassed by serious fell-walkers. Thankfully, its remoteness meant that tourists tended to leave it alone too. The early sunlight had lost the battle against the cloud and seemed happy to let a light overcast rule the sky. A westerly breeze cooled the air, but had no effect on those descending the path. Far below, the dark waters of Scythe Tarn rippled invitingly and sheep grazed with hardly a murmur. Castle Rake was familiar to countless walkers, but was an environment suitable only for the experienced. Paul had entered the obvious downward slope with due caution and respect, watching for the worst of the erosion. By choice, he was leading the way, with Rebecca and Jason a few yards behind. They were making progress, but it was not as quick as he had first hoped for. Above them, the top of the path was little more than two hundred feet away and they had taken nearly twenty minutes to descend just that. Rebecca was not an accomplished walker and Jason, despite his cheery disposition, was far from fit after his ordeal. As he turned and went down another of the switchbacks he could hear the two of them chatting above. Then, a faint, but distinctive manmade noise wafted over the top of the cliff and filtered down to them. The sound brought him to an immediate stop as he strained to listen for it. Rebecca sensed he had tensed and stopped too.

"What is it?" she called, adjusting the rucksack on her back. In reply he held up a hand to silence her, straining his hearing against the rush of wind gusting up the face past them. With a growing unease he silently cursed their luck. The all too obvious 'thwack-thwack' suddenly pierced the air above them. All three looked skywards as the increasing volume of noise burst over the edge, with just feet to spare. The Bell Jet Ranger helicopter swiftly, yet deliberately, flew outwards into a left hand arc to bring it back into line with the cliff face. Paul looked down and could only just make out the partially obscured path as it disappeared from sight beneath them. There were still several hundred carefully placed steps to go and absolutely no cover. The helicopter was level with them and he threw caution to the wind. In an effort to divide the attention of the crew, he began a headlong dash down the scree-covered slope. With his feet just keeping him upright on the shifting sea of loose rock, he reached the subsequent downward turn of the path. There he slipped over and slid the next thirty feet on his stomach before dragging himself to a stop with his hands. He quickly struggled to his feet, ignoring his badly grazed knees and palms, in an attempt to be moving again. A hail of bullets peppered the rock face inches to his left and brought his crazy descent to a halt.

The loud mechanical buzzing of the helicopter filled the air and Paul could see it hovering about forty feet from the cliff just above him. It had rotated through one-hundred and eighty degrees so that the open cabin was facing them. The current of air, channeling up from the ground far below, made the machine bob in its position. Paul could clearly see the sniper, sitting in the open cabin, with a radio headset on and a semi-automatic rifle pointing in his direction. As if defeated, he slowly made the point of raising his arms above his head. It would pass as a show of hopeless defeat, although he still had the automatic pistol in his pocket.

Watkins grinned with evil satisfaction at the early find and capture. He spoke coldly and confidently to the pilot through the microphone.

"They're in the bag. Give the word, Smithy, and Sayers is dead."

"Patience," Smith calmly replied, deftly moving the helicopter closer to the face of Scythe Crag. As he looked back through the large expanse of cockpit glazing he could see Paul, standing with his hands on his head and with a canvas bag slung over his back. Just above he could also see the other main prize, the woman Storn so much wanted. Both were cornered like animals in a trap. He was satisfied and smiled too. "He's brought them the wrong way. They're ours for the taking. I'll call it in and see what they want to do."

"Okay, I'll keep him covered from here. He's not carrying any weapons."

Smith keyed an outside radio channel. "Air one to ground, over."

The crackle of static filled their headsets before the familiar voice of Myra acknowledged them. "Base here, one. What do you have?"

"Three rats in a barrel, over."

"Whereabouts?" came her excited reply.

"They're stuck halfway down Castle Rake. There's nowhere to hide or go. What do you want us to do? Over."

The voice in the headphones immediately changed to the more powerful tones of Storn. "Kill the boy, now! Then shoot the woman in the legs. It will serve to keep Sayers there. If he tries to run, wound him too. I want them both alive. Understand?"

"Backup?"

"Coming," Myra added.

"Roger that. Over and out," Smith firmly replied, and switched back to the internal intercom. "You heard it, Dave. Do the kid and kneecap the bird."

"You bet," he replied, with obvious relish. Rebecca and Jason were standing side by side like two targets lined up at a fairground sideshow. Casually, he clicked the weapon from automatic to single shot and nestled his eye in along the sights. "Up a bit, Smithy."

"Will do," he said, and skillfully manoeuvred the Bell as it rode the current of air.

From where she was, Rebecca could see and sense that the aircraft was coming up to their level. If anything, one or both of them was the intended target. She had begun to form a plan of preventing the attack, but knew it would take an awful lot out of her to succeed. In a last moment of desperation she reached out to Paul's thoughts and saw that he was already ahead of her. Instead of executing her own idea she concentrated on deflecting the attention of the helicopter's occupants.

Paul had no idea that Rebecca was aware of what he was doing. He could see only that the sniper had switched his attention away from him. With the helicopter rising he guessed they were about to shoot Rebecca in a bid to prevent her leaving. Several drops of cold sweat ran down his face, despite his exertions, as the reality of the situation hit home. There was just one chance, with their attention momentarily diverted. He withdrew the automatic from his pocket and locked both hands firmly around it. It took less than a second to aim and fire twice.

Watkins, with his thoughts subdued by Rebecca, had blanked Paul from his mind for several fatal seconds. He had coldly lined up Jason in the crosshairs and was speaking to the pilot. "Okay, Smithy. One shot. What are yer giving?"

Smith eagerly replied to the sickening challenge. "A hundred to two if you take the left eye cleanly."

"Done. Have yer wallet ready." With precision, born out of endless practice and cold calculating ease, he settled his breathing and looked down the sights one final time. The boy was as still as a statue and Watkins smiled in evil confidence. "Say goodnight," he whispered.

The words were the last he spoke. The first shot tore through the top of his head, pitching him over backwards into the open cabin, splashing blood all over the seats. The second bullet slammed harmlessly into the padded roof area above the pilot's head, making him whirl round. Smith was taken by complete surprise, but was even more shocked by the sight that greeted him in the cabin. The sprawled, bleeding, and obviously dead Watkins was lying across the seats. The bearded face still held the evil smirk, even though the top of his head had opened out like a flower and his lifeless eyes stared heavenwards in pure astonishment.

"Oh shit!" Smith swore, glancing to the path below.

"Get down!" Paul screamed, trying to be heard above the heavy drum of the helicopter's rotor blades and gestured to the two above. Rebecca sensed the words, rather than heard them, and immediately dropped to the ground, taking Jason with her. Paul was reassessing his target and taking aim at the rear of the machine. With the sniper dead, and the knowledge that he was armed, Paul knew the pilot would swiftly vacate the area. However, he only needed a few seconds to hit the right target, the rotor on the rear boom. He knew enough to know that it prevented the whole thing from spinning round on itself and that a good hit would make it un-flyable. With the best aim he could make, he emptied the remaining rounds from the pistol into the whirling rotor and tail-shaft.

Smith had a perfect view and realised that he was not the target, but his machine was. He again swore loudly, at everything and everybody, while his hands played instinctively over the controls of the Jet Ranger. It was an aircraft he knew well and he felt the uncharacteristic twitch in the tail as he kicked it round and down to the right. The grey cliff face was momentarily lost to sight in the turn as he opened the throttle. It was too late though, the shots had found a mark. Several of the rounds missed, some passed harmlessly through the skin, but a vital linkage was torn apart, making the Bell totally unstable.

Paul watched the helicopter descend past him as it turned into the sheer cliff below. It seemed far too close to be a deliberate turn and he shouted down at the doomed aircraft.

"Fly it now, you bastard!"

At the controls, Smith was fighting a losing battle with the Bell as the horizon spun around in a blur. Just briefly he looked out through the top of the Perspex canopy and caught sight of the indistinct figure looking down.

"You son of a bitch!" he yelled, uselessly, as a fleeting second later the main rotor blades collided with the unforgiving rocks.

Paul watched the aircraft slam solidly into the cliff some two hundred feet below them. It disintegrated rapidly as the fuel tank ruptured. It exploded into a searing fireball that grew in magnitude as it rose upward. He realised it was coming straight for them and bellowed out a sharp warning to Rebecca and Jason, who had come to the edge to witness the demise of the helicopter.

"Get down now! Cover your faces!"

They disappeared from sight as he dived for cover. A scant moment later he felt the rush of burning aviation fuel run past him in a mushroom of flame and smoke. Once it had cleared he stood up, with a huge sigh of relief. Beneath Scythe Crag, at the base where the path emerged onto the grassy plateau, he could see the littered remains of the Jet Ranger. It was scattered over a wide area and had even reached the tarn. Very little of the machine was recognizable, apart from a large mechanical section that appeared to be the turbine. Paul's only concern was the fact that the pilot would have alerted others to their position. They could easily be surrounded within the hour. Time was crucial, especially with Rebecca and Jason in tow, and he looked up into the sky. If there was another helicopter it could be on them in a matter of minutes. He ejected the empty magazine from the pistol and kicked it over the edge. A fresh one was retrieved from his pocket and he made sure the safety catch was off. Next time he would be ready.

"What now, Paul?" he heard Rebecca call from above. She appeared unruffled by the episode, or was good at hiding it, and was looking over the edge with Jason. They both stood, waiting for his lead, and he took a deep breath. The descent would still take about an hour, much too long with Storn's people alerted, and he knew it was a futile direction in which to continue. He pointed back upwards, towards the summit of Dunter Fell.

"Back up! Quick as you can! They know we're here now!"

At least back on top there was room to spread out and see the danger coming. With luck they might even fool them by doubling back. He took another look at the smouldering wreckage below, before steeling himself for another few miles of walking.

281

Chapter 59

The telephone in the control room burst into life while Myra was still trying in vain to raise the helicopter by radio.

"Where can they be?" she asked, frustrated, as only static answered her calls.

"Yes?" Scott-Wade greeted, sharply, snatching up the ringing telephone. For several seconds he listened, before replying. "Get over there quickly."

"Well?" she asked.

"Search party three is near the summit of Rough Crag, about two miles from Dunter Fell," he replied, despondently. "A couple of minutes ago they saw a fireball rise up above the fell." He shook his head, angrily. "Somehow, Sayers has downed the chopper."

Storn did not react at all, his face remained unmoved. Then, inexplicably, he strode without word from the control room. Only the sound of his heavy footsteps, disappearing down the corridor, indicated that he had left.

"Son of a bitch!" Myra cursed. "Why don't we just kill Sayers now?"

Scott-Wade looked at her angrily. "You try."

"If Storn gave the word I'd go now!" she almost screamed back at him. "The bastard took my man. Remember? He owes me."

"Richard's old news," he retorted. "Search three also found Joe Hiller; dead at the bottom of some rocks."

"Dead?" she said, incredulously. "I don't believe it?"

He nodded, in some reverence at the loss of a friend.

"What was he doing out there on his own? How did Sayers get the better of him?"

He turned his back to her and Persephone, who was sitting by the door.

"I alerted Joe last night, just after we received word that Sayers was near Padrigg. I knew he was the best man for the job, I'd hunted with him many times, he was a good friend," he explained.

"How did Sayers get past him though? Joe Hiller would've been ultra-cautious."

He shrugged. "We'll never really know now. I personally told him to be wary of Sayers and treat him like any other dangerous prey. He was to just shoot him in the legs as soon as he saw him. Joe was the best, exceptional sniper, wildfowler, poacher, hunter, and gamekeeper if asked. He excelled, and proved it by finding that bastard overnight, only to die doing so. What a waste."

Myra glanced over to Persephone and saw a half smile on her face. The smugness seemed all too evident and it suddenly infuriated her.

"You'd better tell me exactly what you're thinking, Daughter, or I'll personally slap you till you beg me to stop!" she lashed across the room at her, causing Scott-Wade to turn too.

"I've always believed she knows more than she says."

Persephone remained indifferent to the threat and instead seemed remarkably calm. "I see the same as you. Yet why do I see more?"

"Explain?" Myra blazed.

Persephone pushed the hair back from the corner of her mouth. "Anger blinds you all, don't you see that? Hatred of Paul Sayers, fuelled heavily by Storn, has turned you into an avenging mob."

"Go on," Myra urged.

"Storn has his own agenda. Our lives mean nothing, unless it's serving his needs. What he really wants none of us will ever know." She stood up. "All he wants at this moment is the Guardian. And he'll sacrifice everything you've built for him to get her. And I mean everything, Mother. He's manipulating all of us and using Sayers as the tool, by making sure you keep him alive to take her. Face facts, Scott-Wade, you could kill him from a distance without effort."

He nodded. "That's true; we could've taken him out months ago. Only Storn's orders keep him alive."

"Then why's it so difficult to just capture him?" Myra butted in, eager to explore the obvious concept offered by her. "We've a powerful, well equipped organisation behind us to do it. Sayers is a loner, a deadbeat, yet he makes us look like fools and is reducing our numbers by the hour."

Persephone smiled, weakly. "Love."

"What do you mean?"

"Love," she repeated. "Sayers and the Guardian are in love. They've become inseparable, like two spirits coming together as one. It gives him strength and an inner confidence that would normally never surface in an individual. You have to realise that he's no longer the rank amateur you've repeatedly called him. He's got the Guardians on his side and powerful allies they are."

Scott-Wade was almost enlightened by what she had said. "It fits."

Myra looked her straight in the eye. "I'm proud of you, my child. You seem to have gained a new awareness and insight from your encounter with him."

Again she half smiled and lied. "Don't expect more than just flashes."

"I won't."

"Tell me what you'd do with him then," Scott-Wade added.

"If Storn say's you can't kill him, there's only one other option," she replied. "Leave him alone."

Myra's face darkened. "Oh no, Daughter, I'll never do that. I intend to spit on the grave of Paul Sayers. I swear it."

Chapter 60

The sun broke through the partial cloud cover and bathed the fells in bright yellow warmth. It was late in the afternoon when Paul, Rebecca and Jason stood looking down on the lush green valley of Stydale. The village of Stydale was on one of the main north to south roads bisecting the district. Because of this, and its central position, it was a popular tourist trap. Paul eagerly cast his eye over the familiar territory and felt relieved that they had made better progress since the incident with the helicopter. They had travelled northwards over the old corpse road before going completely off the known paths across the fells. There had not been another helicopter, thankfully, and they had deliberately avoided contact with other walkers. Also, Rebecca was able to project her thoughts outward and sense anyone before they got near. Even so, it had been close on several occasions. They had hidden amongst rocks twice to avoid detection from Storn's search parties. Paul guessed, with the weather being so good, Stydale would flood with people coming in for the weekend. With walking gear on, and the family unit they appeared to be, he hoped to be able to slip in and out without trouble. His thoughts though were broken when Rebecca slipped an arm around his waist. She gave him a brief squeeze and he looked into her depthless blue eyes, sensing that she was not happy.

"Is there a problem?"

"I can pick out several of Storn's followers down there."

"Even from up here?"

"You are forefront in their thoughts, Paul. So many minds are thinking of you, it is quite amazing."

"Nice to be wanted," he replied, casually.

"There is a teashop at the end of this lane, Paul. There are two there watching all those coming and going and several others are roaming the outskirts of the village.

He nodded. "It's risky and we're all too tired to go any other way."

She whispered in his ear. "Jason needs to sleep."

He knew she was right and felt too tired himself to face dodging Storn's people.

"You're right."

"What shall we do?"

Like most Lakeland towns and villages there were farms scattered all around the periphery of the main settlement area. Several were close to where they were, but lower down, and he pointed to one that had some sturdy looking outbuildings away from the main farmhouse.

"We'll find a comfortable spot to hide for the night. Hopefully by morning they'll have dispersed a bit."

Rebecca felt he was being careful and agreed with his tactics. If they had gone into Stydale it would be impossible for her to deflect all of the attention they would receive.

"Anything you would like me to do?" she asked, as they set off in the general direction of the farm.

He smiled. "I think you'd be better popping down there and getting us something to eat and drink. Can you do it undiscovered?"

It was her turn to smile. "I think I can, by myself."

He patted her on the bottom and pushed a twenty pound note in her trouser pocket.

"Off you go then and don't spend it all on sweets."

At the next fork in the path they parted. Paul and Jason made a beeline for the first building while Rebecca continued into the village. She was quite sure she could pinpoint Storn's followers and avoid them or deflect their thoughts. There was also the added factor that they were looking for three of them and not her alone. Once she reached the bottom of the descending path she glanced back to see the progress of the other two. They were already out of sight and she turned her attention to the task at hand.

Chapter 61

Saturday 29th May 1993

Paul had woken early in their hiding place. The outbuilding was secure and, more importantly, not in immediate use on first inspection. Some baled straw was used to build a wall to hide behind and more spread on the floor to provide a place to sit and lay. Rebecca had returned with refreshments and fish and chips. Afterwards, Jason had settled down and quickly fallen asleep. Paul assumed it was the effects of the drugs he had been given and the distance they had walked. Rebecca assured him the boy was well and they too settled down for the night. They had talked quietly into the early hours, before tiredness overcame her. After a few hours sleep, Paul had woken and found them both still peacefully sleeping. He decided to let them lie and had dozed himself until way past eleven o'clock. Only then did he wake them up with the intention of moving on.

Rebecca stood next to him as he looked across the fields to the village. In amongst the houses the square tower of the parish church was visible and the sound of bells could be heard. Behind them Jason was eating and had told them he felt fine.

"What can you sense?" Paul asked.

"There is now just one at the teashop and two more in a car at the far end of the village."

"Good," he said, scanning the houses. "They've obviously dispersed in the hope of finding us. We'll make a move now in case they come back in numbers."

"The one at the teashop?" she asked, looking up at him.

"I'll go another way."

"And us?"

He turned round. "You ready Jason?"

He nodded. "Say when."

Paul pointed across the fields to a small wooden, shiplap structure. "The bus shelter," he said. "You two make your way over to it and I'll meet you shortly."

"What are you going to do?" she asked, suddenly concerned they were parting.

He smiled and winked. "I'll get us a car or something. I'm already fed up with walking."

"Please be careful."

Affectionately, he kissed her. "Don't fret, I'll be okay." With that, he hefted the canvas bag of weapons over his shoulder and headed off into the village. Once amongst the houses he calmly made his way into the centre in search of transport. There were plenty of parked cars and the road was busy, but he realised there was no chance of getting anything in such an exposed position. The main street was bustling with tourists, walkers and locals, all occupying themselves amongst the numerous shops and attractions. Although no one appeared to take any notice of him, he felt distinctly uneasy surrounded by so many people. As he walked past a newsagent's, he saw his own face, in black and white, staring out from the front page of a national newspaper. He did not even pause to read the headline and quickly turned down a side street to avoid possible recognition.

There were more cars, yet all were locked and too visible to attempt to break into. Starting one would be easy, but forced entry would give him away. Without much success he found himself at the bottom of the lane leading up to the church. The bells had stopped and there were cars parked alongside the wall of the churchyard. Paul looked again at the church and realised it was a wedding. He took the opportunity to make his way along the line of cars when he saw that everybody was inside. His heart began to quicken as he tried each door in rapid succession.

"Bingo," he whispered, finding the one outside the gate unlocked. He swiftly got in behind the wheel and tossed the canvas bag on the passenger seat. As expected there were no keys in the ignition and he took the pistol from the pocket of his jacket. With two swift blows he smashed the plastic steering column cowling and exposed the ignition switch. He knew from his work on the Wolseley that it would just be a matter of finding the correct feed. His pocket-knife soon bared the most likely looking wire and he touched it across each of the others in turn until the dashboard lit up.

"One down," he said, quietly, and looked through the windscreen. There was still no sign of life in the lane and he glanced at the church to make sure no one was coming out. He stripped another wire and touched it against the two he had joined. The engine fired once and revved at his use of the pedal. Seconds later he was heading down the lane to a rendezvous with the other two.

A net curtain twitched in the front window of the cottage opposite the church gate. The elderly woman watched as the car disappeared from sight. Only moments earlier she had glanced out and seen the man get into the car. She knew for certain he was not the driver and from the short distance away his face seemed familiar. Satisfied that it was obviously a theft, she sat down with the telephone. As she heard it ringing at the other end, she picked up her morning newspaper and looked again at the photograph on the front.

"Police house," the constable on duty answered.

"Good morning," she greeted. "Mavis Reeves here in Stydale."

"What can I do for you Mrs. Reeves? I'm busy with urgent matters today."

"I've got something very interesting to tell you."

Chapter 62

The fact that she was a Guardian, amongst mortals, made no difference, Rebecca still felt completely out of place whilst at the same time knowing she had to appear totally casual. The little wooden bus shelter felt like a coffin as they sat waiting. Every few moments she would discreetly poke her head out and glance to either side. Each time she did was in hope of seeing Paul coming. It was an odd sensation, because she could tell before looking he was not near them, but still on the other side of the village, as she could sense him there. That fact could not ease her troubled thoughts and neither could the simple truth that Storn's followers also sat unaware of their presence. She realised she was feeling a new emotion, something mortal, anxiety. Jason sat on the bench beside her, casually swinging his legs backwards and forwards, oblivious to her discomfort. The shuttle bus had arrived only a few moments after they had sat down. The doors had opened and the driver had looked at her, questioningly. She had mumbled out the excuse that she was waiting for her husband to join them before catching the next one. Much to her relief the driver had happily accepted it and drove off.

As she again sat back, a quiet, smooth-running car glided to a halt in front of them. Its appearance caused both her and Jason to sit bolt upright in startled attention. The gleaming, nineteen-seventies Jaguar XJ6, with polished chrome bumpers and wheel trims, glinted in the weak afternoon sunlight. The snow-white ribbons that adorned the bonnet and door handles stood out brightly against the cherry-red bodywork of the luxury saloon. As she sat, wide-eyed at the sight of the wedding car, the lightly-tinted passenger window slid down on a silent electric motor. The face she saw, grinning from behind the wheel, was familiar.

"Wanna lift, gorgeous?" Paul called, in a deep salacious voice.

She was immediately up on her feet, seeming to ignore the manner of the invitation, and pulling Jason behind her.

"I have been very concerned," she said, opening the rear door for Jason. "Where have you been?" she added, jumping in the front beside Paul.

"The wait was worth it for a bit of class, wasn't it?" he cheerily replied, patting the dashboard as if he had just bought it, instead of stealing it.

She shook her head as he accelerated from the village. "You are getting worse Paul."

He stole a glance and winked at her. "I've got the car, Jason can be best man, and all we need is a vicar with a church."

She gave him an incredulous look, which needed no faking on her part. "Is that all you have been thinking about at a time like this? Paul, just look at the danger we are in."

"Go on," he urged. "Best offer you'll get today. I'm at my peak in life. It'll be all downhill from here." He spoke in an easy manner, which apparently showed little or no concern for their situation. In truth he was trying to keep relaxed while he put distance between them, the church where he had stolen the car, and Storn's people.

Rebecca could only shake her head, unable to respond sensibly to his proposal of marriage. He reached over and gently patted her knee.

"Shall we say another day then?"

"We will see," she quietly replied.

He slid the window down. "We won't need these then," he said, reaching out and pulling the bow off the door handle. He passed it to her. "Do your side, my angel, and you do the back please, Jason. Stuff 'em under the seat when you've done."

Rebecca untied the bonnet ribbon, dragging it in as it flapped in the slipstream.

"Now what?" she asked.

"A bit more deception I hope," he replied, with another wink. "You two slouch down a bit in the seats so you're not so visible."

The lack of conversation that followed did not bother Paul, as he headed out of the Lake District. The smooth ride soon had

Rebecca and Jason asleep, despite having slept the evening before. He felt stiff, rather than tired, with aches and pains all over, but dared not stop. There was just one place he had in mind to go, a place of safety, Rosemary's.

Chapter 63

The towering figure of Storn was like a stark silhouette as he stood with his back to the windows. He was completely oblivious to the majestic beauty of the manicured gardens outside. Instead he was totally focussed on the control room. Larger scale maps of the Lake District had been freshly pinned to the walls and the computer link was watched over hungrily for any scrap of useful information. Myra had spent the entire day awaiting the next sighting of Paul. Reluctantly, she had grabbed a few hours sleep the night before, but since then had been more or less rooted to her seat. She was carefully thumbing through a sheaf of papers the printer had spewed out just moments before. There had been no sightings since the loss of the helicopter and angered frustration had given way to just frustration. They were awaiting confirmation of a possible sighting in Stydale, earlier, and that was the only sniff of a lead they had.

Although she was playing little part in the search process, Persephone was in the room too. Dressed in a loose top and denim skirt, she watched them go about their various tasks. She did not possess the ability to pinpoint him, not yet anyway, but she could sense Paul, on the move, somewhere beyond where they were.

Scott-Wade had been on the telephone for only a few seconds. He replaced it and quickly crossed to one of the maps. "It's definite," he said, sticking a red pin in the centre of it. "Sayers has stolen a Jaguar from Stydale church."

"Why has it taken so long to confirm?" Storn barked. "You had that report forty-five minutes ago! What is happening out there?"

He calmly faced Storn, realising he was about to blow up into another rage unless he was placated. "We're lucky. The local copper's our man. He had to go and confirm the sighting with the old woman and convince her it wasn't Sayers, but some known car thief. Also he had to deal with the irate Jag owner and wedding guests at the church. The fact he's done it all and got back to us in this short space of time is better than we could've hoped for."

"Sayers has been on the run for all that time," Storn remarked, in a more even tone. "I want everyone out of the fells, immediately, and joining the road search teams. There will be no one to help them this time and we will not make the mistake of involving the police. I will personally deal with Sayers the moment he is brought here. Then I can take what I want from the Guardian bitch at my leisure and be done with them both."

Myra nodded in agreement, but Persephone felt an urge to leave the room. A sudden feeling of sickness in the pit of her stomach forced its way to the surface and she knew she had to go.

Myra saw her going to the door. "Where are you off to?"

It took a supreme effort of will to paint a false smile on her face. "Just going for coffee, would you like one?"

She shook her head, reaching for the telephone. Persephone quickly went out and closed the door behind her as another searing pain went through her. She fell heavily against the opposite wall and propped herself up. The pain had grown in intensity. It was far greater than anything she had suffered before, like her period pains. She desperately wanted to cry out, but deliberately bit her lip to stifle any noise other than a whimper. Through the pain she could hear the voices of the others behind the closed door. Their chatter was inaudible to her, not that she felt in any mood to eavesdrop, and she slowly pushed herself upright. There was nothing else to do other than summon up the strength to make it down the corridor to the relative privacy of the kitchen. With her senses in a blur she staggered with leaden steps all the way to it and, mercifully, found it empty. For some unknown reason she crossed to the worktop and switched on the kettle. But she almost passed out and sank to the ground in a loose heap. Her entire body began to shake, uncontrollably, as if she was suffering a severe fever or convulsion. The agony inside was the worst she had ever known and she knew instinctively where it had come from. It was an inner power, one she had been unaware of until it had been triggered by her first fateful meeting with Paul Sayers. The encounter with the soul of Tessa Fisher had added to it, and now she could feel that the raw energy Storn possessed had fuelled it to the point it had broken free. Now that she had it for her own benefit she would have to control it and, moreover, not allow him the knowledge of her potential.

For over five minutes she lay helpless on the floor, until the shaking subsided to a level where she could physically see and hear once more. She was wet, soaked in sweat that had seemingly flowed from every pore in her body. Her life had changed and would never be the same again. The first thought was for Paul, the man who had somehow been the key, the man she shared a distant past with. If there was a power, she would first use it to gain that past, a place she had briefly touched before, yet wanted to visit again with a desire that hurt. It was not so much a memory, but a consciousness of existing in another body that was not hers. However, it was hers to feel and see through. She closed her eyes and allowed her senses to break free of the normal boundaries they were limited to. At once, the scent of the sea filled her nostrils and she breathed it in, in a way far stronger than the scant snatches she had experienced before. Then, as if impelled by the wondrous smell, the rest of her senses came alive to the reality and she could hear the wind across the shore, feel it ruffle lightly through her long hair, and then taste the salt it carried. She felt elated, but scared too, scared to imagine where she was and what she would see if she dared to open her eyes to the new world around her. But she knew she had to and properly take a step into the new world only she could inhabit.

When Persephone at last opened her eyes, she was standing on a beach of sand and shingle. The sea filled the panorama and the dull red disc of a setting sun sat just above the horizon in the evening sky. She ran down to the water's edge as a white-topped crest struck the shore and carried a fine mist into her face. The cold salty water washed around her bare feet as she put her hand over her eyes to look out over the incoming waves. With eager anticipation she scanned the foam-lined breakers, trying to catch sight of the boat. Then she saw it, broaching the swell, the white-painted hull of the fishing boat, Victoria Lynn, pushing its way towards the shore on the rise and fall of the unceasing sea. It belonged to her twin brother, James, and was also worked by her intended husband, Albert. Both were strong fishermen, he rowed while James stood erect at the tiller, expertly guiding them onto the beach as she knew only he could. A cold realisation washed over Persephone and she felt she was herself again, staring at the scene from a past life. James was her twin, yet the face she saw looking towards her was that of Paul Sayers. The reason they felt so close together was obvious, they shared something in spirit that had found a link through time.

Above her, on the worktop, the kettle switched itself off as steam issued from the spout and pulled her back to her own reality. The saltiness still assailed her senses and she reluctantly dragged herself to her feet. Briefly, she felt at her cheek and, looking at the palm of her hand, she saw that it was damp with saltwater spray.

Chapter 64

Sunday 30th May 1993

It was comfortably cool inside the air-conditioned incident room at Clayborough police station. Helen Bradshaw was idly studying a large-scale map of the British Isles, affixed to the wall, while around her a team of eight men and women sat working. They were ranged around a series of desks equipped with telephones and computers. A slow methodical interpretation of all the data they were steadily accumulating was being made. They were experts in their field, patience being an acquired skill, and sifted through everything, no matter how trivial-looking. Being involved in a nationwide manhunt was a new experience for Helen. Previous cases had never been so high profile and she studied the map thoughtfully. It felt strange to be wondering where Paul was, or looking for the Galloway boy, and at the same time hoping he would remain at large. There had been numerous sightings from eager members of the public, thanks to the media interest, ranging from one end of the country to the other, all of which had to be pursued. The only real clue they had was the discovery of the car he had taken from Norfolk and left in the Lake District. Any real positive leads after that had simply dried up. She had spoken with David Pryce and, unsurprisingly, he had remained tight-lipped about the whole affair. The story he had concocted seemed to bear little relation to the suspected truth and she believed he too was firmly on Paul's side. If he wished to paint himself as a victim, to protect his family, she could see no point in pressing him further and exposing them to Storn. There was nothing else to do but wait for fresh information and she knew the patience game too. She turned from the map and looked at her busy team. Again she found herself resting her gaze on the figure of Carter, seated in the corner with his back to her. He was unaware that she was close to arresting him. All she needed were the results of the blood test and she would make the move. Also the notes he was copying onto a pad were being written left handed, another piece of evidence pointing to him being the murderer of Sally Marcroft. She mused over the note taking, wondering whether or not it was for them or Storn's benefit he was doing it. It felt anomalous to have somebody close to her working primarily for someone else. The situation gave her a new insight into the value of truth and trust. An officer behind her called out, breaking Helen's inward train of thought.

"Ma'am, I've a caller wishing to speak to you personally."

"Who is it?" she asked, crossing to her.

"Won't say," she replied, holding her hand over the mouthpiece. "He won't speak to anyone else and says it's in connection with a little girl in Leicester."

"Bradshaw," Helen said, taking it.

"Good morning, Helen. Working Sundays I see," came the voice she expected. Strangely, a sense of relief that Paul was safe and still alive washed over her.

"What can I do for you?" she continued, in a firm tone.

"Oh, like that is it?"

"Yes."

"I thought you'd like to know I've got the boy with me and that he's in good health."

She breathed a sigh of relief. "I understand that."

"Keep it under your hat."

"I will. Is there anything else?"

"Pour every good copper you can muster onto a farm at the end of Padrigg, in the Lakes. The place was hit by lightning on Thursday night. It's in a bit of a mess, but was used by Storn's lot to hold all the victims. If they've not cleared it up it may yield useful evidence."

"I might just do that."

"There were at least three bodies in the rubble to my knowledge," he continued. "Also, if you've heard about a helicopter crash in the Lakes on Friday morning, that was my handiwork too, I'm afraid."

"I hear what you're saying," she replied, in a non-committal way while mentally noting what he had been through. How had he dealt with so many, and a helicopter, without help?

"I'll call again if possible," he finished, and she heard the line buzz in her ear. Glancing across the room she saw Carter, twisting in his chair to face her.

"Has something turned up?" he asked, eagerly.

She shook her head. "Not worth talking about."

"Maybe not, but who was it?" he asked, more insistently.

She was about to reply when again the officer near her handed her another telephone.

"It's external, Ma'am, the lab."

"Yes!" Helen snapped, taking it.

"Good morning to you too," came Maggie Watts' voice. "I'm breaking my ass to get your results and you bite my head off."

"Sorry, it's a tiring time," she immediately said, in a softer tone. "Any news?"

"Your blood sample is a match."

"No doubts?"

"None, but it won't get you a conviction on its own."

"It'll do for now. I owe you," she said, and grabbed the attention of the officer who had just got up to stretch his legs. "Sergeant Morris, would you come with me while you're on your feet and bring one of your men."

He looked bemused for a moment, before indicating to the nearest seated constable to join him. The rest of them stopped their various tasks and watched as the two men followed Helen to the other side of the room. When she stopped at the desk Carter occupied, he was looking up at her, a puzzled expression on his face.

"What's this?" he asked.

"It may have taken time to get to the bottom of this mess," she began. "But, in the light of new evidence, I'm placing you under arrest for the rape and murder of Sally Marcroft."

He was stunned into silence and just stared at her as she

continued to inform him of his rights. When she finished, the room was in hushed silence and she stood aside for the two officers to lead him away. Once they were gone she called Cunningham's office. It was answered in less than a couple of rings.

"Bradshaw here, Skipper. I've just arrested Carter for the rape and murder of Sally Marcroft."

A notable pause followed before he spoke. "Are you certain?"

"It's positive on the blood sample. I'll get some fingerprints and we can wait for the DNA."

"What do you want to do now?"

"I want permission to abandon the hunt for Sayers and the media to be immediately informed of the new arrest."

"Are you sure? What of his involvement in the other investigations?"

"If we clear the pitch for him now I'm sure he'll come in to help us sort it out. Plus I've spoken to him and he has the boy safe."

"You're joking."

"Far from it Skipper. We need to do this quickly."

"Okay Helen, it's in your hands," he said, firmly, and put down the phone. She did likewise and turned to face her waiting squad. Above all else, she felt immense satisfaction that she was back in control of the whole situation.

It was a little over twenty minutes later when the news reached Pelham Hall. Carter was in custody and the hunt for Paul had been called off. Myra sat in silence while Scott-Wade paced the floor.

"I knew it was too damn complicated," he spat. "Now he endangers us all."

Storn occupied his normal position by the window and spoke calmly in response. "It does not matter; we will continue looking for Sayers."

"But Carter..." he started.

"He knows better than to say anything. I will make sure of that." He turned to face them. "Your primary objective is finding Sayers and the Guardian. If the official hunt for him is over he will no doubt come out of hiding. Therefore, Scott-Wade, tell me where it is he will likely surface."

For a moment he just stared into space. "Commonsense would tell him to walk into the nearest police station with the boy," he eventually replied.

"He doesn't use commonsense Tony," Myra butted in. "He's always coming at us from the side."

"Precisely!" Storn said, forcefully. "So where will he go?"

Scott-Wade was quiet for a few seconds, before a smile crossed his face. "Well, if I were him, I'd return to where it all started."

"Clayborough," Myra said, in expectation.

"I'll move every team we've got southwards, straightaway, covering as many routes as possible, and then position them on every road and track into Clayborough. It's a gamble, but this way we'll spot him," Scott-Wade added.

"Do it!" Storn ordered, and watched as they immediately went to work.

Chapter 65

The afternoon traffic was light when the Jaguar left Begdale and headed south-east into the Yorkshire Dales. That morning, after ringing Helen Bradshaw, Paul had applied grey primer paint to the car, removed the wheel trims, and applied a different number plate. Most of the bright red paintwork was now covered and, to all but close inspection, it looked like an old Jaguar. He had chosen to stick with it, not wanting to steal yet another car and add to his crime tally. The news gave him some hope too. He was no longer being hunted by the police or being charged with Sally's murder. However, he knew Storn's people would grant him no such goodwill. Rosemary's hospitality, as always, had lifted all their spirits. The hot bath had been relaxing, but Rebecca had seen him removing his shirt and had been shocked by the bruising. He shrugged it off; the beating in the cells earlier in the week had produced most of the discolouration in his ribs. But the fall off the crag, when he had jumped on the hunter, had also left his shoulder badly bruised and sore. They had slept separately at Rebecca's request. She said he needed the rest and not the distraction of her close to him. He had made no argument of it, guessing she was following her Guardian rules.

After lunch with Rosemary, they opted to carry out his original plan and go to Saltmarsh. He had toyed with the idea of going immediately to the police or home to face Helen at Clayborough. However, something nagged at his good sense and both ideas were rejected. At the wheel of the big saloon, Paul felt reasonably refreshed and better than he had done for days. Rebecca was studying a road atlas, unaware of his thoughts. She looked contented, even after the rigours of the previous few days and for the length of time she had spent in her mortal guise. He had never known it be so long, not that he was complaining, and she had even eaten well at Rosemary's. He had woken to hear her in the bath, but resisted the urge to go in and have the pleasure of watching her bathe. Instead he was happy to see her blue eyes sparkle with magic at the breakfast table. With a brush she had done wonders with her fawn blonde hair and he could not help but keep stealing glances in her direction. Behind them, on the rear seat, Jason too sat freshly groomed and well fed. Without complaint, he had devoured everything Rosemary had put in front of him and had slept all night. He could only think that it was the effects of the drugs they had used on him and the walking. A set of clean clothes had been sourced by Rosemary, along with some football magazines and a large bar of chocolate for the journey to Norfolk. Again, they had spoken with David Pryce and Jason's mother and father, assuring them of his safety. The whole family were overjoyed and, on David's advice, awaiting his return by Paul. For the man who had rescued their boy they had more than a little trust. With some reservations, over the distance they had to cover, Paul hoped the trip to Saltmarsh would be trouble free and that no one would even guess they were heading there. The weapons he had liberated from the farm had been securely packed away and hidden at Rosemary's. All he had with him was an automatic pistol and two spare magazines.

"Which way are you intending to go?" Rebecca asked, looking up from the map and breaking the silence in the car.

"We'll need some fuel soon or this thirsty old girl will run out. Then we'll do a zigzag, south and east on the back roads until it gets dark."

"Do you expect trouble?"

He shrugged. "Who knows. We've just got to hope Storn's lot are spread pretty thin searching for us. The constant change of direction should see us through, especially if we head over to the eastern side of the country."

She looked thoughtful for a moment, before returning her attention to the map. Ahead of them, rounding a bend, he saw an approaching car that made him tense behind the wheel. Beside him, she sensed it and immediately looked up. An Isuzu Trooper 4x4, complete with nudge bars, was heading towards them.

Melanie and Stephen Howat were heading east towards

Begdale and the end of their search pattern. It had been the fifth time that day they had returned on the same route. Between them they had swapped the task of driving at each turn around. It was to be the last run that afternoon, because they had received the call from Myra earlier to make another two passes of the main road before taking a slow southwards run down the motorway to Clayborough. The repetition, for two days, had been numbing and, with little sleep between them, they were exhausted. However, she became instantly alert when she saw the Jaguar.

"Stephen!" she shouted. "There's a Jag coming our way!"

He was semi-dozing in the passenger seat, with a map and clipboard in his lap. But he snapped awake and immediately focussed on the approaching car.

"Not our colour or number by the looks of it," he muttered.

"Could've been changed," she said, as the two cars passed each other. From her higher seating position she could easily look down into the big saloon as it went past them. The two individuals occupying the front seats were instantly recognisable to both of them. They had studied the photographs for hours and there was also the boy on the back seat.

"It's them!" she screamed, in victorious relief.

"Got the bastards," he said, snatching up the telephone. "It looks as if they've daubed the car grey and fitted another number. Get after them, Mel, while I get reinforcements."

She glanced sideways at him, questioningly.

He shook his head, knowing the meaning in her look. "Let's not get stupid, Mel, he's too bloody dangerous. The others have tried alone and failed. We'll do it right."

She nodded in agreement, as an entrance to a field appeared on their left. Without slowing too much, she stamped hard on the brakes and threw the steering wheel hard over.

The Jaguar passed the Isuzu with Paul attempting to look as casual as a man out for an afternoon drive. However, the expressions on the faces of the two people in it told him they had been recognised.

"Bugger it!" he cursed. "We've only just left Begdale." He

glanced in the rear-view mirror and saw the brake lights of the 4x4 come on. They were turning as he moved out of sight round the bend. "Here we go again," he added, as both Rebecca and Jason turned in their seats to watch the other car. The engine growled with renewed vigour as he stabbed the accelerator to the floor and picked up speed. "You're going to have to navigate fast for me, my angel, if we're to get out of this."

The road ahead was twisty, but good, and he quickly accelerated to nearly eighty miles an hour. Rebecca again glanced over her shoulder.

"Can you get away from them?"

He shrugged, without looking at her. "In this I've got the edge for speed. Possibly size too, if they want to tangle. Remember though, Storn's got a lot of people around here. I can't believe they're not already reporting the fact they've found us."

She nodded as he weaved past another car, crossing the solid white line to do so, and causing an oncoming van to brake and flash its headlights. Undisturbed by the near miss, he continued accelerating.

"Any ideas where you want to go?" she asked, sharing her gaze between him and the open page of the map in her lap.

"Not yet," he replied, slowing for the car in front. "But we won't get far on this road."

As the Jaguar dipped into the next bend he caught a brief glimpse of the Isuzu, a long way behind them.

"I know where I am," he added, as a tree-lined turning appeared on the right. He aimed for it, braking hard and slewing across the oncoming traffic. The tyres squealed in protest, but he wrenched it in line and gunned the car hard down the side road. He could just see the main road in his mirror, as they rapidly left it behind, and saw the three cars he had overtaken, followed by the Isuzu, pass away from them.

"You've lost him, cool," Jason said, looking behind too. Rebecca glanced hopefully at Paul.

"It won't be for long," he replied, to the unspoken question. "They obviously didn't see us come down here, but it won't take long to figure out where we've turned off."

She went back to the map as he raced as quickly as possible along the country road.

"I think we must be about here," she said, after a few seconds of study, and pointed to a spot on the page. "If you continue to head this way you will eventually come to..."

"The M6," he finished for her.

"So you know this road?"

"I do now I'm on it," he replied, quietly, as several strong memories ran through his busy mind. "There's a garage down here we can get fuel from. The owner owes me a favour."

"That sounds fine," she said, with a growing smile of relief on her face, until he pulled the pistol from the door pocket.

He looked at her sideways and winked, with a wicked smile on his lips. "Payment."

Chapter 66

At a distance of some five miles behind the Jaguar, the Howat's were just turning into the road Paul had taken minutes before, but from the other direction. As predicted, it had not taken them long to figure out that they had disappeared far too quickly to be ahead. The twisting single carriageway they had traversed countless times in two days had far too many vehicles on it for the Jaguar to overtake and get away. They also had a reasonable idea of how many vehicles Paul had overtaken since they had turned to follow. Sensibly, they had taken the decision to head back to the only junction they had passed in that time. It was a gamble, but a calculated one. Already the control room at Pelham Hall had been alerted to the fact that they were in pursuit and heading east. If by chance they were wrong, several other teams were already converging to intercept ahead of them. As they raced along the presumed course of the Jaguar, Howat was attempting to get back in contact with Myra.

"Can't you get through?" Melanie asked, as the trees beside the road whipped past at increasing speed.

"There's no signal on the phone," he said, with a shrug. "It's a bad reception area with all these hills."

"Keep trying," she urged. "We should be on them soon if we're right."

"You hope," he replied, and again hit the memory recall button.

Chapter 67

The control room at Pelham was deserted, except for the seated figure of Myra, waiting expectantly by the telephone. A cigarette smoked heavily from her lips as she drummed the top of the desk with her fingertips. She paused for a second to take it out and exhale in a long sigh. Behind her, the door opened and she turned to see Persephone enter. She was carrying a cup of coffee and placed it carefully in front of her. Then, with a look of disgust, she shook her head.

"When did you start on those foul things again?"

Myra looked away and crushed the cigarette out in the already half-full ashtray beside her. "I got them from one of the guards," she began to explain, before rounding on her. "Look, we've been in here for hours and I need something. Not your holier-than-thou attitude."

She shrugged. "It's your funeral."

"It is."

"Is there any word?"

Myra shook her head. "Nothing. I assume Mel and Steve are still following. Their first call was slightly broken up and now we can't make contact. But they're sensible enough not to tangle with Sayers without backup. What about the others?"

"After that first call, Storn and Scott-Wade disappeared in the BMW with everyone else trying to keep up. They seem to believe they've got them this time."

Myra whirled round and stood up to face her. "Why do you sound so convinced that they won't achieve anything again?"

She shrugged.

"What is it you're not telling me?"

She failed to answer, her face showed little emotion, and Myra felt maddened.

"Just what's going on inside that head of yours, my girl?" she demanded. "I want answers."

Persephone spun on her toes and paced back to the open door before turning to face her again. Both of her hands were clenched in tight fists against her chest and her features flushed red.

"I don't know, Mother!" she wailed, unclenching her fists and running her fingers roughly back through her blonde hair. "Something's going on inside me that I didn't ask for and have no control over. It's scary."

"No control at all?"

She glanced at the floor, realising that in her outburst she had perhaps said too much. Sadly, she had long since realised she could never really trust her mother, a mother who would have allowed her father to rape her and then sell her to show loyalty to Storn. Only her empathy with Paul Sayers had kept her from that fate.

"It comes in flashes that are beyond understanding. Just feelings really," she whispered.

"I've suspected something's been troubling you for some weeks now. Will it prove useful to us?" Myra asked.

"Maybe, in time," she replied, still without looking directly at her, knowing that 'us' meant Storn.

"Is it always Sayers who causes these flashes?" Myra pressed.

"Yes," she lied.

"So you think Sayers will evade us again?"

Slowly she looked up and nodded. "I believe so. He possesses the uncanny ability of making us look ridiculous," she replied, making the point of including herself.

"Tell me about it," Myra retorted, in disgust. "Why we just don't kill the bastard and be done with it is beyond me."

"Storn won't allow it. Whatever it costs the rest of us."

"You're still certain of that too?"

"Sayers will be kept alive while he fulfils a need."

Myra picked up her coffee and went across to the wall that had the maps pinned to it. She glanced first at the ones of the Lake District and then to the one showing the Yorkshire Dales. It was covered in a seeming confusion of coloured pins marking out the mobile search teams and potential target areas to wait in. It had all been carefully set up by Scott-Wade, to cover all possibilities, and had been in the process of being broken up in the move south to Clayborough. Now everything was converging on the main road eastwards. The whole area looked totally wrapped up, despite Persephone's words of caution, but they had lived that scenario before and Sayers had slipped out of their grasp.

"If he breaks out of this lot, which I doubt, where will he go?" she asked, turning to face her daughter. "Care to share your thoughts?"

Without thinking she crossed to another map and tapped a spot with her finger. "There."

Myra moved next to her. "North Norfolk Coast again? Why? There's no connection. If he evades the net he'll go back to Clayborough, just as Scott-Wade believes, surely?"

"You asked."

"We're putting everything into this push south and the set up at Clayborough. It's a lot of manpower."

"I know."

"It makes no sense to go there, Sephie. The boy's from Norwich and Sayers'll get no welcome in Saltmarsh. Why go to the coast?"

"Fishermen will always return to the sea," she replied, inexplicably, and turned to leave.

After Myra watched her go, she pondered their conversation for over a minute. The decision to pull a two-man team off the Clayborough setup would be hers and she would stand by it if quizzed by Scott-Wade. Without further thought of changing her mind she picked up the telephone.

Persephone was glad to be away from her mother, and hopeful that she had not let too much slip about her burgeoning abilities. The thought of her knowing, and passing on such knowledge to Storn, was as frightening as the powers were. She passed down the corridor, into the entrance hall and up the staircase, taking little notice of how quiet the house was. Lost in thought, it was not until she reached the top that she sensed someone was there, blocking the way onto the landing. It was Payne, one of Storn's guards who had remained to look after the house. The smart, dark suit was worn neatly on his tall muscular frame and only thinly disguised the shoulder holster. The expression on his face told her all she needed to know.

"Get out of the way," she said, as he towered over her.

He grabbed her arm, locking it in a vice like grip. "You know no one's here and mummy's busy downstairs, little slut. It's time for you to spread those legs for me."

She tried to shake loose, but it was in vain. "If Storn hears of this..."

He locked his other hand over her mouth, cutting her words in mid-sentence. "But he won't, will he? Because you're not going to tell anyone," he hissed, in a threatening whisper. "I'll kill you long before he does anything to me. Get it?"

Her eyes widened in horror, because she knew he meant it. Releasing the grip on her arm he ripped open her cardigan, tearing the buttons off, to reveal the bra she wore beneath. In the next moment his hand was inside it, pulling it aside, and clasping her right breast. His face was close and she could smell the tinge of alcohol on his breath.

"Com'on," he urged. "You're aching for it. You blonde tarts are all the same. Scream blue murder then lay back, eager to get wet."

In that moment, when she should have felt the most terrified at the prospect of being raped, a sense of calm overtook her. It grew from nowhere, a peaceful inner sense of control. Her new talents were taking over, or perhaps just enhancing what was already there. The tranquillity released her mind to go into Payne's. She could see through his eyes, at herself, vividly see, in all its humiliating detail, what he wanted to do to her. It was in the downstairs kitchen that she could see herself, naked, apart from a pair of white stockings, bound across the table top with nylon cord. He was there, still immaculately dressed, advancing to have intercourse as she lay incapable. She switched places, so she could see his face, the evil perversion that was etched there, and waited. As he began the degrading sexual act she reached deeper inside him and began to reassemble the fantasy in his mind. It was easy, with her new talents, to take control of his thoughts and change the naked image of herself on the table.

Payne froze, paralysed in horrified shock as the dominant image projected by Persephone flooded his thoughts in the most unwelcome way conceivable. His long-held fantasy of having her tied to the kitchen table, to be subjected to his every sadistic whim, was quickly being replaced. Instead it was filled with the very real image of him having sex with a filthy grey, rotting corpse of an old woman. It still had her eyes, torturing him with a vile stare, and her sickly yellow hair was running with lice. As he realised what was happening the putrefied head moved, the decaying hands, free of their binds, reached out and dragged him towards it in the act of kissing. The hellish face opened its black, maggot-filled mouth to welcome him with a stench that caused the contents of his stomach to well up in anticipation of vomiting.

Persephone pulled his hands off her breast and away from her mouth. He was sweating profusely as his eyes snapped open. The feeling of paralysis remained, her cold, uncompromising stare cutting right through him. She reached up and clasped her hand over his lower face, burying her fingernails deep into the flesh of his cheeks.

"I don't need Storn to do my punishing. Every time you look at me you'll suffer that vision." She did not wait for him to acknowledge her; instead she pushed him down the stairs. "Tell the others too," she added.

At the foot of the stairs, some feeling finally returned to Payne as he lay groaning. Briefly he closed his eyes, but the image of the foul hag seemed burned into his senses and he quickly opened them again. Persephone had moved out of sight, but for several minutes he remained in a heap, watching the point where she had stood, realising she was not to be messed with again.

Chapter 68

The rundown garage remained unchanged from Paul's memory. The last time he had pulled into Owens' petrol station had been just months before. It had almost proved fatal as Owens was one of Storn's followers.

"Here we are," he said, drawing up to the first pump. "Lay across the back seat Jason, pretend to be asleep if you have to, but keep down."

"Okay," he replied, eager to be in on the deception.

From the shop, and to his surprise, Paul saw a youth ambling across to them.

"No Owens," he said, glancing at Rebecca. "I don't know if there's a connection between them. Can you cloud his thoughts a bit?"

She nodded. "Go ahead."

With deliberate ease he stepped from the car and tucked the pistol into the waistband of his trousers at the back. He left the car ticking over and consciously kept his back to the approaching youth. The position on the forecourt also gave him a good view of the road they had come down and he could see for several hundred yards.

"How much do you want?" the youth asked.

"Whatever it'll take," Paul replied, eyeing the overweight teenager as he activated the antiquated pump. He breathed a little easier as the drum figures slowly clicked over and petrol splashed into the tank. "Where's Owens today?"

The youth looked blankly at the pump face. "He's been out for a couple of days with my dad. They're mates."

"What are they up to?"

"Do you know 'em?" he replied, without looking.

"Yeah, we go back a bit."

"I'm not supposed to know, they consider me too young at the moment, but I overheard a lot of it," he freely answered. "They're out hunting for that bloke who's been on the telly. He's a right bastard. He's caused a lot of hassle for Dad, Mr. Owens, and their friends."

Paul smiled and briefly looked in at Rebecca, making a sweeping motion across his forehead with his hand. She understood and relinquished her hold on the mind of the youth.

"The bastard's not to be trusted then?" Paul said, after a few moments.

He glanced at him. "No, not at all." Then his eyes widened as he saw the muzzle of the pistol levelled inches from his face.

"When that balding little shit Owens comes back, tell him Paul Sayers sends his love. Got that? Paul Sayers."

He nodded, dumbly, as the colour drained quickly from his spotty face and fuel gushed from the Jaguar's filler pipe.

"Now, if I were you, I'd run!" Paul roared, pointing the automatic down the road.

He took no further goading and proceeded to flee from the garage. Carefully, Paul sealed the filler cap before resetting the pump and clipping open the trigger. He laid it on the ground and within moments there was a healthy flow of petrol gushing out across the forecourt and down the slope to the road. Then he stood waiting, for over two minutes, until he saw the Isuzu appear. The growing pool of fuel was expanding rapidly, with the stench of petroleum fumes filling the air, and he quickly got back in behind the wheel. The big saloon pulled away from the pumps to the far edge of the forecourt, furthest away from the spillage.

"What are you doing?" Rebecca asked, as he pushed the cigarette lighter in. At the same time he used the switch on the centre console to drop her window.

"Wait a second," he replied, pointing the way they had come. "Our pursuers have finally caught up."

"Then we should be going," she cried, urgently, as Jason sat up and stuck his face against the window.

"In a minute," he soothed. The lighter 'pinged' in its socket. "This is the place I called at last year after rescuing you."

She nodded.

"Owens is one of Storn's men and was the bastard who stuck a pistol in my face. He owes me a tank of fuel."

"I see."

"Apart from paying him back, we can unsettle this pair too," he added.

"There they are!" Howat cried, when they both saw the garage ahead of them. "It's the Owens place, he's waiting for us"

"Why?" she asked, puzzled, but still pushing the car hard towards where the Jaguar was. Instinct told them both something was wrong. In cold realisation, Howat pointed beyond the windscreen towards the road in front of them.

"Shit, Mel! He's covered the road in petrol. Stop!"

With her heart rapidly filling with dread she stamped hard on the brake pedal. In front of them the Jaguar began to pull away from the garage.

At the edge of the forecourt Paul was accelerating when he saw the nose of the Isuzu dip under braking. As they moved he snatched out the glowing cigarette lighter and tossed it out through the open window. The cherry-red element arced away from the car and landed in the pool of fuel. The Jaguar raced away as, behind them, the spilt petrol erupted in a huge, incandescent wall of flame. The road, forecourt, and pumps, were immediately engulfed in the expanding fireball.

"Business closed," he casually remarked to Rebecca, and glanced in the mirror. Before the scene disappeared from sight he saw the Isuzu appear, out of control, from the conflagration. The tyres and bodywork were ablaze as it slammed into the dry-stone wall on the other side of the road.

Jason was looking back too, until they rounded a bend. He poked his head between the front seats. "Barbecued."

Paul looked back and grinned. "Totally."

"You're wicked Paul," he added, before settling back in his seat.

Chapter 69

The dark of night had succeeded in enveloping the roads of North Norfolk in an almost cloying blackness. A low bank of cloud was already covering the sky, although rain seemed unlikely. Several hours of tension had passed since they had left the blaze at the garage, with Paul switching and dodging across the country on any and all minor roads he could find. Finally, they had parked in a secluded lay-by until night fell and he could make a more direct run to the coast. Only then had he relinquished the wheel to Rebecca and taken a chance to rest. She had kept the speed down and was following the coastal road from Hunstanton to Cromer. For the first time that day she felt relaxed, now they were closer to their goal, the village of Saltmarsh, and it filled her with a sense of success. She was wearing a summer dress, given to her by Rosemary, and a white cardigan. The Jaguar passed through another small village, although she missed seeing its name. Like several others they had passed it appeared devoid of life at that hour, tucked away in the desolate marsh area of coastline. She glanced across at Paul, slumped asleep in the passenger seat. Likewise, Jason was fast asleep in the back. Despite Paul having rested at Rosemary's, she could see the strain of the preceding week etched on his tired face. The almost erratic course he had taken to get out of the Dales had clearly taken it out of him. Now she was driving she felt they would complete the journey in peace. She glanced down at the clock on the dashboard. It was just past one in the morning and she knew they would be with David Pryce within half an hour. The road ahead straightened out as she left the lights of the village behind and once more the surrounding countryside was plunged into darkness. As she settled into the seat her eyes were drawn to the rear-view mirror and the set of headlights approaching from behind. It made her concentrate on her driving, remembering Paul's advice to keep calm and do nothing to arouse suspicion. After a couple of minutes she noted the following car had drawn nearer, yet seemed in no hurry to overtake them. Carefully, she eased off and slowed the Jaguar to thirty miles an hour. She hoped it would encourage the other driver to pass and restore her peace of mind. Again she glanced at Paul, still asleep, wanting to tell him, but deciding not to in case it appeared silly.

Two of Storn's followers had sat in the Range Rover for over five hours, after a long drive down from the Pennines. They had both been involved in the original search on the fells of the Lake District and were totally exhausted. Their diversion by Myra to the North Norfolk Coast seemed like a fool's errand and they considered it purely an outlandish whim. For the entire evening they had sat in a field entrance, watching cars enter and leave the village of Thorpe-by-the-sea until night fell. As the hours ground by they had sat cursing Myra and Persephone with every insult they could think of. But now, in the early hours, the whole picture had suddenly changed into one of adrenaline-pumping action. Steadall and Carpenter drew closer to the rear lights of the Jaguar while eagerly exchanging glances and excited words.

"It has to be them, Mick," Carpenter said, pounding his fist against the dashboard. "Look, blotchy painted Jag, even the number fits with what Steve Howat passed on. That little Stanford bitch was right."

The Range Rover pulled ever closer to the car in front, illuminating the rear with its own headlamps. Steadall grinned. "It's them alright, John, call it in."

Carpenter nodded, reaching for the telephone. "Let's give the good news."

There followed a brief pause before he heard the tired, but still alert, voice of Myra answer. "Who is it?"

"Carpenter," he responded. "We're on their tail."

"Give me your exact position," she swiftly ordered.

"We've picked them up on the coastal road between Hunstanton and Cromer. We're passing by the marshes."

"Are you certain?"

"Of course we're bloody certain," he swore. "I wouldn't be wasting my time and yours otherwise."

"Okay, give me best position."

"We're heading in the direction of Cromer, just past Thorpe-by-the-sea. But remember, we're solo," Carpenter added.

"I know," she replied. "I'll get what I can over to you."

"It'll take hours," he warned.

"They might be heading for Saltmarsh. Stop them if you can, but don't take any risks. The bastard's too dangerous. There've been too many foul-ups already, Carpenter. Don't add to them."

"We'll keep tabs on them and inform you of anything different happening. Okay?"

"Give me a couple of minutes then call back. I want you on the line the whole time. Understand?" she warned.

"Noted," Carpenter replied, and the line buzzed in his ear. After replacing the phone he reached into the back and retrieved an automatic rifle.

"What she say?" Steadall asked, seeing his partner check his weapon.

"Myra wants us to keep talking and following. I say stuff the reinforcements. Let's bag 'em now."

"Now you're talking my language," Steadall said, with an evil smirk. "I'll pull alongside and you can spray the tyres. It'll stop the son of a bitch in his tracks."

Carpenter lowered the window and levelled the rifle out of it. "Let's kick ass!" he spat, as Steadall accelerated and moved to overtake.

Chapter 70

Rebecca once again glanced at the car that was following her. If she had knowledge of such vehicles she would have realised it was a 4x4, the sort favoured by Storn's followers. She did not though and to her it was simply a set of headlights. However, she could not help but feel a little apprehensive. She made up her mind to wake Paul, but everything changed when the car moved to pass her. By instinct she cast her senses in the direction of it while at the same time gently coaxing Paul awake.

"Wake up darling, please."

He semi-jerked into consciousness, puzzled by his situation, yet his subconscious mind was alert to the tone of her voice. As his eyes focussed he could see her face dimly lit in the glow of the instrument panel lights.

"What's the...?" he began to mumble, but already his attention was drawn beyond her and to the Range Rover overtaking them. She too was turning her gaze to the same spot, her mind invading the open thoughts of the two men in it. Despite the lack of light, Paul could see the face of the passenger along with the deadly outline of the assault rifle.

"Paul!" Rebecca screamed, clearly seeing their intentions.

However, his reactions were already taking over, moving rapidly on the offensive. In one move he reached across her and grabbed the steering wheel. She let go, as if stung, and watched helplessly as he wrenched it hard over.

Steadall was taken completely by surprise as the Jaguar veered violently across the front of them, blocking the road. There was no restraint shown in the manoeuvre and he could do nothing to stop it slamming into the side of him.

"Shit!" he cursed, as they were forced onto the verge.

Beside him, the jolt succeeded in throwing Carpenter off balance, just at the point he opened fire. The one and only burst from the weapon tore across and upwards, shattering the front tyre and peppering the Jaguar's bonnet. The Range Rover nosed off the road first, bouncing wildly over the uneven verge, and caught its front bumper in the soft edge of the ditch. The momentum flipped it over in a somersault and smacked it hard into the other side of the saltwater-filled dyke. For a second it teetered on the edge, before sliding backwards into the mucky water. The Jaguar careered onto the verge too while Paul was wrestling to get it back onto tarmac. The soft ground and tattered front tyre only added to the difficulties of steering. The low front end caught the lip of the dyke, at speed, and the force pitched the saloon downwards and over. The car effortlessly tumbled, nose over tail, clearing the ditch in one bound and landing in the field the other side. With a bone jarring bang the Jaguar slammed down hard on its wheels. Everything fell silent, the engine died, and the lights flickered out.

Paul sat temporarily stunned as he regained the use of his senses. The rude awakening and duel with the Range Rover had taken only seconds to enact, but still flashed through his immediate thoughts. For a scant moment he thought it was a dream, but knew it was real. In the darkness, he flicked on the interior light causing Rebecca to snap her head round to look at him. She looked ashen faced, her hair hanging loosely across her wide open blue eyes. The rapid series of events had been too quick even for her to take in.

"Are you alright?" he asked, grabbing her hand. She just stared at him, dumbfounded.

"Are you alright?" he repeated, more forcefully.

"Yes," she replied, weakly. "I think so." She glanced away from him. "I am sorry Paul. I have ruined everything."

"Rubbish," he quickly retorted, surprised by her self-criticism. "It's amazing we've got this far." As he spoke he glanced into the back, where Jason was strapped in. Amazingly he was still asleep. "For Christ's sake, doesn't anything wake that kid?"

Absently she found the ability to smile, but he was already climbing from the car.

"You did us proud old girl," he said, patting the side of the now useless Jaguar.

The ditch was a little over thirty feet away from where they had landed and Paul crossed to see how the other car had fared. It was upside down and half submerged in the green-tinged, foul-smelling saltwater. Surprisingly the headlights were still on, illuminating the immediate scene, but he could see no movement from either it or the surroundings. He remembered the pistol was still in the car and turned round. Rebecca was getting out and he waved to get her attention. Behind him, the ditch erupted as Carpenter sprang from the water and grabbed his legs. Caught unawares and off balance, Paul toppled backwards into the murky water with him. Hopelessly, he struggled to find his feet in the glutinous mud and also fought hard not to swallow the water that threatened to fill his lungs.

Rebecca was still getting out when she saw Paul fall backwards into the ditch. At such a short distance she could easily feel the murderous intentions of Carpenter.

"No!" she shouted, and began to run across to the other car.

Carpenter was up on his feet and using it to keep an advantage over Paul. Roughly, he pulled him out of the water by the front of his shirt and punched him hard in the face.

"I'm gonna kill yer now, yer bastard son of a bitch!" he spat, and again punched him.

Still spluttering for air, and with his head ringing from the blows, Paul fell as Carpenter lost his grip. In a reflex action Paul kicked upwards as he sprawled on his backside in the water. With some satisfaction he connected with his attacker's groin and heard a loud 'whoof' as he expelled air. Amidst much cursing Carpenter staggered back, allowing Paul the chance to roll over and finally find his feet. It was only a scant reprieve from the attack and Carpenter was already punching him again. Paul barely had time to deflect it and chop down on his arm with his own right hand. However, it was a feint and Carpenter slammed his left fist into the unprotected side of his face. Once again Paul was off his feet and into the swirling filth of the ditch.

"Choke on it, fucker!" Carpenter swore.

Paul pulled himself up and spun round to face him. In the light he caught the glint of steel in his outstretched hand. The knife was about eight inches long, with one side razor sharp and the other viciously serrated.

Carpenter swished the knife in a slashing movement, purely for effect. "I'm gonna carve you up into dog meat, Sayers!"

Instinctively, Paul flexed and loosened his body, waiting for the attack that would surely follow. He knew, with no defensive weapon, it was a certainty the knifeman would inflict serious injury. He waited only a moment before Carpenter moved. The first attack was a feint, followed swiftly by a probing lunge. Paul half fell to onside to avoid it as Carpenter stumbled in the soft mud at their feet. With their respective positions changed the two men faced off a second time. The next assault was instantaneous and Paul had little space to fend it off. Carpenter was on him in a flash and he vainly tried to grab the hand with the knife in.

"Die, fucker!"

Paul knew immediately that the blade had gone in. The searing fire of pain flared in his lower left side, just above the waist. He grasped the hand with both his as he creased in agony.

"Yes!" Carpenter howled in delight. "How d'yer like the feel of that?"

Above them Rebecca had reached the edge of the ditch in the few seconds the violent episode had taken place. She looked down and saw the knife sticking in Paul's stomach, the sight of it filling her with horror.

"Paul!" she shrieked, at the top of her high pitched range.

Surprised, by the unexpected scream, Carpenter spun sideways to look. Paul saw the distraction and, despite the agony, punched upwards, connecting squarely with his attacker's chin. It was Carpenter's turn to pitch over backwards into the salty mire, with an audible groan. Even with his knuckles split, from the unrestrained blow, Paul leapt on him and used all his weight to slam him down, burying his knee into his chest. At the same time he grabbed his head and shoved it under the water with both thumbs pushed into his eyes. Carpenter flailed about, wildly, but Paul used every ounce of strength he possessed to keep him under the water. It seemed a lifetime, but Paul stayed on him for over two minutes, until he finally stopped thrashing and went limp.

"Is he dead?" Rebecca asked, shakily.

"I bloody hope so," he replied, clambering out of the ditch. She moved closer, but found it impossible to take her eyes from the knife protruding from his stomach.

"Don't go funny on me now," he warned, seeing the look on her face. "I need you to keep together. I've had worse than this and you know it."

His words had an immediate effect and it made her draw on an inner energy to pull her feelings into some kind of balance. She quickly went to him, reaching out, while at the same time capping her emotions and panic as best she could. It seemed hard to believe that everything could go so disastrously wrong in such an incredibly short passage of time.

"There's a first aid kit in the glove box, Rebecca. I'll need it," he urged, walking back to the car. He was anxious to get her busy and to be moving away from the scene. Without doubt he knew Storn would have again been advised of their position and only time would tell if any others were close. Both cars were useless and they were once again on foot just a few miles from safety. Wordlessly, he cursed the bad luck that seemed to dog their path.

Rebecca could sense the burning agony radiating from his injury and the thoughts racing through his mind. He seemed more concerned that she and Jason were vulnerable to Storn's people than with his own well-being. Such thoughts were either dismissed or consumed in the pain he felt. She wanted to say something, in an attempt to equal his feelings for their safety with her own love for him, but words failed her.

Jason had woken up and was standing by the car. He waved at them when they were closer. "How'd we get here?"

"Long story," Paul replied, and turned his back to him. He then slipped an arm around Rebecca's shoulders and whispered in her ear. "This could freak him out."

She nodded and saw his free hand go to the knife.

"I'll have to remove it now and worry about the mess later." She watched, mesmerised, as he slowly withdrew it from the bloody wound. Sweat broke out on his forehead and seemingly all over his body as the deadly serrated blade came sliding out. An anguished cry wanted to break free, but was silenced as he bit down on his tongue. Rebecca did her best to hold on and channel her love to him, yet it seemed to have little or no effect. All she could feel was the searing pain and the cry he kept silent, but screamed inside. When he finally removed the knife tears were running down her cheeks.

Paul wiped the blade and examined it in the mediocre light. "Combat knife, I think," he muttered. "Sheffield steel, stainless too, at least it's clean." In one movement he threw the weapon away and they both heard it land in the ditch with a splash. He then clasped a hand over the tear in his stomach. "First aid box Rebecca. Please."

She sprang into action and sprinted the short distance to the car, ushering Jason to one side as she reached it.

"What's the matter?" he asked.

"Paul has cut himself," she said, realising she was bending the truth to a certain degree. The first aid kit was in a small red box and she opened it to study the meagre contents. As she did so Paul appeared in the open door, allowing her to see him better in the light.

"There is not much in here," she said, almost apologetically.

"Look the other way," Paul instructed Jason, who had walked round to see what was happening. The boy reluctantly nodded and turned his back to them. Paul then pulled his soaking wet shirt open for Rebecca to examine more closely. She winced at the open tear in his side that was still oozing blood, and also at the foul smelling dirt covering him. There was just one small swab in the kit and she began to clean around the wound with it.

"There is not much I can do, Paul. You need proper attention."

"We're miles from help, just plug it the best you can," he urged. "We can't afford to stay long, not with the chance they reported finding us. I don't want to be caught here."

Reluctantly she agreed and placed a wad of cotton wool over the wound and fixed it with sticking plaster. Then she took the largest bandage in the box and wrapped it around his waist, fixing it with a safety pin.

"It is temporary," she said, closing his shirt. "I'll do something better with it later."

"Good," he replied, pulling her out onto her feet. "Grab what you need and bring it with you. We're going now."

Jason turned to him and Paul just nodded. "Grab your stuff we're moving on."

Paul found his fleece lying in the passenger foot-well, but the pistol had been dislodged from the door pocket and he could not find it. There was no time for delay and his only choice was to abandon it.

"You need medical care," Rebecca said, in a low whisper, as she came to his side carrying her bag.

"No time." He laid a hand on Jason's shoulder and pointed into the gloom in front of them. "Okay, young man, we're in your hands now. Across the road and find us a decent path to the shoreline."

He looked up, astonished at the faith being placed in him. "I won't let you down," he said, and strode off, eager to be at the task.

"Not the road?" Rebecca asked, as they followed him.

Paul shook his head. "I'm not hitch-hiking at this hour in the hope of a lift from Storn."

"I see your point," she replied, taking his hand.

Chapter 71

In the control room at Pelham Hall the atmosphere was filled with yet more anger and frustration. For once though, it did not come from Storn. He sat with his eyes closed in a leather swivel chair, by the window. Outside it was dark and the clock on the wall showed two-thirty. Instead it was Scott-Wade who was furiously cursing their misfortune for the second time that day.

"How could we have them in our hands and then lose them again," he fumed. "And to lose two men into the bargain is beyond belief. Just how does the bastard do it?"

Across from where he was pacing, Myra was taking notes while listening on the telephone. After his outburst she replaced the handset and looked at him. "Calm down for a second, Tony."

"Calm!" he started. "It's another foul up."

"She said calm," Storn added, without looking.

"It was my pulling a team off the intended Clayborough watch that gave you Sayers. You were placing everyone there."

"With good reason," he threw back.

"Persephone gave us the place to find him. Both of you remember that," Storn added.

"True," Scott-Wade said, nodding in agreement. "But they screwed it."

"Not necessarily," she said, waving the sheet of notepaper. "As soon as we lost contact I sent one of the teams from Clayborough, by fast motorcycle, to the last known position."

"What did they find?"

"Both cars are off the road, some sort of collision. Steadall was dead in his car and Carpenter was found drowned in a ditch, his eyes almost gouged out in some sort of struggle."

"Sayers and the woman?" Storn asked, spinning round to face her.

"They're on foot, in the marshes, with a likely injury to Sayers."

"You can't know that," Scott-Wade interjected.

"They found blood near the Jaguar and Carpenter had been drowned in a struggle. They couldn't find his knife. You know he always carried it, and my guess is he used it."

"Wake Persephone," Storn ordered. "See if she can feel anything new."

Myra nodded. "I'll do it when we've sorted the search teams out."

"Good. What are your intentions?"

"We're already doing it," she said, confidently. "All the teams from Clayborough are moving towards the search area now."

"And?"

"We'll co-ordinate them to encircle the marshes and I've also alerted Fleming at Wittering to give us an added edge."

"I didn't authorise that," Scott-Wade blurted, quickly crossing to her. "That's a valuable asset. It's too much so to risk on this venture."

She did not reply to his concern. "If you leave at first light in the helicopter, Tony, you can be on site to oversee the search."

Storn stood up. "That sounds an excellent idea and I trust you agree with it Scott-Wade."

He nodded. "I suggest the teams change into their army fatigues before they move into the area."

"Why?"

"Cover," he replied. "They'll pass for a Territorial Army outfit on exercise. We've done it before, successfully, and we've the right equipment. If they push it they can even get the proper vehicle in too."

"See to it then," Storn said, feeling satisfied. "I will remain here and revitalise my inner-being. Myra will keep me informed."

"I had hoped to go too," she added.

"The need of you here to supervise is greater than your need for revenge," he firmly told her. "They will be brought back to me here."

Both of them realised he would not change his mind once it

327

had been made up and simply nodded in agreement. She hid her obvious disappointment at being excluded from the hunt and watched as he exited the room. Scott-Wade turned to her, a cold hard look in his eyes.

"I don't care what he says," he began. "I'm personally going to slit that bastard's throat."

"Absolutely Tony, make sure you get Sayers, that's all I ask."

He picked up his things from the table and followed where Storn had gone. She watched him go and called out. "Do one thing for me."

He momentarily halted.

"Bring back Sayers' body so I can spit on it."

"No sweat."

"Then you can have me," she added.

"I'll hold you to that," he said, without turning, and continued on his way. For a few seconds she simply stared at the nearest computer screen before deciding on going upstairs to wake Persephone.

Chapter 72

The low cloud cover had begun to break up in the skies over North Norfolk leaving a smattering of flickering stars. A light breeze had blown in off the land lowering the temperature a few degrees, but the atmosphere was comfortable. Only the sound of the waves, rolling ceaselessly onto the shingle-covered shoreline, could be heard and there were few visible lights of habitation beyond those of a distant village. Paul, Rebecca and Jason had quickly left the crash scene by crossing into the marshes that bridged the area between mainland and sea. Paul calculated that walking for at least an hour and a half would put two or three miles between themselves and the Jaguar. It was all he could hope for, a breathing space and the chance to make it to Saltmarsh in the morning. In his own mind though, he knew that the events of the day were just another skirmish in the war against Storn. It felt like a hopeless battle, one against overwhelming odds that he would lose one day. He tried not to think about it too much, it served no purpose to try and second-guess the time he had left or how the end would come. He glanced at Rebecca as she walked alongside him; her thoughts appeared to be elsewhere. There was comfort in the knowledge she would always be there when the end came, to guide him on. But there were unwanted thoughts too. How could he ever stand the pain of leaving her? Essentially she had the ability to be a Guardian for countless years of his time. As he grew old she would remain forever beautiful, those depthless blue eyes gazing youthfully at his aging body. It was a blessing to be in love with such a woman and a curse too.

"Something ahead," Jason called quietly from in front of them, breaking Paul from his thoughts. The boy had unerringly taken them across the marshes and onto the gravel bank. To their right, below the bank, stood a concrete pillbox, one of many that still littered the countryside, an enduring reminder of the Second World War. They caught Jason up as he stood looking down at it.

"Is there anything down there?" Paul whispered to Rebecca.

Briefly, she closed her eyes and delicately probed the immediate area. "I sense it is empty. Why?"

"Good," he said, urging them down the bank. "We can rest until it gets light."

"Will it be safe?" she asked.

"Should be," he replied, scanning the darkness. "I doubt they'll get organised before dawn and I hope we've wrong-footed them."

The interior of the pillbox was almost in total darkness, yet it was clear that it had been used from time to time, perhaps by local children or curious holidaymakers. There was some straw scattered across the floor, along with a fair amount of rubbish and an old mattress.

"Beggars can't be choosers," Paul said, pointing to it. "It'll do for something to sleep on."

"If it does not turn any colder we will be fine," Rebecca said, smiling.

Paul set about trying to make the interior a bit more habitable and was busy with the task when he saw Rebecca talking quietly to Jason by the doorway. She seemed to be explaining something and making movements with her fingers. After a few seconds the boy nodded and went outside.

"What's that about?" Paul quizzed.

She tapped the side of her nose. "Wait and see."

Several minutes later Jason reappeared with a satisfied smile on his face. He caught Rebecca's attention and gave her a thumb's up sign, which she acknowledged in kind. Paul looked puzzled and she almost laughed, despite their predicament. He shrugged, sat down, and took off his shirt. Rebecca took Jason to the corner where Paul had piled up most of the straw and, once he had laid down, she knelt beside him and took off her cardigan. She used it like a blanket to cover his top half and then gently caressed the sides of his forehead with her fingertips. The soothing sensations she transmitted soon had him sleeping soundly.

"Nice work, my angel," Paul whispered, when she joined him.

"He will sleep undisturbed until morning," she said, turning her attention to his wound.

"It's okay."

She shook her head. "Lay back, the bandage is soaked with blood."

"It's okay," he repeated.

"No," she firmly replied, her blue eyes blazing with purpose. "It is not. Do as you are told."

For a moment he saw the stubbornness that had got her into trouble before and realised fighting was a waste of energy. "You win."

Gently, she placed a hand behind his back and made certain he was lying flat on the mattress. In silence she removed the bandage and examined the wound.

"It seems to have stopped bleeding," she said, delicately running her fingers over it. "I cannot detect any serious damage inside you."

"It hurts like hell."

"I know it does, my darling, I can feel it through you. I am afraid this will hurt too."

"Just get on with it."

The tear in the flesh was over two inches long and she concentrated on it with her reserves of inner energy. Then, in one swift motion, she pinched the opening together with her finger and thumb whilst at the same time flooding them with her power. Paul visibly jerked as the burning flared intensely in his stomach.

"Rest still, darling," she soothed, continuing to roll her finger and thumb along the gash with a continuing action. She continued until the process was complete. What remained was a blood stained and discoloured bruise, over a deep red scar. He struggled into a sitting position and she threw her arms around him in an embrace that exuded an excess of affection to take away the pain.

"Thanks," he gasped.

With some reluctance she pulled away and opened the first aid box. From it she took the remaining bandages and began to cover the sealed wound.

"You will have to keep it covered for several days."

"Yes nurse, whatever you say," he whispered. Without word their lips met and they began to kiss, gently at first, letting the love wash over them before the passion flared in intensity. The embrace became tighter and she dug her fingers into his back, although he was totally immersed to ever notice or even care. The sensations went beyond the briefly snatched cuddles they had shared before, filling each of them with fast flowing emotions. Reluctantly, Paul gently pushed her away.

"What is wrong?" she whispered, huskily, her eyes blazing intensely with excitement and her body aching with a passion she had never known.

"I mustn't. I made a promise," he said, shaking his head. "I didn't know it would be like this."

"Just once Paul," she begged, the look and longing in her face tearing at his basic instincts and also at the promise he had made to Charlotte. "I want to know how it feels. I know what to do."

"I can't..." he began, but she interrupted.

"Charlotte cannot see us here, if that is your worry."

He seemed puzzled and she smiled, wickedly. "But I thought."

She shook her head. "I had Jason draw a few codes in the dirt outside. It will cause enough of a disturbance to give us privacy and it is small enough not to bother me."

His expression changed, the longing in her face matching that of the deeply suppressed yearning he had always had, to make love to her. The opportunity had been handed to them and, despite the events of the day; he would not waste their one and possibly only chance. He pulled her close, the anticipation almost unbearable, and ran his hands through her hair, pushing it away from her glowing face.

"I'm a bit out of practice. Celibacy has a price."

She whispered in his ear. "Come on big boy, fuck me."

He laughed, quietly, but she was already lightly pushing him back down and undoing his trousers. Without word she pulled them off and straddled him as he reached up to undo the buttons on the front of her dress. She waited, patiently, while he undid each one in turn until he could slip his hands inside and push the dress off her arms. There was plenty of time, but she felt urgency, the fear of discovery and the trepidation of doing something she was not allowed by Guardian law to indulge in. Yet she felt no shame for her voyage of self-discovery with the mortal man she loved. She reached behind her back, pulling the clasp of her bra apart, but he was already pushing the straps off and reaching for her firm breasts. Eagerly, she lowered herself on top of him pushing the panties she wore over her hips. She was kissing him as he played with her erect nipples, lightly kneading them between his fingers and thumbs. Then his hands were on her back caressing, stroking, and then in one flowing motion onto her bare bottom, squeezing the flesh there. For Rebecca it was simply a cascade of inner fire she had never previously touched. Even when she had been close to him before it had not felt like this. She could feel the stiffness in his groin pressing into her and some buried instinct made her pull away from the passionate exchange of kissing. Paul did not stop her moving into a kneeling position across him. It was a moment in time he had only dreamed of, fantasised about, a stolen time fate had dealt them. Her body felt as if it was trembling against his, but she was warm on the makeshift bed. Carefully she moved down onto him, her eyes flickered, but never opened, as she experienced the sensation of him entering her for the first time. Again her reaction was instinctive as she began to easily move up and down, letting the intercourse begin and allowing him to caress her breasts. The sensations running through her body seemed to also touch her spirit, a blissful almost euphoric delight in being close enough to join together. It seemed incredible to him, but she managed to somehow tune herself to the waves that were rolling onto the shore just a few yards from where they lay. It was a rhythmic movement he had never experienced in love making before and he wanted it to last a lifetime.

"Gently," he whispered. "Easy going my angel, let it last."

She opened her eyes, sweat pouring from every pore in her body as he sat up.

"I will."

He reached for her, wrapping his arms around her as she locked her lips over his mouth. It felt close, the almost electrical thrill flooding up and down her body and blazing in her genital region was about to explode, and she wanted to scream. She denied herself the luxury of it and rocked wildly on him without letting go or drawing away.

"No," she moaned, again digging her fingers into his back as the rush of orgasm they shared came swiftly to her. No longer could she hold back and screamed out as her body shook uncontrollably. She fell against him, her breath coming in short ragged gasps that left her unable to speak for several long moments.

"Worth waiting for?" he whispered, but she was already kissing him again, running her fingers down his back as her body still quivered. The actions made her intentions clear and he was not about to disappoint her. He gently ran his fingertips down the smooth skin of her neck, pushing her head backwards until her breasts rose up to meet his hands. As his tongue moved over and around her nipples, gently exciting her, he could hear the sighs of delight as she writhed to the intimate touch. When she could take no more of it she clasped his head and pushed his face into her cleavage, kissing him through his hair.

"Again darling, please, do not stop now," she panted.

"I wasn't about to," he replied. "Give me a minute and I'll see what I can do for an encore."

She laughed, a happy fulfilled sound filling the empty ruin of a building. "Do you ever stop joking?"

"Not if I can help it." He found himself gazing into her shimmering blue eyes, dazzled by the intensity and depth he saw there. "You're so sexy. Did you know that?"

"No teasing," she gently chided, running her hands down the sides of his face.

"I'm not," he added, as her touch worked its magic.

Around them the night was starlit and quiet, except for the unceasing motion of the sea against the shore. For the two lovers their cares and troubles were forgotten, the rest of the world ceased to exist. Their souls and bodies were one, sharing a special bond of love that should never have been theirs. The forbidden fruit was indeed very sweet.

Chapter 73

In her private rooms Charlotte lay relaxed on a support of softly pulsating energy and was lost within a state of meditation. As always, a part of her was still aware of her surroundings and became alert to the fact someone had entered. She opened her eyes. Chantelle was brushing a loose strand of long brown hair from her face and smiled when she saw Charlotte looking at her.

"Sorry for disturbing you," she apologised, in a musical voice, and clasped her hands together.

"What is it?" Charlotte asked, without rising.

"We, or should I say I, have lost them," she said, truthfully.

She sat up. "Are you sure?"

Chantelle nodded. "As instructed I have looked in on them every so often to make sure their journey was still going as predicted."

Charlotte stood up, allowing the energy bed to shimmer noiselessly into the floor, and pulled her robe together. "What happened? They had cleared every obstacle and had a trouble free trip ahead."

"Evil took a hand, somehow. I located the car they were travelling in, abandoned in a field, some distance from the Pryce house."

"Storn?"

"Involved," Chantelle replied. "Also, I discovered at the same location another car belonging to his followers. The two occupants were dead. One died in the accident and the other in a struggle."

"Paul?"

"It would seem so," she surmised, as Charlotte gathered up her long red hair and put in a band to hold it in place. "However, I cannot see them even though they cannot be too far away."

"Shielded?" Charlotte asked, puzzled by the very idea of it.

"That is a possibility, but for what purpose?" Chantelle answered, equally as puzzled. "None of Storn's people are nearby in force. Two men have discovered the location yet seem reluctant to move from it."

Charlotte nodded. "They will be awaiting further orders."

"Then what am I to do?"

She placed an arm across her shoulders. "Do not blame yourself Chantelle. I am to blame for this, believing they were safe. I should have known better and placed a full watch on their progress."

"Cerestina and her restrictions?" she offered.

"Whenever something involves Rebecca, she is so obviously set against it, despite the evil she and Paul have to deal with."

"I cannot see how such an attitude achieves much for us here."

"Neither do I. However, something tells me they are safe at the present moment. Let us wait for morning to come there before getting overly concerned."

"Perhaps the shield is something they have devised between them so we cannot see where they are." Chantelle speculated, catching Charlotte's thoughts of Paul and Rebecca together. Her eyes widened as the notion of what she had said sunk in. "But did not Paul promise?"

"Rebecca could easily sway him, despite what we know about him. He is, after all, just a mortal man with all the weaknesses they possess. It would not take much with the way they feel about each other."

"Can they be stopped?"

"We are jumping to conclusions without evidence, Chantelle. There could be a quite simple explanation as to why we cannot see them," she concluded. "We must have some trust in them."

Her reply was a wry smile. "It would be too late now, I guess."

Charlotte nodded. "Let us hope nothing terrible has befallen them." She indicated for them to leave. "We will both go to the viewing chamber and see if we can detect a shield anywhere near to the car. If we do, I will go there myself."

"That is a good idea."

Together they made their way down through the labyrinth of

gently glowing corridors to the viewing chambers. As they rounded the corner they were surprised to see Cerestina already standing there, waiting with two of her closest Guardian sisters, Cristal and Felia.

"Dressed in a meditation robe Charlotte?" Cerestina began. "What has brought you here so urgently?"

"We appear to have temporarily lost contact with Rebecca," she replied, stepping up to the senior Guardian, who was wearing a long white dress flecked in dazzling silver. "I was about to conduct a search of the last known position to see if we can determine what happened."

Cerestina was shaking her head as she spoke. "Can you not see what this foolish girl is doing? She is running around as she pleases and you are allowing it."

Charlotte remained calm. "You gave permission for her to go to aid Paul against Storn."

"But not to this degree, Charlotte. I expected you would show a certain amount of good sense in this matter. She has brought nothing but trouble since her involvement with that mortal and it can only mean difficulties here. In future you will confine her to duties in this realm. Our laws are set that we do not meddle in the affairs of mortals. Go back to your meditation and you, Chantelle, revert to your normal duties. If Rebecca returns you will immediately take away her means of travel and confine her to this place. If this is not clear enough I will undertake these matters for you."

Calmly, Charlotte did not show any sign of weakness. "If Storn becomes strong in any realm he has the opportunity to dominate and rule over spirits everywhere."

"A common misunderstanding, he has no such ability."

"I disagree."

"What is your point?"

"Rebecca is helping one lone mortal combat the spread of evil started by Storn. Would you not agree it is a just cause?"

Cerestina tried to intimidate by authority. "Do you oppose the declared ruling?"

Charlotte would not back down and chose her words carefully. "I oppose no one Cerestina, it is not our way. My loyalties are to this realm and the sisters I serve with. Storn needs to be kept in check if we are to remain strong."

"I will decide who needs to be kept in check," she retorted, firmly. "You will return to your meditation. Leave the disruptive Rebecca to sort out her own mess. If she does not return, so be it. She will have no more help from anyone here."

Chantelle fixed her in a cold stare which almost frosted the space between them. "You would leave a sister Guardian to the possible fate of capture by Storn for a second time?"

"You will return to your duties!" she snapped.

Chantelle spun on her heels and strode away. "I did not think you could be so heartless."

Cerestina almost took off after her, but Charlotte blocked her way. For a brief moment they stared each other down, neither one giving the other an inkling of their thoughts. She broke the silence first.

"If you defy me, Charlotte, I will have you stripped of your position."

"And just how will you go about that?"

"You are not above the laws of this place. I will call a judgment on you. Understand?"

"I will comply with your wishes," Charlotte conceded, realising defiance was not the answer. Reluctantly, she gave a respectful bow to her senior and headed back in the direction of her rooms. When she turned the corner the wall beside her shimmered and Caroline stepped out.

"Did you hear all that?"

"Yes, every word, Charlotte. What can we do?"

"We will do as we are told at the present. I only hope nothing has happened and all is well. She has Paul to look after her and I have much faith in him to protect her."

"Then we await her return?"

"Yes, or hope Cerestina changes her mind and allows us to make a move."

"If it were possible, I would say, 'Do not hold your breath'."

Despite the circumstances Charlotte smiled at the obvious mortal statement.

Chapter 74

Monday 31st May 1993

Early morning sunlight was streaming in through the gun slits of the pillbox. Paul slowly opened his eyes, allowing them to become accustomed to the brightness. A glance at his wristwatch showed it was just past seven and he was surprised not to have woken earlier. An unwanted thought, that Storn's people were possibly close, filled his waking senses, but he fought the urge to panic. The old mattress had been amazingly comfortable and he felt reasonably refreshed. Although the wound in his stomach had been sealed, it still gave some discomfort, like a burn in the process of healing. In the doorway he could see Rebecca, standing with her back to him, idly looking out over the sun-kissed fields and enjoying the freshness of the morning. She wore a simple slip, where it had come from he had no idea, and framed by sunlight it was transparent. Again he felt the stirring of passion as he gazed at her. As if aware of his thoughts she turned. The sun almost made her hair seem ablaze with gold, even though it was ruffled from the exertions of intercourse and sleep. She sensed the pleasure he gained in just admiring her naked body through the thin clothing she wore. Unashamed, she dropped her arms and allowed him to see her breasts, pushing firmly against the see-through material. His pleasure matched her sense of fulfillment from the intimate night before.

"Good morning, Miss," he greeted. "Do you often drop by ruins in your scanty underwear?"

She smiled and shook her head.

"Are we safe for the moment?" he asked, guessing she would be able to tell if anyone was close.

She nodded and crossed to where he was lying. Without word

she knelt down beside him, tenderly took his face in her hands, and kissed him. When she drew away he could see in her expression a mixture of love and emotion.

"It seems silly, yet I do not know what to say," she eventually said, unable to find any words to relate her feelings to the man she loved.

He brushed the hair back from her face and smiled. In that moment she seemed more of his world than the Guardian one she belonged in. Emotion; a human weakness?

"You could say you enjoyed it," he offered. "I did, it was the most wonderful night of my life."

"I..." she was about to start, but Jason was getting up.

"Are you two awake?" he asked, with a beaming smile.

Paul nodded. "Isn't it obvious?"

"Are we going to Uncle David's now?"

"In a minute," Paul replied, as Rebecca hurriedly retrieved her dress and passed Paul his trousers. "Are you up to a walk?"

"Is it far?" he asked. "I'm hungry."

"There are a few things in my bag," Rebecca said, tossing it to him before doing up her buttons.

"Great," he chirped, delving immediately into it. "Are you two getting married then?"

Paul pointed to the open doorway. "Outside now, young man, and clear away those marks you put down last night."

He lowered his gaze and slowly passed between them with half a packet of biscuits in his hand. Paul followed him with a serious stare until he had gone from sight then turned to her.

"I didn't tell him to say that."

She tossed him his shirt. "It is dry, but like you it smells a bit."

"Charming," he replied, pulling it on.

"How is your wound?"

"It smarts a bit."

She stood up, gathering their belongings together. "Do you believe we will be okay?"

He smiled. "We're not out of the woods yet. There's still a fair walk this morning. But it's a Bank Holiday today and this place will be swarming with people within the hour."

Beyond the doorway she gazed out at the rising sun. "You think Storn is out there?"

"If they haven't already they'll soon find the two wrecks from last night. After that it's anybody's guess as to their next move. If they don't make it soon they'll get tangled up with the public."

Chapter 75

The area was relatively deserted for the reasonably early hour, but on the road, about half a mile away, vehicles could be seen going about their business. Paul, Rebecca and Jason had left their refuge and were making steady headway along the top of the banking. The sea-defence was a considerable structure, built entirely from piled gravel. It was nearly as high as a house and equally as wide. On the side facing the sea it was stepped in two descending sections, while landward it was a sloping bank. A pair of gulls wafted by, gliding on the breeze, and one squawked loudly at the trio below. Rebecca walked hand in hand with Paul while Jason strolled on a few paces ahead.

"I sense you like being here Paul."

"I've always been drawn to this part of the world," he said, looking around at the familiar landscape. "From the first time mother brought me here. Now I know of my previous life, as James Cooke, I suppose those feelings make sense. They're deep rooted in my soul somewhere."

"What brought your mother here?"

"Father, I guess. When she met him he was a keen sailing enthusiast and had a boat, not a big one. I think it was kept up at Blakeney."

"Do you miss him?"

"Can you really miss someone you never knew?" he replied, openly. "I miss Mum a lot. I've never really spoken to anyone about him, though. I miss the chance of knowing the man, seeing how alike we are, do we think along similar lines, that kind of thing. Then again, we could've hated each other. I'll never know."

She squeezed his arm. "Why did your mother not keep it?"

"Money. Boats need it for upkeep and she didn't have enough

to spare. She sold it after he died. What else could she do with it?"

He looked wistfully across the waves. "The Sea Witch."

"Pardon?"

"That's what he called it, The Sea Witch. Mother said he always wanted to buy an ocean going craft and sail her around the world. What a dream to have."

She smiled. "What about your dreams, my darling?"

He shook his head and laughed. "I couldn't sail across a duck pond, let alone around the world. I'd be a lousy yachtsman. Best if I stick to dry land and you'll have less to worry about."

Ahead of them Jason had come to halt. He was scanning the sky.

"What is it?" Paul called out.

"I can hear a plane coming," he shouted back.

They halted and Rebecca let go of his hand to join in the search for it. Apart from a few small clouds the sky was clear and a low rumble heralded the approach of the aircraft.

"It's a jet," Paul surmised, as the noise became louder.

Jason suddenly let out a yelp of delight. "There it is!"

They both followed to where he was pointing directly down the shoreline. The bat-like shape was growing in size and it appeared in no hurry as it flew towards them. The outline of the plane became recognisable as it drew closer.

"It's a Harrier!" Paul shouted, as Jason continued to point.

"How do you know?" Rebecca asked, studying the approaching jet with some curiosity.

"Interest in machines I guess. You just get used to seeing them over the Fens on a daily basis. Don't you remember? I won a gliding holiday three years ago as part of a marketing promotion."

"I was not this close to you then," she quickly reminded him.

"I know, but weren't you watching over me? Keeping me safe?"

"I do not watch you constantly, Paul," she said, indifferently.

"I'll remember that."

As they spoke, the drab-green fighter cruised past at a little over one hundred feet, travelling just below two hundred knots. As it came level with them it quarter-rolled so they could see the upper surfaces of the wings and the pilot inside the cockpit. Once past it levelled up and carried on its way.

Squadron Leader John Fleming had crossed the coast minutes earlier, at Happisburgh. His intention was to make a deliberate slow pass over the beaches and fields bordering the seashore, looking for signs of the three fugitives. In truth he had not expected to see anyone at all. He knew someone could easily jump into cover at the sound of the approaching jet and his being there was just an excuse to placate Storn. It was pointless and dangerous too. To get a fighter put on the line on a Bank Holiday, purely on the pretence of a flight test, was endangering his rank and career, but he would not argue the fact out of fear of punishment. If Storn wanted a jet fighter, flying up and down the coast on the hopeless task of finding a needle in a haystack, that was what he got. Above the seaside town of Sheringham the land flattened out into fields and then salt marshes. He knew the crash point of the car and where the ground teams were beginning their searches. His intention was to follow the shore past the town and then over-fly the marshes. The helicopter was also due in the area and he would gladly relinquish the sky to it and carry on with his cover sortie as planned. With such expectations in mind he was more than a little surprised to see a group of three walking on top of the banking.

"It can't be," he said, slightly rolling the Harrier to get a better look. "Damn, it's them."

Paul watched it continue on its heading along the coast before it banked and turned inwards over the land. The manoeuvre took just a few seconds to complete, but it had covered a large area of sky. The new course was now bringing it back towards them.

"What is it doing?" Rebecca asked, slipping an arm around Paul's waist.

"Search me. I didn't think they flew on Bank Holidays."

Jason began to jump up and down in excitement as it came back over them. "He's seen us!" he shouted above the roar, as it flew low over them.

Rebecca clasped her hands over her ears to subdue the noise. The helmeted head of the pilot could be clearly seen looking down at them, before it flew out over the sea.

"Wow!" Jason called out, without taking his eyes off it. "Did you see that?"

"At least someone is happy," she cheerfully whispered to Paul. However, she soon realised he was not listening.

Fleming grinned with evil satisfaction beneath the tinted visor of his flight helmet, while at the same time flicking on the radio. The frequency was their own and only Storn's control room, the helicopter, and the search teams on the ground were listening.

"Air two to ground. Are you receiving? Over." His voice sounded muffled in the face mask, but was clear over the microphone. The earphones crackled static for a brief moment before he heard Scott-Wade respond.

"Ground, we're receiving you. What have you got?"

"I have your three lost sheep. They're walking along the top of the banking about two and a half miles from your present location. Over."

"Excellent, air two, we're returning to the vehicles now. Over."

Fleming nodded to himself and began to turn back in towards the shore. "What do you wish me to do, ground? Over."

Before Scott-Wade could answer, the unmistakable voice of Storn carried harshly across the radio. "Pin them down and scare them into staying there."

"Understood. Over." After hearing the radio return to static he aimed the nose of the Harrier at the point he had just flown over.

Rebecca was acutely aware that Paul's thoughts were elsewhere and reached out with her mind to feel what he was thinking.

"What is it Paul? What is troubling you?"

"Maybe nothing," he quietly replied, without looking at her. Instead his face seemed clouded with uncertainty as he followed the progress of the Harrier. She too began to look afresh and saw it flying back in their direction, a scant fifty feet above the waves.

Apart from settling at a lower height, it was also accelerating, the noise level increasing as it swiftly zeroed in on them.

"What are you thinking?" she asked, taking hold of his hand.

"Worst nightmare," he replied, glancing to where Jason was still excitedly watching the incoming jet. "Storn's got followers everywhere, in every walk of life. If they're in the services, getting a solitary fighter plane to search for us could be possible."

"Would they?"

"Oh shit!" he swore, as the dreadful realisation dawned. "If it's cannon armed it'll cut us to pieces in one burst." He turned and started running, unceremoniously dragging a startled Rebecca with him. Jason looked sideways and saw them both bearing headlong down on him.

"Run Jason!" Paul yelled, at the surprised youngster. "Jump down the right side of the bank!"

The boy immediately responded and disappeared over the edge as Paul glanced out to sea. A cold sensation ran through him as he saw the Harrier turn slightly to come into line with them. Then he saw the brief flash from its belly whilst at the same time he dived over the side with Rebecca. The cannon shells ripped greedily into the gravel scant moments later. Paul twisted his body to cover Rebecca, but Jason was several yards ahead of them. All three clung desperately to the side of the bank as the air filled with noise and gravel rained down all around them. A second later the Harrier roared over the top, less than twenty feet up, and continued inland. Paul was swiftly back on his feet dragging Rebecca, all gentleness forgotten in the fight for survival.

"Get up Jason, now!" he yelled, stinging the stunned youngster into action. "Get on the top and run!"

For all three of them it was like running in slow-motion as they scrambled against the steep side of the bank. The gravel shifted like water and every step was an effort. She could feel him physically pulling her, willing her to get up, and sweat broke out on her face at the sudden exertion.

Chapter 76

At a point roughly two miles up the coast, in the marshes, and away from the fleeing trio, around thirty men and women were quickly assembling at their vehicles. They had begun searching the vicinity just after first light and had already covered a large area. All but a few were dressed in combat fatigues, giving the impression it was legitimate Army business or Territorial manoeuvres. The news that the Harrier had spotted their targets though had sent them rushing back to their transport. Scott-Wade had not waited for the helicopter to take him to the search area. He had travelled down in the early hours, impatient to be with the teams at dawn. The helicopter was due at any time and now that they had them in their sights he wanted to transfer to it quickly. He was one of the first back at the meeting point and was standing on the bonnet of a Land Rover, scanning the coast ahead with powerful binoculars. They had all heard the Harrier and he was eager to see what was happening. As he picked out the plane the brief buzz of cannon carried over the marshes.

"Get him back on the radio, Evans," he ordered one of the men nearest him. "He's made a strafing pass and I want to know the outcome."

The man did as instructed as Scott-Wade jumped down. Around him they were waiting for instructions and already another man was unfolding a large-scale map. They gathered round while he quickly appraised the new situation.

"Three ways into the target area," he began, indicating on the map the tracks that went through the fields to the shoreline. "Divide into three equal groups. Smithy take the first route, I'll take middle, and Vinny you take the last."

Everyone nodded and there were a few words of encouragement.

347

"Keep on the radios at all times, I want constant updates from everyone, and we'll pincher them somewhere out on the beach. I'm buying a case of best Scotch for whoever wings that bastard Sayers. Now move!"

A chorus of positive jeering rippled through them and, stirred by his words, they quickly went to their vehicles. The man Evans reappeared with a hand-held radio and passed it to him. "It's the Harrier."

"What's happening?" he snapped, without formality.

The reply was muffled with static. "I'm trying to pin them in against the beach, but I can't keep it up. I'm going to draw attention pretty quickly so get here fast. Over."

"We're moving now. Out."

The vehicles were already starting up when the distinctive sound of a jet, turning under power, rumbled towards them.

"He's not got long over there, hurry!" Scott-Wade shouted. "Post a man at each entrance and keep the public out, make an excuse! Go, go, go!"

Paul had steered the other two to the very edge of the bank and they ran while he kept a constant watch on the Harrier. The only chance they had was in using the bank as a shield and judging when the attack would come. Rebecca was panting and sweating behind him, her hand still firmly locked in his.

"Can you stop it?!" she called out, between gasps.

"Have you got a shoulder launched missile in your handbag?"

"No, I have not," she replied, seriously, missing his sarcastic humour. "Do you think he intends to kill or just make us stop?"

It homed in on them for another pass. In the shifting sea of loose gravel, Paul could feel his legs turning to jelly as the muscles worked overtime. "Well, if he's trying to scare us he's doing a bloody good job of it. Now!" he yelled, and all three of them tumbled down the side of the bank. They landed with a crash amongst a shower of stones, but he was already forcibly dragging Rebecca into cover. The cannon shells could be heard tearing into the sea defence just a few yards to their right. He saw the Harrier as it tore over their heads with seemingly inches to spare. There was no time to waste and he knew it. Quickly, but also a bit shakily, he was on his feet and dragging the still uncomplaining Rebecca behind. Jason was clambering back up the side of the bank and they followed him. With the roar of the jet moving away from them Rebecca kept her hand firmly in Paul's. She could sense his sheer frustration and helplessness at being unable to do anything against the attacking aircraft. However, his mind was working overtime at the possible outcomes and chances they had. For the first time she realised how much he had changed in the ways he thought and acted when under pressure. Somehow his mind had become much quicker and adept at dealing with such situations. The stumbling, unprepared Paul, who had blundered into the Fox at Kirkham, had gone for good. But events had changed them both since that day.

"And it was such a good morning," Paul muttered to her, unaware of her thoughts. The boy was on his knees a few feet from them, totally exhausted. "Get going."

"No. I will not leave you."

He held her by the arms. "You must Rebecca, please, it's over."

Along the shoreline they could see the jet descending in a shallow dive. It was lining up with the top of the bank and there was nowhere to run.

"He'll do a proper job this time," he said, turning to gaze into her sweat stained face. "I want you away from here when it happens."

"No," she repeated, her voice remaining calm. Strangely, it contained so much love it silenced him. In those few moments they felt as if they were sharing an eternity together. Both felt the overwhelming passion of their shared and forbidden night of love. Never before or ever again would they be fulfilled as they had been in each others arms that night.

"Tell me how it works?" she whispered.

His face looked puzzled. "How what works?"

She turned to face the Harrier. "Tell me how that weapon of destruction works."

"Can you stop it?" he asked, incredulously, picking up the positive tone in her voice.

"Yes. Now tell me, quickly."

He realised she was deadly serious and quickly explained the rudiments of how an aeroplane was controlled. They both looked up and saw it drawing closer.

"Get behind me Paul. I will deal with it," she added, confidently.

He took several steps back and squatted down next to Jason.

"What's Rebecca going to do, Paul?"

He slipped a reassuring arm across the boy's shoulders. "Not sure, but keep down."

They both watched, in rapt fascination, as she opened out her arms, fingers outstretched, and seemed to welcome the fast-approaching danger. With her eyes closed, Rebecca divided herself into two equal parts. One part stepped outside her inner-self and began gathering the elements of nature as if she were picking wild flowers in a summer meadow. The other part placed its energy inside the cockpit of the fighter. At once the other two became conscious of a breeze stirring the air up around them. Within seconds it was growing at an alarming rate that rushed past and over them towards where she stood. The whirlwind quickly drowned out the noise of the jet and Jason buried his head in Paul's chest. Paul could see Rebecca, clothes flapping crazily in the force of the vortex as it tore past her and up into the sky.

In the enclosed world of his 'safe' cockpit, Fleming began a controlled pull out of the shallow dive he had started seconds before. Through the front of the bubble canopy he could see them. She was opening her arms out as if to greet him. A malicious grin cracked his face.

"You silly bitch," he snorted, into the face mask. "If I open up now you'll be food for the gulls."

Mentally, he was judging the point at which he would pull the nose up right above their heads and induce that final moment of ultimate fear. But then the aircraft encountered the first buffet of wind.

Back on the ground Paul could hardly believe the strength of the maelstrom Rebecca had created. A powerful gale was blasting violently past them and sweeping up all the debris and rubbish from the beach. On unseen and ferocious currents it rose in twisting spirals above her.

The 'safe' world Fleming was used to suddenly felt cramped and confined for the first time in his professional life. It was as if he was sharing the cockpit with someone else, but it did not make sense. The buffeting was growing increasingly worse as he descended towards the beach and he worked the control column to keep from rolling over. Pure instinct and training had him fighting the plane to correct every single jolt it took. It was scant moments later that he realised it was not under his control at all. Somehow the throttle was opening against his backward hand pressure and the plane was gradually rolling onto its port side.

"Straighten up you tub of shit!" he cursed, as it continued against full stick pressure to fall onto its back. All thoughts of the trio on the beach vanished as he used every ounce of his strength to check the uncontrollable jet. Then, without warning, the column was snatched violently from his grip and the plane snapped over. The complete three hundred and sixty degree roll took less than a second and hardly waited for correction before repeating. The second time it was even faster and the G-force pinned Fleming into his seat. His world was fast becoming a kaleidoscopic blur that hurt the eyes. The plane was rolling faster than it was ever designed to and would quickly fall apart.

Paul clung tightly to Jason, doing his best to shield him from the effects of the hurricane-like vortex. The air around them was being whipped into a frenzy and he could taste saltwater spray filling his mouth and nostrils. Ahead of them, Rebecca remained with her arms outstretched despite the violent atmosphere around her. Above, the jet was arcing towards the spot where she stood. However, he could see it spinning at a rate of roll that was far faster than normal for such a machine. There was no cannon fire coming from it and he realised it was doomed.

His head was pounding like a hammer on an anvil and all Fleming saw was a spiralling whirl of red blur. The blood vessels in the backs of his eyes had burst under the excessive G-force and his suit held him in a vice-like grip. In such a state he found it hard to think straight, let alone figure out how to regain control of his aircraft. However, a self-survival instinct forced one hand to the ejection seat handle between his legs. Against the unremitting force, though, his fingers were just too far away.

With a ringside seat to the terrifying spectacle, Paul stared, with his heart pounding as the spinning blur powered directly at them like an arrow. It was unrecognisable as an airplane and a sickening metallic screech tore through the sound of the vortex. One of the wings was ripped off the fuselage. At that moment Rebecca threw her right arm out in the direction of the sea. The Harrier reacted instantly to her command and snapped away from its original course. Shedding pieces everywhere, the self-destructing fighter slammed like a huge fist into the water just yards from the beach. Paul reacted on reflex and threw himself over Jason to provide him some protection. The explosion rang loudly in their ears as the force of the blast passed over them. It was followed by a shower of seawater, gravel, and pieces of debris raining down around them. Miraculously, or by Rebecca's will, he was not sure which to thank, nothing touched them. He stood up and looked to where it had impacted with the water. The sea had boiled up into a frothy-topped swirl that had disrupted the early morning calm. Apart from a patch of burning fuel floating on the surface, nothing else remained. It had sunk quickly in the shallow water, the sea willingly claiming the prize. Further along the beach the torn wing lay where it had fallen to earth. It would remain as a marker for the investigators to find the plane and recover the body. In his heart he could find no pity or remorse for the loss of a man he had never met, a stranger intent on their demise, and, sadly, he realised he was becoming cold-hearted. He bent over and prodded Jason. The boy rolled over, dazed, and opened his eyes.

"Are you alright?"

"I think so," was his weak reply.

It was enough for Paul to know that he was not hurt and

around them the violent vortex was rapidly diminishing. He glanced up to where Rebecca still stood and saw her arms drop loosely to her sides. Then she sank to her knees as her head flopped down. Filled with a sudden dread he quickly sprinted to her. Within seconds he was in front of her and lightly taking her by the arms. Without word she sagged against him.

"What's the matter? Are you hurt?" he quietly asked, stroking her ruffled hair and keeping a lid on his own anxiety.

Her answer was barely a whisper. "I am fine, my darling. I am not used to such an enormous effort in this mortal form. It has taken it out of me a bit, to say the least."

"It was bloody amazing."

She slightly pulled away from him while still allowing him to support her. A brief smile came to her lips. "It was nothing."

He brushed the loose hair back from her face. "You're a marvel, my angel. Have I ever told you I love you?"

The smile broadened and she tapped the end of his nose with her index finger. "Yes, and I think I told you, you are lucky to have me."

Despite the situation he managed to laugh. "Rebecca, when are we going to have one whole peaceful week together?"

"We will, my darling, I promise."

He glanced up and saw that a significant patch of burning jet fuel had developed on the water and it was sending a highly visible plume of black smoke skyward.

"We're giving ourselves away, pretty lady," he said, facing her. "We'll have to be on our way before Storn's posse gets here."

"I need a little time to regain my strength. You two get on your way and I will follow shortly."

His eyes widened. "No way, I'll help you." Without letting go of her hands he got to his feet and pulled her up onto her own. The strain of her efforts was still evident and she quickly grabbed at him for support.

"I will not get far."

Paul did not reply, but instead bent down and looped his arm under her legs. With a surprised gasp from her, he effortlessly scooped her off the ground.

"You were saying."

A loving instinct made her put her arms around the back of his neck. "Oh, nothing."

"Right then, let's get out of here."

Jason was quickly at his side, carrying their bags. "Are we still going along the top?"

"No," he replied, immediately descending the steep sided bank to the field below. "We're sitting ducks now. I can't believe the Harrier wasn't seen and heard in the last few minutes. This place will be crawling with people shortly, good and bad, and we need transport, quickly."

They crunched their way down the slope and Jason trotted on ahead.

"Head for the road," Paul called after him. "But keep your head down."

He nodded and made a beeline towards the narrow track that divided the two fields to their left. Paul followed, carrying Rebecca, happy to let the youngster lead them towards the road. As they walked he glanced down at her.

"You're lazy, for an angel. Did you know that?"

"What makes you say such a thing?" she replied, wounded at his unexpected statement.

A broad grin crossed his face. "Maybe it's because I always seem to end up carrying you somewhere."

"Oh stop teasing," she said, sensing the lack of malice in his tone. Their relationship may have been unique, yet it was as loving as any normal one could be. The last time he had carried her was when she had been trapped in the darkness of her own soul. Then she had weighed nothing, because it had been a spiritual world. In what he thought of as the real world she was her own bodyweight and it would slow him. However, he did not mind, she would never be a burden to him. She lightly ran her fingertips down his cheek while at the same time transmitting the feelings of the love they had shared just hours previous. The warm, intimate sensations rapidly stirred his basic male instincts.

"Now that isn't fair, precious," he warned. "I can't do anything with an erection while in this position."

Mischievously, she giggled. "Oh I am aware of that Paul. It is for calling me lazy."

"Really," he countered, and deliberately moved over to the deep channel of dirty-green saltwater running alongside the track and feigned to throw her in. "You'll take an early morning bath in a minute young lady."

"No! Paul!" she laughingly screamed, in mock horror. "I was just teasing."

He shifted her in his arms, preventing her from saying more, and their lips met. Everything they had shared was held in it for the passing of a few seconds and then they parted. Without taking her eyes from his, she ran her fingers down his face and whispered; "Thank you for last night."

"It was you who made it easy, made it feel so right."

"You were kind, gentle, and considerate, my darling, everything I imagined a lover should be. I now know completeness, Paul. We will always be one."

"I know what you mean," he replied. "I just hope Charlotte never finds out."

"Shush," she said, putting a finger to his lips. "What Charlotte does not know will not harm her."

Their brief interlude was broken by Jason, running back towards them.

"Up ahead," he called, breathlessly. "I can see the road."

"Stay there then," Paul called out. "We'll come to you."

Being taller than the boy he could see above the crops in the field and to the road ahead. A white coloured van was passing, southwards, but it did not appear to be slowing down. There was a mixture of emotion that perhaps help was close, but also that Storn was near too. They needed to be wary and he noticed Jason was still sprinting on ahead.

"Slow down Jason, wait for us. I'd hate to blunder into something unseen."

"Okay," he called, and stopped.

"Expecting trouble?" Rebecca asked.

"It's never far away." he said, glancing back over his shoulder. The plume of smoke was falling behind them and to their left. He reached the spot where Jason was waiting and his blood ran cold. On the road, and heading towards them, were several off-road vehicles and a couple of military trucks. Because of her closeness to him Rebecca could sense his change of mood. She did not need to see to know things had gone awry.

"They are coming."

"Yes," was all he said, as the first two vehicles peeled off at the track that was furthest away from them. The next group would be on top of them within a minute.

Chapter 77

Scott-Wade was in one of the cars and was peering hard out of the windscreen.

"Radio's dead on the Harrier," Evans informed him from behind.

"Shit," he cursed. "How on earth did he lose it? All he had to do was circle above them, the stupid bastard."

"Perhaps it was Sayers," Evans added, tossing the radio onto the seat and picking up an automatic rifle in its place.

Scott-Wade spun round, anger flushing his face. "Shut up! I want that bastard's head on a pole."

"Look, smoke," the driver interrupted, and they turned to see where he was pointing.

"I told you. The bastard's brought him down."

"Here! Here! Turn down here!" Scott-Wade shouted, as they drew level with the track. "They'll be somewhere here," he added, snatching his own weapon. "Send just the one wagon and car further down and we'll deploy the rest here. Get the helicopter here fast, this place will soon be crawling with the wrong people."

The 4x4 stopped, just a short way down the track, with the others closely following.

"Post one of the uniformed men here and tell him to keep onlookers at bay," Scott-Wade ordered, as they deployed.

Evans jumped out. "Will do, but we've literally got just minutes to do this."

"Then let's do it now and bag them," Scott-Wade added, slamming his door shut. As they quickly assembled a nagging doubt entered his thoughts. Had Sayers really brought the Harrier down? It seemed impossible, but he vowed to be on his guard when they finally came face to face.

Chapter 78

"Get into the ditch now!" Paul shouted, when he saw the vehicles turn off ahead of them. He fell onto his backside and slid into the saltwater channel with Rebecca in his arms. Also taking immediate heed, Jason jumped wholeheartedly into the stinking green water and disappeared up to his chest. It was cold, even for Paul with his trousers and boots on. The level came up to his waist and it meant Rebecca was dipped in the water too. She gave him a wry smile and he attempted a shrug.

"Sorry about the wet bum, precious, but you'll have to suffer it I'm afraid."

"I am a burden to you both, leave me."

"No," he retorted, but paused, looking at her thoughtfully. "I'm an idiot. Why don't you just shoot back to Charlotte and I won't have to worry."

She shook her head. "Sorry, darling, but I cannot go back in this condition. It would be dangerous for me. I need a little time to recharge myself before it is safe."

He looked defeated. "You'll have to suffer my company for a while yet then."

Jason had slowly waded back to where they were. "Is it them?"

Paul nodded. "Yes. The Harrier would've been in contact with forces on the ground. Judging by how quickly they've got here they must've been close."

"What shall we do?" Jason asked.

They were hugging the edge of the ditch closest to the crops in the field. It was oil seed rape, several feet high, topped with yellow flowers, and he wordlessly indicated Jason to climb out of the ditch into it. The boy did so and Paul helped Rebecca into the cover behind him. Once they were lying flat he carefully re-arranged the crop around them.

"Keep still and quiet," he whispered, and dipped out of sight.

"Keep safe," she whispered, but he was already gone.

Moving as quickly as possible and keeping low, he moved along the channel until he reached an outgrowth of weed and rushes. It was quite dense and he slid himself in amongst it until just his head was above water. Moments later he glimpsed several sets of boots swiftly heading towards the gravel bank. Luckily, the men and women of the search party were fanning out as they passed the point he had left the other two. He quickly went back and waited until they were out of sight before pulling Rebecca out. Jason followed and all three waded to the end of the field. The channel made a right-angled turn and then continued along the other edge, only a hundred yards from the road. A section of old fencing provided cover for Paul to drag himself out of the water. There were three 4x4s, a camouflaged army truck, and behind that a Vauxhall Frontera 4x4. To both his left and right he could hear the search teams crossing the area around them. He knew any action would have to be swift if they were to stand any chance of escaping. For several long moments he studied the scene, looking for the opening he would need to get the other two out of the ditch and into a car. There appeared to be just the one man with the vehicles and he was armed. Dressed in army fatigues he seemed intent on keeping watch on the entrance and not what the others were doing as they progressed towards the banking. Paul rapidly made a plan of action and slid back into the water, where Rebecca and Jason were waiting.

"Here's how it goes," he whispered. "The only transport is theirs, so we're taking one. There's one guard. When I silence him, out of the ditch and keep yourselves low, use the cars as cover, okay?"

Both nodded.

"Are you feeling strong enough?" he asked Rebecca.

"I can crawl out of here," she replied.

"Good," he said, climbing out of the ditch.

Chapter 79

The armed skirmish line was carefully, yet swiftly, making its way to the point where the last vestiges of smoke were still rising. At the head of them, Scott-Wade pulled a trilling mobile from his pocket.

"Yes," he snapped, as they continued to thread their way through the crops.

"We need an update," Myra's familiar voice began.

"It's falling apart rapidly," he replied, truthfully. "We're out of the cars and heading to where the Harrier went down. But this place will be crawling with the authorities shortly. If we don't spot them in the next five minutes I'm dispersing everyone."

"But they could be close by."

"Do you wanna come here and run this!"

"If I have to!" she shouted back. "Find them."

"Get off my back, the chopper'll be here in a minute or two and I need to speak with it."

"Then report..." she continued, but he was already cutting her off. The man closest had half heard the conversation and glanced at him.

"Trouble?"

He shook his head. "Bloody woman, I know exactly what she needs."

The man snorted once and they relentlessly moved forwards.

Behind them, Paul was out of the ditch and moving across to the blind side of the guard. The vehicles were parked in a line and he was standing by the last in the row, the Frontera. Paul kept close to them so their bulk masked him from the sentry. However, he seemed more intent on watching the road than his rear. He obviously assumed the skirmish line would prevent anyone coming from behind. Paul just hoped the cars had keys in them or that the man carried a set in his pocket. All he had to do was eliminate him and they would be away. The army truck was next in the line and he rolled underneath it for cover. Strapped to the chassis were various tools and he removed a pointed shovel. Behind him Rebecca and Jason had reached the edge of the ditch and were peering over the top. She could see the guard, with his back to them, and his thoughts were solely on the road. Over to her left she saw Paul roll out from the underside of the truck carrying a shovel. His thoughts were quite clear too and she unceremoniously dragged Jason down into the ditch so that he would not witness the attack.

Hillson again scanned the road with his binoculars. There was some activity on it, but no one seemed to be taking much notice of what they were doing. Further down, a car had stopped and someone appeared to be studying the marshes. Scott-Wade had warned of police involvement and that was the concern for all of them. However, he was hungry, having not eaten at all that morning. Like the others, he had spent several tiring days searching in the Lakes, without a result. With little rest they had then driven down to Norfolk in the early hours to start the hunt again. More than anything else he just wanted a meal and a bed. As he was about to have a closer look at the car on the road, a noise from behind took his attention. With reactions dulled by tiredness, he turned, expecting to see one of the others returning. However, the man advancing swiftly on him in long, almost noiseless strides was instantly recognisable.

In the time it took to register, Paul was on top of the guard and already swinging the makeshift weapon. With binoculars in one hand and his assault rifle hanging uselessly from his shoulder, he was at a disadvantage. The man was ducking, but it was too late. Without thought of restraint, Paul slammed the spade hard into the side of his head, scant moments before a fending hand reached any point of usefulness. Hillson collapsed, uttering no noise as his head exploded in a flash of pain. Paul went down on one knee beside him and swiftly scanned the ground behind. The heads of the skirmish line were still visible as they neared the bank. There was no time to waste and the sound of a distant siren could be heard. He could see Rebecca, climbing out of the ditch, and she appeared unsteady on her feet. With a brief wave he motioned her over and she reached down to help pull Jason clear of the ditch. Both were sopping wet and covered in smelly slime.

Realising there was no time to lose; Rebecca did her best to jog with Jason to the rear of the truck. Paul was already there and had dragged the unconscious body of Hillson behind him. She knelt beside him, exhausted from her exertions.

"You're an ugly bitch," he swore, coldly, and grabbed her hand. Her eyes widened at the unwarranted outburst, shocked by his harsh words. Paul saw the confusion in her expression and, without explaining, pushed her hand against the side of Hillson's face and let go. In her confusion she had dropped all her mental shields. On touching the body she immediately drew out his life's energy and soul, turning it into a tinder black corpse. Jason gagged at the shocking sight and staggered to one side to throw up. Rebecca, realising what Paul had done, looked astonished as the energy surged through her body in a tingling sensation.

"Sorry about that precious," Paul apologised, lightly taking her by the arms. "I had to find a way of recharging you, so to speak. He was already beyond help and your need was greater than Casserhan's."

"I cannot believe what you have just done."

"Needs must, as the saying goes, or something like that," he replied, reaching for the pale looking Jason. "Sorry, young man, but..."

One of the men in the line had halted, briefly, to take a drink from his water bottle. As he did so the sound of a siren could be heard in the far distance. He turned to look at the road and could still see their vehicles parked at the far end of the field. For a second he could not believe it, but his blood ran cold and he dropped the water bottle to the ground.

"They're behind us!" he yelled, while at the same time firing twice into the air.

As if one, the whole line turned to see what the commotion was. The reaction was immediate and they all began a headlong run back through the crop to the vehicles.

Scott-Wade was quickly in front, yelling as he went. "Open fire, you dozy bastards! Drop them!"

"Oh shit," Paul swore, grabbing Jason by the arm and propelling him past the truck. Rebecca looked confused, again, and he pushed her forwards too. "Get into the blue car at the end!"

She needed no further prompting and swiftly ran ahead of them to the Frontera. On reaching it she snatched open the passenger door as Paul caught up. Shots were already pinging into the ground near them and she ducked as he pushed Jason over the front seat into the rear.

"War's broken out," Paul muttered, as the boy fell out of sight. "Keep on the floor Jason," he added. At the same time he grabbed her by the arm and hoisted her up into the passenger seat. "Keep down."

"I will!" she shouted, as better-aimed shots began to creep nearer to them, one bouncing off the bonnet scant inches away. As he was shutting the door she briefly grabbed his hand. "I understand why you did it Paul."

"Good," he countered, slamming it. A moment later a bullet hit him high up in the right thigh causing him to buckle against the side of the car. A second one followed, almost instantly, into the same leg below the knee. He gritted his teeth against the burning pain, knowing they had little time to dawdle. Shots were starting to come in from every direction as he hobbled to the driver's side. As he opened the door a bullet passed by so close he almost thought he felt it and the window shattered, showering him with glass.

"Nasty," he muttered, jumping up into the seat. Rebecca had bundled herself up into a ball on the floor and was looking at him with grave concern. Unperturbed, he gave her a lopsided grin as the window next to him frosted and blew inwards. Jason, lying on the floor too, gave a scream of disapproval as the glass covered him.

"A typical day at the seaside for the Sayers family," Paul said, winking at her, and twisted the ignition key. "We have some laughs, eh precious?"

Despite the awful situation she could not help but smile at his attempt at humour. The Frontera burst into life as he floored the throttle pedal. The tyres of the 4x4 chewed up the loose surface of the track and they were quickly moving.

In the fields and on the track, Scott-Wade and the others had covered two-thirds of the distance back to their vehicles. Some of them were firing on the run, while others stopped to take better aim at the fleeing targets. However, they did not need binoculars to see the Frontera drawing off and bouncing towards the road. Scott-Wade cursed, loudly, for having let them get past so many men without detection. Fortune it seemed smiled on Sayers. He stopped, while the others continued, and pulled a radio from his pocket.

"Get after them, but be bloody careful!" he ordered the ones heading to the other 4x4s. "The rest of you get in the truck and bugger off out of here! I can hear sirens!"

The exertion had been too much and, panting heavily, he spoke into the radio whilst shouldering his rifle. "Air one, this is ground, come in."

The static crackled. "Ground, this is air one. ETA to shoreline is two minutes. Over."

"Good," he replied. "Pick me up on top of the banking."

"Okay. Over," came the reply, and in the distance he could hear the drone of the approaching helicopter.

Chapter 80

The relief and elation of escaping was not lost on Paul, it felt good to be on four wheels. He turned out of the track and onto the main road. The Frontera felt powerful and tough as he accelerated away and slipped on the seatbelt. Only the front and rear screens had glass left in them, but the tyres were still up and it had half a tank of fuel. Still bundled up in the foot-well, wet and dirty, Rebecca studied her man.

"You can get up now," he said. "You can too, Jason. Be careful of the glass and strap yourselves in."

The two of them were only too glad to get out of their cramped positions and be in the seats proper.

"Will they follow?" she asked, clicking on the seatbelt.

"Yes. If we hadn't been spotted I was going to let their tyres down."

She looked behind for a few moments and then straight ahead. When she was not looking he glanced down at his right leg and the pain he could feel there. His trousers were wet and mucky and there was a small pool of blood staining the carpet at his feet. His examination was unexpectedly broken by Rebecca, shouting at him.

"Paul, you're on the wrong side!"

He jerked up, pulling the car back onto the right side of the road as they entered a sharp bend. It was too late though to avoid the collision. The little blue Renault was being driven by a woman and she braked in panic as the big Frontera clipped her front wing. The force peeled it back and punched in the door as they passed. The steering wheel bucked in Paul's hands and they slewed sideways from the impact, coming to a halt in the middle of the road. The Renault had come to a rest too and he could see the young woman rubbing at her face in disbelief. She seemed unhurt and he screeched away without waiting, leaving wreckage in the road.

Rebecca was studying him as they drove on, a puzzled expression on her face. He smiled, wearily, while at the same time erecting a barrier between his thoughts and hers.

"Sorry, a lapse in concentration," he explained

Her eyes widened when she sensed the mental block and was dumbstruck by it. "What is wrong Paul?"

"Nothing," he replied, returning his attention to the road. There was no real conviction in his tone and she easily picked up on it. Reaching out she laid a warm hand on his. Although he could block her from probing his mind, he could not prevent her feeling the pain in his body. In an instant her eyes snapped down to his legs and she saw the blood staining his clothing.

"You have been shot!"

"I know."

Desperately, she gripped his arm and the mental barrier crumbled. She could see he was more concerned with their welfare than his own. In fact it seemed as if he had tuned out the pain so it would not disturb his concentration.

"We will have to do something about it Paul, please," she pleaded.

"I've been shot before. I must make a good target."

"Will you be alright?" Jason asked, leaning between the seats. "Can I do anything?"

"I'll be fine. We'll be in Saltmarsh in minutes."

It was more than Rebecca could take in. She sat, open mouthed, staring at him, her love reaching a new sense of understanding. He was prepared to suffer and do anything, without word of complaint, in order to see them safe. She wished she knew how he managed it.

Ahead of them a tractor was being followed by several cars and he had to slow down. It was a steady moment and he saw her still gazing at him.

"Take my belt off."

She looked puzzled.

"A tourniquet, Rebecca," he urged. She quickly understood and leaned across his lap to remove it. The Frontera nosedived under braking. He had accelerated past the tractor, only to see the sign for Saltmarsh right on the bend.

"Hang on," he warned, grabbing her with one hand. The tyres squealed in protest as he raced into the junction. He gave her arm an affectionate squeeze. "Sorry, precious, nearly missed the turn, didn't want to lose you."

The sign for Saltmarsh said six miles. Rebecca looped the belt around his upper thigh and yanked it tight. He moaned, audibly.

"Sorry, my darling," she apologised. "I know it hurts."

"It's okay, not far now."

"There's a helicopter coming in behind us!" Jason yelled, breaking their conversation. Rebecca twisted in her seat and saw the low flying machine zeroing in on them.

"It must be spotting for the cars," Paul said, casually, unable to see it himself. "They must be near."

"Will they try to stop us?"

"I doubt it. He won't get too close for fear of hitting something."

The helicopter was easily outpacing them and swiftly drew alongside. Paul glanced at it and then in the mirror. Rebecca saw the pursuing car at the same time he did and felt the adrenaline rush inside him. The Toyota 4x4 was fast making ground with a second one directly behind it. As Rebecca watched it she felt Paul take hold of her hand.

"You'll go now," he said, when she turned to look at him.

"No," she replied, firmly.

His response was even firmer, almost ordering her. "No arguments, Rebecca. Go!"

"No, Paul, please let me stay."

The first car had closed to within yards of the rear bumper and he could see the determined faces of the men in it.

"Now, Rebecca. You promised."

She saw the agonised concern in his face as tears streamed freely down her own. "I am deserting you."

"No, you'd never do that."

In a fleeting moment she saw something he had always managed to keep hidden from her. The fear that haunted him, the horror of what Storn would do to her if he captured them. It was nothing like the expected outcome, yet she could see it was more than he could bear to let happen. She squeezed his hand. "I love you."

"I know."

She reached over and took her bag from Jason. "Be good," she whispered, gently running her fingers down his cheek.

"I will," he replied, with a weak smile.

Paul saw her clasp her bracelet and in an instant she was gone. Only then did he breathe a sigh of relief.

"Is it much further?" Jason asked, climbing into the vacant front seat with a canvas tool-bag.

"About three miles," he replied, deftly passing a slower car in front. He was sweating, profusely, and guessed it was due to the gunshot wounds. "What have you got there?"

The boy pulled a black sphere from the bag and showed it to him. "Is it a grenade?"

Paul grabbed it, disbelievingly. "Yes, for heaven's sake. Where did you find it?"

"There're six in here and a box of bullets."

Paul glanced in the mirror and weighed the ball of death in his hand. "Get down Jason, the fireworks are about to begin."

Chapter 81

The pursuit continued at high speed towards Saltmarsh. Paul had remembered David telling him about their important visitor that day, but he had no idea at what time it would occur. The one hope was for plenty of police to be in the immediate area. Surely the pursuing cars would not tangle in the village? His thoughts blurred and he glanced again to the Bell Jet Ranger, keeping close to their right.

Inside the helicopter, Scott-Wade was becoming increasingly agitated by the lack of action. He turned and barked at the pilot.

"Can't you get this thing down and push him off the road?"

The pilot shook his head, incredulously. "This ain't a movie and I'm no stunt pilot. There are trees and telegraph poles down there. If we go in at this speed we'll pile it in."

"Shit!"

"It ain't worth dying for," the pilot added.

"What can you do then?"

"Keep pace with him. It's up to the ground boys to stop him."

Scott-Wade nodded and quickly spoke into the radio, without formality. "Webb, are you there?"

"Yeah," was the sharp response.

"You'll be in the village in a couple of minutes. Whatever it takes, stop the son of a bitch, kill them and get out of it fast."

"Will do," was his eager acknowledgement.

"Don't fail," Scott-Wade added, and turned his attention again to the car with Paul at the wheel, just yards to their left. "Bastard," he muttered, and then spoke to the pilot. "If they cock it up, get out of here."

"I heard that."

Paul glanced in the mirror and saw the gunman leaning out from the passenger front window of the following car, weapon at the ready.

"Here it comes!" he shouted, as Jason scrunched down in the front foot-well. At the same moment he saw the police car edging out of an entrance only yards ahead of them. He decided not to even attempt to brake. With a twist of the wheel he avoided a major collision, although he clipped the front of it and tore off its bumper. The impact slowed their progress, briefly, and he knew for certain the officers inside would be alerting the forces inside the village to their arrival. A second after the collision, a burst of gunfire raked across the back of the Frontera, shattering the rear window. A single bullet thudded into the dashboard just to his left and he stared at it for several seconds. The grenade was sitting in his lap and he smiled, coldly. Holding it between his knees he pulled the pin and tossed it out of the shattered side window. It hit the tarmac and bounced sideways, detonating harmlessly in the grass verge. However, it did little to put off the following cars and another fusillade of shots hammered into the rear. Paul began weaving and at the same time held out a hand to Jason.

"Give me another."

Without word, he passed one from the bag. Paul removed the pin, waited, and then casually dropped it out. The Toyota, behind, swerved to avoid it as it tumbled down the road towards them. Likewise, the second car missed it too and it exploded behind them.

"Lucky sods," Paul cursed, as the rear of the car erupted in noise. A full magazine from the pursuing car shattered the Frontera. Almost at once the left rear corner went down and Paul had to fight to keep the car straight. Within yards, the bullet ridden tyre ripped off. He floored the throttle, determined to keep going, even on just the rim. Another burst tore through the car and the windscreen shattered like crazy paving. Frantically, Paul punched at the mess obscuring his view, until a section of glass fell away in front of him. The rush of air, noise, and broken glass stung his face. With his left hand dripping blood, from the shards of glass imbedded in it, Paul reached across to Jason. The grisly sight made the boy gag and he could also see blood oozing across Paul's chest. A bullet had passed through the back of the seat and straight out through his left shoulder. He seemed not to have noticed as he shakily placed a grenade in the crimson stained hand.

"And another" Paul said, firmly, as another burst took the right rear tyre out. The Frontera's two rear wheels screamed in protest on the tarmac. Jason nodded and put a second in his hand.

"Pull 'em."

With his hands shaking, Jason withdrew both pins at the same time. Paul counted to five before dropping them from the window. They both rolled under the first Toyota, without harming it. However, the second was not so lucky. The two grenades detonated simultaneously, just under the front of it. A fountain of metal, plastic and glass accompanied the car as it was flipped effortlessly over in a somersault. The twisted wreckage cartwheeled into the hedgerow, burning fiercely.

"Bingo!" Paul cried, and put a bloodied thumb up at Jason. "That's one down."

From the helicopter, Scott-Wade saw the demise of the second car and three good men. He cursed, silently, and looked ahead through the wide expanse of canopy. They were almost on top of the village and he could see police cars blocking the road.

"Get out of here," he ordered the pilot, without looking.

He nodded, relieved, and banked away heading north.

Scott-Wade clenched his fists, fighting hard to suppress the anger and frustration he felt. "One day, Sayers," he muttered, bitterly. "My turn will come. I promise."

Chapter 82

The road leading into Saltmarsh took on a rather blurred appearance as Paul passed the village sign. He realised, belatedly, that his injuries were rapidly catching up with him and his body was going into a state of shock. However, his driving force was to get as close as possible to the community centre. The Frontera was in bad shape too, but, despite its condition, he kept the speed up to sixty miles an hour. Ahead there were two police cars blocking the road. Positioned around them were several officers, all in cover except one. He was out in front of the roadblock with an outstretched arm. Despite this, Paul did not slow down.

The officer leapt out of the way when he realised the Frontera had no intention of halting. The others too were quickly moving from behind their cars and Paul saw weapons in the hands of two of them. He aimed at the small gap between the cars and pushed the throttle pedal to the floor. A colossal bang followed, accompanied by tearing metal, and they ploughed through the makeshift barricade. One of the armed officers had kept his full attention on the scene. Primarily he could see the man leaning out of the following Toyota with an automatic rifle. Fortunately, for Paul, he aimed his own at the more dangerous target and fired several times. Webb, the driver of the Toyota, died instantly. The big 4x4 clipped the rear of one of the police cars and spun into the front garden of a nearby house. The gunman was thrown clear and quickly surrounded by armed officers.

Paul continued into the village. He was frantically searching a memory that was being increasingly dulled, looking for where he thought the building should be. Thinking he knew, he turned left, mounting the kerb and tearing through the corner of a garden close to the road. Another police car was blocking the road ahead, but he was past caring and drove along the pavement to avoid it. One of the officers with it was armed and opened fire, but the rounds missed their target. Less than a hundred yards further down the street he saw the roof of the new complex and realised he was on the wrong road, they were at the rear of it. The Frontera had almost had enough of the demands being asked of it, as clouds of steam poured from under the bonnet edges and a loud knocking noise could be heard coming from the engine.

"It's buggered," he muttered, to himself more than the badly shaken Jason.

A tall wooden fence shielded the back of the community centre. Again, Paul mounted the pavement and slammed straight through it. Inside the grounds of the complex things were happening fast, as the police were alerting the security staff within. The happy, expectant chatter, as the First Lady mixed with the invited dignitaries and locals, soon died away. The police and her own special service agents swiftly descended on her when the Frontera crashed noisily through the fence. It demolished a section over twelve feet long before coming to a rest in a raised garden area. At once screaming and shouting took over as the engine spluttered to an inevitable stop.

Sue Pryce grabbed David by the arm, startled by the appearance of the car. "What's happening?"

He was rooted to the spot, despite the confusion around them, and was staring hard at the Frontera. There was movement inside it and he recognised a face.

"Oh dear Lord," he whispered. "It can't be."

The melee behind them continued; with the First Lady being bundled rapidly back inside the building. Security staff were trying to cover the retreat while guests fled in every direction from the scene. However, two agents stepped from the general confusion and were drawing aim on the shattered Frontera. David saw Paul almost fall out of the car at the same time the men were preparing to fire. It took a fraction of a second to realise they were not going to give any sort of warning and horror filled his senses when he saw Jason's head appear over the top of the dashboard.

"It's Paul and Jason," David mumbled to Sue, before wildly

setting off towards the nearest armed man. "Don't shoot!" he shouted, and charged into him, knocking the pistol from his hand.

Sue was running too, screaming. "There's a child in the car!"

In such a stunned state, Paul was oblivious to the confusion around him. He staggered clear of the car, only to be confronted by the second agent just yards in front of him.

"Oh shit," he said, in tired defeat.

The single bullet tore through the left side of his chest, the force picking him off his feet and throwing him backwards onto the ground. The screaming was renewed as the shot echoed around the enclosed area. Jason dived from the car and sprawled on the prone figure of Paul. He was shouting too, at the top of his voice. "Don't shoot!"

David was back on his feet, running past the agent who had fired the shot, and falling to his knees beside Paul. Sue was close behind, almost hysterical at the rapid change of events. Jason looked in a dishevelled state, tears streaming down his face.

"He saved me, he's done nothing wrong."

"I know," David soothed, and beckoned Sue closer. Jason threw his arms around her and began to cry afresh. She looked over David's shoulder and saw Paul for the first time. He seemed covered in blood and she gagged at the sight of the gaping wound in his chest. David laid a hand across Paul's forehead. Amazingly, he saw his eyes flicker open and could not believe that life remained in such a badly wounded man. "Get an ambulance here, quickly!" he called, to the few people remaining by the entrance.

A blood-spattered hand weakly grasped him by the arm and David looked down.

"Keep hanging on Paul, there's an ambulance on the way."

The reply was a cracked whisper, blood trickling from his mouth. "Ever heard the expression, getting there is half the fun? It's a load of bollocks."

"Keep quiet Paul," he urged.

The grip on David's arm lessened until Paul slipped into unconsciousness. He looked desperately at Sue.

"Where's that ambulance?"

Chapter 83

The office was quiet for a few minutes and Helen took the offered opportunity to relax. Picking up the remote, she flicked on the small portable television sitting on top of the filing cabinet. It was nearly one o'clock and although she knew about it, she wanted to see what the media were reporting. As expected, the disruption to the First Lady's visit and Paul's finding of Jason Galloway, were the top stories.

"Dramatically, this morning, the escaped suspect, Paul Sayers, crashed into the grounds of a community centre being opened..."

She smiled. "Trust him to do it in style."

"With him was missing Norfolk youngster, Jason Galloway..."

As the newsreader continued, she sipped at her coffee. A shadow fell across the door and she turned the television off as it opened. It was Cunningham and he closed it behind him.

"Sorry, Skipper. I didn't know you were coming down."

"Thought I'd pop down and see how it's progressing."

"It's only just starting. There's a lot to do before we get to the bottom of this."

"Have you got anything on those ritual killings?"

She shook her head. "No one person to point a finger at yet, we're still gathering evidence. The place at Padrigg is yielding useful information, but they seem adept at covering their tracks."

"How adept?"

"Very," she replied.

"Still, the Galloway boy's safe," he added. "And we've Carter for Marcroft's murder."

"Yes, a definite on that Skipper. And they've got one of the men from the car chasing Sayers."

"Are you intent on dropping all charges against Paul Sayers?"

"You're saying I shouldn't?"

His expression was neutral. "There are a lot of unanswered questions, Helen. There are all those dead bodies and a helicopter down in the Lakes for starters. And a Harrier crash off the coast."

"The RAF is there now. There's nothing to link him to it."

He gave her a sideways look. "I don't believe in good guys Helen, especially ones who break the law. How's he doing?"

"Last word was he's still in theatre. They don't let on much, but, reading between the lines, his chances aren't good."

"A pity, he could've proved useful. Can you put anything my way concerning Scott-Wade?"

"No. But he's dirty, Skipper."

He nodded, and made to leave. "Keep this open, Helen, and dig carefully."

"I will."

Down in the cell area a heavy door swung open and Carter looked up from where he sat slouched on the bed. He recognised Renton as he stood in the doorway.

"Aren't you supposed to be suspended?"

"There's a manpower shortage. They still need me."

Carter nodded. "And what about the other two?"

"The same for them, but they're not on duty today. Anyhow, you've been sent a lawyer." As he spoke he stepped to one side and allowed a woman to step in. "I'll leave the door open Ms. Call when you're ready."

"Thank you," she muttered, as he left.

"Who sent you?" Carter asked, without getting up.

Without replying she sat down on the end of the bed, next to his feet. He studied her while she opened a small briefcase on her knees. For a moment he almost thought she was someone he knew, but dismissed it as an idle thought. However, she had gone to great lengths to hide her true identity, with a long black wig, glasses, and heavy make-up. He was about to sit up, when she produced a silenced pistol from the case. Ruthlessly, she fired twice into his head before he could even move. As he slumped, she sprang up and dragged him down the bed by his feet. Then she rolled him onto his side and covered him with the blanket. After calmly slipping the pistol back inside the case, she stepped out of the cell and called down the corridor.

"I'm done for now, officer."

Renton was standing at the reception desk, with another constable. "I'll get it Kev," he said, setting off towards her. "Then I'll be off on my break."

The other nodded. "Okay mate, see ya in half an hour."

Casually, Renton made his way to the cell. He looked in at the prone figure of Carter, closed the door, and winked at her. "Sleeping?"

She only smiled as together they made their way up through the station and out through the staff entrance.

"Are you leaving now?" she asked, when they were outside.

"Too bloody right we are. I've been ordered out with Barker and Matthews. They want no one connected with this farce left in place."

"What will you do?"

"I'm being picked up in a few minutes. We're going down to Lavington to beef up security at the farm. Our days in the force are over."

"Good luck," she said, when they reached the bottom of the steps.

"Thanks."

Without delay, she went to the car park behind a parade of shops, two hundred yards from the station. It was where she had left the Honda motorbike. Working quickly, she strapped the case to the rear carry rack and pulled a pair of leather trousers and jacket from the tank bag. Close by was a rubbish skip, which she slipped behind and changed; depositing the wig, glasses, and skirt in it. Once done she returned to her bike and started it up. Moments later she was astride it, watching the station from the other side of the road. Storn despised failure and, in his eyes, the three of them, along with Carter, had played a major part in the breakdown of the operation. The promise of sanctuary at the farm was hollow. Like Carter, they were best out of the way, permanently. As the Audi, containing the three men, passed her, she took out a mobile phone. The six figure number was already keyed in and she only had to press send. Ten seconds later the explosive charge detonated next to the fuel tank. A successful conclusion to an assignment was all that mattered to her. She cared little for those she killed or were injured by the blast.

A sense of satisfaction filled her as she rode away from the chaotic scene of devastation. The loose ends at Clayborough had been tidied up and it left only the man in police custody in Norfolk to deal with. He would be harder to take out, but he was less important in the scheme of things and she had time on her side.

Chapter 84

The afternoon turned out warm and sunny. Although inside the intensive care department of the Royal Norfolk Hospital, the patients had no cares or worries about the weather. The surgeon who had carried out the operation on Paul, for over three hours, stood outside the room where he was being looked after. David and Sue Pryce appeared in the corridor and made a beeline to him, anxious for news.

"How's he doing?" David asked.

The surgeon shook his head. "It's not good I'm afraid. Is there any family we can contact?"

Sue answered. "There's no one that we're aware of. Paul seems to just have himself." She paused, looking at David, who nodded. "But that's not strictly true. It would take too long to explain, but we're the closest thing to family he has."

"Then I won't give you any false hope," he replied, and motioned to the glass partition. Beyond it, Paul was lying on an intensive care bed. He was sedated, with drips in both arms, a machine to help him breath, and several monitors attached to his body. "We've done our best, but the ventilator is keeping him alive at present." He turned and looked at them. "I have to be honest with you. He's not expected to live beyond the next few hours."

"Isn't there anything you can do?" David asked.

"It's out of our hands. We've done as much as we can. To be truthful, he should've died before he got here. It's testimony to his strength he made it this far."

"He's a special individual," David added, gazing through the glass.

"There were two bullets in his right leg, one shattering the shin bone. If he lives we'll possibly be amputating it within a day or two. Another bullet went through his left shoulder, causing bone and tissue damage..."

Sue felt ill and turned away.

"The left hand was cut to pieces and filled with splinters of glass. But, by far the worse injury is to the left side of his chest. The tissue damage is beyond repair, as well as the loss of the lung that side."

David nodded. "I know. I saw the agent shoot him at almost point-blank range."

"That would explain the damage, but you should make some noise about it."

"Why?" Sue quizzed, turning round.

"Because the bullet I pulled out was a hollow point."

"A dumdum? Aren't they banned?" David asked, incredulously.

"They're banned by the Geneva Convention. They'll stop a man dead in his tracks and, close up, usually fatal."

"What a rotten trick."

"You're right. However, what's done is done."

"Then we must pray for a miracle," David concluded.

"That's all you can do," the surgeon replied, with a shrug.

Chapter 85

Gradually, Paul became aware of his situation and opened his eyes. Looking down he saw he was wearing a loose gown.

"Hospital," he said, out loud. "At least I made it this far." He then studied the surroundings. "But this isn't it."

Around him was just the essence of a soft white glow, without any sense or feel of depth. In fact there was no perspective of any kind to relate to.

"I'm dead and gone to heaven," he finally surmised. "Hang on though," he reconsidered. "Where's Rebecca?"

"Hello, Paul Sayers," a female voice greeted.

Undisturbed by the melodic tone, he turned. She sat on a cube of pure white light, raised from the floor, with one dark nylon-clad leg crossed over the other. She wore a black mini-skirt and purple satin blouse, which hinted at the sensual curves beneath. Smiling, she ran a hand back through her short black hair and waited for him to speak. Her beauty was something to be appreciated and a stirring in a deep part of his memory surfaced. In a scant moment he remembered every detail of their previous meeting.

"Hello, Chimelle. What are you doing here?"

"Passing by," she replied, with a wink. "I couldn't resist saying hello."

"Passing? From where to where?"

She smiled and wagged a finger. "Now, now, Paul Sayers, that inquisitive streak will bring trouble."

"It usually finds me."

The seat dissolved into the floor as she stood up. "It has a habit of doing so. Yet you excel in dealing with it and enjoy it, even if you won't admit it."

"It's my lot in life to suffer."

"If you believe you're suffering."

"Aren't you pretending to be someone else?" he asked, as she turned to leave. "Isn't that what you usually do?"

"Not always. I'm here by choice, Paul Sayers. Casserhan doesn't call you today."

"What about Talid myths?"

She laughed, without looking at him. "A different story altogether."

"Who are you really Chimelle?"

"Anyone I care to be," she answered, turning.

"Very clever," he commented. "It's almost perfect."

"Of course," Chimelle replied, not only in Rebecca's body, but also with her gentle voice. "I choose who I want to be. There are no limitations to visual masking." Slowly, she walked back over to him and slid her arms around his waist. Their lips met and he did nothing to resist. The contact was tender, the sensation loving, but she did not possess Rebecca's magic sparkle. He pulled away and found himself gazing into the face of someone completely different.

"So it was you?"

Chimelle had transformed into the old lady from the high Pennine road. "Yes."

"Why?"

She smiled and reverted to her true self. "It will not harm to tell you, because, like before, you'll not remember me on waking. The young woman you rescued was under my personal protection."

"I thought the Guardians were responsible for that sort of thing?"

"That is true." she said, while smoothing her hair back with her hands. "But certain souls are special and need extra vigilance."

"Why did you want me to help her?"

"Goodbye, Paul Sayers," she said, ending the conversation. "You're in safe hands."

He watched as she slowly walked away and seemed to melt into the glowing light.

"Who was she, Chimelle?"

The reply was barely a whisper. "My mother. Thank you. Until the next time."

Driven by an unknown instinct, he strode off in the opposite direction.

Chapter 86

At midnight the duty nurse cast an expert eye over the various monitors surrounding Paul's bed. Satisfied that all was well, she sat back down in her seat at the foot of the bed. Dealing with patients in intensive care was a task she had grown accustomed to. The life and death struggle brought out the best in both patient and staff. However, with him she felt they were simply waiting for the inevitable. Opening up her day-old newspaper, she turned to the crossword and became happily engrossed.

Moments later Rebecca walked into the unit, pausing only to smile at the nurse and brush the hair back from her face. The nurse returned the warm smile and immediately went back to her puzzle, where at once the clues seemed clearer than ever before. Content that she was distracted and unaware of her presence, Rebecca went to Paul's bedside.

"My darling, I have come to make you better," she whispered, tenderly kissing him on the cheek. From her shoulder bag she took out a crystal sphere, about two inches in diameter, and sat on the bed next to him. Once she had closed her fingers around it the colour began to pulsate from within. She then placed her hand a scant fraction above the chest wound and the healing power flowed through her fingertips. For over five minutes she did not move her hand until the process was complete. Then she moved onto the next damaged part of his body, to flood it with healing energy. For over half an hour she worked methodically from one area to the next, leaving the bandages in place to protect the tender flesh. Finally, she removed the respirator mask and ran her fingertips down his cheek. After only a few seconds of her gentle touch his eyes flickered open.

"Welcome back, my darling."

He reached out and laid a hand on her cheek. "I really don't deserve someone as beautiful as you."

"I cannot believe the man I love does so much for others without a thought for himself."

"He's a fool."

"That is not true. It is because he knows how to love."

He glanced around. "Is this a hospital?"

Rebecca nodded. "Margaret says they have done an excellent job, but you also needed some of her help too. She prepared a sphere and instructed me in its use."

"It was bad then?"

"They are expecting you to die."

"Charming," he added, and looked at the nurse. "Is she seeing any of this?"

"Nothing she will remember."

Carefully, he pulled himself upright in bed. "Has Charlotte asked you about the other night?"

"No. Too much has happened for her to be concerned about such a small incident as not being able to see us," she replied, and kissed him tenderly on the lips. "I must be going Paul."

"Have a safe trip."

"I will be back later."

"And her?" he asked, pointing to the nurse.

"When I have gone, you will only need to speak to her to bring her out of it."

A moment later she was gone. Paul made himself comfortable, sitting up, and cleared his throat with a cough.

"Excuse me," he called to the nurse. Duly startled, she dropped the newspaper, complete with finished crossword, and stared at him, wide-eyed. "Is there any chance of something to eat? I'm starving."

385

Chapter 87

Tuesday 1st June 1993

The door to the private hospital room opened and Paul looked up from eating his lunch. It was Helen and David. They crossed to the bed and each warmly grabbed a hand.

"I prayed for you to stay with us Paul, but it's a miracle. There's an entire medical team out there who're flabbergasted, to say the least," David began.

"It's good to see everyone in less harrowing circumstances," Paul replied, and smiled at Helen. "I guess I should thank you for the armed coppers crawling all over this place."

She nodded. "I need to look after you. And don't worry; I've personally selected each one."

"I hear you lost Carter."

"They got into the cell and shot him. Also, the three responsible for doing you over were killed in a car bomb."

"They're clinical, Helen. I hope you're watching your back."

"I am, but the investigation will continue. We'll need to talk at length."

"I'll tell you everything I can."

"You could still face charges," she added, seriously. "My superior doesn't believe in letting the good guys get away with anything."

Paul smiled. "Understandable. I hope you don't expect me to incriminate myself."

She laughed. "I doubt you would."

The door opened and Rebecca stepped in, dressed in a floral print summer dress. She greeted them all with a smile and David kissed her on the cheek when she joined them.

"Lovely to see you again, Rebecca."

"And you."

Helen winked at Paul. "We'll talk a little later."

"You can buy me lunch," he said, as she made to leave.

Briefly, she held Rebecca by the hand. "Angels. It's mind blowing. Thank you for showing me the truth."

"You would have seen it eventually. I had to make it quick for Paul's sake."

"Look after him; he's one in a million."

"I always try to."

Helen grabbed David by the arm and steered him to the door. "Com'on, I'll treat you to coffee."

"No questions?" he asked, as they left.

"Oh plenty," she added.

Once they were alone, Rebecca sat on the bed next to Paul and they embraced.

"Can we sneak out of here and go somewhere quiet for a couple of days?" he asked, when they had finished kissing and parted.

"I thought you would never ask."

He raised both eyebrows. "Can we?"

"Yes," she whispered. "Are you ready to go?"

"Let me put some clothes on and we're out of here," he replied, eager to be going.

"One more kiss, my darling, and I will follow you anywhere." Their lips met and a new feeling of life flared in Rebecca's spirit.